Philip Cecil Lumley, born in Ballycommon, Co. Offaly, started to write 60 years ago when he was in "digs" in Ballyshannon, Co. Donegal.

Since then he has written a motley collection of plays, short stories and radio plays – not to mention bedtime stories (verbal) for his sleepy-eyed children.

As a drifter in Canada/USA for a number of years he imbibed the styles of Hemingway, Scott Fitzgerald, tough-guy, Raymond Chandler, and the much underestimated, John P. Marquand.

"Caulfield" is the first of a trilogy of novels.

CAULFIELD

Philip Lumley

C a u l f i e l d

Pegasus

A CIP catalogue record for this title is
available from the British Library.

ISBN 978 1 903490 28 0

*Pegasus is an imprint of
Pegasus Elliot MacKenzie Publishers Ltd.*
www.pegasuspublishers.com

First Published in 2008

**Pegasus
Sheraton House Castle Park
Cambridge CB3 0AX England**

Printed & Bound in Great Britain

Dedication

To my wife Victoria

In memory of

Rev. Robert Lumley MA
(Caulfield)

Chapter 1

Murphy, Henley-Smith & Caulfield

4.30 pm.

The referee blew his whistle. The match was over. A tall woman dressed with casual elegance in a Russian mink coat and hat, intently watched the players enter the pavilion. Around the perimeter lights appeared in buildings as students opened their textbooks and rehashed their notes. It was Saturday evening, an October Saturday evening.

A small man, in late middle-age, remained on the touchline. He was well dressed with a cashmere coat and Burberry scarf. He had quick intelligent eyes. Small though he was, he exuded a certain presence.

The tall woman put away her notebook and walked over to the small man. She exchanged a brief word and moved on.

Dusk crept across the rugby pitch, and pockets of mist gathered in places. The spectators drifted away and only the dedicated lingered. Girlfriends of the players, mothers of the players, old college chaws who had played there fifty years ago. They reminisced of heroics in the past and battles long ago.

Two girls were gushing about Henley-Smith.

'Isn't he gorgeous?' one said. They whispered to each other and giggled. They spoke to one of the old timers that they knew, Dr. Kelly.

'Wasn't that a great try that Henley-Smith scored?'

He looked at his companion, another doctor.

'What do you say, Jones, was that a great try?'

'Yes,' said Jones, nodding his head sagely, 'a very good try.'

They looked at each other sardonically.

It was not yet dusk, a typical October Saturday rugby afternoon. The players started to leave the pavilion in twos and threes. The little man retreated to the dark shadow cast by the library. He looked carefully at each player as they passed and then came the last three speaking in the loud, confident tones of students everywhere. He knew them by sight – Murphy, Caulfield and Henley-Smith.

Two of them were tall and athletic. Murphy appeared smaller but stronger.

'We'll have a few jars,' said Murphy as they went by the man, lurking in the shadows.

'OK,' said Caulfield, 'Let's go to Slats.'

The little man watched them and then followed.

The tall woman stood by the college gates and saw them leave.

The usual crowd was in Slattery's College Bar, otherwise known as 'Slats.' A chorus of cheers greeted the trio.

'Great win,' shouted someone, half-stupid with drink. Another fool slapped Henley-Smith on the back. He winced. Henley-Smith was tired, not the pleasant tiredness that follows a tough game, but what starts in the head and the mind.

He knew he had slipped up marking O'Neill, but there was no need for Murphy to say what he did. It was damn awful, and Cynthia and her sister were standing there and heard every word. You could bet that Capt. Fitzhaugh would know of it next week.

At least he had scored a try, but it gave him little satisfaction. He supposed it would go into the books, and perhaps the Monday papers might give it a run. His mother could read it if she wasn't in bed with one of her headaches. Some dopey girl from Mount Anville or Wesley would drool over his photo. But it was all nothing. Caulfield made it as Caulfield made everything.

Caulfield and Murphy were talking vigorously about the pack.

The door opened, and a small man came in, well dressed in a cashmere overcoat. He moved to the end of the bar where he was on his own.

Henley-Smith watched the man as he ordered a hot whisky. The coat reminded him of his father, Commander Henley-Smith, RN, a man who he loved and hated.

Stiff necked, overbearing and unloving; Henley-Smith loathed it when he used to take him on a tour of their house.

'You can learn the history of Britain,' he would boom, 'in these pictures.'

Henley-Smith knew what was coming next.

'Britain and the Royal Navy,' his father would boom again. 'What's the difference between them?' and Henley-Smith would answer dutifully 'There is no difference.'

'Well said!' his father would bark, and reward the small boy with a clap on the back.

Henley-Smith looked again at the little man in his cashmere coat, and the memory of the coat reminded him of his father, as he pointed out the past heroes of the family: Captains, Rear Admirals, Commodores, their decorations, their victories.

Henley-Smith gritted his teeth. He did not want to be a hero and he wasn't.

Caulfield was pulling at his coat.

'Wake up, man, have something to drink.' Henley-Smith ordered a beer.

'What great thoughts are you having?' Caulfield asked him quietly.

'Nothing,' said Henley-Smith. It was uncanny how Caulfield could read his mind.

Henley-Smith lowered his voice. 'By the way, Caulfield, thanks for that try.'

'It was nothing,' said Caulfield.

But Henley-Smith knew it was something. Caulfield made the opening, took the hard tackles, spoon-fed him with the right pass. He didn't know why Caulfield did it for him, but it was his only chance to escape from that night of terror and shame.

Henley-Smith the international winger could bury Henley-Smith the coward.

7.00 pm.

Murphy was in great form. He was a legend in the college, and he boasted of his Kerry blood. Any Kerry man, he claimed, can drink twenty pints without having to relieve himself.

He proved it.

Later he smuggled a goat into the college and locked it in the Junior Dean's car.

Now he was balancing a full pint on his forehead. Caulfield was leading a slow handclap.

A small man pushed by, wearing a cashmere coat and scarf. He smiled benevolently at the roistering students, went outside and waited.

Murphy balanced the pint on his forehead with practiced skill. His attention was ostensibly on the pint glass, but his mind was elsewhere. Out of the corner of his eye he saw Henley-Smith.

What a creep, he thought.

Henley-Smith was trying to be one of the boys. He had an idiotic half-smile as if he didn't know whether to laugh or cry. One day mixing it with the fellows, the next day too good for them. He did not know what he was or what he wanted.

A big fat slob, thought Murphy, now barely controlling the glass. It was getting heavier and the perspiration started to trickle down his neck.

In Murphy's opinion, Henley-Smith was no good to the team. If it wasn't for Caulfield who carried him, and did all but push the ball into his jockstrap, he would be nothing. *A slob*, thought Murphy, *with just a bit of speed.*

He could see Henley-Smith with his patronizing half-smile. Murphy felt the bile rising in him as the balanced the pint glass. You would think Henley-Smith was a landlord addressing his tenants, which of course he was.

A rage seemed to possess Murphy, and then he remembered. He called out –

'Daddy's in the Navy, Daddy's in the Navy.'

There was a sudden silence. Caulfield groaned and cried to himself, *why does Murphy have to be such a bastard? Henley-Smith doesn't deserve it again.*

In the previous year Henley-Smith had been asked what his father did. Unthinkingly, he said, 'Daddy is in the Navy.' Why did he not say that his father was in the navy? But 'Daddy is in the Navy' had become a catch cry, and was thrown at Henley-Smith in every bar in Dublin.

Even at the Colours match, when he threw himself bravely on the ball and saved an almost certain try, he heard it coming from the touchline, 'Hurray, hurray, Daddy's in the Navy.'

As Henley-Smith heard again the hated sneer from Murphy, he gave away to blind fury. He jumped forward and lashed out with all his strength. Murphy was sent flying, the pint crashed to the ground, scattering broken glass and beer all over him.

Murphy was taken completely by surprise. Apart from the suddenness of the attack, he was taken back at the power of Henley-Smith's punch.

Groggily he got to his feet.

'OK, Sailor Boy,' he whispered, 'Get ready for a beating.'

The crowd fell silent. The barman knowing how quickly a rugby crowd could wreck a bar, vaulted over the counter and tried to restrain Murphy.

Caulfield felt sick. He threw his arm around Henley-Smith and cried, 'Back, back,' he roared, 'get back!'

Surprisingly, the barman was able to restore order. 'Shake hands,' he said.

'Go to hell!' said Murphy.

Murphy and Henley-Smith looked at each other, their chests were heaving and sweat rolled off their faces, they trembled with latent fury.

'Shake hands,' repeated the barman.

Murphy spat on the ground and walked away. Caulfield had enough. The whole scene made him sick. He remembered that he had nothing to eat since breakfast. He pushed forward through the pub door and outside the raw October night hit his face with a slap.

The street seemed to spin around and, as he grasped the railings, he realised to his horror that he was throwing up. Around the steps of the pub his vomit splashed out. The street seemed to heave and turn, and as his legs gave away the road rose to meet him. He felt a pair of strong arms catching him from behind. It was a small man in the cashmere coat.

'Take it easy, Caulfield,' he said. 'I have to speak to you.'

10 pm.

They had been walking and walking. Caulfield stumbled over the kerb, but the little man held him. Caulfield didn't know how long they had been walking, but he guided him expertly over footpaths, around corners and across busy streets.

He paid no attention to his low, even conversation. In any case he could not make out what the man was saying, or even where they had been walking. His voice sounded as if it came from a distance, echoing like a drum.

Do I know this man, thought Caulfield, *and what is his angle?* Although he knew himself to be drunk, he knew he didn't have to go with him. He was curious about the little man and what he wanted. Whatever he wanted it was not money. Sometimes when

Caulfield was short of money he would go to church on a Sunday where his cousin was the minister and, with a bit of luck, get taken home for lunch.

No, this man is going to be sorry if he thinks he can get anything out of me. I haven't got tuppence. He felt momentarily sorry for himself. *I am beginning to get tired of this walk.*

Perhaps he could push him away, and crawl back on his hands and knees, barking like a dog, and ask jeering youths where College Green was.

The man had stopped and was pointing at something in a tenement building.

'Do you see that window?' he said, pointing to one with broken glass. 'In that room I was born, 85 Dorset Street, on the fourth floor.

Caulfield screwed his eyes to see better.

'I see.'

What was he supposed to do? What was he supposed to say? Did this man bring him halfway around Dublin to show him a broken window in a tenement?

Caulfield started to say something, and then he lost the thread of his remarks and ended in a confused mumble.

'Let me show you,' said the man.

They crossed the road, and with his key the man opened the door. Inside it was very dark. There was an inch of thick dust everywhere. The stairs, which led all the way to the top, creaked alarmingly. Caulfield was the worst for wear, but he recognized something familiar. The sweep of the stairs and rear windows reminded him of a great house near Templemore, the home of a great family.

The little man kept climbing. 'When I was a boy I used to climb these steps three at a time in thirty-five seconds.'

The steps creaked and groaned as they reached the fourth floor.

It was a little brighter on the top floor with light from a broken skylight.

'Come here,' said the man.

Caulfield moved to the door.

'In there lived five people – three children and two parents.'

'Do you know what this is?' said the man. He pointed to a three-inch piece of wood fastened diagonally on the doorframe.

'I have seen it before,' said Caulfield, 'something to do with the Jews.'

'Yes,' said the man, 'it is known as mezuzah. Inside the mezuzah is a small roll of paper called the shaddai. On the shaddai is printed the holiest words in the Torah. 'Hear, O Israel, the Lord our God is one God'.'

The man kissed the tips of his fingers and touched the mezuzah, pushing open the door. It creaked, and dust fell to the ground.

'Is this one room?' said Caulfield. 'How do five people sleep in one room?'

'With difficulty,' said the man. 'My parents slept in a double bed in this corner. My bed was here by the wall. My brothers, David and Ken, had another double bed. The kitchen was at the end. A lavatory in the corner.'

'No bath?' asked Caulfield.

'None,' said the man, 'but we had to wash ourselves down every day from top to toe.'

That wasn't much fun, thought Caulfield.

As if he knew what Caulfield was thinking, the little man said, 'In cold water.'

'In the middle of the floor stood the sewing machine. This machine, and the man who worked it, fed five hungry mouths. It paid for schools and shoes, it paid for shillings for Ger Flanagan, the alcoholic postman across the landing, who was never refused bread or tea. It paid for books. All the world was in this little room.'

'Did your father ever feel that he was poor?'

'No,' said the man, 'he had three sons.'

The man smiled at him, 'I can tell you that plenty of times the sons felt poor.'

'The children of a strong man are like arrows in his quiver'.

'Well said,' said the man.

Caulfield went to the window and looked through the broken glass. The street lights were on. The chipper was doing a good business.

Caulfield felt better, but his mind was disturbed. It had been opened to a world he hardly knew. They left the room and the building. The man took him by the arm and they crossed over, continuing to walk down Dorset Street, to Amiens Street. This was new Dublin. Old slums replaced by new slums. Old slums had life, children, uncles and grannies.

New slums reeked of poverty that had no energy, mired in a deadness of spirit so that its people could do nothing. Where was family, old and young, helping one another? Those left behind were the weakest, waiting for the grim reaper to take them away.

They kept on walking and found themselves outside the Custom House. Caulfield's voice was clearer now, but his stomach still growled.

'What are we doing here?' he asked.

'It wasn't meant to be a grand tour,' said the man.

'I have seen more of slums that you will ever see. Where do you think medical students learn the ropes?'

'I suppose so,' said the man.

'The question is, what are we doing here?'

The man lit a cigarette and sat down at the base of a pillar.

'We will move on in a few minutes,' he said, 'and get something to eat, and then we will talk or perhaps we won't talk.'

'It's possible,' the man continued, 'that we will retire to our respective mansions, and failing this we can take to our tents, O Israel.'

The man spoke in a dream-like manner. Caulfield was getting interested.

'Where I want to go,' said Caulfield, 'is to bed, and a crust of bread where love is. Can we head in that general direction?'

The man threw his cigarette away and stood up.

'Let's go, then.'

They walked on and came to O'Connell Street.

1 am.

They came to an Italian café. The manageress was a faded woman with tired eyes. She looked at them without any great interest.

'What do you want?' asked the waitress.

'My name is Hemingway,' said Caulfield – and then he lost the thread. 'I have come here,' he continued, 'I have come here… to eat the big chip.'

'So that's chips,' said the woman, not batting an eyelid.

'Just coffee,' said the little man.

'Only coffee,' said the woman.

Caulfield looked at him.

'What about chips?' Caulfield said.

'Just coffee,' said the little man.

'This is the chips capital of the world,' urged Caulfield.

'Let's sit down,' said the little man.

The two men sat down and tried to sum each other up.

Caulfield looked closely at the little man. He noticed the ring, the Rolex watch, the Royal Cotton shirt and silk tie, the Magee suit, the cashmere coat and Burberry scarf.

This fellow is no bum, thought Caulfield.

The man looked closely at Caulfield. His shoulders were wider than he thought. He looked at his hands and wrists. They were the hands of an athlete.

When Caulfield stooped to pick up a napkin the pack of muscle in his shoulders moved in unison.

He is fantastic, said the little man to himself, *even when he is drunk.*

Caulfield looked around the café again. He noticed the portrait of Toscanini.

'Ah! the divine Toscanini,' he called out.

He started to hum Beethoven's Fifth.

'Da da da dum,' he called out. 'Join me,' he said to the man, 'da da da dum.'

The man ignored him.

Caulfield turned to the table where two women were sitting.

'Sing Beethoven!' he shouted, 'da da da dum, da da da dum!'

The women looked affronted, not sure to be indignant or amused.

'I beg your pardon,' said the manageress to Caulfield. 'Please keep your voice down in this establishment.'

Caulfield looked goggle-eyed at her. The little man nodded his head vigorously.

'Yes, madam,' remarked the little man. 'This is a respectable establishment. I can see for myself that you don't allow misbehaving.'

'Absolutely,' said the woman, looking gratified, 'No misbehaving, no spitting on the floor, no taking the Lord's name in vain.'

'That's what I call a good establishment,' said the little man.

'Do you allow dancing?' asked Caulfield.

The woman looked scornful, and then she hesitated and a far off look came into her eyes.

'Dancing,' she said, thoughtfully. 'I never thought of dancing. I must mention it to Mr. Luciano.'

The little man made an approving noise.

'Of course, it must be respectable dancing.'

Caulfield shook his head 'I can't stand unrespectable dancing,' and to the woman, 'I hope you won't allow that class of dancing.'

'Absolutely,' said the woman, drawing herself up. 'Only the best class of dancing would be allowed.'

Caulfield looked around. 'If you took out six tables,' he said, 'you could have a nice little dance floor.'

The woman served them with chips and coffee. She had something to think about.

The little man said 'Isn't it strange? You talk about something completely stupid, but when you start thinking then perhaps there is something to it.'

Caulfield pondered. 'This could be the Palais de Dance di Luciano. It all started here.'

'Absolutely,' said the man.

'I was thinking of your home in Dorset Street and how your father brought you up, you have come a long way,' said Caulfield.

'A long, long way.'

'How did you make your first big deal?'

'By doing a man. By lying to him.'

Caulfield looked at his eyes. They were steady. He didn't avert them. No sign of shame was on his face.

Caulfield said, 'You are very frank. Can you justify your action of cheating and lying?'

'I can,' said the man. 'It's very simple. I never lied to anyone who first didn't lie to me. The first man to lie to me I destroyed. The honest man who was stupid I put on his feet, and gave him some advice.'

'What was the advice?'

'I advised him not to be stupid again.'

'That sounds like sensible advice,' said Caulfield.

Caulfield seemed to be an age chewing over one chip, and then he spoke.

'Alright, sir, vot is it you vont, and vot is going on?'

The little man looked at him under hooded eyes.

'I want you,' he said, 'but not for myself.'

Caulfield looked at him in puzzlement.

'It's a very special job.'

Caulfield looked pained and shook his head in disbelief, as if to say, '*this is the end.*'

'Do you think,' said Caulfield, 'that I need a job? Do you not know that I am going to be a doctor?'

He pushed himself to his feet and wagged his finger in the man's face.

'A doctor, do you hear that! Not only a doctor, but a medical protector.'

He stumbled over the words 'a medical protector.' He got it right the third time.

'A medical practitioner.'

He thundered out the words. The man turned away as the diners listened. The customers were hoping for an argument, perhaps a few blows struck. The manageress rushed up, she hated trouble late at night.

'Sir,' she called out, 'I thought you were a gentleman.'

'Oh, but I am,' said Caulfield, clutching his chest. 'I am the perfect gentleman, not an ordinary gentleman, but the perfect gentleman.'

'Do you know,' he said in a confidential voice, 'do you see this man?' They looked at the little man. 'I found him in the gutter. I picked him up. I put a coat on his back and shoes on his feet. I arranged membership for him in the National Geographic Society. He had seven children – I sent them away to Mrs. Caulfield's orphanage, where they got fresh bread every day, and butter and jam on a Sunday. I did all this for him, and now...' he paused, '...and now he has turned on me.'

Caulfield raised his hands at the ingratitude of it all. Life can be so unfair.

The man sat there looking pained.

'But do you know what I am going to do?' he patted the manageress on the back, 'I am going to have an office and I am going to spend the rest of my life treating old ladies for ingrown toe nails.'

There was a titter from one of the other tables. The manageress looked anxious, it was two in the morning, and she was on her own. Caulfield continued to yell.

'I'll have a surgery in Harley Street, and all the Duchesses and Royal Highnesses will queue up for me to fix their damned ingrown toe nails.'

The little man looked unamused. Almost as if he realised what an exhibition he was making, Caulfield sat down quickly and quietly said to the man,

'Now you see why I don't want a job.'

The two men sat back in their chairs. Minutes passed as the pair sat in silence. The manageress relaxed a little. Caulfield chewed another chip. It was cold and soggy.

The man sat there with folded arms, as if he was asleep. The two women paid for their tea and left, and then the little man spoke.

'There is no good in me saying anything to you in this state. I want to see you in the Shelbourne at 10.30am. on Wednesday.'

Caulfield looked up in amazement.

'You want to see me, sir, at 10.30 in the Shelbourne?' he asked with heavy sarcasm.

'Yes.'

'At 10.30 am.?' his voice rising to a crescendo, 'and I'll be there at 10.25 am. for I wouldn't like to keep an important gentleman like you waiting, would I?'

'Shut up, Caulfield.'

'And I'll have to shut up, sir. I'll have to do what I'm told, sir. Won't I, sir?'

The man looked up and down.

'I can have no respect for anyone who can't hold his liquor.'

Caulfield jumped up as if electrified. He grabbed a handful of chips and flung them at the man's head. He missed and the chips went flying over the ground. The manageress screamed and grabbed a sweeping brush, but the little man was quick. He shoved something into her hand and she looked at it. It was a 50 Euro note.

'I'm sorry for your trouble,' he said, and she smiled in relief.

'It's alright, sir. Thank you, sir.'

He went back to his table. Caulfield had collapsed, he was devastated.

He moaned. 'What am I doing? God almighty, what am I doing?'

The little man laughed and patted him on the back.

'Let this be a lesson to you, Caulfield. Don't skip your breakfast again.'

He nodded.

'For the last time, I want to see you on Wednesday morning at 10.30 am.'

Caulfield replied in a barely audible voice. 'I have lectures on Wednesday.'

'No, Caulfield, you have no lectures on Wednesday. You are not walking wards on Wednesday, you are not fixing toenails on Wednesday, you are not screwing nurses on Wednesday. You are off all day Wednesday. I know, because I checked it.'

'I give in,' said Caulfield.

The man took an envelope from an inside pocket.

'In case you feel like changing your mind between now and Wednesday I am giving you a deposit. If you are not going to do it, bring back the deposit. If you are I'll pay you ten grand along with this.'

Caulfield's hands shook as he opened the envelope. Inside was twenty 50 Euro notes.

'Is this legal?' asked Caulfield.

'Quite legal.'

Before Caulfield could do or say any more the little man rose quickly to his feet and walked out. As he did so, he was nearly knocked down by Murphy and Henley-Smith as they charged in.

Henley-Smith looked after him. 'Who is that little guy? I think I have seen him somewhere before.'

"What are you doing here?" asked Caulfield.

"We are temporarily and financially out of funds," replied Murphy, "and we searched high and low for you.

Caulfield took out an envelope crammed with 50 Euro notes. "See these."

I earned them from the sweat of my brow. I will have to think about them and then do nothing."

In the meantime I will go to bed."

"Divide by three," said Henley-Smith, "after all that's what friends are for."

Chapter 2

Caulfield & Herzog

It was almost 10.30am. Caulfield had twice walked around Stephen's Green, bringing a nice flush to his complexion.

He was not sure what to wear. Perhaps he should have a suit for the Shelbourne. But he had only one and it was shiny, with two buttons missing.

He checked his watch. It was 10.30 as he climbed the steps. Henley-Smith and Murphy had promised him moral support, and they took their stand on the far side of the road.

In the long sitting room of the Shelbourne the little man was waiting. In front of him a silver pot and two coffee cups and saucers.

He rose to shake Caulfield's hand. 'We meet under happier circumstances.'

Caulfield smiled and said, 'Sorry about last Saturday.'

For some reason he felt ill at ease; the little man was in full control. He lifted a finger and a waiter came and poured out two coffees.

'It is wonderful what money can do,' said Caulfield, a little sourly.

'Exactly,' said the man, 'people in my position never inherit respect, we always have to buy it.'

Caulfield had decided that he would let the little man do the running. He lifted his cup and sat back. He said nothing, and glanced around the room.

Two prominent politicians were talking earnestly. Farther on, a vicar just up from the country, was talking horses to two jolly looking girls. A sales rep. opened and closed a briefcase, looking out for his contact. A couple of tweedy women chattered in loud voices.

An exceptionally attractive woman sat by a window. Not only attractive, but expensive. She was dressed in a sage green unlined linen jacket. Her skirt, an inch below the knee, was in a matching fabric and colour. Unlike the jacket the skirt was fully lined. It gave a soft rustle when she moved. Her champagne camisole top was surely pure silk. Caulfield looked at her basket weave peep-toe shoes in rich tan. She carried a small suede leather tan clutch bag. On the right lapel of her jacket was pinned a gold mosaic multicoloured peacock brooch. She sat down, and crossed her legs elegantly, and flicked her hair into place. In general Caulfield knew nothing about women's fashions, style, clothes or jewellery, but even he could see that this woman had it all.

Her complexion suggested Greek, but she couldn't be, as she was too tall when she stood up. Caulfield found himself catching his breath and cursing as she moved. Passing him by, she left the room.

Caulfield looked at the little man to see if he had noticed her, but apparently not. In fact, he seemed to be struck by a young fat waitress with lipstick all over her face.

Caulfield sank back into the cushions of the sofa and waited. He closed his eyes and thought of ankle jewellery, long legs and olive complexions. He thought diamond clasps, pearls and gold necklaces. Someone tapped his knee. It was the little man.

'Are you dreaming?' he asked, 'are you dreaming about ingrowing toe nails?'

Caulfield smiled bleakly. 'I guess I am back in the real world,' he said.

The man opened his wallet and took out a business card. 'You might as well know who I am.'

Caulfield read 'Isaac Herzog.' Suddenly his memory jolted to a casual meeting in Henley-Smith's home some years before.

'Does it mean anything to you?' said the man.

Caulfield read the name again. *Isaac Herzog.* 'Don't you have something to do with a bank?'

'Yes,' said the man, 'I own a bank. In fact, I own two banks.'

Caulfield said, 'This is a bit too rich for my taste.'

'Just call me Isaac,' said the man, 'and don't be bowled over by my owning a bank. It's like owning a grocery store, only you sell money instead of eggs.'

'I want to tell you, Isaac, that I am no use to you. I can't pull off deals. My financial acumen is confined to dividing my weekly allowance by seven. If my weekly allowance doesn't come I have to divide zero by seven, multiplied by the cost of not being able to eat. It never seems to work out.'

Herzog was one of those people who can laugh without moving his lips.

'You understand,' said Caulfield, 'that I don't own two banks.'

Herzog threw his arms out. 'Good heavens,' he moaned. 'What sort of a place is this? Meeting someone who doesn't own a bank!' Then speaking seriously to him, he went on, 'I want you because you are the only person qualified to give.' He waited, and then went on. 'I dare say your friends Mr. Murphy and Mr. Henley-Smith might have been suitable. Physically they are fine people, ethnically I have no complaints, intellectually I am sure they are first class, but you have that something extra. Consequently it must be you.'

Said Caulfield, 'I feel confused.'

Herzog beckoned to a waiter for fresh coffee. Caulfield was struck by the obsequious manner of the waiter as he moved to serve.

A hotel guest came into the room and recognised Herzog. He hesitated, as if to stop and speak, but seeing him engaged reluctantly moved on.

Caulfield said again, 'I feel confused.'

They drank their coffee. Caulfield thought again of the woman. Would she come back? Would he get a whiff of her perfume as she walked by, what sort of precious stone was in her bracelet, which matched so perfectly with her suit?

He gave a slight groan: *these things don't happen to me.*

'Are you listening?' said Herzog.

'Yes, Isaac, every word.'

'I'll get to the point,' Herzog continued. 'I have a wife, Abigail, and I am glad to say I love her dearly and she loves me. I am in a position to give her anything she wants and she gets it. Houses, boats, cars, clothes and jewellery. We travel the world. Through my company we entertain the leaders of the nations, big and small. My wife is welcomed by crowned heads.'

Caulfield said in what was almost a whisper, 'And a few minutes ago she was sitting by the window and sizing me up.'

Herzog sat back with a jolt. 'Yes, you are right.'

Caulfield took a couple of deep breaths.

'OK,' he said, 'Carry on.'

Herzog continued, and his voice became increasingly intense. The two politicians stopped talking and strained to listen.

'My wife and I have received honours from the UK, France and the Nordic countries. I have endowed chairs in more than twenty universities. In your own country, in this city, in your own college, I financed a research unit for applied science at a cost of fourteen million dollars.'

Caulfield winced. Now he recognised it. He passed the building every day. 'I am sorry,' he said. 'I should have known it.'

Herzog continued, 'In Israel, an entire university is called after my wife.'

'Alright, alright,' said Caulfield, 'I believe your every word. I am tremendously impressed. Don't say any more.'

The intensity of Herzog's tirade seemed to flatten him. 'Just one question, Isaac. If this is all true, as I know it is, what were you doing in a cheap Italian café last Saturday night?'

Herzog leaned forward and grasped Caulfield's arm in an iron grip. 'I want you to provide my wife… with a child,' he said.

Chapter 3

Murphy

Murphy and Henley-Smith stamped their feet against the cold. They were getting tired waiting for Caulfield to come out, from his meeting with Herzog.

'What's keeping him?' said Murphy, 'he must have sold his soul by now.'

They decided to leave and walked down Dawson Street to College Green. Murphy was troubled. It was strange, to say the least of it, that the two of them were walking together like puppies, waggy-tailed and friendly, after the events of Saturday night. Everything had happened so quickly.

The sight of Henley-Smith standing with clenched fists and a scowling determination had made him think. Had he taken on too much? He had felt fear on Saturday.

He took a side-glance at Henley-Smith. He must be six foot four inches and weighed in about sixteen stone. If he wasn't yellow he could have been a dangerous fighter. At rugby, if he went for the line with a bit of determination, he could have walked on to the Irish team. But Murphy knew he had made a mistake on Saturday, pushing him too far.

As for that stupid catch-call of his, he had better forget it.

And now they were together again, as happy as Larry.

They passed Davy Byrne's and Henley-Smith said, 'How about a pint?'

'No, thanks,' said Murphy. He only had eight cent in his pocket, and he knew he could not stand his round until Saturday.

'Come on,' said Henley-Smith, 'I'll stand you.'

Murphy gave in.

There were times when Murphy quite liked Henley-Smith. On his own he was alright; he wasn't mean, he didn't have a bad word to say about anyone, he didn't throw his weight about – not much – and the pint he stood you was first class. *What's wrong?* he thought, *is it me, or is it Henley-Smith? One minute I am all over him, the next minute I'd love to bury him.*

But Henley-Smith always liked to put people in their place. Mention anyone – say the Dalai Lama – and he would say, 'Oh yes, I was at school with him,' or Joe Stalin – 'Oh, I was at school with him.'

At times Murphy could not stand Henley-Smith's manner. Say something to him, and he would look you up and down with that half-sneer, as if to say, '*what the hell do you know about it?*'

It made Murphy cringe. Despite his size, Henley-Smith was forever atremble, terribly anxious to be liked. If he told a story and if it fell flat, he would almost cry.

Daddy is in the Navy, said Murphy to himself, *but if he is, why is this lump of lard not in it as well?*

'I wonder where Caulfield is now?' said Henley-Smith. That was it, everything ended up with Caulfield. Without Caulfield, they would hardly have spoken to each other. Each of them wanted Caulfield.

Murphy felt relaxed and at ease with Caulfield, his jokes (usually outrageous) were funnier, the time passed quickly. He felt he could unburden himself to Caulfield, he was a man's man, yet sympathetic and practical. The women in college were mad about him.

Caulfield ruled a man's world. On the rugby pitch the raw power seemed to surge from his boots. He seemed to fill those boots until he strained the top lacing. The man's world was not open to women, it was a world they could not enter or understand.

Henley-Smith was looking at him.

'What are you thinking about, Murphy?'

Murphy shook his head, he could not answer. He knew that in the blackness of his night Caulfield would come.

Nobody but Caulfield knew of the fears that might strike at Murphy, of the convulsions that tightened his body to a scream.

Henley-Smith finished his pint. Murphy had not even tasted his. Henley-Smith looked at him again. *I don't even know this guy.* Henley-Smith left.

Murphy remained in Davy Byrne's for over an hour. He barely sipped his drink, which anyway had gone flat. He started to think of Henley-Smith again. *I might be mixed up, but he is more mixed up. That fellow came to college after leaving the Navy.* There was something shady about Henley-Smith; perhaps he might have got the Admiral's daughter pregnant. Murphy did not know much about the Royal Navy, but he knew it was not something that you just left. His thoughts turned to the match to Henley-Smith on Saturday.

Wanderers were ten yards from the goal line. Henley-Smith was on the blind side, he was supposed to be marking, their winger. He had the reputation of being dirty. Tackle him in that position when he was going for the line and you would get a knee-full of him into your mouth. Murphy smiled grimly, he had tried that on him last year and he left him stretched. The fellow had to be carried off.

The referee could have sent Murphy off, but he had seen the winger before and he knew what the score was. He just awarded a penalty and frowned at Murphy. This time Wanderers won the put in, and it was clear as anything they would play the blind side. The scrumhalf dummied, as if to open the middle. Every dog in the street could see the dummy coming, but of course Henley-Smith pretended to buy the dummy, ran to the middle, leaving the blind side open. It was going to be a soft one for him, but he stumbled, and Caulfield, racing across managed to tackle him into touch at the corner flag.

Murphy clenched his fist until it whitened. What bugged him was Henley-Smith, running over always a bit too late. Full of action when it was all over. Caulfield had saved his bacon then, and would continue to do so.

Why? he asked himself, *why?*

Murphy was a bit tall for prop forward, but he had the strength. He was strong enough to bring down the scrum. He knew it was illegal, but not easy for the referee to see, and you had a good chance of getting away with it.

He grabbed a young barman by the arm.

'What was Henley-Smith doing when we were leaving our guts on the pitch?'

The young barman was startled. 'I don't know,' he said.

'I'll tell you,' whispered Murphy, 'just between you and me. Henley-Smith is my vote for Jerk of the Year.'

The barman nodded and backed away.

'And all he did last Saturday was to waltz up and down the touchline and show his backside to those girls from Loreto.'

The barman did not know what to do or say. A senior man came over and said, 'Excuse me, sir, but he has some work to do.'

'Of course, of course, I should have known.' Shouting at the top of his voice, he roared to the senior barman. 'That's a fine young fellow. You give him a raise to-morrow, won't you? Will you give him a raise to-morrow?'

'Sure.'

Murphy cried, 'That's good. That young fellow will go far.'

One would think that Murphy was drunk, but in fact, he had no drink. He was cold sober but he was being possessed by a profound sadness. He shouted to drive away the demons. He looked in the mirror of the bar and saw his mother. She was crying and shouting. She was hitting him. He cried and tried to run away, and then he saw the horror and the devils. The lake and a boat. His little sister was in the boat. She was smiling, the sun shone through her golden hair, and then she fell into the water. She cried, but he could not rescue her. He was afraid. He did not know that the water was only two feet deep and he ran away; he ran and he ran. His mother was beating him and he ran; he ran as far away as possible until he could run no more and collapsed sobbing on the ground.

In the evening mist he saw his little sister, the light was still shining in her hair. She was smiling and held out her hand, but he could not move.

She faded away, and then his mother came and she beat him.

The bar was silent. A woman left. There was no sound but his sobs. And then Murphy felt a comforting arm around him.

It was Caulfield.

'Come on, Murph,' he said, 'let's go home.'

After taking Murphy home, Caulfield stayed with him and put him to bed. He was not yet a doctor. He asked one that lectured him in the hospital to come in and give Murphy a shot, and he spent a restless night. He never stopped muttering, talking to his grandmother, long since dead.

The next morning Murphy was soundly asleep, snoring away. Caulfield decided to telephone Murphy's parents. He had met them once at the college races with Henley-Smith. Murphy had always put out that he was a rough diamond, born in the Kerry Mountains to poteen makers. In fact, his father was an economist in a government department in Limerick. His mother lectured in French literature.

He knew their 'phone number and called them. They were both at home. His father answered, but very quickly handed over to his wife. Caulfield gave her a brief description omitting the part she played in his fantasy.

She listened coolly, almost indifferently. Caulfield felt like hanging up. He explained that he was a medical student – she was not to be influenced by his opinions – and then went on to talk about Murphy, fluctuating widely between extremes. He lived in the past and then was pushy to day.

She listened in silence and when Caulfield was finished, said nothing. He waited for her to day something, anything. Caulfield felt he had to ask one question and get an answer.

'Mrs. Murphy, I must ask you this. Did you have a little daughter who died in infancy?'

Again, there was no answer from her, and she hung up.

'Damn the bitch!' said Caulfield.

It was Thursday. He remembered about lectures. He let Murphy sleep on and rushed away to the hospital. If he was in early enough he could get a good breakfast. There was also a pretty girl from the north, and he always enjoyed her friendly smile and banter.

Caulfield was back in his rooms by eight o'clock. He was not too surprised to see Murphy up and about in the kitchen frying rashers.

'How are you?' he asked.

'Fine,' said Murphy, 'Overslept a bit, had some weird dreams, but that was the bad beer.'

'I'm going to play doctor. Come on, be reasonable, let me take your temperature.'

'There's nothing wrong with me,' said Murphy.

'Yes, there is, and don't ask me what it is, but yesterday you were a sick man.'

Murphy said nothing, but stood still. Then he turned off the gas and sat down on his bed. He was trying to figure out what, if anything, had happened. He knew Caulfield was not a scaremonger, but there was a missing twelve hours in his life.

'Two degrees over, and that's two degrees too much,' said Caulfield.

'I remember being in the pub,' said Murphy, 'I must have gone on a bender. I think you left and you wanted to come back here, so you quit and I stayed. Henley-Smith came in and we had a few pints, and then he left. I suppose I must have had some more, though I don't know where I got the money.'

'You remember me being there?' asked Caulfield.

'I sure do,' said Murphy.

'Murph,' said Caulfield, 'I wasn't there.'

Murphy sat still on the edge of the bed. He tried to figure out who was with him. It was very complicated, the little pieces of the jigsaw did not make the picture, and now his head was beginning to pain.

'Caulfield,' he whispered, 'I have a headache.'

'I wasn't with you,' said Caulfield, 'and you were only with Henley-Smith for one pint. You were with nobody except yourself, and it's no fun to be with yourself. You travelled back twenty years and you relived a Sunday afternoon. Do you remember, Murph, the sun was shining, the children were playing...'

'Stop it, Caulfield!'

'You must face it, Murph. It won't go away. You remember what happened. What happened, Murph?'

Murphy lay back on the bed and covered his face.

'There was a little girl,' he sobbed.

'The little girl,' said Caulfield, 'was she your sister?'

'No,' said Murphy.

'Are you sure?' asked Caulfield.

Murphy's body shook. Caulfield could not tell if he was crying or not.

'Are you sure?' asked Caulfield again.

'Yes.' yelled Murphy, 'She was my sister. I killed my sister.'

He stood up. 'I don't want to talk about it. I don't know if I was even there. I don't know anything.'

'OK,' said Caulfield, 'that's enough, I'll get you something for your headache.'

He came back with some aspirin but the room was empty. Murphy had gone.

Caulfield ran down the steps two at a time and raced out to the quad. Murphy was not there; he went out to College Green but saw nothing.

40

A familiar voice spoke behind him. It was Herzog.

'Are you looking for Mr. Murphy?'

'Yes,' said Caulfield.

'Well then, join him in the Shelbourne. I told him to go there and have a good feed.'

He caught up with Murphy in the Shelbourne, and Murphy was arguing with a waiter. He had forgotten Herzog's name and the waiter was not inclined to serve him.

Caulfield quoted Herzog and the waiter smiled.

'God bless the Sons of Israel,' said Murphy.

They had a good meal and it was nearly 10 pm. Caulfield left Murphy in the hotel, he wanted to call Limerick, reverse charge.

It took some effort to get them to accept a reverse charge call.

'Mrs. Murphy, this is Caulfield again. Pardon me for calling so late, but I want to speak about Kevin.'

'I don't think it's any business of yours.'

Caulfield felt he had overstepped matters.

'Look, I am sorry. I just rang you up to find out about Kevin, he was in a bad way yesterday.'

'Alright,' she said, 'I can't say anything now, but I'll suggest to Kevin to ask you down to Limerick for the summer. Perhaps we can get an opportunity to talk.'

'Thanks, Mrs. Murphy.'

Caulfield went to bed. It was then that he remembered about Herzog. A cold shower was not as cold. When he was finished with Herzog on Wednesday it seemed quite reasonable. Herzog was a man of means, well spoken, sane, a brilliant academic record and he undoubtedly had a beautiful wife.

The whole thing was legal, if not too respectable; the Medical Union could not object, he was not a doctor yet and even if he was, she was not his patient. Basically, it was very, very simple.

And yet something nagged. There was a fear of the unknown. He was walking into something that he could not handle. There was

41

something that Herzog had not told him, and he had his own problems that Herzog did not know.

Supposing the whole thing went wrong? Did Herzog and Abigail have some ulterior motive? Had they planned to make a cat's-paw out of him? Caulfield was conscious of his inexperience in the company of these worldly, sophisticated high-flyers.

Basically, he was just a country-boy; he could be used and made a laughing stock. The glossy magazines would write him up as *'Mr. Deeds goes to town'*, a simple minded hayseed holding a rugby ball, open-mouthed and confused.

Would Herzog and Abigail be capable of planning such a thing?

Caulfield rose and went to the window; he gazed out on the sleeping city. His mind travelled to the sleeping countryside, to Ballynale and Tipperary.

It represented decency and friendship and truthful living.

He had not given a straight answer to Herzog. The issue was not settled. He would have to check out Abigail, who he had barely seen. He felt Herzog was straight, but a man did not get where he got by playing goody-two-shoes.

After all that, he would have to check out himself.

Chapter 4

Herzog
Flash Back, 1951

Herzog enjoyed walking. Even in the city, he could stroll without bumping into others and a favourite walk was from the Shelbourne down to College Green, to Dorset Street where he could stand wrapped in thoughts and return back as he had come.

When he bought the building ten years ago he had left the windows broken as they were, so that the world would remember Kiev.

An hour of walking and thinking, he stood for some time and he could almost hear the clickity-click of the sewing machine. That place would always be his home. Now he preferred to stay in hotels – the King David, Shelbourne, Savoy, Plaza – with his bags half-packed, a thousand or so dollars in the room safe, his shoes polished from the night before. From his earliest day he left quickly.

He looked at the windows again and he remembered Kiev. His father had often reminded him and his brothers of that madness. The pogrom started when the synagogue was torched, and a bonfire made of the holy books.

Then it was the turn of the little shops – his grandfather's kosher butcher, the saddlers, the tailors, the home for Jewish widows.

Then it was their house. The stones came through the windows. His father told him how he fled to his mother's bed for security.

The next day the unspeakable. Old women were stripped naked and tied to lampposts. His grandparents were forced to scrub the pavements of Kiev with their own excrement. His father, Emmanuel, said that one of the worse things that he felt was when he asked his father what wrong they had done to deserve this, he said he did not know.

His father told his parents that they must get out, there was no future in Kiev, but they would not leave its familiar streets. In the end they let him go. He refused the meagre help they could offer but he took what were most valuable, names and addresses of relatives, friends, cousins, uncles, aunts across central and northern Europe. It stretched to Chernivov, Kalinkovich, Warsaw, Budapest, Vienna, Frankfurt.

They took him in, fed and clothed him, wept over him and sent him on his way.

Isaac Herzog looked again at the fourth floor of 85 Dorset Street. Speaking to the ghost of his father, Emmanuel, he said, 'You travelled all that way to end up here.'

Herzog had remembered the day he got sick. It was his eleventh birthday. For his treat he was allowed to sleep in his mother's bed. It was a fine sunny day and the happy sounds of children floated up from the street.

He cried, and Emmanuel his father came to him. 'Voszhe iz kleyn yingl?' he asked him in Yiddish. 'What is it, little boy?' He replied in Yiddish, 'Ikh filn zikh salafkeyt.' 'I feel sick.' Emmanuel sat down and stroked his hands. Isaac Herzog noticed his father's hands; they were as small as a girl's. His thumbs particularly fascinated Herzog. He could bend them backward to a U shape. He often felt like asking him how it was done.

Herzog felt that he was his father's favourite son. The idea was pleasing, and yet from time to time it worried him. It was a burden he was carrying, even as a child. Emmanuel Herzog was starting to reminisce. He would remember Kiev. The smell of orange groves, the dog he had, the sight of men fishing who sometimes let him hold their rods.

He didn't remember everything, but it was always there, like sand in an oyster.

Emmanuel's description of his flight across Europe was one that always bored his son Isaac. A meaningless list of names, cities and relations who he never saw again.

'I came here,' said his father. He stood up, went to the window, and looked down on the street. 'I came here,' he said again, 'and met your mother. Sanovich, the piano tuner, sent her around here. He was her uncle. Three children were reared in this room. Your two older brothers and you.'

Herzog started to feel sleepy, but his father droned on. Emmanuel was a scholar at heart. Although leaving school at twelve years of age he longed for the company of books, ideas, the conversation of the teachers – any type of learning. Denied the company of the learned, he would go down to the synagogue and listen to them as they discussed the law and the latest books.

He was encouraged to join in, although his contribution was naïve and ill-informed; but they indulged him and understood. They smiled benevolently, nodding with agreement. His great pride was that his mother was descended from the medieval scholar, Weisek of Prague. This increased his standing, but constant reference to Weisek tended to lead people to yawn.

All his ambitions fell upon his children. His two eldest sons disappointed him. Instead of Leviticus, they talked about football. They left school as soon as they could, went into commerce at which they excelled. They were dutiful sons and vainly tried to persuade their parents to move to a pleasant bungalow.

Emmanuel's attention was focused on his youngest son, Isaac. Small for his size and thin as a whip, he was forever getting sick. However, Isaac brought joy to his father.

45

Hardly ever without a book in his hand, he read everything and raced home quickly after school to steal an extra hour in the public library.

As a special treat, he went to the synagogue with his father, to listen and dispute with the learned elders. His father almost burst with pride to hear him argue a point with style and authority. It did not take Isaac long to discover that the alleged erudition of these men was not what was claimed, and all they tended to talk about was the old days in Poland, rather than the fine points of the law.

Isaac won every prize at school. He was unequalled at mathematics as he was at languages, history or English. He astounded his math teachers by working out geometry problems in his head. He had proved to be an outstanding student and scholar. At the university, he won, as a matter of course, every scholarship and exhibition for which he was eligible.

Emmanuel's cup was filled to overflowing. With every academic success, his father toured all the establishments in Dorset Street, finding excuses to call to the bank, the library, the dry cleaners, even the bookies owned by Passchier, his wife's cousin. They all listened open-mouthed, and expressed their admiration at Isaac's success.

There was hardly any more to win. But Isaac said, 'Only one – the gold medal.' Yes, his father had heard. The elders knew of it and occasionally inquired to Isaac if he was sitting. One of their nephews had won the great prize ten years ago, and was now in Harvard.

If he won, his name would be on the Achievements Board in the Examination Hall, for all generations to see. Isaac Herzog would be immortal. Doors would open for him across the world. Invitations would flood in from Yale, Princeton, Heidelberg, the Sorbonne, Oxford, Cambridge, Jerusalem. He would dine with the provost. But Isaac knew that defeat was not just possible, it was also highly probable.

McNight was also sitting the examination. He had tried last year but withdrew. He was being talked about as the favourite this year. Isaac knew he had only one chance. If he failed once he knew that he did not deserve another go.

Isaac thought he had the measure of McNight. His false cordiality stuck in Isaac's throat. He could not stand the sight of him in his tweed suit and scarlet cravat. It got under his skin to listen to his ascendancy voice with an underlay of Belfast. Isaac admitted to himself that McNight was a good scholar, but he lacked a spark – there was something missing. McNight was all grind and all swot.

Isaac wanted to win. He wanted to win for the sake of a little man back in Dorset Street, for his mother who lived in her own silent world, for his aunts and uncles who saved his life in the ghettoes, for his grandmother who screamed for pity from the thugs of Kiev. For all his people who were kicked like dogs from generation to generation.

The year before he sat the exam, Isaac went to see for himself what it was like. There was a mob of people at the Notice Board; the different candidates were there with their supporters, friends and followers. Some parents appeared but they were shooed away, tradition dictated that they could not attend. All the candidates, of course, were loudly claiming that they had no chance and were already commiserating with themselves.

The winner was a dark horse, H.H. O'Driscoll. Isaac was glad it was O'Driscoll, he liked O'Driscoll. He used to take Isaac to his parents' house for a hot dinner. Occasionally he had to borrow a fiver from O'Driscoll, and when he returned it O'Driscoll would claim that it *had* been returned and was not due. Then Isaac had to struggle to push it into his pocket.

O'Driscoll was carried around the quad in triumph. Cheers rent the air, and then the provost appeared.

'Congratulations,' he said, shaking O'Driscoll's hand, 'We were very impressed with your paper. I hope you will dine with us tonight.'

'Yes, provost. Thank you, provost.'

Slats was packed all day long, a tribute to O'Driscoll's popularity.

The following year Isaac sat the examination. He came home that night, his face drained. He was hungry yet couldn't eat; he went to bed but could not sleep. As in the old days, his father came to him, sat by him and rubbed his hands.

'A dank tate.' 'Thank you, father,' he said in Yiddish.

'Bless you my son,' said his father. 'Zeige gebensht meine zun.'

The examination results, according to custom, were announced on the first Monday of May at 10 am. The Proctor would bring down a piece of paper with one name on it and pin it to the wall. That was last year, this year was this year.

At the last moment the day was changed to the previous Friday as the Provost's father had died and the funeral was on Monday.

Friday felt like a dental appointment. The previous Sunday Isaac's father tried to downplay the event with the familiar mantras: *it's not the end of the world, you can have another chance, you can go for scholarship in June.*

'Yes,' said Isaac, 'It's not the end of the world.' But he knew it was, and so did his father.

Friday morning 9 am. Isaac straightened his tie and indulged in the extravagance of two shirt changes in one week. He shook hands. 'Good-bye, Father.' His father grasped his coat.

'Isaac,' he said, 'you will win to-day, and when you do there will be celebrations, yes?'

'I suppose so.'

'You will buy people drinks, perhaps buy champagne?'

'Father, what are you on about?'

'Just wait.'

He went to a vase, plunged his hand into it and took out a £50 note. 'This is for you.'

'Please, I can't take it. You have worked hard for this all your life. I can't spend money you have worked hard for.' His voice trailed away. He was overcome by a powerful emotion.

'Yes, you can,' said his father. 'This is the most important day in your life. It is also the most important in mine. Please take it for my sake.'

Isaac's voice choked, he could not speak. He took the £50 note and fled from the room.

Because of the funeral of the Provost's father, a smaller crowd than usual waited for the result, and the happy buzz of previous years was lacking. McNight was there, attempting to dominate the people waiting but his bon mots fell flat, and he looked around at gloomy faces, tired and hostile.

He was not with friends, nobody was. Everybody's hand was against the other. They could win if everybody else failed. McNight glanced at each of the faces.

Most of them had no hope; a few posed a danger. He knew them from lectures – they were good, but not good enough. McNight knew he could handle them until he came to Herzog, and a spasm of rage went through the man.

He exchanged glances with Herzog and he sensed the Jew's contempt. *How dare he,* thought McNight, *to look at me like that! He has no right to parade within these ancient walls. Let them build their own college and award medals, good enough for a nation of pawn brokers.*

O'Driscoll showed up. He came to Herzog and shook his hand warmly. 'Best of luck! I know you will make it.'

They embraced and he left. McNight looked sick.

The Proctor appeared. A dead silence fell over those assembled. It was as if an execution had been announced. The Proctor caught Herzog's eye and nodded to him.

What does that mean? thought Herzog. *Does it mean 'Congratulations, you have won' or does it mean 'Hard luck, you*

49

have lost'? Those who had gathered there read the name, and then walked quietly away.

One person was left. A pleasant, rather plain looking girl. He didn't know her well, but they used to exchange smiles every time they met.

She went to the notice board and read the name, and then came to Herzog. Putting her hand gently on his arm, she whispered 'Isaac, you must read it sometime. Read it now.'

So Isaac went to the notice:

Winner

ISAAC HERZOG

Herzog walked through the college. He met hardly anyone he knew. He saw McNight training on the rugby pitch. He stopped to say something, but McNight turned his back. He sat down here and there and tried to control himself. It was a fabulous honour for someone whose mother tongue was Yiddish, but if it is why am I not jumping for joy? He headed for the canteen for a cup of coffee. It was usually packed at that time. Surely the news would have gone around. He would go in, there would be a moment of silence and then an explosion of noise: claps, cheers, whistles.

He reached the canteen. It was closed – for repairs. Then he heard cheers. Eagerly he looked around – a group of about twenty men were whooping and hollering. They came up to him smiling. He braced himself for thunderous slaps on his back, but they walked through him without any notice.

He stopped one of them and asked, 'What's going on?'

'Have you not heard?' he replied, 'Baxter has been chosen to play for Scotland next Saturday in Murrayfield. Actually he will be playing against Ireland.'

He hated all athletics, especially football, with their brainless shouting. Kipling's words came to mind '…flannelled fools at the wicket, muddied oafs in goal …'

Herzog stood there as lonely as any man can be.

He left the college and walked home. He saw a man sitting on a bench in O'Connell Street and sat beside him. The man looked suspiciously at Herzog, and then got up and walked away. Herzog didn't know how long he was sitting there. Feeling something in his pocket, he pulled it out. It was a £50 note. He remembered, and looked at for a long time. The £50 note was for him to celebrate and rejoice, to buy champagne, to fill Slats pub with his pals. Then he tore a tiny bit off the note and threw it up and the wind blew it away. Then he tore another bit off and the wind blew that away. And then another bit, and another, until all the note was gone. And then he said to himself, *'They never gave me a kid, that I might make merry with my friends.'*

Chapter 5

Young Caulfield
Flashback 1940

Years later Caulfield could recall that summer. Would Abigail, Herzog's beautiful and future wife, have been a tomboy, playing hide and seek among the haystacks, or would she have been a little madam. Little did Caulfield know of the part she might play in his life.

He was nearly twelve years old, his college years sometime ahead. He was beginning to tower over his contemporaries. In summer, he cycled to Roscrea and played in the Tipperary Tennis Championships. He won first prize in the Juvenile Section, beating players two to three years older than him – and was starting to be talked about.

He never had a lesson. The only help he had was a tattered booklet called *Elements of Tennis* which he found in the church basement. He practised until his backhand was better than his forehand.

Caulfield settled into the rhythm of North Tipperary. He walked all over the place. He liked cattle. He liked to stand among them, and as they chewed the cud he felt that the cows were thinking of something. He felt relaxed. He felt safe.

He whistled for them to come over. They came as cattle always do. He would talk to them and they would look at him with their big gorgeous eyes. He stood among them, slapping their backs. He thought he might like to be a farmer, but the thought of sending away his friends, the cattle, to the meat factories was too upsetting. *Cop yourself on,* he said to himself, *they are only cattle.*

They were more than cattle.

Caulfield would leave after breakfast, walking over the fields, talking to people. At night he would go into some farm and ask if he could sleep in their haggard. Of course, they wouldn't hear of it, he must have a bed. After breakfast, he would do some chores for the farmer's wife – collect water or stack turf, as a 'thank you' for the bed.

As a society, they did not seem to use much money. They made and exchanged, and grew and picked. The pig hung in the kitchen. Thick ham and rhubarb was on the table. Home baked bread and yellow butter that was always fresh. Milk straight from the cow was deliciously hot. At Christmas, old fashioned celery that had to be scrubbed with a brush, the squawking of the turkey hinted that their most hated enemy, the fox, was near.

His Uncle Sam in the Co-Op had some special ideas. One was that school children should never work on their holidays 'Childhood was for children,' he said. Adventure was for boys, college was for falling in love. So Caulfield had a free hand for tennis, for reading, for climbing trees, for swimming in the river and for hanging around.

Caulfield could come and go. But, there were two exceptions – Wednesdays and Sundays. 'You can do what you like on Wednesday,' Uncle Sam told him, 'but you must be back in time for the prayer meeting.'

Uncle Sam was a genuinely religious person. He had a religious experience at seventeen and he had felt that God had called him, but his brother had gone to college and the mission field, and he was wanted at home.

The weekly prayer meeting was on Wednesday at eight o'clock. Caulfield did not say much at the prayer meeting, but he liked the voices of the honest farmers, the murmur of the women, the silences of people at prayer. It seemed to him that people escaped from the humdrum and ordinary. They put aside their cattle and milk and corn, and had a glimpse of the eternal.

Sunday was the day that was special. Shopping even for essentials was frowned upon. Everything about it was special. Their fields were not tilled, the butter was not made, the cattle were not counted. The clothes they wore were different and better. The preacher was invited for lunch (called dinner).

It was a day when many things stopped. The land seemed to rest. It was a day for church, morning and evening. The radio was on only for the news, a gardening talk and hymn singing in the evening.

The church was simple, not beautiful except in the mind's eye. Their ancestors had built the church. A careful people. They were never fashionable. No landlord paid the bill.

Caulfield remembered the day when some relation from England was staying and the sense of shock when he appeared dressed in a sports jacket and grey flannels. Sunday best should have been Sunday best.

One of the big days in the life of the church was Overseas Mission Sunday. The Methodists were justly proud of their missionary outreach – it stretched from China to the South Seas, through Africa and India. Overseas Mission Sunday was most talked about after Caulfield's performance.

Usually the service took the form of a visiting missionary leading worship and telling the faithful the heart-warming message of mass conversions to the gospel.

On this occasion the visiting missioner failed to turn up. No doubt, mechanical failure of the car or sudden illness was to blame, but the minister of the church became anxious. The expectant congregation stirred restlessly.

The minister, speaking from the pulpit, said, 'It appears that the missionary, the Rev. James, has been delayed.'

He licked his dry lips. 'I wonder if there is anyone here who has knowledge of the mission field in – eh – Ceylon, and would like to tell us something of it?'

A voice spoke up. 'Is that where the tea comes from?'

The minister responded eagerly, 'Yes, yes. Do you …?'

The voice said, 'No.'

The minister appeared to close his eyes. 'What about – eh – Africa?' He left the question in the air.

Caulfield became aware that people were looking at him. A whisper spread about the room, and a buzz of conversation developed. The minister looked around at Caulfield. His face brightened up.

'Of course, of course, it's Caulfield! You have been born in Africa on the mission field.'

Caulfield felt some resentment, as he thought the minister said he was born in a field. But the minister continued.

'I am sure we would like to hear, Caulfield, of your experiences in Ghana, where your father laboured for – eh – some years.'

Caulfield pressed himself back into his seat and tried to look invisible.

'Come now, Caulfield, we would like to hear you,' said the minister, and turning to the congregation, 'wouldn't we all like to hear Caulfield, who will tell us something of that – eh – beautiful country?'

There was a confused response from the congregation, it could have been 'Yes.'

The minister took Caulfield's hand and led him up to the pulpit.

'Now, let's start at the beginning, Caulfield, when were you born?'

'I was born,' said Caulfield, 'when I was three.'

The minister nodded enthusiastically at this. 'So, you were three.'

It became obvious that a new atmosphere permeated the church. Men, who had lolled disinterestedly, were now on the edge of their seats. Women stopped fixing their hats. Two ten-year-old girls exchanged anxious looks.

'And tell me, Caulfield, what friends had you to play with?'

'Yes,' said Caulfield, 'I had three little brothers to play with – M'wana, Bigamo and B'moto.'

The minister thought he heard wrongly, but it was essential to keep going.

'Tell me, Caulfield, what was Sunday service like? Much the same as here, eh? Did you sing the same hymns?'

'Sometimes,' said Caulfield, 'at Christmas, everyone brought their spears.'

'Spears?' said the minister, weakly.

'Yes, spears,' said Caulfield. 'We had a big fire, we danced around the fire. We threw pigs from one side to the other and threw spears at the pigs. Anyone who speared a pig was called Burambo-Borono.'

'Burambo-Borono,' said the minister mechanically.

'Yes,' said Caulfield, 'It means Little Jesus.'

'What?' said the minister, tottering back, ashen faced.

'Yes,' said Caulfield, 'you see, it was Christmas.'

The minister opened his mouth to say something, and then left the church for a glass of water.

When he returned Caulfield was in full flow. He discovered that he had a natural gift of eloquence. Some of the congregation was rhythmically banging the floor, while three men at the back stood on pews for a better view.

Not since the time of Wesley was there so much excitement.

Caulfield continued, 'I must tell you about Zambusi. One day I went into the jungle to kill a leopard which was killing our cheetahs. After I shot him, I found a gorilla with a broken leg. I brought him back to our camp, made up a splinter, and bandaged his leg. Ever after he became my faithful friend and followed me everywhere. I called him Zambusi which means ...' He stopped and thought deeply, and then in a flash of inspiration, said '...Faithful Monkey.'

'What does that mean?' asked a man.

'It means Zambusi,' said Caulfield.

'Do you know,' shouted Caulfield, getting more worked up, 'I made a Christian out of Zambusi.'

There were cries from the congregation. Some booed, women screamed and the two little girls clapped their hands delightedly.

'Faithful Monkey!' shouted a young man.

Caulfield looked sternly at him and banged the pulpit; pointing his arm at the youth he cried out, 'There is a special place in hell for scoffers!' Caulfield was amazed as the youth turned pale and crumpled up.

There was a turning of heads in the church. It was the Rev. James who had just arrived. He was looking around in bewilderment, and the minister staggered up to him. He pointed with a trembling hand to Caulfield, but Caulfield had found his voice and vocation and would not be stayed.

'Do you know what I learned?' he asked. 'I learned the gorilla language.'

There was a gasp from the congregation. Caulfield walked from one side of the pulpit to the other.

'And do you know what I taught that gorilla? I taught him...' and he paused to create maximum effect, '...I taught him – the Lord's Prayer. In gorilla language, it goes like this: grunt, grunt – pause – grunt, grunt, grunt.'

The congregation was now suffering from an excess of emotion. Some left the church and stood outside talking in low voices.

'Finally,' said Caulfield, 'finally, my dear friends, I must end on a sad note. I lost my best friend, Zambusi. He was attacked by a polar bear and carried off into the jungle. I jumped on a passing zebra and we rode after him, but it was too late. The polar bear and a crocodile had finished him off. The crocodile attacked me, and I fought with it for two hours. Eventually we found ourselves in the mighty Zambesi River, and we were swept over the waterfall to five thousand feet below. Fortunately I could swim, but the crocodile was drowned.'

Caulfield bowed his head at the finish, left the church and went home.

CHAPTER 6

*The Tennis Court
Flashback 1952*

Caulfield had an abiding affection for Tipperary. Most people thought of Ireland as rain, turf and whiskey.

But Caulfield, either in his vacant or pensive mood, thought of Tipperary as summer evenings, the smell of hay and friendly people and greetings.

His father was in a state of mental collapse when he returned from Africa with the young boy Caulfield, aged three.

His brother, Sam, who ran the North Tipperary Co-Op Society, agreed to take in Caulfield and bring him up with his daughters.

It was an ideal place for an adventurous boy. Rambling corn sheds, broken down bicycles and farm machinery. Hens ran all over the place and never seemed to lay an egg.

As he progressed through boarding school, college and the adulation of crowds of fifty thousand he felt that his roots were never far away from a land of small towns and tidy farms.

Caulfield went to the Protestant National School. He was an object of curiosity to the class. Sometimes he might be asked questions about Africa. Modestly, he would tell how he raced camels through an equatorial rain forest, and then fought a lion with his bare hands.

Being a minister's son, it was deemed that he could never tell a lie. When he did slip up, the shocked onlookers could see the gates of hell opening.Recreation in summer was confined to one tennis court, which had been built by voluntary labour. An enthusiastic

Church of Ireland curate had organised a work party years before, and a contractor who was tarmacadaming the church car park was persuaded to do the same for the new tennis court, free of charge.

Caulfield played every morning (except Sunday) with the rector's son and his own cousins.

The tennis court had no name. It was just the tennis court. There was no president, treasurer or secretary. There was no membership fee. It was open to the town.

And yet it was not quite open to the town. It was open only to the Protestants. The Catholics could not play there.

There was never a meeting that made the decision that only Protestants could play.

It was never thought or considered for a moment that Catholics were not fit to mix with decent Protestants.

In fact, they mixed every day (except on Sunday) in the course of their business and ordinary neighbourliness.

Nobody, not even Catholics, questioned the right of a Protestant tennis court, it was just part of the great, profound, universal scheme of things.

When a newly appointed bank official saw the tennis court and innocently said he would like a game, there was an embarrassed silence followed by looks of panic.

If any Catholic was ill mannered enough to ask why only Protestants played there, he was met with bewilderment and confusion. There were some questions that could not be answered.

The nearest people got down to discussing the fundamentals of the issue were late at night in a public house where sectarian differences tended to dissolve.

A Protestant farmer was challenged on the issue. After pleading ignorance, which was dismissed out of hand, he said something about the difficulties of people playing on Sunday.

When the conversation travelled the Protestant grapevine, there were mixed opinions. There was general disquiet that a Protestant should frequent a licensed premise where alcohol was freely available. Many of them showed their displeasure to this man.

But his excuse that opening the tennis court to all comers might result in Sunday tennis touched a raw nerve.

It justified the Protestantization of the court. The very word of God was on their side. If Sunday tennis got a grip who knows what would happen to the moral fibre of the nation?

The terrible example of the Gaelic Athletic Association was considered. The G.A.A. played all their matches on a Sunday, including the cup finals in Dublin. The Protestants knew that large crowds attended these matches, where the spectators indulged in shouts, cheers and boos.

The spectators even directed remarks to the referee who, whilst not a Protestant, did not deserve to have aspersions cast on his name, his sight and his knowledge of the game. It was also unfair to accuse him of being bribed by the opposition, or to express views regarding his parentage. To do this on any day was bad enough, but to do it on the Lord's Day was to invite the devils of Satan to do their fearful work.

The mark of a true Protestant was to attend church services twice on Sunday, in the morning and the evening. If he went to a football match on Sunday, how would he get back in time for the evening service?

There existed a dark suspicion that the Gaelic Athletic Association was a sinister organisation devoted to the destruction of Protestantism.

The battle lines were drawn.

The tennis court stayed closed on Sunday.

In the village was a man who claimed to be an agnostic. He told the Catholics that St. Peter was never Pope, and to Protestants, he cast doubt on the inerrancy of the Bible.

Strangely enough, the village was rather proud of him. He was looked upon as harmless, and no threat to the established order. His presence was proof of the broadmindedness and sophistication of

61

the people. It was, perhaps, not the Left Bank of Paris, but near enough.

As he did not want to be identified with one group or another, he bought his groceries from Bradshaw's Stores (Protestant to the core), and his petrol, hardware etc. in O'Shea's (a true son of Rome). His own son was sent to the Protestant National School, and his daughters to the convent school.

Seeing one day a Protestant and a Catholic in the street having an amiable conversation, and perhaps arranging for one to help the other about something, he put to them a question.

'Why is it that you men cannot step ten feet to the left and play a game of tennis?'

The question was Machiavellian in its subtlety.

Within an hour, this was being discussed behind closed doors and the finest brains of the village grappled with the issue.

The Protestants felt that it was incumbent on them to answer the question as they were responsible for the court in the first place, and they sought an answer that would be reasonable, magnanimous, truthful, Christian-like, openhearted and firm in the belief that the court was only open to Protestants.

Dermot Flynn.

Dermot Flynn lived with his parents in Patrick Pearse Street, Ballynale. His father worked on the railway and cycled to Nenagh every day.

His mother was renowned for her cooking and spent a few hours in the rectory kitchen most weekdays. Dermot was inclined to be timid; he stood back if there was a shouting match. He did not like loud noises, especially at night-time. He didn't make friends easily. He liked to climb trees and look down at people, sometimes listening to their conversation. One day he overheard a man proposing marriage to a young woman, who shook her head and ran away. He told his mother and they both laughed.

Dermot was a reader. He asked the rector if he could read some of his books; the rector told him to come any time he wanted.

He read *Treasure Island, Captain Marriot, Ivanhoe, Huckleberry Finn, Just William.* He read books about Napoleon, Hannibal and his elephants. From the staunchly unionist library of the rectory he read books about Wolfe in Canada, Clive in India, Cecil Rhodes the hero of Africa – all makers of the British Empire – as well as a history of Mexico and the collected sermons of the Bishop of Oxford.

Dermot met Caulfield when he was trying to mend as puncture on his bicycle. Caulfield was not handy with his hands. The plaster came off the tube, and then he found it difficult to get the tyre under the rim. Caulfield had asked his uncle if he could bring it to O'Shea, a man who fixed tyres for only one Pound. Uncle Sam told him to fix it himself, and gave him a bicycle repair kit. When Dermot saw him struggling to mend the puncture he offered to help, and then fixed it in a jiffy.

From then on the two of them were friends. They went everywhere together. They sold ice cream at a ploughing competition. They painted the back of Bracken's shop. When Bradley's cow got loose they carefully herded her back to her stall. They cycled to Roscrea and paddled in the river, jumping from one stone to another. It was a great summer.

Then Caulfield heard he was being sent away to school. Dermot was not going. He would probably go to the local technical school and learn welding or block laying. They both grew sad at the thought of parting.

The day came when Caulfield had to leave. Caulfield told Dermot he would be home soon for Christmas, and then it would be the same. Next summer would be a great summer.

In December, Dermot called into Uncle Sam's. He was told that Caulfield would be back on the 15th. He already knew it – he had asked the same question twice before.

He knew that the train would stop at Nenagh about ten o'clock. He decided to wait until the afternoon; Caulfield would be back by then. Maybe they could cycle over to Mangan's farm and ride the ponies. He wished that Caulfield could come sooner.

Caulfield's Aunt Hilda baked lovely biscuits with flaked almonds and chocolate; she always had a plate of them when Dermot called. Dermot called at two o'clock and she went in to fetch Caulfield out.

He came out. Dermot was stunned. It was his pal Caulfield, but it wasn't Caulfield. He was taller and different. He was wearing flannel pants with a nice crease, and a blazer with a funny thing on it. His voice was different and there was something calculating in the way he looked at Dermot. Dermot tried to say something to Caulfield in the old, easy way – but he couldn't.

Dermot knew it would never be the same again.

Caulfield's aunt brought out a plate of her almond and chocolate biscuits. Taking one, Caulfield said to Dermot, 'Gosh, they taste good – eh, Flynn?'

Dermot said nothing.

Chapter 7

Stoneyhurst College,

Clitheroe,

Cumbria

Dear Mumsie,

Thank you for the fruit cake you sent over. Fr. Paulus asked for a slice and thought it was delicious. Many thanks.

Two of the priests here are Irish. I do not like them much. They seem to have it in for me. I told one of the fellows in my dormitory that they were both born in a stable. Unfortunately, they heard of it from someone, and they are out to get me.

You will never guess whom I met in the train. A chap called Caulfield, who is going up to Wesley a Dublin School.

He is the chap I beat in the final of the Championship Tennis last summer. Well, I did not actually beat him, but I had him beaten, but the umpire was so biased that he gave him the match. If anyone wants it that much he can have it. I told that to Fr. Paulus and he seemed to agree.

After meeting that fellow Caulfield, I started to think about the tennis finals. I was so confident that I would win, especially as I got through to the final without any trouble.

Unfortunately I told Father that it would be a walk over, and if he wanted to see me play to come early as I might have it won by then.

He came early all right, but by then I was beaten. I tried to explain to him that there is no point in winning some matches, but he started shouting at me, with the usual guff. To see Caulfield knocking up, you would know he had no style. He hit the ball as if he was beating carpets, and his serves were so crude. He just threw the ball in the air and gave it a lash. The problem was that he could put it down each side of the area very accurately. It was difficult to play against.

I can remember the first set. Right enough I know I lost it, but I did not mind that. It was four all. I nearly won the fifth, but two wrong calls by the umpire killed it, and Caulfield was damn lucky with a backhand volley.

I could kill that umpire – a half-blind bank manager – giving the wrong calls. He was trying to light his pipe when Caulfield was serving. No wonder he got two aces.

When he served the second one, the so-called half-blind umpire had to ask a ninety year old woman asleep in a deckchair if it was in or out. She nodded her head, and he gave it in.

Actually, she had not a clue. She was nodding her head all afternoon, and I believe she died two days later.

If I were not a gentleman, I would have torn strips off that umpire.

So I lost the first set, but that did not bother me. I felt I was getting on top of my game. My eye was in and Caulfield looked worried.

I had the service and I was ready to use my secret weapon. It had lightening speed with a hell of a sidespin. I had been coached in it by this fellow Father brought down from Carrickmines. He told me not to use it in social tennis. It was too difficult to play against and it spoilt the game for everyone.

Ah ha, spoil the game for everyone, will it? We will see if it spoils the game for a certain Mr. Caulfield.

I sent down one of the finest serves in my life. It was so fast that you did not see it until it crossed the net. It kicked like a horse and it ended in the pavilion.

I wish Mumsie that you and Auntie Miriam were there to see it. Auntie Miriam would have given me one of those slobbery kisses that she used to send me to bed with.

What a serve! I sauntered to the far side of the court, singing a little tune 'Happy days are here again.' Then I could not believe in what I saw. Caulfield was down on one knee, with his tennis shoe in his hand. He was peering into it.

The umpire called to him 'Are you ready to start, Caulfield?'

'Yes, sir,' he said, 'I thought I had a nail in my shoe, but it was only a stone.'

'Sir' he called him. Remember, Mumsie, Uncle Roslyn? – you did not like him because he drank all our whiskey – but he used to say, 'you can tell a railway porter by the way he says 'sir'.' Everyone said he was a great wit, but when I asked him once what it meant, he said I was stupid. I was only a little boy, and I cried until Auntie Miriam gave me a kiss.

To go back to the tennis match, this so-called umpire asked me, 'Are you ready to serve, Henley-Smith?' 'I have served,' I told him. A little bit of sarcasm is never lost on the lower orders.

'I have served, and the score is fifteen nil.' The umpire pursed his lips and gazed into the distance, as if he saw something interesting on the roof of the pavilion. He waited for some time. Caulfield and I waited.

'The score is nil, and you have yet to serve.' I could not believe it. I had hit a perfect serve and he did not see it. I was getting furious. I could not control my anger at a terrible injustice.

As that one-eyed gardener we used to have – Paddy something or other – would say, I was buckin' mad and rightly so.

'Henley-Smith, it's your serve.'

I gritted my teeth. OK, you half-blind umpire and Caulfield, you Tipperary thick, I am going to show you a thing or two. Caulfield will have no answer to this.

I bounced the ball. There was fear in his eyes. I bounced the ball again – he licked his lips. I bounced the ball again and he turned pale. I served; it went over the net like lightening. It also went over the base line, the wire netting, the ladies' court, into a clump of laburnums.

The umpire said, 'Love fifteen.' I could hear the jeer in his voice.

I knew my justifiable anger had upset my concentration. I also knew that the umpire and Caulfield were now working together. I should have buttered up the umpire before the match.

There was no way I could beat the two of them; why bother to play when they were making it impossible? I stopped trying to win. I would save my energy and skill for another match when I could trash Caulfield. I felt sorry for him. I could feel the fear in him already. He would have no answer to my serve.

Your loving son,
James.

***

Caulfield returned to Ballynale, bearing a precious silver cup, as Juvenile Tennis Champion. He was not elated by his win. He felt sorry for his opponent Henley-Smith, especially as his father berated him in public for lack of effort.

'It's a nice cup,' said Aunt Hilda. 'It will look well on the piano.'

'I suppose so,' said Caulfield.

Later that evening Caulfield asked his Uncle Sam what sort of people were the Henley-Smiths.

'A very old Catholic family,' said Uncle Sam. 'They were chief of the O'Herlihys and owned all the land down to Limerick. They are to be respected for they maintained their religion and at the same time took the King's shilling. They, and people like them, built the British Empire; consequently they hold their land, all two-and-a-half thousand acres. The last of the O'Herlihy's was ennobled after Trafalgar, and another led the cavalry at Waterloo, but they left only one daughter, Lady Emily O'Herlihy, who married an impecunious navel officer, James Arthur Henley-Smith, R.N., whose descendant you beat at tennis this afternoon.'

'I suppose there will be rejoicing in Paris to-night,' said Caulfield.

Uncle Sam blinked. He didn't quite get it.

Chapter 8

The Death of Emmanuel Herzog
Flashback 1940

Emmanuel Herzog died in his sleep at 85 Dorset Street, Dublin. His sewing machine had been in use the day before his death. The finished garments were completed and neatly folded.

His life's work was over.

His sons brought him down in honour to his grave.

In accordance with Jewish custom, he was buried the same day. Shiva was the following day in the home of David Kent, his eldest son.

David lived in a modern two stories house, with garden back and front, parking for two cars, a hedge neatly clipped, a small flowerbed tastefully surrounded by lobelia.

It was home.

In the back garden there was a football net for children, two apple trees, a border for shrubs, a forsythia splendidly in bloom for two weeks in spring, three rose bushes and a grassy area showing signs that a golfer had been practising his six-iron.

It was home.

The house itself had four rooms upstairs – or three bedrooms and a study, or two bedrooms, a study and a baby's room, or two bedrooms, a study and a boy's room with posters of Everton F.C.

Downstairs was an L-shaped room, a room with a table (called a dining room) and a hatch to the kitchen, a large tv. set, two lavatories (called toilets) upstairs and down, books family photographs – two of them showing graduates in caps and gowns with their beaming parents (why shouldn't they?) – a carpet only a little bit worn.

It was home.

It was a house that tens of thousands in Dublin would give their right arm for; convenient to the building society, the bank (snooty lot, they were), a butcher, a hardware with a lawnmower outside that seemed to have been there for years. Buses (used to be trams), a short walk to the Spar, the pub, the hairdresser, a fruit and veg. shop (where the proprietor spent most of his time gazing soulfully down the street at nothing), a dog who slept in a tool shed and who wagged his tail and barked or whinged if he wasn't taken for a walk.

This was home.

The tens of thousand of bread winners (male and female) who came home every night, closed the gate, closed the door, put on their slippers, turned on the TV, ate their tea (called it dinner), put up their feet, read their paper/book/magazine, felt sleepy at the fire.

It was home.

A tyrant could oppress the poor, the homeless or even the wealthy, but if he oppressed these people in their three or four bedroom houses and modest gardens, then his days were numbered.

David and Kenneth Kent lived within about five-minute's walk from each other. When they left school at sixteen their ambitions were not in the rarefied world of scholarship and culture, which their father valued. Simply they wanted to make money.

They were not avaricious or greedy. At school, they could see the boys with better bicycles, other boys with older ones. They had none. They could see those with the cleaner shirts and newer shoes, who were so confident they could push their way into the classroom and claim the better seats. The seats were no better than any others, but the fact that they claimed them (and got them) convinced everyone else that they were better.

There was a subtle atmosphere in the classroom caused by something different and alien.

Jews.

Some looked Jewish. Others were no different. One thing above all marked them out. They didn't play rugby. This was partly due to their Sabbath falling on a Saturday, which was the day for inter-school matches.

When school was out, the better-off cycled home. Mothers in small runabout cars collected others. The Herzogs tramped through the puddles – they didn't even have a penny for the tram.

The Jews played cricket, which seemed to suit them, but it intensified the difference between them and the Gentiles. They played cricket, but not rugby – there was something unhealthy about this. The Gentile boys could not figure this out. The fact was that they had become more unlike them. If they played one game, why did they not play the other?

Sometimes the Gentile boys would exchange lurid facts about the Jews. 'Give them a job,' said one, 'and within five years they will own the shops, your house and everything.'

The Gentiles expressed respect and fear for the intellect of the Jews. They admitted they were brilliant, especially in science. Scholarship winners were more likely to be Gentiles than Jewish.

If a Jew was good at games, even cricket, it made a big difference to his standing. If he chose to ignore the teaching of the Law and play rugby on a Saturday his popularity would shoot up, and he became virtually an honorary Gentile.

The Gentile boys had never heard the word anti-Semitism. They felt no great antipathy against them, except that they were different and stuck together. A source of difference was that the Gentiles were mainly boarders and the Jews tended to be day-boys; the boarders enjoyed the ineffable sense of superiority over all day-boys, Jews as well as Gentiles.

When Caulfield was twelve he left the Ballynale National School and went as a boarder to Wesley school in Dublin, built for the education of Methodist families. It ultimately created a division between Caulfield and those who stayed behind in Ballynale.

Seated in front of him in Class Pre A was a Jewish girl, Leah. Caulfield scribbled a note asking her to come with him to the school party. She turned red, and shook her head sadly.

Years later, he was to meet her uncle, one Isaac Herzog. Neither was to mention the incident, but it was remembered.

Herzog, Abigail and Caulfield, three in one. Their lives entwined.

David and Kenneth Kent found home in this suburban Elysium. While at school, they saw the difference and longed to be able to buy what they wanted, and to be respectfully received at the bank.

They saw that philosophy would never butter parsnips, that culture was OK but could you buy and sell it? Scholars were admired for being poor. They wanted to be admired for being rich.

They found it difficult getting that first job. Once people had heard the name 'Herzog' that knowing look came into their eyes, and their job was gone. They went to their youngest brother, Isaac Herzog, who was just beginning to go to school. It seemed incredible that an eight-year-old was asked for an opinion, but they were afraid of worrying their father.

'He refused you work because he heard the name Herzog?'

'Because he knew that we were Jews,' said David.

'But it was the name that told him you were Jews.'

They nodded.

'Well then,' said Isaac, 'change your name.'

It looked so simple. They sat in silence and then they started to laugh.

'Brilliant!' they shouted.

So they became David and Kenneth Kent. For a while they were afraid to tell their father, but when they did, they were surprised at his calm acceptance. Names were nothing to the Jews.

73

If they were Polish their names ended in 'ski', Russian 'evh', German 'man', English anything. Nationality was nothing to the Jews. There was only one people, one nation, one God, one promise, one land was theirs to go in and possess.

The Kents started in business. They got jobs in a small warehouse on the docks. Their employer was a Quaker, even more clannish than the Jews. They sold yeast, salt, dried fruit, almonds, cherries and everything that a baker wanted.

The business was dying a slow death. The Kent brothers were distraught. They felt sorry for the proprietor, a harmless man who knew who they were but did not mind, as long as they were not Catholics, Church of Ireland, Methodist or Presbyterian.

The Kent brothers decided to go and look for more business. They used to sell 25 kg bags of salt that was purchased from a salt merchant called Crampton. They went to Crampton's premises and saw salt being delivered by Telford Salt Company, Telford, UK.

They wrote to Telford's for a price, but were told that they could not supply, as they were not more than sixty years in business.

One day, they saw the man who delivered the salt to Crampton's. They followed the man to a pub, followed him in and bought the man a pint, and then another one, and asked where Telford's got their salt. He told them that Telford's was no more, they were buying it from the North British Salt Company, Belfast, and Wycherley, UK. They telephoned the company in Belfast to see if they could quote for twenty-ton lots. They did. It represented a fifty- percent discount on what they had been paying to Cramptons.

They bought candied peel and cherries from a jam manufacturer. One day, a young man from the country came in and asked if he could supply these goods, as he was recently established as a fruit preserver.

'Price?' they said.

He gave a price that was thirty-one percent cheaper. He got the order.

One day the Quaker did not come into work. His wife 'phoned that he was sick.

'Please come and see him,' she said.

They came out to his house in leafy Mount Merrion. She met them at the door.

'Thank you for coming.'

She had a manner that was restful and at peace.

In his bedroom, he waved his hand at them, and they went and shook it.

'I am going,' he said, 'I have asked God to take me home.'

He died the following day, and they called to his house to express condolences.

She handed them some papers.

'He signed them last week. For you two, the business is yours.'

***

Kenneth and David stood outside the door of the house, and welcomed all that called. Neighbours, members of the congregation, business people. Neighbours from Dorset Street, college associates, family relations and Isaac Herzog.

Isaac mourned his father more than he mourned his mother. The three brothers shook hands. They thought of the little man who they had buried yesterday.

'He was a giant,' said Isaac.

In the house, Kenneth and his brother put on their yarmulke, and Kenneth started to recite his father's deeds. He spoke of the early days in Kiev, good friends and neighbours.

The friends and neighbours in the house who knew a little of the pogrom shifted uneasily, with bowed heads they exchanged glances.

'Of course, it could not happen here,' Kenneth continued. 'He survived the horror of a pogrom. As a small boy, he journeyed

75

across Europe. He was offered work here and there, but pushed on until he came to Dublin. He became a Dubliner.'

David glanced at Isaac, who tightened his lips.

They both knew that their father was never a Dubliner, and never would be. Nobody recited the Passover prayer with more feeling, 'Next year in Jerusalem.'

***

The Shiva was over and everyone drifted away. They would meet again for the next six nights, and again for Annual Prayers, the Yahrzeit, when thanksgiving would be offered up for Emmanuel Herzog's life.

With everyone gone, the house fell silent. Isaac Herzog, Kenneth and David Kent remained, and sat with tea and bagels, which Kenneth's wife provided. The three brothers sat in silence, as if exhausted. Their wives and their children sat in the kitchen and talked of this and that. Instinctively, they knew that they should leave the three brothers alone. Both parents were now dead. The sadness was over the final breach of the family. The brothers had lost their father and mother, who was now going to be the family head? The person they could grumble at, dispute with, moan and groan about everything, but love and obey – most of the time.

The other religions had their cathedrals, their spires, their stained glass windows but they had not. They had the family who was stronger and warmer than any flying buttress. The family was their buttress, when one failed, two helped.

'What are your plans?' asked Kenneth. He looked at Isaac.

'I can think about nothing else,' said Isaac. 'To be honest, I have to make some changes, big ones.'

'Since you got that Gold Medal there is nothing much left than a doctorate.'

Isaac smiled to himself. David knew as much about doctorates as Isaac knew about icing sugar.

'How long would it take to get a doctorate?'

'A year,' said Isaac, 'or perhaps a lifetime. 'I nearly had a brain storm working for the Gold Medal. It was for the old man that I did it. I would not have put in the same effort for myself, or even for Mother when she was alive.'

The brothers sat quietly, trying to digest the bad news. It was similar to having to accept the news that he was giving up the faith, marrying a Christian, and denouncing the state of Israel.

'Don't rush this.' Kenneth said, 'You have to follow your own instinct. Do what's best for yourself.'

They ate more bagels and drank more tea. Isaac looked at his father's yarmulke. It was threadbare from much usage.

'You can see the threads in it,' said Isaac, looking closely, 'they are very bare. And that,' said Isaac portentously, 'is where we get the word *'threadbare'*.'

Kenneth banged the armrest of his chair. 'Good heavens!' he cried, 'Is there no end to this man's profundity?'

They all laughed.

'You don't need a doctorate!' said David.

The question of Isaac's future lay heavy on their minds. Both Kenneth and David had made good use of Isaac's success. It had circulated around the Jewish community. The Ashkenazi Jews of Eastern Europe were always looked down on by the Sepitardi of Portugal, Holland and the Middle East.

The Herzogs were Ashkenazi, but Isaac's success had given them a lift, and they walked tall. Even outside Jewry, the achievement was known. The concerns of Kenneth and David were not entirely altruistic; they both wanted the distinction of having a brother who was a Doctor.

David's wife came in with apple strudel. She had good legs and a trim figure. Her ash blonde hair was thick and curly. Isaac was sleepy. He lay back with his hand over his eyes. He watched

Rebecca, and saw her smile quickly at Kenneth as she held the plate for him, her leg for a second brushed against his.

Damn fools, thought Isaac.

Already he felt he was Head of the Family.

The evening was drawing to a close, and the setting sun lit up the room. Isaac stood up and spoke seriously to the other two.

'I have more or less decided,' he said, 'that I will sit my Masters, and then call it a day. Then I will go out and have a look at our world, and see what's in it. A lot of letters after my name is not going to conquer it.'

Kenneth and David gloomily nodded in agreement.

David said, 'This is the end.'

'No, Dave, it's the beginning and at the end I hope our father will not be disappointed by any of us.'

As he spoke, he glanced quickly at Kenneth.

***

Isaac Herzog walked back to Dorset Street. It was a good hour's walk. It had been raining in the inner city and the pavements glistened as if scrubbed and washed. He thought of the day, and wondered if he ever would experience anything like it. The previous day he had found his father asleep. His father was dead, and with him died Kiev, the ghettos of Europe, the small child who remained small all his life, the small man who reared with his deaf and dumb wife three sons who would rise up and call him blessed. The little man who, on hearing that his youngest had won the Gold Medal, had run from the room to the waste ground at the back, so that he could weep tears of joy and gratitude.

Isaac walked the whole distance. On reaching Dorset Street, he stopped and looked up to the fourth floor, at the room. Somebody had thrown stones, and the windows were broken.

'I am home,' said Isaac Herzog.

Herzog hesitated on the side of the street. He didn't feel like going to his room but wished he had someone he could chew the rag with. He tried to think where he had heard that stirring phrase. It must have been trans-Atlantic. Ah yes, it was that straw-haired Swede from Minnesota, with the innocent freckled face; not quite the same as the broody Jew from the Ukraine.

Herzog had formally thanked the Swede for this gift to his vocabulary, and who with great generosity had given him another at absolutely no cost, the immortal *quit stallin'*.

Yes, said Herzog to himself, *I should quit stallin' and go and chew the rag with someone.*

Instead he went to his room and found a letter which had been delivered that day. He recognised the handwriting; it was his second cousin, Eli, writing from Australia, who after a lifetime in Shanghi and a peregrination that took in Singapore, Macau and the Indonesia, had come to rest in Melbourne.

He put the letter in his pocket unread, left his apartment and caught the first bus that was going to where he knew not where. It brought him to Howth. Seated on a bollard, he read his cousin's letter. It irritated Herzog considerably. Cousin Eli was almost a generation older than Herzog and his marriage to another cousin had been without issue. The main tenor of the letter was that Herzog should get married, preferably to one of his own kith and kin.

His cousin, Eli, had suffered almost every misfortune that a man in business can experience. Nonetheless, he had done it with style and panache and he was not slow to offer advice to his relations, much of which had little value. "Get married," he wrote, "and if you have a problem in this world of the goys I have the woman for you." Herzog groaned – there is nothing worse than unsolicited advice.

Eli went on to extol the attractions of the unknown beauty living in the city of Melbourne whose good fortune had decreed she was to be Herzog's wife (so Eli wrote).

A minor problem, Eli said, was that she was already married. Abigail Liebnecht was on her way to solving this problem.

Herzog crumpled the letter in his hand and threw it into the waters of the harbour. It bobbed on the outgoing tide and was not seen again. *What sort of an idiot,* he thought, *can advise me to go to Australia when my finances are strained by going to Terenure?* Also, the effort of seeing an alleged beauty in a foreign hemisphere – on the advice of a second cousin with a renowned reputation for folly – wasn't worth thinking about.

Herzog strolled around the harbour admiring the trawlers unloading the catch, the weather-beaten fishermen, and the seagulls squawking overhead.

In his mind he scoffed at Eli's naïve marriage broking. It was nonsense, yet he couldn't ignore it.

This Abigail Liebnecht was a nothing, a nobody – why then could he not forget her?

Chapter 9

Henley-Smith

Caulfield was in Ryan's shop in Cloughjordan when Henley-Smith drove up. Caulfield greeted him, but Henley-Smith had acquired the gift of his class of being not able to see someone standing three feet away.

'Petrol!' shouted Henley-Smith, to no one in particular.

He carefully got a fill of petrol. His father thought nothing of spending small fortunes on his house or gardens, but was parsimonious to a degree in buying petrol. If an attendant in a filling station let petrol dribble on the body of a car he became enraged and roared at the man for having permanently disfigured his car, and/or for overcharging for the wasted petrol.

The Commodore was a typical example of his time. He was a domestic tyrant. He addressed people as if standing to attention. Orders given to the gardening staff were like the final words to the men before going over the top. Standing on the steps of the house, or on some elevation in the garden, he stood stock-still and his piercing glance swept the horizon as if seeking the dastardly enemy. The Commodore was not to be trifled with.

He had a particular dislike of petrol companies. They always seemed to be owned by Americans, and he had a longstanding antipathy to Americans. Americans had the crashing bad taste to build a larger navy than the Royal Navy. They should know that there was nothing more absurd than an American fleet. If they wanted protection they should have known that the Royal Navy would protect them, as they had done so for one hundred years.

As he was a very fair-minded man, he was prepared to admit Americans were first class builders of covered wagons, axes for cutting trees and arrows (not the bows, they were British). Anyone who wasn't British was a foreigner, and most of them were damned foreigners.

There were nations, like the French and Spanish, who had put up a token resistance to Britain and had interfered with Britain's God given right to rule the seas. This list included the Germans, whose navy was to be pitied more than anything else.

The pathetic effort of these nations to challenge the Royal Navy was a source of national disgrace to their peoples. Magnanimously, Britain never rubbed it in, except perhaps when renaming the streets of their cities as Waterloo, Trafalgar, Agincourt, Armada, etc.

The Commodore's distrust of foreigners (including damned foreigners) was aggravated by their inability to play cricket. As it had been proven beyond doubt that cricket strengthens the backbone of the nation, the failure of foreigners to play this game has contributed to the moral degeneracy of countries like France and the United States.

Henley-Smith paid for the petrol. He was surprised that his father had allowed him to drive, and given him money for the petrol. The attendant had left him slightly short and he had eight pence change, which he had invested in two bars of chocolate.

Big deal, he thought, *big, big, big deal!*

He was already sixteen years of age, and big for his age. His knees banged off the steering wheel. Like most sixteen year olds, he was confused about who he was. He had practically no one of his own age to talk to. His Mumsie and Auntie Miriam irritated him.

He was confused in other ways. He was a Catholic, the pride of Stonyhurst. He had foolishly said to a Jesuit there that he thought he might become a priest.

Father Paulus had cornered him in the science laboratory.

'You would make a marvelous priest. We want men of your class and standing.'

'Eh, yeh?' said Henley-Smith.

'Would you join us in a prayer group?'

'I dunno,' said Henley-Smith. The priest persevered, but hope faded.

What am I? said Henley-Smith to himself. *I am an Irishman. I talk like an Englishman. I am a Catholic, but I mainly know Protestants. I am an O'Herlihy, but I am also Henley-Smith. I like games – rugby, cricket, tennis, but I am too big to be any good. I am bone lazy about most things, but I can come alive digging a well, ten hours a day.*

He revved the car up and down, until the attendant came out and asked what he wanted.

'I'm fine,' he said.

The man looked at him curiously, and went back into his shop.

'That fellow is an odd bod,' he said.

'His name is Henley-Smith,' said Caulfield.

'I know him now,' said the shopkeeper. 'He lives in a big house near Nenagh.'

Henley-Smith drove away.

What am I? thought Henley-Smith, *am I Irish, or am I English or am I British?*

When he landed in Liverpool on the way to Stonyhurst, he knew beyond doubt that he was not English. Despite the Irish influence there, he knew he was not Irish. He knew it even more so when he talked to the man at the petrol pump. It was not his accent or his looks. It was not the shop with the dirty window and the floor inside that cried out for a clean up. That was Irish, he was not that Irish.

Henley-Smith came to the entrance of their house and the estate. Two children ran out of the gate lodge to open the iron gates, but he decided to drive on, down to the lake where he parked the car.

Henley-Smith stretched his legs, and started to ponder again. *When I was Irish, and when I was English.* He recalled an afternoon in a pub in Dublin. There was a programme of World Cup soccer on the television. England was playing West Germany, Italy was playing Brazil. His sympathies were all for England. After all, he spoke English, he went to school in England, and he played the English game of rugby. True, he did not play the English game of soccer (which was exclusively for the working class) but he was grateful to the English for inventing a gentleman's game.

However, he did not mind watching soccer on television. England scored against the Germans, and it was received with apathy, but when Germany equalled against England the crowd in the pub erupted with cheers.

Henley-Smith sat slumped in the car, and tried to reason it out. Is it the sign of a great Irishman to hate England? If Ireland was playing against England at rugby, then the issue was clear-cut – he felt Irish and sincerely rejoiced at an Irish win.

However, if France was playing England the situation was a little muddled; he hoped that England would win, but if France won he did not exactly rejoice for France, but he didn't mind too much that England was beaten.

Henley-Smith said this over a few times to himself, but he felt he was going nowhere; he shook his head. He thought of his father, and all the Henley-Smiths who went back to the O'Herlihy's three hundred years ago. The O'Herlihy's had fought for Charles I and (clandestinely) for William III, but would that loyalty have survived another three hundred years? Probably yes, because class is usually stronger than nationality. The first James Arthur Henley-Smith, and all his descendants to the present day, took the King's shilling. They were loyal in a way that even baffled the English. Although they were descended from the O'Herlihey's, they were never completely accepted by their tenants and neighbours, big and small. There was a latent hostility, sometimes benign. It was part of the air they breathed.

It was no wonder when Britannia started to spread her empire that she sought for her colonies the younger sons of Irish squireens to rule vast tracts of Africa and India, such men were used to living amidst a hostile population.

Henley-Smith remembered when a Jesuit superior came from England to stay with them (he was his mother's nephew) that a dinner table discussion revolved around this very point. The Jesuit commented: in Africa they found themselves amongst blacks, in Ireland they were brought up amongst greens.

Henley-Smith had been subjected to a number of snide remarks from his neighbours and even indefensibly from members of the grateful tenantry. His father had complained to Captain Fitzhaugh that he could not understand why Fitzhaugh's family got an easier ride than the Henley-Smiths from loose-lipped politicians, etc. bearing in mind that the Fitzhaughs remained Black Protestants in comparison to Henley-Smith.

'They admire us,' said Fitzhaugh, 'because we stuck to our religion.'

Henley-Smith gave up.

Back at the village petrol station, Caulfield was standing and thinking. *Henley-Smith! I remember him in Roscrea, the fellow with the so-called cannon ball service. He strode around the courts declaiming in that accent they teach them in Stonyhurst. He had to be told twice to keep quiet when someone was serving.*

Henley-Smith was not used to being told to keep quiet. He fancied he had a devastating answer to anyone who tried to put him down. He would look fixedly at a point just above his head, and drawl, 'I beg your pardon?' This riposte was effective up to a point. The previous summer he had a nasty experience when a very common type lit a cigarette with a flick and snarled, 'Button your lip, buster'. He was so taken back by this piece of gutter talk that he retired to the men's changing room and tried to think of what was happening.

It was not exactly the fall of the Roman Empire, nor was it the arrival of Lenin at the Helsinki station – it was, as a bishop said in church, 'a sign of the times.' He sat in the changing room for so long that people kept coming in to see if he was all right. He answered such questions with what he considered was admirable sang-froid:

'Fine, thank you; fine, thanks.'

He felt wounded and bruised; a perfectly civil answer to a rather impertinent question had invoked this low type of person to come out and sneer at him. If it happened in Stonyhurst, he would have been entitled to take that brat to his room, and lash him with ten of the best. The priests would have supported him, and perhaps added another ten.

What was the good of education if this type of moron was going around? Was there no respect for people born to rule the country who, because of their superior birth and situation, were equipped to control the manners and conduct of their people?

Henley-Smith felt he would like a smoke, but he did not have any cigarettes, and anyway did not smoke.

Chapter 10.

Henley Hall, Tipperary.

Dear Caulfield,

I was pleasantly surprised to bump into you in Roscrea last week. I hope you are keeping up the tennis, and that your backhand is as lethal as ever.

I am writing to see if you would like to join a tennis party at the above next July 12th? It happens to be my birthday, but please, no need to bring a present, unless you really feel you must, and then make it something small but costly. Ha, ha, of course I am joking.

Actually, if you want to be even more middle class than you are, I would like nothing more than ten cigarettes. I have decided that I am at a social disadvantage by not smoking. I seem to be having a run in with some awful people, both here and in England. I notice that it is no good verbally flattening these untouchables if they can come back snarling with a puff of smoke. I will be able to smoke next year in Stonyhurst, so I want to get in some practice.

I have had little tennis this year, and my life is in turmoil. Being a Henley-Smith means I am down for Dartmouth – I am filled with dread at the thought of life at sea. I always get seasick, and it's no comfort to know that Nelson also suffered seasickness.

The worst part of it is that the old man might be serving on my first sailing. He is impossible at home, but what will he be like cooped up on some floating tin can in the North Sea? I would prefer some more pleasant task like cleaning blocked sewer pipes.

As you know, my mother enjoys bad health. Her long-suffering doctor was in with her last week, and mentioned that you were talking to him about life as a quack. Bully for you – you can put me down as your first patient.

We will have about eight people for tennis, but another dozen or so will come for dinner. The men have stopped dressing for dinner, so a collar and tie is fine.

You probably won't know my mother's relations who are staying here. You might know the local P.P., who fancies himself as a tennis player, and the solicitor chap Brady, of Brady & Brady (did you ever see such presumption?) I was in with him a few days ago leaving some papers, and mentioned that I was on school holidays. 'Oh', he said, 'do you go to Clongowes?' 'Is that the school at the top of the town?' I asked him. He practically bared his teeth.

I should mention a peculiarity of our tennis party. My Auntie Miriam likes a game (singles) with whom she considers is the best tennis player in the party. I should say her age can vary between eighty-nine and one hundred and nine.

It is very likely that she will pick on you. It is essential to remember that

1.   *She can't run, and only walk with difficulty*
2.   *She serves underarm, and it is actually the best part of her game*
3.   *She thinks she is entitled to three serves*
4.   *If she hits the ball out in your half of the court, just remember that it was in*

The most difficult part of the game is to get her to win two games out of the set. Anything less than that and she might accuse you of cheating.

See you soon.
Henley-Smith.

Caulfield was not sure if he wanted to go to Henley-Smith's birthday tennis party. He only asked me because I am a good tennis player, and anyway it is too far to cycle and he would have to borrow Uncle Sam's car.

He knew that Uncle Sam was the most agreeable of men alive, but his agreeableness seemed to stop short of his car. He had a prejudice, shared by adults, that young people wanted cars for speeding, exhibitionism and – perish the thought – for occasions of sin.

'Can you not take the bus to Henley Hall?' he asked him.

'I can,' said Caulfield, 'but it is a two-mile walk up to the house.'

'Can a strong fellow like you not walk two miles?' he asked, with a rhetorical flourish.

Caulfield groaned, and scuffed his feet irritably.

'What about your bicycle?' asked Uncle Sam.

He gave an air of trying to be immensely reasonable, searching for an answer in good faith.

'My bicycle,' said Caulfield, 'take a look at my bicycle!'

Uncle Sam had seen the bicycle one thousand times. There was no need to look at it again. However, he turned around and looked at it with new interest.

'The bicycle,' he said.

'Yes, the bicycle,' said Caulfield shortly.

'The bicycle,' repeated Uncle Sam. 'It looks like a good bicycle, after all it...' and he stopped.

Caulfield waited resignedly. He knew that one of Uncle Sam's witticisms was on the way. Uncle Sam liked his jokes; a really good one was not to be tossed carelessly away but to be savoured, like a wine producer tasting his vintage. Not that Uncle Sam drank wine.

Repeating himself, he said, 'It looks like a good bicycle because... it has two wheels.'

Uncle Sam's laugh boomed out across the street. Even Caulfield gave a smile and a short laugh.

Caulfield felt pleased, he knew that Uncle Sam would lend him the car. Uncle Sam was in a good humour and would usually let Caulfield have his own way.

'All right, all right,' he said to Caulfield, 'you can have it. I suppose you will bring it back with three wheels.'

He gave a little chuckle as if it was a follow up to the first joke.

'Thanks, Uncle Sam.'

Uncle Sam was in a good humour. Caulfield was his only nephew, and he had no sons. His two daughters benefited from Caulfield's company. At boarding school, the girls shared in the reflective glory of Caulfield. From the girls' gossip, while on holidays, he could tell the other girls' hearts beat a little faster at the mention of Caulfield.

At age sixteen, Caulfield was nearly six-foot tall. Junior Captain of rugby, cricket and just about everything else. Next year he had a good chance of being senior captain in rugby and cricket, and was in line for the Leinster schools' interprovincial honours. What pleased Uncle Sam was Caulfield's easy manners and pleasant disposition. He was popular with both men and women. He was the life of the party.

Caulfield, in his own way, tried to please Uncle Sam. He knew he had been left virtually an orphan, and his uncle and aunt had given him a welcome that was both warm and sincere.

Uncle Sam had felt the approval of the congregation in the way that Caulfield attended church functions, youth meetings and services. Uncle Sam was to be congratulated in his good influence over Caulfield, and Caulfield was praised for his influence over his two cousins and other young people.

Some people said to him that he should be a minister, but, after a week in hospital when a bad rugby tackle had torn his cartilage, he had time to see the bustle of hospital, the pretty nurses, the hush when consultants did their rounds, he knew this was to be his life.

Uncle Sam was secretly impressed that Caulfield was invited to Henley Hall. It was only twenty miles away, but it was a lifetime in another world.

Uncle Sam knew something of Henley Hall. They came sometimes in a jeep, to leave a large order. Henley-Smith sat in front with the chauffeur. The chauffeur would blow the horn loudly and Uncle Sam had to come out to collect the order.

Once Uncle Sam asked the chauffeur why did he not come into the shop and collect the goods, and he was icily told that Henley-Smith did not go into grocery shops and neither – sniff, sniff – did he.

Uncle Sam knew that Caulfield could handle himself in Henley Hall. If they tried to patronise him, he would smile, tell a joke, smile again until they laughed. They dare not do it again.

Caulfield packed his bags for Henley Hall. Fortunately, his whites were clean – they were the first things his aunt had washed after coming home for holidays. His racquet was in a wooden frame. He looked at the frame. What was it supposed to do? Everyone said it was to keep the racquet from warping. How did it do that, was it necessary? He remembered that the Wimbledon players never had them on their racquets.

They did not need them. The whole thing was a bit of nonsense. He threw the frame out of the window.

He packed his bag and shoved the racquet in. It didn't look right. He undid his bag, shoved in the racquet so the handle stuck up about ten inches, and repacked the bag. It now looked the real thing.

The children came out again from the gate lodge and Caulfield drove through. He was a little apprehensive – what sort of people were Henley-Smith's guests? Would they pepper him with questions: who was he? what did he do? what did his father do?

He could always say that his father was in Africa. It sounded better than saying he was in a nursing home in Co. Derry. He might change it and say he was into horses, buying horses for the Mexican army. Did that sound a bit hairy? No, it sounded reasonable. He lived in Africa and brought horses to Africa, where he broke them in before selling them to the Mexican army. It was brilliant.

The Henley-Smiths knew nothing about him. They could not contradict.

He came to the house with an open grassy area in front. There were a few cars, and a man standing on the steps. The man made no effort to move.

Caulfield parked his car, took out his bag, and looked around. There was no sign of anyone.

He walked over to the man on the steps. He climbed the steps and said to him, 'Good afternoon.' The man neither moved nor blinked.

Caulfield opened the door and went in. There was a slight hum from a distance. To the right was what looked like a large drawing room. He went in, saw an elderly woman reading a magazine, and looked over her shoulder.

She was reading a 1927 copy of the *Illustrated London News.*

She, too, did not move or speak. Caulfield sat down. He leaned back in his chair and looked around.

On the wall was a display of native spears, arranged according to size, with the tallest spears in the middle and smaller ones on each side. It looked like the pipes of an organ.

A painting showing a cavalry charge by the Hussars, the leader pointing a sword at a group of terrified semi-naked natives, the title of the painting *'British Gallantry'.*

The biggest painting was a naval battle scene with burning ships, various flags of the nations, the figures of nineteenth century sailors and a familiar figure lying prone, *The Death of Nelson'.*

Caulfield wondered where the tennis was. It was three o'clock and the tennis would end at six.

***

In the distance he could hear the sound of the plopping of tennis balls.

He went out. The man standing had disappeared, and Caulfield felt unsurprised. He walked around the house and found the tennis courts. Henley-Smith was having a desultory game with a woman. She missed his serve and the ball sped past. Caulfield caught the ball and returned it.

'That's frightfully kind of you,' she called.

'Not at all,' said Caulfield.

'But it's actually terribly, terribly good of you.'

Caulfield smiled.

'It is really so good of you, and thank you so, so much.'

Caulfield said, gallantly, 'It is my pleasure.'

'Oh is it, that's super isn't it, it's absolutely super.'

Caulfield's eyes narrowed; he looked up at Henley-Smith. He was bouncing a ball on his racquet – he was oblivious of Caulfield, who wondered what had happened to his manners. Why did he not come over and welcome him?

Perhaps he could teach him a little lesson. He said to the woman, 'Would you like to come for a walk, and see the gardens?'

'Would you really, are you absolutely sure? It would be too, too wonderful!' She dropped her racquet.

Would you take me for a walk?' she asked. Caulfield nodded and smiled his nicest smile.

'I've dreamed of this,' she said breathlessly, 'all my life I've dreamed of someone taking me …' she hesitated.

'For a walk,' suggested Caulfield.

'Yes, yes that's it, for a – what did you say it was?'

'A walk,' said Caulfield.

'Ah yes! That was it, a walk. That is absolutely super, a super walk.'

She slipped her hand into his.

They walked down a narrow path. He walked on the grassy verge to let her walk on the path.

'I saw that,' she said with glistening eyes, 'you let me walk on the path.'

Caulfield smiled.

'I think that is absolutely super of you. Do you know,' she whispered, 'no one has ever let me walk on the path like that.'

Caulfield did not know what to say.

'All these years,' she said with a sob in her voice, 'I have had to walk on the grass.'

She snuggled closer to Caulfield and looked up to him.

She went on, 'I have met you and you have been so lovely to me, so lovely.'

Caulfield thought it was time to return to the tennis, but she was already walking ahead, and they came to a greenhouse. Outside was a bed of rhubarb.

'Did you ever see anything so lovely?'

'It's rhubarb.'

'Yes, of course, but is it not incredibly lovely? These beautiful colours! I love the blue coloured rhubarb.'

'Blue?' questioned Caulfield.

'Yes, blue, my darling. Blue.'

Caulfield tore a leaf off the rhubarb.

'What colour is that?'

'Oh! What a lovely pink,' she murmured.

'We must return to the tennis now. Henley-Smith is waiting.'

Caulfield led the way back, careful, to walk on the grass, unconsciously carrying the leaf of rhubarb.

They came to the tennis court. Henley-Smith was there. He looked crossly at Caulfield.

'Where have you two been?'

The woman took Caulfield's arm.

'We were looking at the gorgeous rhubarb, it was just too lovely. It was too lovely, lovely rhubarb. Show him the rhubarb, darling.' Caulfield held up the rhubarb leaf. 'And this is the lovely pink rhubarb.' Smiling at Caulfield, she cuddled up to him.

'It's not pink, it's green, my darling.'

Henley-Smith looked at Caulfield. He frowned. He didn't know this fellow well. Pink rhubarb sounded odd.

A mixed doubles had started. The parish priest and Fitzhaugh's daughter were playing Brady and the notorious Mrs. Fitzherbert, famed for her amours.

Henley-Smith came over to Caulfield. 'Do you mind telling me what this is all about?'

Caulfield looked at the clinging woman by his side.

'You tell me. I came in and stood at the end of the court and you said nothing. You ignored me, as did the military gentlemen on the steps this morning ignored me. Even in Ballynale they would find that hard to take.'

Henley-Smith gawped.

'What! I'm awfully sorry, old boy. I never saw you. Please, I am terribly sorry.'

Caulfield was gracious. He held up his hand.

Henley-Smith said, 'Look, you have your stuff here. Come upstairs and change.'

They left, leaving the woman behind.

'I'll be back,' promised Caulfield.

'Make it soon, darling.'

Caulfield half expected to find the house in an advanced state of decay. Actually, it was in pristine condition. A sweeping staircase, which he was to see repeated in years to come in 85 Dorset Street, Dublin, was polished and carpeted.

On every landing, oil paintings on the wall of various heads of family, sometimes holding a telescope, or with a background of a four masted man-of-war.

'I could get used to this,' said Caulfield.

Henley-Smith led him into his room. It overlooked the tennis court and gardens. The woman was talking volubly to the priest, who in his turn was trying to serve.

'Henley-Smith,' said Caulfield, 'I hope you don't mind me asking, what is the story of that woman?'

'Story?' he said, 'What story? There is no story.'

'She must be family, otherwise you would not be so loyal.'

'She is my only sister.' He went to the window and looked down at her. 'She is still a child. She lives happily here. Happy in her own little world. Sometimes she lives in another sort of a home. Her name is Elizabeth.'

'Was she always like this?' asked Caulfield.

'I'm not too sure,' said Henley-Smith, she was born before I was. She was my father's pet.'

Caulfield had a good view of the gardens. The herbaceous plants were a blaze of colour. The Commodore had collected trees and plants from all over the world. A tartar with men and discipline, he humbled himself before the smallest flower.

Caulfield was silenced before the glory of the garden. As he looked out a small man strolled into view. A small man, obviously not a tennis player, smoking a cigarette.

'Who is he?' asked Caulfield.

'I don't know,' answered Henley-Smith, 'some Jew. I think his name is Herzog. He does business with the old man. His wife Abigail is a knockout, but she is not here to-day. I heard him tell the old man that she is sick in hospital, somewhere in Australia. I don't know why she had to go to Australia for a hospital.'

Caulfield looked at the little man, *he is* ...he tried to think, *he is not ordinary.*

He changed his clothes. He discovered he had packed only one white sock – Henley-Smith loaned him one.

A voice was heard. 'Hello-alo.'

Henley-Smith went to the door and looked out. 'You must be Kevin Murphy, eh?'

'I am Kevin Murphy eh.'

He came in and let his bag fall to the ground.

'Murphy,' said Henley-Smith, introducing him to Caulfield, 'and this is Caulfield.'

'Bully to you, Caulfield.'

It was the second time that Caulfield had met Murphy who had played for the Munster Senior School boys rugby when he was only sixteen. He won a senior cap although the referee wrote to the Abbot of Glenstaf after the match, complaining of Murphy's play.

Caulfield had played for Leinster School boys in the same match.

Caulfield had the feeling that Murphy had come to look for trouble. He was not as tall as himself or Henley-Smith, but he was broader, and with a head lower on his shoulders he looked like a young bull.

'I'm delighted you are here,' said Henley-Smith.

'Oh, I am terribly delighted,' said Murphy, 'I feel quite overcome with delight.'

He unzipped his bag and pulled out his tennis clothes in one grab.

'If I was back in Limerick I would be getting in some serious drinking instead of playing pat-a-ball with the vicar's daughter,' he said.

'There are no vicars' daughters here,' said Henley-Smith, 'and Caulfield here can give you a good game of pat-a-ball.'

'We will see,' said Murphy.

He went to the window and looked down on the courts.

'So you have two tennis courts?'

'We only use one to-day. It's the best one,' said Henley-Smith.

'I suppose the servants use the other one on their day off.'

'They prefer to play polo on their day off.'

'That is witty.' Murphy pretended to double up in laughter.

Caulfield tried to read Murphy. He had heard something about Murphy of Limerick. The father was a dry-as-dust boffin in a government department.

97

Henley-Smith was not going to let him off.

'I can send down a few cases of beer to the kitchen. If you are missing some serious drinking, you will find the servants there great company.'

This stopped Murphy. 'OK, OK,' he said, 'we will call it quits.'

Caulfield relaxed, as did Murphy. Henley-Smith was on edge. It was his birthday, and he did not want to have to cope with this thick, and who was he? He was here because his mother had been friendly with Mumsie. He decided that he did not want anything to do with him. He could shag off and mind his own business. He could take his bad humour out on someone else.

They changed into their tennis whites and went downstairs. In the hall, they met Lady Mary.

'Mumsie, this is Kevin Murphy.'

'How do you do?' said Murphy, shaking hands.

'And Caulfield.'

'Oh, Caulfield.' Caulfield stood with hands behind his back.

The elderly woman who had been reading the *Illustrated London News* came out of the drawing room.

'Auntie Miriam!' called Henley-Smith, cheerily, 'this is your new boyfriend, Caulfield.'

'You are Caulfield,' she said in a quivery voice. Someone was right, she sounded about one hundred and nine.

'I am going to challenge you for the house championship,' she said, 'many have come in hope, but they left in tears.'

'So I heard, Aunt Miriam. I'll have to ask you not to be hard on me.'

'Oh, ho, ho, ho!' she cackled, 'I will have no mercy on you, Mr. Caulfield.'

Caulfield looked at Henley-Smith. He looked bored at the elaborate jesting of the two, where they were saying the exact opposite of what they meant. She was probing Caulfield to see if he could handle her oh-so-cute rallies. He returned her ball without any trouble.

She toddled to her room.

'See you later, Mr. Caulfield.'

'Not bad,' said Henley-Smith, 'you handled her well.'

'I didn't think I was handling anyone,' said Caulfield irritably.

'Oh tut-tut,' said Henley-Smith, 'no need to get touchy. Look at Murphy there, he is not a bit touchy.'

What was Henley-Smith trying to do? He had come to play some harmless tennis on his birthday, and now he was being measured against the best people.

As they went down the steps of the house, Murphy pulled at Caulfield's arm.

'You should have shaken hands with her,' he whispered.

'What?'

'You should offer to shake hands with a woman. It's *her* choice to take your hand or not.'

Caulfield looked at Murphy. He was grinning.

'Stick with me, Caulfield, and you won't go far wrong.'

Henley-Smith overheard Murphy.

'Don't mind him,' he said, 'those Limerick people are fearful snobs. We hired Murphy to teach us manners.'

Ignoring Henley-Smith Murphy continued, "When you are walking in the street with a woman you must walk on the outside."

"You don't say."

"And when you are dining in mixed company, you talk to the person on your left."

"Suppose there is no one on my left."

"Just shout," said Murphy.

'I must remember,' said Caulfield.

'Remember what?'

'I must remember about not eating peas off a knife.'

'On the whole, it's frowned upon,' said Henley-Smith, gravely, 'it's eating them with a soupspoon that's definitely out.'

Caulfield grunted. Henley-Smith pointed, 'Over there are my cousins, Wendy and Prudence from London. I want you to go and completely wow them.'

'I hate them already,' said Caulfield.

Henley-Smith introduced them to his two cousins and their mother. They were charming, friendly and good looking. They made Caulfield feel completely at ease. Then he thought to himself, *are they at ease with me?* As he listened to their cut-glass accents he wondered, *what do they think of my accent?*

Their accents were the litmus test of gentility. They chatted away, but at the back of Caulfield's mind was the question, *where did I hear about cut-glass accents? I must have read it somewhere.* It was not in North Tipperary. Although when he thought of it, he did notice when he came back from school in Dublin at term end the people of Ballynale had a slightly different accent than before.

Caulfield said to himself, *don't panic, count to ten, breathe deeply, keep smiling.* They exchanged some chit-chat and he could sense they were falling his way. For his part, he became quite enchanted with their cut-glass accents (there it goes again), and then he remembered – it was something to do with the London Stock Exchange. Still, he wondered about his accent. *Were they terribly polite and pretended not to notice?* He supposed it would not have mattered if he was speaking with a Scottish accent – like the fellow on television – or a Welshman speaking with a Welsh accent, all up and down like a Welsh valley. Perhaps they were a bit odd, and they actually liked an Irish accent?

Perhaps, but he did not convince himself.

The Parish Priest, Fr. O'Neill, double-faulted his serve and hit two balls into the shrubbery. Caulfield excused himself and went to look. When he came back, the two girls were speaking in low confidential tones, which they broke off the moment he returned.

'Found the balls?' one of the girls brightly asked.

'Yes,' said Caulfield, 'no trouble at all.'

Wow, the sparkling wit of the conversation.

'Do you come from around here?' asked Prudence.

That was it, the gentle but ruthless interrogation that would tell them all they wanted to know in less than two minutes. Caulfield knew that there were three main approaches: 'Do you come from here?' 'What do you do?' 'What does your father do?'

'Do you come from here?' she asked.

'No,' said Caulfield, 'I come from Ballynale, about twelve miles away.'

Almost immediately, he could have bitten his tongue off. He was culchieland. He might as well have said that he came from the far side of the bog.

But Prudence was brilliant. Her eyelashes only flickered for a few seconds. Wendy did not have Prudence's social graces. Her smile was fixed, frozen.

It had to come again. Caulfield was expectant.

'Does your father live here?' Prudence asked.

The answer to the question could reveal to the skilled interrogator (a) who his father was, (b) job, religion, housing, acreage of his farm (if he had one), social position, educational standard.

Caulfield was ready. He had it rehearsed since he left Ballynale. Briefly, he had it that his father lived in Africa (Ghana), Caulfield sends out horses to him, he breaks them in and trains them and sells them to the Mexican army. It had the beauty of being almost impossible to check.

But Caulfield hesitated. It was, as the fellows would say, a bit much. Would they buy such an outlandish story? Considerable publicity had been given in England to Irish chancers (i.e. a thief who tells lies) and when questioned, invariably state that they are 'in horses.'

Caulfield shrewdly decided that he would not be 'in horses.'

He replied, 'No, he does not live here. He is in prison.'

The girls jumped to their feet, delightedly.

'A prison, how wonderful, how exciting!'

'Please,' said Caulfield, 'keep your voices down. The Special Branch are all over the place.' He looked nervously around; 'They might be here, perhaps up a tree, behind a bush.'

Prudence tiptoed behind a laburnum. 'Not here!' she whispered.

They looked up a tree. 'I see something.'

'No, it's nothing – only a branch. Perhaps a Special Branch?'

She squealed with delight, 'Do you get it, Caulfield? It's a special branch.'

Caulfield got it all right. He was beginning to regret. The tennis players were glaring at them. Brady was serving, and he liked a captive audience to admire his service. The girls hushed up. Brady served, and it left the P.P. standing. The girls clapped, 'Well done, well done!' Brady modestly acknowledged the applause.

'Tell us, Caulfield, why is your father in prison? It sounds frightfully exciting.'

Caulfield took a deep breath and looked into the far distance.

'Exciting yes, but dangerous more so. I am not allowed to give any details. Scotland Yard has my number. Even the FBI in Washington have me on file.'

'The FBI!' The girls were almost panting.

Caulfield looked suitably grave. 'Yes, the FBI,' he said, 'they never really trusted me since that trouble in Budapest.'

'Budapest!' cried Prudence.

'Budapest,' whispered Wendy.

'What happened in Budapest?' they cried.

Caulfield stood up, looking carefully around. He went to an old oak tree, walked around it twice, and looked up into the branches. Returning to where the girls were, he picked what could have been the broken spout of an earthenware jug. He examined it, brushing off some clay, and then he spoke into it a few words before slipping it into his pocket. He went back to the girls and sat down.

'Budapest.' With mouths opened, they nodded.

'Budapest,' said Caulfield, 'that's where we killed Kransky.'

There was a sharp intake of breath from the girls.

'Poor Kransky,' said Prudence.

'Yes,' said Caulfield, 'he was my oldest friend. But Washington insisted. *Kill Kransky*, they said. It wasn't easy,' said Caulfield, sighing deeply.

The girls turned away. Instinctively they put their arms around each other. With drooping heads, they mourned for Kransky.

After the girls dried their eyes, Prudence spoke, 'But that doesn't explain why your father is in jail.'

Caulfield thought as quickly as he could. 'That was before the Obelensky affair. It's classified as top secret.'

'But your father is in jail, why should he have gone to jail?'

'I should have gone to jail,' said Caulfield, 'after all, I lost the blueprints. But he asked MI5 if he could take my place. I never knew how much he meant to me until then.'

'It was very noble,' said Prudence.

Caulfield nodded in agreement, and tightened his lips to control his emotion.

'But what are blueprints?' asked Wendy.

For a few minutes Caulfield realised that he had not much idea what blueprints were.

'They are,' he said, speaking slowly and disjointedly, 'pale blue things that are... printed on, on... things that are sort of paper... that's blue.'

'I see,' said Wendy, 'they are blue things printed out and...' pause '...that is why they are called blueprints.'

'Very good!' said Caulfield, enthusiastically. 'Isn't Wendy very clever, fancy knowing what blueprints are?'

'She is a genius,' said Prudence, with a sarcastic look at him. 'Nearly as good a genius as you.'

Prudence had seen through him. Caulfield felt it was a good time to play tennis. The existing mixed doubles came off the court. Brady looked well satisfied. His partner congratulated him and thanked him.

103

'Now,' said Henley-Smith, 'what about a foursomes between Caulfield and Prudence and Wendy and me?'

It was unanimous.

He must think he is better than I am, offering to play with the weaker of the girls, thought Caulfield. *Well, we will see.*

Prudence served. She had a good first service, but a weaker second one. She also had a stronger forehand, and a weaker backhand. Wendy was quite good all round. She seldom had a killer shot, but she didn't miss anything too easy.

Caulfield was upset at his partner's manner. She played in silence, refusing to reply to his chat or jokes. She hit the ball with a dogged disinterest.

Henley-Smith could see there was a hostile silence between them, and wondered what it was.

Elizabeth came along with her racquet and dressed for tennis. Caulfield greeted her cordially and she watched, and then started to keep score. The score was love/fifteen, but she called out thirty all; fifteen/thirty became love-forty. Caulfield's thirty/fifteen was advantage out.

Prudence tried to keep her sense of balance. After all, they were cousins and had been warned to humour her, and they were guests in the house.

Henley-Smith made no effort to control his sister, and eventually they were playing a game without an end. It went on and on. Eventually, after a five-minute rally, Prudence called to her.

'Well, that end's that game. Thank you, Cousin Elizabeth, you were a very good umpire.'

'Thank you, Cousin Prudence. Is the game all over?'

'Yes, Cousin Elizabeth. It was a lovely game.'

'Yes, it was a lovely game, a really super game – was it not, Caulfield?'

Before Caulfield could reply, Prudence burst out, without mentioning his name, and she asked, 'It was a super game, eh? The same as you could play in Budapest? Tell us what it was like in Budapest, eh?'

'It was raining in Budapest,' he said calmly.

'Oh ho, do you hear that?' she turned to the others who had been playing. 'He had been playing in the rain in Budapest.'

Henley-Smith and the others were perplexed at this exchange between them. Prudence continued, with growing sarcasm, 'Who did you play with in Budapest? Did you play with MI5, or perhaps somebody from Washington DC?'

'No,' Caulfield replied, 'that was in Beirut, and we used hand grenades instead of tennis balls.'

She stopped suddenly. In Bridge terms, he had aced her king. She turned away from him, and he saw her shoulders shaking.

She was giggling and then laughing. They all laughed, not knowing what they were laughing at. He spoke to her direct.

'I am sorry, Prudence.'

'Oh, Caulfield, you are impossible.'

'Could I make it up to you by showing you the gardens? They're nice at this time of year.'

'Another damn lie!' she said. But she linked his arm and they walked away.

It started to cloud over. The light was going, and the balls were getting dirtier.

'We have had the best part of the day,' said Henley-Smith. 'We can finish up with a doubles.'

The women had disappeared and the hardy four were left – Murphy, the priest, Henley- Smith and Brady.

'Suppose Kevin and I play Fr. O'Neill and John Brady,' said Henley-Smith. The two of them agreed with mutters, they neither agreed nor disagreed.

Murphy said nothing. He looked sourly at Henley-Smith. *Nobody asked me if I wanted to play them,* he grumbled. This was the first time that Murphy had met the other two.

Caulfield, Murphy supposed, was all right, although he disappeared for an hour to go necking with that English dame. It was considered bad form in Limerick to do that. If you were asked to a person's house you went and mixed around and did your bit. You were expected to chat up the plainest girl in the party, which was an example of true Christianity.

Caulfield and the English dame had slipped away, as if they were going to steal apples. Was this their party?

No, it was this fellow Henley-Smith – a slob if ever there was one. Pity he did not play rugby against him, he might get a chance to walk on his face.

Henley-Smith twirled his racquet.

'We won!' he cried, and then to Murphy, he asked, 'Do you want to serve?'

Murphy knew that Henley-Smith was going to serve. It was his tennis court, his birthday, his tennis balls and he was going to serve. Murphy looked at Henley-Smith. 'No,' he said, 'you serve.'

Murphy stood back on the base line. He knew this was wrong, he was supposed to stand at the net and try to cut off the return.

'Please stand at the net,' asked Henley-Smith.

Murphy knew there was a certain kind of Englishman who could insult you by the use of the word 'please.'

'I prefer to stand here,' said Murphy.

'I prefer you stand at the net,' said Henley-Smith.

Murphy knew from watching Henley-Smith in a knock-up that he stood an excellent chance of getting a tennis ball behind the ear.

Reluctantly, he shuffled up to the net. He stood well out, almost off the court.

'Come in more,' said Henley-Smith.

'I am in far enough,' said Murphy.

'You can't expect me to score,' said Henley-Smith, 'if you don't stand in.'

'I don't expect you to score anyway,' said Murphy.

Brady and the priest stood listening; they were acutely embarrassed. What had happened between the two?

Prudence and Caulfield came back, hand in hand.

Henley-Smith served a double fault. He looked at his racquet.

'Something wrong with your racquet?' shouted Murphy. Henley-Smith glared at him.

The match continued, and the priest/Brady won six-one. Murphy was guilty of discourtesy. He deliberately double-faulted, hit the ball into the net, claimed a ball being in when it was out.

'It will be better next time,' said Murphy to Henley-Smith.

'There will be no next time,' said Henley-Smith.

For the first time, Murphy flushed and appeared hurt. He flung his racquet into the shrubbery and walked away.

Prudence went into the house, and the men stood around discussing whether another game was possible. When it started to rain, they decided to call it a day.

Caulfield happened to look up at a high window and a woman's hand waved to him. He waved back. His heart gave a leap. Prudence had come into his life.

Life was only beginning.

Chapter 11

Prudence

Caulfield washed his hands and sung an old chorus. He sounded a very happy man.

'What's all the peace and joy in aid of?' asked Henley-Smith. Caulfield smiled, and kept on humming.

'It wasn't the tennis,' said Henley-Smith. 'You only had a few games. You were very gallant asking Elizabeth to play. I must have heard the word 'super' a dozen times.'

Caulfield kept on humming, and he sang to himself:

I am H-A-P-P-Y,

I am H-A-P-P-Y,

I know I am, I'm sure I am,

I am H-A-P-P-Y.

'So you are happy, eh?' said Henley-Smith. 'Well, isn't that terrific! Let's see, you are happy because you beat the stuffing out of me.'

Caulfield stopped humming for a second, but then resumed.

'OK,' said Henley-Smith, 'so it's not tennis, then. Brady of Brady and Brady has taken a fancy to you and is going to make you into a pillar of respectability, a....'

Caulfield said, 'A solicitor – no.'

'So it's not Brady. I take it it's not the parish priest? He is very broadminded, he didn't mind too much having to play with a Protestant.'

Henley-Smith went to shower, came back and rubbed himself down.

'That only leaves my well bred English cousins.'

Caulfield stopped humming.

'I don't believe it,' said Henley-Smith, 'Is it Prudence? Are you serious?'

'You are looking at a man who is in love.'

'You are crazy,' said Henley-Smith, 'she is not that great a tennis player.'

'Cut out the jokes, Henley-Smith. I am truly, completely, absolutely over the moon, head over heels, madly in love.'

Henley-Smith shook his head sadly.

'Why don't you lie down for a few hours?' he said.

'Don't joke,' said Caulfield, 'this is the real thing. We both feel the same. We went for a walk in the garden, and it suddenly hit us. She sort of fell into my arms, we did not say that much. It's a strange thing, Henley-Smith, but do you know what it is like when you are overcome by your feelings to a woman and you can't find the words, your heart is just bursting ...'

'No,' said Henley-Smith, 'I don't. Now, go in and take a shower. Your feet are beginning to smell.'

Caulfield headed for the shower. 'I only hope, Henley-Smith, you meet the love that I know. You can know the sweetness, the overpowering feeling that you are not the same person, that you are lifted to an elevation ...'

'Take the shower!' roared Henley-Smith, 'and another thing, I can't take any more of this crap.'

Caulfield pushed his head out of the shower. He gave a beatific smile.

'I don't blame you, Henley-Smith. How can you know Heaven if you have never been there?' He went back into the shower.

Henley-Smith walked across the floor, carrying a shoe. *This fellow has gone bananas.* He looked out of the window; the dusk was gathering, the scent of the lilac tree came through. *It was all too much for him,* he thought. *He wasn't used to this sort of party. Even Brady would not have bothered talking to him before now. Perhaps he got hit with a tennis ball? Would Elizabeth have upset him? Did the PP. insult him, he is a very plainspoken man. And what happened to Auntie Miriam, she never appeared to play her tennis match. Perhaps that was it, Auntie Miriam didn't want to play. He didn't offer her his hand, the way Murphy did. She saw Caulfield wasn't top drawer, and Caulfield felt the snub, and somehow he flipped the lid.*

Caulfield came out of the shower. He stood in the middle of the room, the water dripping, making a puddle all around.

'It might be an idea to dry yourself,' said Henley-Smith. In an absent-minded sort of way, Caulfield started to dress.

'Do you know what I was thinking when I stood in that cold shower?'

'I would prefer not to,' said Henley-Smith.

Caulfield appeared not to hear him.

'I was thinking,' he said, 'that right across the world there is one woman who is your soul mate, and how do you meet her. What do you think, Henley-Smith, how do you meet her?'

Henley-Smith did not answer. He put on his trousers, socks and shoes, his shirt, made his tie, put on a Stonyhurst blazer, combed his hair and leaned back on his bed, put his feet up and closed his eyes.

Caulfield said nothing more, and finished his dressing.

'OK, boy,' he said, in his favourite funny-man Cork accent, 'time to move!'

Henley-Smith slowly arose. He looked Caulfield up and down.

'Will I make it?' asked Caulfield.

'Provided you don't speak rubbish. No more talk about the fairies in the glen, or how Lovey Dovey found True Love.'

Caulfield shook his head sadly. 'Pathetic!' he said.

There was a hum of conversation from below and going down the stairs Henley-Smith, in a low voice, said, 'It might not be a problem, but if you have to introduce people introduce the new comers to someone already there; and the men to the women, and a younger person to an older.'

'You don't say!' said Caulfield, 'but that's the way we always do it in Ballynale.'

'For goodness sake, keep your cool,' said Henley-Smith.

'As a matter of fact, only yesterday I had to introduce a Duke to an Archbishop; they were arguing over the price of a bullock.'

'I don't know why I bother,' moaned Henley-Smith.

***

The drawing room was full. Caulfield knew all the tennis players, which included Cynthia Fitzhaugh. She was very nearly pretty, married to an amateur jockey who had ridden twice in the Gold Cup.

The Bradys were new to all this. Brady had handled work for the Henley-Smiths and had more or less soaked up the ambience. His wife was from the purest Republican stock, and was torn between old loyalties and her new social ambitions, which she felt, were her due.

The Murphys had travelled from Limerick. Murphy was the sort of man who never seemed to sweat. He was a doctor of something or other but never flaunted it, or insisted on being addressed as 'Doctor'. Their son, Kevin, refused to go to the dinner, and borrowed their car to drive into Roscrea.

Tom Ronayne, SC., was usually invisible. He took small, safe unloseable briefs. From time to time, solicitors would ask if he was still alive. His main concern was to prevent his wife from getting drunk in public.

Captain Stokes was a relation of the Henley-Smiths. He was commissioned in Iraq and the War Office put him in charge of a bar in Iceland.

Dr. Dowd was doctor to the Henley-Smiths; an amiable fellow, who had long since stopped trying to keep up with medical knowledge. Consequently, he was the best doctor in the country.

The guests were arriving and were met at the door by the butler and a maidservant, who took their coats. The butler escorted them to the drawing room where the Commodore and Lady Mary were waiting.

The butler announced each guest to the hosts.

The butler announced Caulfield. Many eyes were on him as no one had ever heard of him before. His striking good looks and impressive build caused a hum of conversation.

Commodore and Lady Mary greeted him and shook hands with a marked politeness. This time Caulfield offered his hand it was enough, and no more.

Caulfield stood by himself, with his back to the unlit fireplace. He felt in his bones that he had made a good impression on these people. He pretended not to notice that many were looking at him, whispering and trying to ascertain his background. He didn't know whether he was nervous or just uncomfortable. He definitely felt gauche in the company of the upper classes, and tended to flinch at their booming voices and high-pitched laughter. Against that, he had the confidence of one who excelled in athletics, studies; a well-cut figure, handsome, genial.

As he stood there, Caulfield saw the butler sound a gong. 'What's that all about?' he thought, 'nobody has made a move into the dining room.' Stopping a woman who was carrying a tray of Sherries he asked her, sotto voce, about the gong.

'That's for dinner in half an hour. When dinner is ready he will sound the gong again.' She looked at him sympathetically. 'I think you know Mr Caulfield. It won't take you long to learn the drill!'

Caulfield could have taken umbrage, but in a pleasant tone he said, 'Ah yes, Mrs McCabe, I thought I knew *you.*' She smiled and moved away.

Henley-Smith and Elizabeth, with Prudence and Wendy's mother and Auntie Miriam were announced. Caulfield thought he had never seen such a vision as Prudence.

She was radiant.

Caulfield had felt a surge in his heart and something that words cannot tell. He was hopelessly in love. Everything was different. He lived only for his darling's look, her voice, the touch of her hand. He loved her because she loved him. He loved her because he would die and sacrifice for her, as she would for him.

She was looking around the room for him, and when their eyes met, it was as if two hearts were locked together. Caulfield felt a strange ecstasy possess him, it was almost spiritual.

They both felt that their love was pure, that it would last forever; nothing could shake it, that it was eternal for all time. How could he be so blessed? Theirs was a happiness that no one had ever felt.

She smiled up at him as they came together. He couldn't understand his good fortune.

He couldn't understand the happiness that overcame him. He did not care what people said, or if they stared or gossiped. He was not bothered by envy, spite, or small talk. He only knew that he and his darling had seen heaven and were together.

***

Commodore Henley-Smith, RN, and his wife, Lady Mary, moved through their guests. She was the daughter of an earl and could trace her title back to the Tudors. It was the first time that day she appeared in public. Her headaches were famed throughout the county, and resulted in her taking to her bed twice a week. Other days she might suffer an attack from one of her numerous allergies. Living in the country she was, naturally enough, susceptible to hay fever and asthma and was advised by Dr. Dowd to desist from the consumption of lettuce, parsley, rhubarb, new potatoes, leeks, carrots, chicken, white bread, cake containing sultanas, sugar, soft boiled eggs and oatmeal.

The hosts came to where Caulfield and Prudence were standing. Prudence made no secret of her feelings for Caulfield. She looked up at him with adoring eyes, and her voice trembled when she mentioned his name.

Lady Mary scrutinised Caulfield. He met her approval. She had been briefed by Henley-Smith on his background which made him quite impossible, but that didn't matter at the moment. Prudence was only sixteen, but it was holiday time and, for the present, Caulfield would make her an excellent companion. When Prudence returned home she would have many other beaux, and Caulfield would sink without a trace.

He offered his hand.

'How do you do, Mr. Caulfield?' said Lady Mary.

'How do you do?' said Caulfield, shaking her hand and slightly bowing, almost instinctively.

Where did he get his manners? thought Lady Mary.

Isn't he gorgeous? thought Prudence.

Good cut of a fellow, thought the Commodore.

'I believe you are very handy at tennis,' said the Commodore, 'You gave my son a right hiding two years ago.'

'Oh, that was the Tipperary Championship. It was a very close thing. And I think the umpire's decision was – eh – debatable.'

'Nonsense!' said Henley-Smith, 'I think you are too damned polite.'

Caulfield felt this was getting difficult. He glanced around the room to see where Henley-Smith was. Fortunately, he was well out of earshot. If he agreed with the Commodore, he was more or less agreeing that he had thrashed his son in the match. If he disagreed who won, he could see a storm blowing up for the Commodore was noted for his choleric temper.

Lady Henley-Smith was looking steadily at him. There was no sign of ill health in her stance. There was silence as the two men faced each other.

'It seems to be advantage out,' said Caulfield.

They all laughed.

The Henley-Smiths moved on. Prudence squeezed Caulfield's arm. 'As Cousin Elizabeth would say, 'super'!'

Caulfield was aware that there had been a pause in the conversation. The party had listened to the match between him and the Commodore. It was game, set and match for Caulfield.

He was almost unconscious of this. All he knew was that the most wonderful person in the world was on his arm. He could have spent hours simply looking at her. Her smile was simple and unforced. Caulfield could only think one thing: 'Darling, I love you.'

***

It was the first dinner party for six months. Henley-Smith had asked for it, on his birthday. It had been easy enough to select the first guests to invite. Wendy and Prudence and their mother (Lady Mary's sister) had chosen themselves. The family were Elizabeth and Auntie Miriam. The Commodore had asked for Herzog. The local crowd were Brady and his wife. Lady Mary was glad she had invited Brady's wife, she was so common, she was a scream. She rather liked her – she reminded her of the old woman who sold eggs outside Egan's Pub. At least, she spoke her mind and was good for a laugh. The Murphys were supposed to be top of the pile in Limerick. Her friendship with Olive Murphy went back many years, when they were both students in Prague, but a lot of the fun seemed to have left Olive since. Olive's husband was supposed to be something of a nerd – he could calculate the square root of four digit numbers in his head.

The guests moved into the dining room. Caulfield of course escorted Prudence. He wondered why he found it so easy, then he remembered all the old bound volumes of *Punch* which he read in the Rector's study, and the cartoons which educated him into Victorian high society. To his intense annoyance, he was not seated with Prudence, but between Elizabeth and Mrs. Brady.

After the PP. pronounced grace they took their seats and Caulfield saw that Prudence was several places away on the far side of the table.

They made love to each other with their eyes.

MENU: Soup

'In Scotland they call it Cock-a-Leekie.'

'We call it plain Irish leek.'

'The potatoes help it.'

'Absolutely super.'

'The soup is souper.' (Laughter)

'It always tastes better when the vegetables come from your own garden.' (Murmur of approval).

Henley-Smith was sitting opposite Caulfield. He leaned across the table and hoarsely whispered, 'Eat, eat.'

Carmel Brady looked at Caulfield.

'What's he talking about?'

'He is telling us to eat the soup.'

Caulfield had learned enough from his Aunt Hilda.

'He is telling us to eat the soup and not drink it.'

'How can you eat soup?' she asked, her voice getting louder.

'With a fork!' said Henley-Smith, laughing like an idiot.

The whole table was now listening. Carmel's face got redder and she did not know how to answer. Caulfield got angry also. Henley-Smith was being abominable, and he could see himself being dragged into some sort of unpleasantness.

'Eat, eat again,' said Henley-Smith, and then went 'Ho, ho, ho!'

He is drunk, thought Caulfield. Caulfield could have kicked him until he saw Prudence and felt the radiance of her smile. He forgot the asinine behaviour of Henley-Smith. He smiled to her and life was wonderful, and the birds sang.

Henley-Smith dragged him back.

'Want my fork, eh, Madam Brady?'

Carmel controlled herself, and asked Caulfield, 'What's this all about?'

He answered, 'It's about eating soup. Apparently, in polite society they…' looking at Henley-Smith, '…don't talk about drinking soup, they only *eat* soup. And then if they eat soup, should you use a fork to eat soup? The whole thing is pathetic.'

'It's pathetic,' agreed Carmel.

She looked gratefully at Caulfield. He had wised her up on this soup business, but without patronising her. She had learned some valuable tips, which could prove useful next September at the Ladies' Golf Dinner. She must make sure that soup would be served, and she could settle some old scores.

As she finished eating her soup, her hand fell down on his thigh and gently stroked it. Caulfield hoped that Prudence was not watching.

Henley-Smith turned his attention to Mrs. Ronayne, beside him. 'The other way, the other way!' he shouted. She was finishing off her soup by tilting her plate backwards.

This was all too much for the Commodore. He stood up and barked at Henley-Smith.

'Your behaviour is disgraceful on your birthday, you are acting like a hooligan! Stand up and apologise to everyone here.'

Caulfield was surprised at the way Henley-Smith crumpled up; he looked like a whipped dog. He felt Henley-Smith had no backbone of any sort. He did not expect him to assault his father, but he could have stood up for himself a bit more.

He said, 'I apologise. I have had too much to drink.'

117

The assembled party applauded. Mollified, Henley-Smith sat down. He returned to Mrs. Ronayne. 'Away from you, madam, not to you.' He reached over to her empty soup plate. 'When you are finishing it off, tilt it away, like that – not to you, like this.'

He was at it again. Although speaking in a conversational tone, he could be heard by everyone at the table.

Caulfield looked at the Commodore. He looked like a man who had not been to bed for three days. He could hardly believe what his son was putting him through.

Caulfield wondered about this dysfunctional family. He looked at Elizabeth beside him, she was miserable.

'Are you not happy, Elizabeth?'

'Yes,' she said, mournfully, 'I am so happy.' She was almost crying.

'That was a nice game of tennis we had.'

Her face lit up. 'It was wonderful. It was so wonderful!'

'Perhaps we can have another came sometime.'

She was smiling. She had not a care in this world. She was the happiest of happy women.

'It would be super – eh- …'

'Caulfield,' said Caulfield.

'Oh yes! I know you are Caulfield. I was so happy to see you play cricket today.'

'Actually, I was playing tennis.'

'No, I saw you playing cricket, you are a super cricket player.'

Caulfield said nothing for a while.

'I am glad you enjoyed the game,' he said.

The Parish Priest told a story about a bishop and his housekeeper. (General laughter).

Tom Ronayne asked if anyone knew what was a boy's best friend and a man's best friend. A boy's best friend is his mother and a man's best friend is his dog. (Laughter).

Cynthia Fitzhaugh asked if any knew where the word 'tennis' came from. (Subdued exclamations).

Brady told a story about a Kerry jury. (Laughter).

Murphy had a story about an Irish missionary. The natives captured him and they put him into a big cooking pot and made a broth of a boy.

Captain Stokes told a story about a lion keeper, but got confused and never finished it.

Beef

The beef was ceremoniously carried in. 'This is O'Herlihy beef,' said the Commodore, 'descended from a bull that chased St. Patrick.' There was laboured laughter all round. Nobody knew what to expect, most of the party wanted to get away as soon as possible.

The butler put the platter of roast beef on a side table and commenced carving.

Captain Stokes was telling Prudence and Wendy about the Iceland sagas which he studied whilst there. They did not even try to look interested. They knew Captain Stokes as a tiresome bore who inflicted them on family occasions.

'Do you like beef?' asked Caulfield.

'It's so, so lovely,' said Elizabeth.

'What do you think of the beef?' asked Caulfield of Carmel.

'It's alright,' muttered Carmel Brady. 'I'm not going over the moon. We have it every Sunday, and I have proper homemade gravy. It's just like this damn family. You never know whether it comes off the dish or out of the packet.'

Caulfield thought it sounded brilliant. He tried to be as nonchalant as possible. Prudence could be watching, and opposite Henley-Smith was very quiet. Was he listening? Could he hear anything?

Conversation died down as people wrestled with the gristle.

'Would you like to make fifty pounds?' asked Carmel Brady.

Caulfield thought he would chance it.

'Carmel, darling, I'll do it for nothing.'

Carmel choked on some meat. She tried to smother a laugh. Henley-Smith looked suspiciously at them, and even Prudence looked down the table.

Caulfield put on his nicest smile, and Prudence relaxed.

'You're quite a boyo!' said Carmel.

'It goes to my head when I sit down beside a beautiful woman.'

'Ah, come on, come on.' Caulfield could see she was pleased. 'I'll pay you fifty pounds,' said Carmel, 'if you fill your mouth with meat, start choking on it, and pull out a piece of string.'

'Carmel, you are absolutely mad. I would not do it for a thousand pounds.'

'OK,' she replied, 'I'll keep my fifty pounds.'

'I want to ask you something, Carmel.'

'Sure.'

'Do you like these people?'

'Hate them!' she said.

'Carmel, people are listening.'

'So what, Caulfield? I owe nothing to them. I don't have to like anyone.'

'Even solicitors want to be liked.'

'Let me tell you something,' whispered Carmel, 'you are a big, fat mammy's boy and so is that fellow across the table.'

Henley-Smith looked up. 'What did you say?'

'Nothing,' she said, 'but I brought my money into my marriage and I don't need to kowtow to anyone. Plenty of people have asked me, and you are not to ask me, where it came from.'

'Maybe you have friends in low places.'

'Aha, very neat, Caulfield!' she looked pleased.

'So, you say you hate them. Is there anything about them that you like? Surely they have style, class et cetera.'

Before she could answer, a servant came around with roast potatoes. They were delicious. He asked Elizabeth if she wanted one.

'Thank you,' she breathed, 'you were the only one to ask me. Thank you so much. Thank you, thank you, Caulfield.'

She took one potato. 'How can I thank you – eh – '

'Caulfield,' said Caulfield.

'Ah, yes, Caulfield,' she said. 'It's such a lovely potato.'

Caulfield turned back to Carmel.

'So you hate them?' he asked.

She closed her eyes for a moment, as if thinking deeply, and then replied in a low voice.

'I hate them. I wish I was them.'

Caulfield, finishing his meal, said something inconsequential to Elizabeth.

Henley-Smith tapped the table with his knife. 'A pencil, a pencil!' he cried. Again, the table stopped. Henley-Smith was off once more.

'What is he at now?' said the Commodore.

'What's the matter?' asked Caulfield. 'Do you want a pencil?'

Henley-Smith reached his hand over the table and grabbed Caulfield's hand.

'My friend, my dear friend,' said Henley-Smith, 'I don't want you to cut your potatoes with a pencil.'

Caulfield didn't get it. He looked up and down the table – could someone help him? Everyone looked baffled, except Prudence. This was a surprise. She knew something, and she looked away. Caulfield felt a coldness affecting him. Prudence knew something that he didn't and she was embarrassed. She could not face him.

'Caulfield!' cried Henley-Smith, 'It's not a pencil.'

He took up the knife and held it. He reached over and cut his potato in two.

'Like this!' he shouted, 'not like this' and he changed the way he held the knife. It was as if he was holding a pencil.

Caulfield saw immediately what his point was. He found himself blushing and his temper flared up. He had been publicly insulted. The diners shared the humiliation. Some of them held their knife correctly, others 'pencil fashion'.

Caulfield was enraged. He was satisfied he had handled himself very well that day, and now he was exposed as an unmannerly buffoon.

He was not going to stay. If he had been insulted he must leave, that was a bit of etiquette that perhaps Henley-Smith did not know. As he pushed his chair back, he felt two arms surrounding him, the perfume of the woman he loved, and a voice that was a voice beyond all voices.

'Don't go, darling. I love you.'

Chapter 12

Gateau St. Honore

All his life, Caulfield remembered that moment. He remembered the silky feel of Prudence's arms, and the effort he made to control his tears. Indifferent to those watching, she covered his face with kisses, and like a mother murmured his name. How easy it was to love such a woman.

When he had calmed down, she returned to her place. Peace was restored, but it was a peace that left the survivors gasping and benumbed. Never had anyone been invited to a house and treated like this.

If they could have left, they would have, but the Henley-Smiths were people of consequence; in a dozen different ways they would have been dangerous to cross. Better stay and let the storm blow itself out.

Henley-Smith slumped in his chair. His face was the colour of chalk. Very quickly he had sobered up. He lacerated himself with guilt. *Why do I do these things? Why do I have to make people hate me. This incident will be told a thousand times over, and they will all hate me, even if they are not here. And today is supposed to be my birthday. God Almighty!*

'A special treat for a birthday!' Lady Mary announced.

One would think that she had slept during the incident. At the most, in her opinion, it was a minor squabble between children.

The diners continued in a sullen atmosphere. Some were afraid that Henley-Smith might turn and expose them to ridicule.

To cap it all, the beef was chewy.

The Gateau St. Honore was carried in to admiring gasps from everyone. It was a circular dish with a base of meringue and sugar icing. Inside was whipped cream and chopped pineapple, pillars of ice cream supported another row of meringue and cream. Over the entire dish very thin strands of spun sugar had been woven.

'Wow!' said Henley-Smith.

'Gee whiz!' said Caulfield.

'Super, super!' cried Elizabeth.

'How do we eat this?' said Carmel Brady, glaring at Henley-Smith.

'With your fingers,' snarled Henley-Smith. He was not yet beaten.

'Will you two take it easy?' said Murphy, 'Otherwise no second helpings.'

'Horace, behave yourself,' said his wife. He retreated into his shell.

The life of the party slowly recovered. It might be possible to salvage something.

Lady Mary felt her headache coming on; it might have been better to take to her bed. But it was too early for her headache, and Dr. Dowd was enjoying himself. He was on his third glass of wine. Lady Mary looked down her dinner table. Olive Murphy was the one she remembered most from the old days. The time they had in Prague together! She had envied Olive for Carlo and his romantic soul.

And then there was Caulfield.

She had been watching Caulfield and also watching Henley-Smith. There was something about Caulfield that she wanted. Henley-Smith was in need, he was weak, he was Mumsie's boy, and he was going to be flung into the sea.

She had a strong feeling that he couldn't make it. It filled her with a cold anger that her pompous, stuffed-shirt of a husband would use him for his own needs.

But there was Caulfield. Only Caulfield could help.

Henley-Smith called out, 'Did you ever hear the story about the Jewish baker?' There was a groan from around the table.

Caulfield said, 'What about a story of a Jewish jeweller?'

Brady winked at the PP.

'Have you heard the story about the Jewish chorus girl and the bishop?'

'Not on your life,' rasped the PP. 'In the meantime, I'd love another piece of that Inchicore stuff.' Its called the "Inchicore stuff" tea because it was made in the kitchen of Lord Inchicore.

Everyone pushed their plates forward for a second helping.

'This has been a big hit,' said Caulfield to Lady Mary.

'You'd think she had made the thing herself,' grumbled Carmel Brady to Caulfield. 'The only thing they can make here is rhubarb and custard.'

Henley-Smith stood up. He cleared his throat and cried, 'A special treat! Mr. Caulfield has performed before the crowned heads of Europe. He is going to tell us the joke about the Jew and the jeweller.'

Everyone leaned back to enjoy the entertainer. They patted their stomachs and looked expectantly at Caulfield. It had been a good dinner, spoiled somewhat by the son of the house, but bygones were bygones.

'The joke,' shouted Henley-Smith, 'I demand a joke!' He clapped his hands. The rest of the dinner party started clapping. They were in a bibulous mood. 'Come on!' they shouted to Caulfield. Reluctantly he stood up, and held up his hand for silence.

'Here it comes,' he said, 'the unfunniest Jewish joke of the season.'

'Once upon a time,' he went on, 'there was a small school boy who walked to school every day. Every day he …'

'That's two every days,' shouted Henley-Smith, 'you can't have two every days…'

There was a chorus of boos directed at Henley-Smith. Caulfield held up his hands, and after silence, continued.

'This schoolboy would gaze into the jeweller's shop window and look at the watches in the window, and then he walked on. The jeweller took a dislike to this schoolboy looking into the window every day.'

'Three every days,' shouted Henley-Smith, 'you can't have three every days.'

'I'm only a beginner,' said Caulfield, 'I am entitled to 'three every days'.'

'Let him have his every days,' interrupted Captain Stokes.

'And on this day,' said Caulfield, 'this day, and not every day...' looking meaningfully at Henley-Smith, '...on this day the jeweller ran from his shop, grabbed the boy by his coat and shook him, crying out, 'If you vant to vay a vatch, vay a vatch, but stop vatching the vatches in the vindow'.'

He sat down. There was a silence. Henley-Smith chortled and clapped delightedly, rubbing his hands, pretending to be overcome with hysterical laughter.

'That's it!' he shouted, 'The joke of the century. Give a big hand to the excruciating Mr. Caulfield, joke man of stage, screen and television.'

Caulfield laughed at the antics of Henley-Smith. He was this time genuinely funny. Henley-Smith stood up again.

'That's it, ladies and gentlemen, your local agent for Jewish jokes. Also, Armenian jokes, Bulgarian jokes, Polish jokes and Dutch jokes.'

The entire dinner table shouted and clapped. Henley-Smith was astonished. They were laughing and clapping. He was popular, and they loved him. Even Carmel Brady reached across the table and kissed him. Murphy slapped him on the back. The small man that Caulfield had seen from Henley-Smiths window – Isaac Herzog – did not laugh or clap, but stared unsmilingly at him.

Caulfield glanced at Lady Mary. She was smiling at Henley-Smith, with tears in her eyes. It would be sometime before she had another headache.

When the ladies withdrew to the withdrawing room, Herzog buttonholed Caulfield. He shook his hand, and made enquiries to him about his life and prospects. Caulfield told him about his ambition for medicine. Herzog asked him if he had considered a career in business and finance.

'Undoubtedly you can help men and women to better health. With money you can do it, without money you can do nothing. If you control finance, you can control the world. We will meet again.' They shook hands.

'By the way,' said Herzog, 'you have not met my wife?'

'I don't think so.'

'You are right, she is not here. She has gone to Australia for a month. But sometime when you come to live in Dublin we might have dinner. Her name is Abigail. We might have an interesting proposition. We shall meet again Mr Caulfield,' said Herzog.

'Thank you,' said Caulfield.

As he turned away he said to himself, *this is a man who never gives anything for nothing, what is he up to?*

Earlier that day, Herzog had met with Commodore Henley-Smith. He had cultivated the Commodore for some time. Herzog was the indispensable go-between the navy and the tin-pot tyrants in South America and Africa. The ageing destroyers and submarines, instead of being scrapped, were tarted up and sold as almost new to the strutting dictators. Everyone gained. The naval dockyards were kept profitably busy, the dictators played war games, the navy got its money. Herzog made a million per warship, and the Commodore opened another bank account.

'I am going,' said Henley-Smith, 'I need another drink.'

'I am telling you something, Mr. Henley-Smith. You have another drink now and you might find yourself in fifty years time lying in the gutter, begging for pennies, with an empty whiskey bottle in your hand.'

Henley-Smith chuckled at the good of it.

'If I listen to any more of your maudlin, sugary ramblings, I will be lying in the gutter next week with an acute case of diabetes.'

He headed in the direction of the drinks tray. Caulfield headed in the direction of Prudence. He refused to wait any longer, she was his to take.

She saw him coming, and left Mr. Brady talking to himself. Her eyes shining, they would have embraced if all eyes were not on them.

Caulfield wanted to ask if he could call on her. He did not know the etiquette of the situation. Did he call on her father, or mother, or both? Did he bring a gift of flowers to the mother or not? When he called, could he sit down immediately, or wait for an invitation to sit and then wait for them to open the conversation?

Caulfield felt he never had such a happy day. A small-town boy had mixed it with much older people, even titled people, and they had responded to his easy charm and manners. Both Brady and Herzog had hinted he would be welcomed to join them in business, and above everything else, he was in love, and not with just any girl, but with the most marvellous girl in the world.

Prudence was looking at him, her secret smile said everything. He ached to sweep her away. The Commodore called her over. Reluctantly she left Caulfield.

Lady Mary moved around the room. A rubber of bridge had started. Henley-Smith had a whiskey in his hand.

'Don't you think you are a bit young for a whiskey?' remarked Captain Stokes.

Henley-Smith put on his best 'old boy' act.

'Not at all, old boy. But don't you think you are a bit old for a whiskey? Ha, ha, ha!'

'Young pup,' said Stokes, moving away.

'Did you hear that?' gasped Henley-Smith, 'He is speaking to me in our own house as if he owned it. He'll spend the next few weeks eating our food, drinking our liquor, chasing boys around the stables.'

'Ignore him,' said Caulfield, 'cut him dead tomorrow. There is nothing worse.'

Henley-Smith stopped and looked at Caulfield. 'You are a shrewd fellow. In fact, you are a pretty smart guy.'

'Ah, now, now.'

'I mean it,' said Henley-Smith. 'I'm going to tell you something. Do you know why I invited you here?'

'To play tennis.'

'Exactly,' said Henley-Smith, 'to play tennis, and for no other reason. I had to make up four for men's doubles. If Jimmy Scott-Green, my pal in Stonyhurst, had come, I wouldn't have asked you, because I wouldn't have needed you. Do you get it?'

'I get it very well,' said Caulfield.

Henley-Smith gave a hoot of laughter. His mother looked over at him.

'Watch it, they might take that whiskey off you.'

'You are a character, Caulfield. What I am trying to say is this, you are quite a guy that I would like to know better. I don't seem to know many around here. Even if Scott-Green had come, I would have found him a bit of a jerk. I only asked him because he asked me to his place in Yorkshire.'

'Seriously,' said Caulfield, 'this particular peasant is more than pleased to be here. Everyone was so pleasant and friendly.'

'Come over, come over anytime, especially if I am here.'

'Thanks,' said Caulfield, 'I'll take you up on that. There is one thing I want to ask you about. It's Prudence. I wasn't acting the mick when I told you I was mad about her. Would it be alright for me to call, and leave my card, so to speak?'

''Acting the mick,'' echoed Henley-Smith, in a tone of wonder. 'How charming!'

'It's the way the peasants speak around here,' said Caulfield.

He no longer took umbrage at Henley-Smith's darts. They were entirely good- humoured.

'You are welcome to call on my beautiful cousin. Remember to present your card.'

Caulfield look across the room; every time he did, three or four admirers, both married and unmarried, surrounded her. She had an extraordinary beauty.

'Did you ever see anything like her?' he whispered.

'Actually, yes, she was a cocktail waitress in the Savoy, a bit old for you – not to mention me. And she was very, very friendly.'

'Shut up, Henley-Smith, is there nothing sacred?' Caulfield felt deeply hurt. How could anyone mock the girl he loved, who was to him life and hope, who made his heart beat faster?

'My sympathies,' said Henley-Smith, 'you have a bad dose of it, but don't worry, it will go, it will pass, and remember she is only fifteen.'

'She is sixteen,' said Caulfield, 'and looks eighteen. I am sixteen as well, what mysterious power brought us together? Isn't there something magical about sixteen?'

***

They walked together on the balcony. It was a heavenly night. If it had been a fine night they could have looked up at the stars, but rain was in the wind as it swept in from the west. Prudence shivered, and he put his arm around her.

'Let me put my coat on you.'

'Caulfield, you are so thoughtful, but it's not fair for you. Let's go inside.'

They made their way inside. Everyone looked at them. They were fascinated by the young couple. Before their eyes a romance had blossomed. The granddaughter of an earl had fallen for the local boy made good. He was handsome, she was pretty.

They were ridiculously young and yet had the self-confidence of anyone else in the room.

The rain lashed the house, and windows banged all round. There was a general movement to go home by those who were not overnight guests.

'It's time for me to go, darling. Can we ever meet again?'

'Oh, please, Caulfield, please.'

He smiled down at her.

'I will ask Lady Mary if I can call.'

'Oh! She will be pleased. I think she likes you.'

'I hope her niece likes me, then I'll have everything.'

She squeezed his hand.

He waited in line to thank Lady Mary. As he was shaking her hand, she made it easy for him.

'Would you like to come over on Friday for tea?'

Caulfield said, 'Thank you, Lady Mary.'

Chapter 13

Afternoon Tea

The drive back to Ballynale seemed longer than the morning drive. The rain belted down. Caulfield could hardly see through the windscreen of Uncle Sam's car.

What was he going to do on Friday? He had no idea how to behave at afternoon teas. Lady Mary's invitation was not one that could be passed up. It was also a great opportunity to see Prudence again. He could hardly wait the three days to Friday.

Three days, he thought, a lot of things can happen in three days. After three days what would Prudence be like? Would she be the same loving girl?

Would she be just polite and friendly in a formal sort of way?

The worse thing would be for her to absent herself. Perhaps leave a brief message, or to take to bed with a chill. Then he would never know, and would suffer agonies.

What would he do if Prudence was cold or absent? Could he be nonchalant or even indifferent? Would it do to laugh it off and dismiss it as something of no importance?

Perhaps he could rub it in a bit, and inquire about Wendy (if she wasn't there) and forget Prudence's name and talk vaguely about 'Wendy's sister'.

'That'll learn her', as Uncle Sam would say. *No,* he said to himself, *it would never be like that.* He would die before disparaging her.

The thought of dying for her aroused romantic sentiments. He read a book somewhere about someone dying of consumption in the arms of his/her beloved. How wonderful and yet how sad.

The thought of this heartbreaking, yet lovely situation brought the sounds of violins, Rachmaninov, orange blossoms drifting in the wind. It was incredibly romantic.

What would it be, if he did die for her? Supposing he was driving a car and he swerved to avoid hitting a child, and killed himself. This noble action would cause a sensation and even the police would remove their caps and bow their heads as the cortege passed.

And everyone would talk with a catch in their voice of the departed one's wonderful fineness of character, which bordered on the saintly.

He could see himself being removed from the crashed car, clutching a rose to his bosom which Prudence had given him. The nurse in the ambulance would sob uncontrollably.

Another tragic but beautiful incident which he tended to linger over was the vision of walking with Prudence and her little dog, along the banks of a river. The dog jumped into the river and found itself in difficulties. He gallantly dived in and rescued the dog, but the effort was too much and he expired in Prudence's arms.

Poignancy was added to this drama, by the little dog trying to lick his face and restore him to life.

He imagined different acts of incredible bravery. There was the time when he climbed up the drain pipe of a burning house, and rescued two small children, and on his third ascent to save the nanny who was screaming hysterically, the house collapsed on both of them.

Today a simple stone commemorates the dead, and every year a young woman in black comes and lays a bouquet of flowers. Behind her black veil, the tears flow down, and a voice muffled by grief calls out: 'Caulfield, Caulfield.'

Sad, sad, thought Caulfield.

The rainy weather drifted away and Thursday looked fine. The forecast for Friday looked good, and Caulfield was filled with anticipation and nervousness.

He combed his hair every twelve minutes and secretly borrowed Uncle Sam's razor, he wasn't due for a shave for another two weeks.

His main problem was his hair. It was a little long, but he dare not go to Ned Horan his usual barber. Ned had a habit of cutting one side only or else leaving him looking like a Prussian field officer. So he washed it, then fluffed it up, decided that he didn't like it and in desperation soaked it in brilliantine.

This looked terrible and he washed it again as it was. His Aunt Hilda noted his frantic efforts to be a girl's dream, but said nothing.

Caulfield longed to have the car again. He asked for it once and he had got it. Could he ask again? He decided no. It would be abusing Uncle Sam's good nature. He remembered the story of a golden goose.

He would have to cycle his much dreaded bicycle. It was impossible to clean. So full of dents and chips that cleaning it would only heighten its imperfections.

Maybe I might look good on it? said Caulfield surveying it with a jaundiced eye. *No,* he decided, *I wouldn't look good on it, and the bike looks terrible, but it's all I have.*

Early lunch on Friday. 'Do I have to bring flowers?' he asked Aunt Hilda.

'No flowers,' said Aunt Hilda.

'Should I say 'pleased to meet you'?'

'No 'pleased to meet you',' said Aunt Hilda.

'What about 'how do yeh do?''

'Yes,' said Aunt Hilda, 'You can say 'how do yeh do?''

Uncle Sam asked 'Why can't he say 'pleased'?'

'I don't know,' said Aunt Hilda, 'but you can't.'

Caulfield's cousin Anna said, 'When you go in, the first thing you should say is, 'I beg your pardon but your slip is showing'.'

'Anna,' said Aunt Hilda, 'go to your room.'

Anna wailed but Uncle Sam said 'Stop crying and sit still.' She sniffed a little and then giggled.

'I read it in *Reader's Digest*.' she told her mother.

Caulfield ignored the interruption.

'A fellow at school told me something about a sheaf of wheat,' said Caulfield.

'A sheaf of wheat?' said Uncle Sam.

'It's nonsense,' said Aunt Hilda.

'In any case we don't have any wheat,' said Uncle Sam.

'What's special about the sheaf of wheat?' asked Anna.

'I don't know,' said Caulfield, 'apparently it is the done thing in Spain.'

There was general hilarity.

'You are not going to Spain,' said Aunt Hilda.

'I suppose so,' said Caulfield sunk in gloom. 'I wish I wasn't going to this Henley Hall.'

'You said the same thing on Wednesday before you left,' said Aunt Hilda 'and remember,' patting his hand, 'you are better than any of them.'

'Thanks Aunt Hilda,' and he left.

He was well and truly exercised by the time he reached Henley Hall. Aunt Hilda said 4pm was the best time to arrive.

He had a wonderful surprise. When he was some distance off he saw someone standing by the door. For a while he thought it was the military figure he saw on Wednesday, but as he approached he realised it was a woman.

It was Prudence.

A feeling of wonderful happiness possessed him, his apprehensions disappeared. He didn't know how long she had been standing, but she had come to meet him.

She was smiling the way she always smiled. How could he have doubted. She pulled the door closed behind her, and went down the steps to meet him. They were alone for probably the only time that day. They tenderly embraced and she led him into the withdrawing room.

'You have met mother and Aunt Miriam…'

They looked pleasant. Caulfield has a crazy idea of kissing their hands, but fortunately let it pass. He had seen some costume dramas in the Ballynale Grand Central Cinema, where a dashing buccaneer had kissed the hand of the Queen of France, but was this the time and place? Probably not.

'…and my father.'

Caulfield uttered one word, 'Commodore.'

He had got that exactly right. Even Aunt Miriam looked impressed. A servant appeared.

'Tea please, Elsie.'

'You came on a bicycle?' barked the Commodore.

'Yes, Sir.'

'Jolly good. Isn't that right, Miriam?'

'I don't know. We didn't ride bicycles in my day.'

'Yes you did,' he shouted at Aunt Miriam. 'I remember you on a bicycle with …that fellow who became a bishop.'

'I was never on a bicycle with a fellow who became a bishop.'

'Yes, you were Miriam. I remember it.'

'Henry, does it matter if she was on a bicycle or not?' asked Lady Mary.

'It does matter. Damn'it, it does! I like to have these things right. Ship shape and so on.'

'What I don't know,' he continued to Miriam, 'is why you are disputing if you, or if you have not, ridden on a bicycle. Surely there is nothing disgraceful about riding a bicycle, eh, Caulfield?'

Before Caulfield could answer he roared on, 'Even in your time, Miriam, a well bred girl could ride a bicycle. You agree, Caulfield?'

Caulfield mumbled, 'Well…'

'Yes, of course you agree, Caulfield. Say you are sorry, Miriam.' Miriam did not reply. 'Apologise to Caulfield,' he blustered. 'Now where is the tea?'

The maid Elsie had brought in the tea. There were two plates of small meringues and éclairs. The tea was poured out and the cakes handed round.

The Commodore drank his tea.

'The tea is cold!' he barked at the maid.

'No Sir, it's not.'

'I am telling you it's cold.'

'I am saying the tea was made with boiling water.'

'It's alright Elsie. It's very nice tea.' said Lady Mary. Elsie left.

'Did you hear that, Caulfield? In my own house, what would you say to that? Contradicted by a slip of a girl. If this was the Navy I would have her clapped into irons, eh, Caulfield?'

'Certainly it would improve the tea,' said Caulfield, 'but I agree with Lady Mary. It is very nice tea.'

The Commodore grunted and went over to a chair, out of reach of the party. If Caulfield knew what was the meaning of "high dudgeon" it would have fitted the Commodore.

Prudence, who had been out of the room, returned and sat down beside Caulfield. She gently rubbed the back of his leg with the toe of her shoe.

Caulfield had an uncomfortable feeling that Aunt Miriam had noticed, he also felt that she generally disapproved of him. Also the Commodore was hard to take, and Lady Mary was an enigma. Only Prudence was with him.

'Do you like the cakes, darling?'

'Very nice,' said Caulfield. 'Actually, my Aunt bakes very nice cakes, and she would like you to come to tea someday.'

'That is so nice,' said Prudence. 'I would love to come,' and she squeezed his arm.

Caulfield felt that Prudence's manner was as warm as ever, her eyes hardly ever left him, he could feel her warm body close by and he felt as happy as ever he did.

'Do you have these afternoon teas everyday?'

'Of course, darling, we would be very hungry by dinner time.'

Caulfield felt humbled, even reprimanded.

'Do you not have afternoon tea every day?' she asked.

'Well, I suppose so, actually most of the time, on the whole yes – I think,' said Caulfield.

Prudence was looking at him, it wasn't quite her usual lovey look; it was a look of curiosity, as if he represented an experience that was new to her.

Caulfield was not inclined to be an object of curiosity.

'There are millions of people who do not take afternoon tea,' he said.

'Really?' she said. She sat very still and looked away. Caulfield had given her something to think about. Her world had gone off centre just the merest tilt.

'What time do you have your dinner?'

'We have it,' said Caulfield, 'at 1pm.'

'What time is lunch then?'

'Lunch is at 1pm.'

'The same time as dinner?' asked Prudence.

'More or less,' said Caulfield.

'Do you not have any dinner at 7pm?' asked Prudence.'

'We have, but we call it tea.'

'You have tea at 7 pm?' asked Prudence.

'No,' said Caulfield, 'we have it at six.'

There was a silence and Prudence lips moved as if she was calculating something.

'The good news,' said Caulfield 'is that we all have breakfast at the same time, and we call it breakfast.'

Prudence started to laugh.

'That's what I call good news. Breakfast is at nine.'

'No,' said Caulfield, 'we have it at eight.'

Her laughter rang across the room. She whispered, 'Someday we can have breakfast together.'

They held hands and Aunt Miriam looked cross. Captain Stokes and his wife came in, as did Elizabeth and Wendy.

The Commodore shouted across the room. 'Tell that young fellow to come over here.'

Caulfield stood up and went over to the Commodore. The Commodore growled, 'Sit down.'

Caulfield pulled over a chair.

'Let me tell you something, Crackerfield.'

'Caulfield.'

'Oh, sorry. Caulfield. The Navy is a tidier up. The damned aeroplane has taken over. We pick up the pieces and carry the planes. It reminds me of one of those damned lorries on the road, which you see carrying about ten cars. That's us.'

'What about under the sea?'

'We have some atomic subs.; to replace them would cost billions of billions. Only the U.S.A. can afford them, and the Yanks are nearly broke. They would have to borrow the money from the Chinese.'

'There is something crazy about all this.'

The Commodore tapped out his cigar and sat up and leaned over to Caulfield.

'You are right, Crackerfield.'

'Caulfield.'

'Sorry, Caulfield. Yes, Caulfield you are quite right. There is something crazy about it all. We are paying little black fellows, whilst they are grabbing our lead and copper mines and so on. It's nuts!'

He leaned back in his chair and smoked his cigar, overcome by the problems and complexities of his world.

Talking to himself he muttered, 'The white man is finished.'

Prudence came over to him. 'My aunt, Lady Mary, wants to talk to you before you leave.'

'Is it about you?'

'No darling, it's not about me, don't worry. I can look after myself.'

Caulfield all smiles, walked over to Lady Mary. She greeted him effusively and took his arm and said, 'Caulfield! Thank you for coming, it's most kind and I believe you cycled all the way.'

'Thank you for asking, Lady Mary. It's a pleasure to come.'

'And now I want you to come with me. I am going to show you something of the house.'

She led him up the stairs where the paintings of the Henley-Smiths were hung, covering a period of three hundred years.

''Theirs not to reason why,

> Theirs but to do and die ...
> Boldly they rode and well
> Into the jaws of Death,
> Into the mouth of Hel ...''

'Very stirring!' said Caulfield. 'Was there a Henley-Smith in the Charge of the Light Brigade?'

'Yes, with Captain Nolan and the Irish. They served the King and kept the Old Faith,' said Lady Mary, 'they fought under Nelson and Collingwood. They were killed in the line of duty in every ocean, Caribbean, South Pacific, North Sea, Mediterranean, South China Sea, Indian Ocean. At Trafalgar they were first to cross the T.'

Caulfield wished he was somewhere else. The roll call of honour was moving, the call of the Empire (now gone) provoked a response, but it was gone. What did Lady Mary want from him? He knew he was not there to enjoy the old paintings of the Henley-Smiths'.

In his boarding school there was a room seldom used for classes, but on one of the walls was a large map titled; The British Empire, coloured in red. It was not difficult to be impressed by the vast size of an Empire spread across five continents which was won and held by a relatively small country.

It always gave him a surge of pride to think that this was *his* empire won by his own people. And his people were Irish people and they were proud to be Irish and proud to go to war for their King. Years later he often thought of this map and why it had moved him. He had not been brought up in an ultra royalist home. He had not been indoctrinated at school or anywhere else in the glories of the Union Flag, in fact as a young boy he read a book dealing with the landlord evictions of the nineteenth century, which filled him with a righteous anger against the system.

Despite this, when he saw the wall map of the British Empire, something stirred within him. Blood was thicker than water.

'Are you not listening to me, Caulfield?'

Caulfield pulled himself together.

'I am so sorry, Lady Mary. I was daydreaming.'

'Alright, Caulfield, I discovered that I was talking to myself.'

Lady Mary continued. 'What I was saying, Caulfield, is that the history of the Henley-Smith and the O'Herlihys before them is a heavy one. It is not an easy one. It was not easy for my husband.'

She stopped. Caulfield did not know what to say. 'It is less easy for Henley-Smith,' said Caulfield.

'Yes,' she said. 'I want you to help him.'

She walked down to the end of the landing, and turned the handle to walk in.

'This is Henley-Smith's room,' said Caulfield.

'Yes, come in.'

The room was shaded and the blinds were pulled down. In his bed lay Henley-Smith. The room was in semi darkness. Caulfield instinctively looked at Henley-Smith's bed. A body was lying there, his head swaddled in bandages, his right arm in plaster. He moved slightly and groaned.

'What happened?' gasped Caulfield.

'What do you think?' said Lady Mary; her voice was expressionless. 'He brought it all on himself.' She opened a blind an inch or two and Caulfield could see more clearly. His head over his eyebrows was a mass of bruises.

'It was after you left on Wednesday. He started drinking heavily, glasses of neat whiskey. The Commodore just looked and let him go on with it. It was deplorable. Then he picked some argument with Captain Stokes, and chased the poor man up the stairs. He tried to hit Stokes at the top, but missed completely, and fell down the stairs one at a time. I thought he had killed himself, he lay there without moving.

Fortunately Dr. Dowd was here, although he was nearly as drunk as Henley. Anyway we got him into bed. He was x-rayed yesterday; it appears that no bones are broken.'

'Thank heavens,' said Caulfield.

'I want to thank you more than heaven,' said Lady Mary drily. Caulfield looked at the comatose body of Henley-Smith and wondered, *what does she want? There is an angle here somewhere. Does she want me to smuggle the body out of the house or what?*

'Caulfield, I need your help.'

'Of course. Anything.'

'Henley,' and she looked at him, 'Henley is not a strong person, he is weak and easily led astray, his life is a list of excuses. Could you take him under your wing? I have noticed you; you are strong and will be stronger. You can be a big help to him.'

Caulfield shook his head. 'I don't think I am that strong, but certainly I will do the best I can.'

She pressed his hand. They left the room and went downstairs again and only Prudence and her mother were there. Prudence smiled knowingly at him as he approached her mother.

'Lady Deborah,' he asked, 'may I speak with you?'

'Why yes, Caulfield.' Prudence drifted away, making a close inspection of a painting.

'I would like permission to escort Prudence.'

'Oh how lovely! You want to escort Prudence. I thought you wanted to take her out.'

Caulfield managed a short laugh but it wasn't easy. *All right* he told himself, *if this old bitch wants to mix it, I'll give it to her.* He gave her one more chance.

'I suppose there's not much difference,' he said pleasantly.

'Oh, no difference, Caulfield.' He waited. One of the men in the corn stores had come across an old magazine with a photo of Lady Deborah. She was listed as being at the centre of the messy divorce action involving a Labour Party Cabinet Minister. Caulfield was shown it. If he had to use it, he would. He had made the last move. It was her turn.

Lady Mary was watching the duel, fascinated.

'Are you from these parts?' Lady Deborah asked.

'No.'

Straight out of Jane Austen, she asked, 'And pray, where are you from?'

'A place called Ballynale.' Caulfield decided Prudence or no Prudence, he would go for the jugular.

'How delightful,' she said, 'we must call on you tomorrow.'

'We are not at home on Saturday,' Caulfield said pompously. 'Possibly on Tuesday.'

'How lovely,' said Lady Deborah. 'I would love to see your gardens.'

'Yes,' said Caulfield, 'my cousin, Alistair Stagg, would love to show you. He is here on holidays. He is with the *Daily Telegraph;* you might remember his coverage of that business in Littlehampton, and what went on behind the church?'

There was a deadly silence. Lady Deborah's face went red and then white. She gave a look of pure hatred at Caulfield.

He felt a bit sorry for her now, but she had it coming. She asked for it and she got it.

Prudence came forward and she took Caulfield's hand. 'OK, Mum?'

Lady Deborah as good as snarled. 'Do what you want,' she said.

'Funny thing for Mum to say,' said Prudence.

Prudence's father (Mr. Wolstenholme) had no title but his wife, being the daughter of an Earl had the courtesy title, and was called Lady Deborah Wolstenholme. The same was true of her sister who was married to Henley-Smith who was Lady Mary Henley-Smith. Prudence was Prudence Wolstenholme, as was the Commodore Henry Henley-Smith.

The tricky part was the fathers, who had no title e.g. Mr. Wolstenholme, and Commodore Henley-Smith who was saved from disgrace by having a naval title.

What fascinated Caulfield was what they called each other in ordinary conversation, was Lady Mary called 'your ladyship' by the servants and also by her husband and children?

Should Caulfield have called Prudence 'Prudence' before he kissed her? It worried him a bit. He hoped he didn't offend her as if she worked in the post office.

When he thought of it, he realised that it was not a major problem. He hardly ever called her by her name, but usually 'sweetheart'.

To come to think of it, it might be a bit risky calling her 'sweetheart'. It sounded as if it was straight out of Texas.

***

For the tenth time Caulfield recited all the details of his visit to Henley Hall. They listened spellbound to his description of the servants, how to open a door, how food was served, who drew the curtains, how women were seated.

'It's a different world,' said Aunt Hilda.

'In the end it's not that different,' said Caulfield.

He was wondering how to break the news of Prudence.

'Lady Mary has asked me over again on Monday.' Uncle Sam looked at Aunt Hilda.

'For tea,' Caulfield added.

'Oh, for tea!' said Hilda.

Uncle Sam said, 'It's a long way to go for some tea.'

'As a matter of fact Henley-Smith might be there, and his cousins Prudence and Wendy.'

'How old are they?' asked Hilda.

'Wendy is about fifteen, Prudence is my age.'

Hilda sensed that she was on to something.

'This Prudence one, is she good looking?'

'She wouldn't like to be known as the 'Prudence one',' said Caulfield.

'Well, Miss Prudence, then.' Hilda was getting nettled by Caulfield. He may be growing up, but she would not put up with disrespectful manners.

'Sorry, Aunt Hilda, but the fact is I seem to have got a bit of a crush on Prudence.'

'Ah hah!' said Uncle Sam, 'now we are getting to the nub of the question. Are you planning to run away with the lovely Prudence?'

'Be serious, Sam,' said Aunt Hilda. 'She is only a pretty girl, isn't she?' asked Hilda to Caulfield. He didn't answer. They were knocking Prudence, they lived in a small town as he did, but only he had seen the vision that was Prudence, and the glamorous world she lived in. Caulfield had never looked so miserable.

'Don't worry,' said Aunt Hilda. 'Why don't you bring Prudence back here? I am sure our tea is as good as their tea.'

***

They walked through the gardens, they looked at the courts where they played tennis barely a week before.

'This is where it was,' said Caulfield.

'Only six days ago, when you told me all about Kransky, poor, poor Kransky,' said Prudence looking up at him with mock horror.

'It wasn't all lies I told you that day.'

He smiled, she smiled. They held each other. They wished for a day that would never end.

They met Elizabeth coming out of a greenhouse, eating a tomato. She dropped the tomato when she saw them, and ran away.

'Poor Elizabeth,' said Caulfield, 'and we have so much to be happy about.'

'That's a nice thought,' said Prudence. 'You do say the nicest things. You are the nicest person I have ever met.'

'You should see me in a rugby match,' said Caulfield.

Prudence hugged him. 'I know you are the nicest rugby player.'

'There is no such animal,' said Caulfield.

'Yes there is,' protested Prudence, 'outside centres are always gorgeous.'

Caulfield stood back. 'How would you know anything like that?'

'I know,' said Prudence. 'I heard Brady talking to you at dinner. He saw you playing for Leinster school boys, against Ulster. Some priest said to him that you were the best player and the most sporting.'

'You shouldn't listen to these stories,' he said, but his heart was warmed.

Leaning against a glass house was a ladies' bicycle, obviously there for some time. Caulfield looked at it. It was in good condition. He looked at Prudence.

'You want to say something?' said Prudence.

146

'Maybe.'

He looked at the bicycle again and again looked at Prudence.

'Do you want me to ride a bicycle?' said Prudence.

'I was just thinking,' said Caulfield. 'I have a bicycle, and you can have this bicycle and it might be fun to cycle around Tipperary. I could show you the sights – such as they are – of North Tipperary.'

'Oh, I see,' said Prudence, and with a schoolgirl's giggle she cycled down the path until she fell off. She pushed the bicycle back, and her eyes were dancing.

'Could we really do that? Cycle around Tipperary?'

'Of course,' said Caulfield, 'and we start on Wednesday.'

On Wednesday the sun was shining and God was in his heaven. Aunt Hilda was doubtful about the whole business. 'She is only fifteen,' Hilda remarked. 'Looks eighteen,' said Caulfield.

Caulfield coaxed Aunt Hilda to make sandwiches and fill a thermos with tea. Hilda was disturbed for other reasons. Caulfield was growing out of his puppy days, it was inevitable of course, still it was a pang. Her own two daughters came through it with less fuss.

Prudence was waiting on her bicycle for him to come. Caulfield never ceased to marvel that she was always waiting, always happy to see him, always waving when he came into view, and the surge of happiness he had when he saw her smile.

The days that followed would remain with both of them all their lives. The little by roads which they usually used, that seemed to lead to nowhere. Their adventures in friendship in the small cottages where they stopped for a glass of water, or to inquire the way. They sat in the cottages and were entranced as the hens ran in and the chicks sought refuge in their feathers. Prudence had seen nothing like it, and almost cried with its wonder.

***

147

Sometimes whole days were spent in one place, Terryglass or Droimneer on the Shannon, where lazy hours passed. Small places with music in their names; names like Puckaun, Paulawee, Cloughprior. In the heat of those days they would find shade under the branches of a noble beech, talking or not talking, holding hands and letting the day drift by.

It was Aunt Hilda who for a second time suggested that he should bring Prudence for afternoon tea. It was elementary courtesy, genuine and sincere, yet flavoured with understandable curiosity. What sort of girl had Caulfield gone overboard on? What did it tell her of Caulfield? Was Caulfield empty headed, because he had gone for an empty- headed woman?

Henley Hall had been ruthless in its examination of Caulfield so Ballynale could take on Miss Prudence.

'Remember,' said Caulfield jokingly to Hilda, 'don't say 'Pleased to meet you.'' In fact she was a little tensed up. Caulfield wondered who was seeing who. Was Ballynale judging Henley Hall or vice-versa?

Uncle Sam was the least bit fussed. He had already dealt with their chauffeur. He was disappointed the chauffeur was not driving Prudence over; he had been looking forward to making him sit in the kitchen, while they entertained Prudence in the parlour. Parlours were the holy-of-holies in country homes. Parish Priests (or Protestant Ministers) were entertained in the parlour. It was always permanently dusted in preparation for important visitors. Housewives were judged on the state of their parlour.

Aunt Hilda had reason to be satisfied with their parlour. Books were prominent, for Hilda was a great reader. Two photographs of Uncle Sam's grand uncles who were in the Connaught Rangers, and who failed to survive Passchendaele. Hilda's two daughters, smiling and happy in their hockey uniforms, holding a large silver cup. A steel engraving of John Wesley. A large mirror over the fireplace, which had been bought for 2/6d. at an auction in Colonel Chamber's place, a T.V. set and a piano.

Caulfield said he would ride out and wait for her about seven miles from Ballynale. Aunt Hilda was doubtful. 'Supposing she gets a lift in the car,' she asked, 'and you are waiting at the bridge?'

'That won't happen,' consoled Caulfield. 'I'll 'phone her that morning to confirm.'

'Well, I don't want to be left making conversation.' said Hilda.

'You make very good conversation.'

'Don't be clever.'

'Sorry.'

Caulfield was beginning to feel edgy. He didn't want this to be a big deal, and yet he couldn't help it if it was. It was not as if he was introducing his wife, or fiancée. All these could be nerve racking. He was only sixteen, his girl was fifteen (looked eighteen) and here he was (in that hideous word) courting and yet not courting. What was he up to? It wasn't his idea to have Prudence for afternoon tea.

Caulfield set out for Barney's Bridge where they agreed to meet. He didn't want to be late for Prudence. He wanted to be first, so she wouldn't go through the mental agony of wondering if he was coming.

He was first, but by only a few minutes. They were glad to see each other of course, but Prudence was unsettled. She wasn't like that when they set out a few days before. He noticed she had her hair done. He dare not say it, but the old style suited her better. The present style looked as if it was for the last night of the Proms. He looked at it and said 'very nice' with a forced enthusiasm.

'Are you sure?' she asked him.

'Of course, darling.' It was the first time he ever lied to her.

'I don't think you like it.'

'Yes darling I love it, it suits you.'

'No,' she said. 'I know you don't like it, because you call me 'darling'.'

He gaped at her.

'You never called me 'darling' before. I know there is something wrong!'

He had an awful feeling. She was right. He never had called her that. The word was not in common usage in North Tipperary. In their public domain nobody called anyone darling.

The tears swelled up in her eyes.

'How could you be so cruel to me?' she cried between sobs. 'I thought you loved me and now… and now…'

Caulfield felt he was in some sort of nightmare. The whole thing wasn't real. They stood in the middle of the road, their bicycles at all angles. He kicked his out of the way and sought to embrace and comfort her.

She withdrew back and spoke haughtily, 'Stop, mind my hair.'

'Damn your bloody hair!' he burst out angrily.

She burst into tears, 'I know now you never loved me. You broke my heart, you made use of me. You never liked my hair.'

Caulfield forcibly held her. 'I love you, you stupid fool. I never loved anyone else. Please believe me.'

She looked at him with a new expression.

'Did you call me a stupid fool?'

Caulfield felt he had nothing to lose. 'Yes,' he said.

She threw her arms around his neck.

'Then I love you,' she said through her tears. 'I know you love me.'

Caulfield felt bewildered, but whatever it was it had worked. He picked up the bicycles, and let the cars pass. Behind them on the road four cars had queued up to get by. The drivers and passengers were open mouthed at this real life drama unfolding before their eyes. Some of the people got out of their cars and were animatedly exchanging information. They even looked around to see if there were movie cameras recording the event.

Caulfield climbed down to the small river under Barney's Bridge where he soaked his handkerchief. So Prudence could dab her face.

'It's lovely and cool,' she said. 'I was getting very hot and perspiring cycling on a sunny day.'

Caulfield said, 'I am telling you the truth, you are looking beautiful. You will knock Aunt Hilda for six.'

'Stay close to me,' she said.

They reached Ballynale half an hour later. The news of Prudence Wolstenholme's, daughter of Lady Deborah, visit to Ballynale seemed to have got around.

They arrived. Caulfield they knew, he could be ignored. Prudence dazzled.

As she slowly free wheeled past the garda, she graciously thanked him, until he was overcome by helpfulness. Going to Aunt Hilda's hall door she turned to the women assembled, smiled a smile so brilliant that they gave away to heavy breathing and fluttering.

Caulfield rang the bell, although he knew Aunt Hilda could have seen him entering the village. The bell rang and it rang again. Caulfield felt his blood boiling, and then it opened.

Aunt Hilda ignored Caulfield, but went to Prudence and the two women kissed cheek to cheek. This surprised Caulfield. In Ballynale women were not big into kissing. Women kissing were like prize fighters touching gloves.

Aunt Hilda led the way into her parlour. Two arrangements of flowers were there, which had not been there before. Some sheet music was on the piano. He could read at a distance something about Mozart. Caulfield felt a surge of gratitude. Good old Aunt Hilda, she would not let the side down.

Uncle Sam came in and dressed in his Sunday best which was a nice piece of tweed that suited him no end. Caulfield felt that they were overdoing it, but on recollection how could Prudence know it was his Sunday best, and not his everyday best.

Good old Aunt Hilda, she scored again.

Uncle Sam made polite remarks about Commodore Henley-Smith. Sam's father used to hunt with the Commodore's father – the old Admiral. Everyone hunted in those days.

The Henley-Smiths were the masters of the fox hounds. They were kept in Henley Hall.

'How thrilling,' said Prudence. 'How absolutely wonderful.'

'We used to meet at Barney's Bridge,' said Uncle Sam.

'Barney's Bridge!' shrieked Prudence. 'That's where Caulfield and I met. Caulfield, did you hear? The hunt used to meet where we met today.'

'Actually I didn't know that,' said Caulfield truthfully.

Prudence went on. 'Darling, I knew there was something about Barney's Bridge.'

Caulfield winced. He did not want Prudence calling him 'Darling' in front of Hilda and Sam. Her eyelids fluttered at Caulfield. He smiled. This could not last more than an hour.

Caulfield knew enough of Prudence's manner to realise that she was overdoing it. She was too gushy, too thrilled, too much smiling, too much absolutely delighted, she loved Ireland too much, she was mad on tennis and horse riding, she loved gardening when she had the time, she had read all the books, she simply loved the Irish authors, especially the divine Yeats, she would have loved to have lived in Ireland and get to know the lovely people. It was a shame that England and Ireland went to war back in 1066.

Aunt Hilda said, 'We must have some tea. I am sure you are peckish after your long cycle over.'

Good old Aunt Hilda.

The tea was brought in on a trolley.

Prudence enthused over the trolley. She was quite right. It was a very fine piece of furniture bought at the same auction of Colonel Chambers.

'It's been in the family a long time,' said Uncle Sam exchanging a look with Caulfield.

Caulfield was depressed. He was anxious that his people would make a good impression on Prudence but he also wanted Prudence to go over well with Sam and Hilda.

Both sides were trying to hoodwink the other. Sam and Hilda's family heirlooms which had been bought at auction, and Prudence and the divine Yeats of which she had never read more than two lines.

He loved Aunt Hilda and Uncle Sam for everything they had meant to him and for the simple goodness of their lives.

But he also loved Prudence for reasons less easy to explain. She filled his life in a different way, she made him complete, she made his heart sing in a way nobody else could, without her he felt he could not live.

He sat back in his chair with an empty cup. In the background was the lively chat of Aunt Hilda and Prudence. Caulfield's mind drifted away to far off places. The background chat fell silent but Caulfield fell deeper into reverie.

Somebody was calling his name. Hilda was at the piano playing Mozart but he didn't hear. Two voices were calling his name, but his eyes closed. Somebody was shaking him.

It was Prudence. She said one word 'Darling.' He came to, and shook himself.

'Darling,' she whispered, 'you have gone a long way away.'

It was time to go back to Henley Hall. They rose and Prudence thanked Aunt Hilda and Uncle Sam. Aunt Hilda with a little regret said, 'We seem to be sharing the one man.'

Prudence kissed her goodbye. Outside Uncle Sam said to them, 'It's madness to think of cycling to Henley Hall at this time of the day. Take the car, put Prudence's bike into the boot, and get back here in one piece.'

'Are you actually forcing me to drive a car?'

Laughter all around. He and Prudence drove away to waves and goodbyes.

153

Caulfield felt a tremendous sense of peace and happiness. The whole thing had gone so well. Prudence had tried her hardest to be friendly and gracious, Aunt Hilda had done her bit to be welcoming in the Irish tradition. Prudence had not attempted to pull rank and had never mentioned Ascot, or the coming out ball which was a fearful bore. Her aristocratic connections were ignored, as was her ski holiday at Davos, when she nearly collided with Prince Charles.

Aunt Hilda for her part showed none of the gee whiz wonder at entertaining an aristo. She was completely natural, talked of things that they had in common: when Prudence brought up the subject of the Kakot Bird which she found utterly delightful, Aunt Hilda was able to tell an anecdote concerning it in the North Island of New Zealand. As Prudence had never been to New Zealand, Aunt Hilda didn't try to rub it in and never mentioned New Zealand again.

As the loyal Irish always do, Hilda was avid for news of the Queen – was she looking tired, Hilda asked, when opening that bridge in Newcastle? Would Prince Charles make a good king? Wasn't the Queen Mother a wonderful woman? A pity about Princess Margaret but, Hilda had to admit, she never really warmed to her.

To all this Prudence enthusiastically agreed. Aunt Hilda asked her did she ever hear anything interesting bits about Buckingham Palace, seeing that she only lived ten minutes away.

Prudence dropped her voice to a confidential whisper. 'Yes.' she said. She had heard on a very good source that Prince Philip was very fond of sausages (often had six at a time) but the Queen put her foot down, and would only let him have them twice a week.

She had learned the news from her hairdresser, who got it from her sister, who was married to a footman in the Palace.

They were doing their best to keep it out of the papers.

Aunt Hilda's day was made.

Altogether it was a splendid day.

Prudence snuggled close to Caulfield as the car chugged the sixteen miles to Henley Hall. She had been apprehensive in her own way of the visit.

Caulfield's Aunt Hilda and Uncle Sam were genuinely nice. She had a lurking fear that they would be dreadful and Caulfield would stand in a poor light. If they were middle class snobs who didn't know who to look down on it would have been worse.

Her Caulfield was still her hero.

They stopped at Barney's Bridge. It was still bright, but there was no one around. They held each other and never again would they feel such love.

The stress and anxiety which they went through before the meeting was gone. The peace, it was wonderful.

They talked the way lovers talk, and he drove her home.

***

The summer was passing. Caulfield had the freedom of Henley Hall, he could come and go like one of the family. Even Aunt Miriam warmed to him as he discovered her birthday and gave her a shawl for the winter days.

Henley-Smith happily restored, had tennis parties every week. Caulfield quickly mixed in, and he was invited back to other courts large and small. Mothers of daughters eyed him critically and made mental notes for the future. Caulfield had eyes for only one person. Prudence was the beginning and the end. If she was there it was a wonderful party, absent and the whole thing was a drag.

Prudence and Caulfield knew that shorter days were coming and August would someday be over. They pretended that they didn't know that everything would not go on forever.

Aunt Hilda had reservations about Prudence. In her opinion Prudence was dangerous. Dangerous in the sense that she didn't know she was dangerous. She reckoned that initially she went for Caulfield for a light hearted summer romance that would hurt nobody, but then got out of her depth and fooled herself as well as Caulfield. She was going to hurt herself as well as Caulfield.

Uncle Sam back in his everyday clothes whistled tunelessly as he moved around the place. Aunt Hilda could often be very quiet at any time, but this time her silence was deafening.

Caulfield debated to himself if he should ask Aunt Hilda what she thought of Prudence. He had already asked Prudence what she thought of Hilda and Sam. They are lovely people, she said. That meant exactly nothing.

Aunt Hilda took the initiative.

'Caulfield,' she said, 'about Prudence.'

'Oh, yes,' he replied (to himself he said, *here it comes*.)

Aunt Hilda went on, 'She is very, very pretty.'

(Caulfield to himself, *'But...'*)

'But,' said Hilda, 'she is miles above us.'

Caulfield said, 'I used to think that about all the Henley-Smiths, but the more I see of them, and especially the more I see of Prudence, I feel completely at ease. I don't think of them as being better than us.'

Aunt Hilda said, 'They have made use of you; you have squired Prudence all summer, that was great for them and for Prudence.'

Caulfield was getting very angry. 'Do you think,' he asked, 'that that's all she meant, just to make use of me?'

Aunt Hilda went to him, and put her hand on him. 'My dear Caulfield, please listen. I know she loves you, I think she is mad about you, she will never forget you, but I think she will be mad about a lot of men in her life.'

Caulfield didn't know what to think; he stumbled out of the kitchen, and down to the haggard, and threw himself on the hay. He was so overcome that he could not even shed tears. He lay for a long time. He thought of Prudence, and saw her face, her smile, her most beautiful eyes. She was saying 'Darling.'

He lay on the hay and then he knew, she was for him, for no one else. Then the tears came.

***

Caulfield and Prudence went for long walks. The bicycling was over. The woods and lake at the back of Henley Hall were showing their autumnal tints and the air was alive with the flocks of swifts as they practised swooping and dipping in astonishing harmony.

Prudence was surprisingly well up on nature. She noticed the beginning of a badger's sett.

Walking through the woods was more intimate than cycling, they held hands all the time helping each other, coming apart and then coming together. There was a sorrow in Caulfield's mind. He tried not to think.

Prudence caught something of the same emotion. They talked about everything except what was on their mind. It was the third week in August. Caulfield came down to breakfast to find one of his suitcases in the passage.

'Try on your rugby boots,' said Hilda, 'see if they still fit.'

He did. They didn't.

'Good heavens,' said Aunt Hilda, 'why can't you stop growing?'

Caulfield had to face the fact. The holidays were over.

The following days were wet and windy. Caulfield was housebound in Ballynale when the phone rang.

It was Prudence. Never before had she 'phoned.

'Can you come tomorrow?' she asked. 'I must see you.'

Caulfield knew. 'Are you going home?'

'Please darling, don't ask. Please come over.'

Caulfield went to his room and threw himself on his bed. This was it. The light was going out. It had to be the end of everything. What was he going to do? He could do nothing. He felt utterly

157

drained; the last week had left him without hope, without laughter, without love, without a future, the poorest man on earth, because he had only one thing and it was going.

That evening he went down to his tea. Aunt Hilda looked at his swollen face.

'They are going the day after tomorrow,' said Caulfield. 'I'll be seeing them for the last time.' As he spoke, the tears welled up. Aunt Hilda went and hugged him; all she could say was 'Caulfield.'

'Thank you, Aunt Hilda. Thank you.'

***

Sam insisted he take the car. He drove it so slowly that it nearly conked out. As he drove it up the avenue, he saw Prudence walking down to him.

How does she do it? he asked himself.

He stopped. She got into the car. Caulfield thought she never looked worse. He parked the car in front of the house where he had parked it the first time. As he got out to open Prudence's door, Henley-Smith appeared.

'Keep an eye on her, will you? She has been crying her eyes out all night.'

Then looking at him, 'You don't look so hot yourself.'

Caulfield nodded dumbly.

'Look why don't you come over tomorrow night? I'll make a drunkard out of you.'

Caulfield smiled for the first time, and for the first time he realised that Henley-Smith was one decent guy. If there is any way that he can do a favour for Henley-Smith, then he would do it. Caulfield opened Prudence's door. She was wearing an ankle length lamb's wool coat. Despite that she seemed to shiver.

'Don't go inside,' she said. 'Let's go for a walk.'

They walked down the familiar paths and came to the tennis courts. They stood at the end of the tennis courts.

'This is where it all began,' said Caulfield.

Prudence burst into tears. She clung onto Caulfield. The two of them wept.

'Look, Prudence. We will meet again. Next summer will be a lovely summer. We will play tennis, we will cycle all over Tipperary, we will go into the cottages and see the hens and their little chicks.'

This brought a fresh flood of weeping.

'We will meet again,' said Caulfield, between gritted teeth. 'We will come back here and they will put on a great dinner party for us, and we will have the awful Mrs. Brady and the horrible Captain Stokes, and we will all know how to eat our soup.' Prudence gave a small laugh. Her tears dried up and she snuggled into Caulfield. 'Oh thank you, darling.'

They walked up and down the same path, arms around each other as if they could make themselves one. They had not much to say, the thoughts of the summer were with them and the golden memories it brought. Their hearts were breaking.

They walked back to the car.

'I am going,' said Caulfield, 'but I don't want to say goodbye here.'

She looked at him.

'You are taking the Dublin train from Nenagh tomorrow. It leaves at ten o'clock from Nenagh. I will stand on the track at the level crossing just beyond Barney's Bridge. I'll stand there and wave goodbye. Will you wave goodbye to me?'

Her eyes shone.

'Oh darling, darling, what a lovely thing to do. Of course I will.'

***

At 10.20am Caulfield stood on the level crossing, a half mile above Barney's Bridge. In the distance came the high whistle of the train.

It came roaring in and he held up his white handkerchief and waved and waved. He thought he saw nothing but in the last compartment of the train he saw a woman's hand with a white handkerchief and it waved and waved, until the wind snatched it away.

The train came and went within seconds.

Caulfield stood there, watching the train disappear into the distance.

His face was streaked with tears.

Caulfield knew it would never be the same again, the sun would never be so bright, they would never be in the meadow, exchanging long rambling conversations, they would never sit in the cottage and watch the hen and her little chicks.

He would never hold in his arms the most wonderful woman that ever was.

Chapter 14

Olive
Flashback 1966

'That Caulfield character seems to have gone overboard on Prudence.'

'They will make use of him,' said Olive Murphy, 'and then they will walk on him.'

The Murphys were driving back to Limerick after Henley-Smiths birthday party. Kevin sulked in the back seat and amused himself by mimicking Henley-Smith, *'that's frightfully good of you, that's frightfully good of you'*.

The Henley-Smiths had pressed them to stay overnight, but Olive Murphy didn't like to be obliged to anyone.

Horace spoke to his son. 'I saw you chatting with that character, Caulfield, and also with Mr. Herzog.'

'Yeah,' said Kevin, 'Caulfield's OK; I played rugby against him in the Munster-Leinster Interpro. Herzog kept talking about his wife, called Abigail. I hear she is a model of the year, or the best dressed something in the R.D.S.'

It was raining heavily and Horace Murphy was a master at stating the obvious.

'It's lucky it didn't rain this afternoon.'

'It will probably rain tomorrow.'

'I'd hate to get a puncture.'

Olive Murphy, by clearing her throat, indicated a 'yes' to these remarks or perhaps she meant 'no'.

'What did you think of her?' he asked.

She didn't reply.

'She looks older than you.'

Again no answer.

Horace Murphy was used to these monosyllabic conversations. Sometimes, he was used to it and he let it run off his back, but there were other times when he felt a resentment building up.

He thought, *why do I have to put up with this?* It was a perfectly fair question for him to ask. An equally fair question was why did he put up with it? He couldn't think of any answer.

At such times Murphy got some relief at imagining himself murdering his wife. In some cases it involved violent behaviour on his part. It often took the shape of attacking her with an axe while chopping an old Christmas tree, or drowning her in a bath. He would arrange a perfect alibi; a dim-witted colleague would be persuaded to play golf. Instead of playing off the first tee, they would creep around the back of the course and jump in at the twelfth and so have a perfect alibi for 16.05 hours which was the time the coroner said she expired.

It was so foolproof that he wondered why no one had tried it.

His favourite fantasy was to imagine them on their honeymoon, which was spent in Switzerland. As it happens they were never in Switzerland on their honeymoon or at any other time. However, for some reason in his mind brought him to – Switzerland.

On the third day of the honeymoon he took her mountain climbing and when they found themselves on a suitable crag, he simply pushed her off. This had the beauty that no witnesses could have seen it, and at very little expense.

A small problem was that some of the guests in the hotel might have been looking through the binoculars provided and unfortunately saw the deed happening. This could be easily overcome by going around at midnight dismantling the binoculars, and so making the whole thing watertight.

These days dreaming brought him great solace and peace of mind.

'We are nearly half way to Limerick,' he said.

No comment.

He could see her screaming as she left the crag and head over heels disappearing into the eternal snows.

Olive Murphy was wrapped in her own thoughts. The snag of travelling in a car was that there was no escape. In her house she could walk out of the room, go to the garden, leave the house, walk the dog, go to church. Plenty of bolt holes for a woman to escape.

She had enjoyed the day in Henley Hall. She wasn't a clothes horse, but she liked to dress up a bit for dinner. As long as she didn't overdo it, like that awful Brady woman, who was covered in fake diamonds, and had her makeup plastered on.

It had been twenty five years since she had seen Lady Mary Good, now Lady Mary Henley-Smith.

They had knocked around in Prague together. It was undoubtedly the happiest time of her life. The crowd was mainly Americans, Czechs, Croats, and some British. Nobody seemed to have much money, but now and then they managed to get a chicken and some potatoes and cooked it over a gas ring. A bottle of wine could be scrounged.

It had been a harsh winter, with frozen pipes, sliding pedestrians on icy streets. But she didn't mind, she was with Carlo. They walked everywhere. They talked volubly about French poetry (her speciality) and Italian writers of the Renaissance, about which he was supposed to be writing a book. She didn't believe him but that didn't matter. She loved him.

He was the first man she loved, because he wasn't either stupid or mean, and didn't try to get her into bed all the time. He was good looking in a nervous sort of way. Every time she saw him, she felt like giving him a good woollen pullover, and mothering him when he shivered.

Olive met Mary Good at a party where somebody had managed to lay their hands on ten cases of Pilsner. She didn't know that Mary Good had a title. It hardly mattered in Prague where everyone was nearly broke. Mary had shrunk back timidly to avoid a loud-mouthed philosopher, (that's what he called himself) who was ranting about capitalism, communism, religion, sex and the profit motive.

Everyone was getting on nicely, even Mary opened up and denounced socialism to deafening applause, when the door was broken down and Polizie stormed in. They tried to arrest everyone for the theft of the beer. In the excitement and confusion most people escaped, taking stocks of beer with them.

The Polizie were only half hearted in their efforts. Many of them had children of their own. However, they did arrest Olive, Mary and Carlo, who they released the next day.

The three of them were part of a crowd of about ten who had a sort of moving feast, drifting from one apartment to another. They became experts in finding free food.

The Mormons had a coffee shop/meeting place which supplied leaflets along with hot strong coffee. The young communists ran the Soviet Friendship bureau, where in turn for listening to a speech you could knock back glasses of Georgian sweet wine. The best of all was the Co-Op bakery, where, in exchange for smuggled copies of *Time* magazine and *La Stampa*, you got the day's bakery returns.

She met Mary on and off. Mary was popular as she always seemed to have some money. Mary made a telling remark to Olive one day. They met and Olive seemed a bit down in herself. Mary asked about Carlo. Immediately Olive brightened up and her face flooded with happiness.

'He is not the only man in Prague,' warned Mary. 'Don't commit yourself too much. All men leave in the end.'

It was years before Olive would speak again to Mary.

Olive got abrupt orders to vacate her rooms which were wanted by one of the apparatchik. Carlo found her another one in the old Jewish quarter. He had a gift for fixing things, whether it was getting off one of the innumerable fines by which the city financed itself or finding a plumber who could repair a blocked lavatory in exchange for a kilo of biscuits.

Carlo read Dantë translated from the Italian to French. Olive had the only easy chair. Carlo commandeered the other chair which bore a resemblance to one that went missing from a café some months before. Those without a chair sprawled around the room, eyes half closed.

From time to time Carlo stopped and explained some of the lines. Olive had a paperback of Dantë's *Inferno*, and she could follow it before Carlo spoke. It was obvious that Carlo bluffed. Half the lines were completely wrong, but she forgave Carlo. It was too much to expect a Czech speaker to translate from Italian to French.

Several times when he stumbled over something, she smiled at him in a motherly, forgiving sort of way. Olive could forgive him anything. Her eyes would mist over as if he was her little pet, trying to come right.

Later in the evening, they walked over Charles Bridge and up the river to Legi Bridge and back down to the quarter.

Once they were stopped on the bridge by a peddlar in one of the booths he called them over and opened a tin in which there were two slices of fruit cake. He gave the slices to them and they were delicious. Ever since they slowed down as they passed him, hoping that he would call them again. He never did.

Carlo had a precarious job teaching history and geography in a girls' school. In summer he acted as a tour operator (part time) and drove buses. His mother married a second time to a man called Blazek and his two elder sisters disappeared after the Russians liberated Prague.

Carlo had large sad eyes and a beseeching smile. After the second time Olive met him, she knew he was for her. She day dreamed about their life in Limerick or perhaps their life in Prague. Her dreams were make believe about a land that hardly existed, where they would never grow old. They might be hungry, but then they would be more in love, and everything they had they shared.

Instead of going back to Limerick for the summer she asked her father to send money so they could explore Europe. They were able to take the train to Vienna and after feasting on Mozart, travelled on the boat down the Danube to Prague again and then to Budapest and Kiev.

Years later she hesitated to talk about that holiday to their friends and families. It was too precious to share.

In her rooms, in the old Jewish quarter, she was fond of looking over the Jewish cemetery as the bodies of generations slumbered. In such a neighbourhood anyone would be conscious of the past. Closed up buildings, the abandoned cemetery, the gutted synagogues reminded one of the vibrant life which existed before the Nazi horror.

Olive noticed after a while that Carlo was reluctant to come into that area. Seeing her sitting in the cemetery, he made an excuse in taking her hand and walking away.

'What's wrong?' she asked.

'Bad memories, bad people,' he said.

It wasn't clear what he meant.

'Were you Jewish?' she once asked him.

'No,' he said, 'and my father denied it several times to the Nazis. They were going to beat him so he told them where the Jews were hiding. They left him alone after that. He saw the trucks taking them away.'

Olive squeezed his hand. 'It wasn't your fault.'

'No,' he replied, 'it wasn't our fault. We didn't do anything wrong. We just did nothing. We only watched the trucks go away.'

Carlo was in the grip of a powerful emotion. 'Bad memories, bad people.'

Olive hugged him. 'Darling, leave it to the past.'

Olive loved talking to Carlo about books, and authors. Carlo opened her eyes to Dantë and how he influenced Wordsworth. They argued how England never produced a Mozart or Beethoven but excelled with Shakespeare, Jane Austen, Dickens.

She spoke French in Prague and to Carlo. She was delighted that she found it easier to speak in Prague than in Paris.

Six months passed and then a year. She asked Carlo if he would like to come back to Limerick to meet her parents and brother.

To her relief he said no. She said that he had been described so often that they already knew him.

He looked doubtful, but said he would wait for her to return.

She never returned.

Olive returned to Limerick with a dark foreboding. Prague had been unforgettable, but it had only been a chapter in her life. She knew that she would probably never meet Carlo again, that after a pause he would meet someone else, a new chapter would start. It would be easy for him with his little boy good looks.

What had she? She was a school marm, she could freeze someone who made an unwelcome advance.

Instead of Dantë they would talk football. The familiar towers of Limerick appeared. She knew that after the greetings and jovial welcomes, she would have to tell. She was pregnant.

Chapter 15

Horace
Flashback 1965

Olive was home about a week when she broke the news. Her mother screamed, cried and then went very quiet.

'We must tell your father.'

He was at the factory. The business had been started forty years ago by her grandfather to make cardboard cartons. It now employed over a hundred people. Olive remembered her grandfather as a grumpy solitary figure. He had never played with her as grandfathers are supposed to do. She was told to keep quiet when he came in. Visits to his house were an ordeal for everyone.

Her father came up from the factory. He looked worried. It was the first time he had been asked to come back to the house.

Her mother was trembling.

'It's terrible!' she said.

'What's terrible?' he asked.

'Olive.'

He looked at Olive. Afterwards he said that he thought she had been arrested for shop lifting.

'What's wrong, Olive?'

'I am pregnant.'

He sat down. Everyone sat down. There was a complete silence. There was absolutely nothing that anyone could say. This sort of thing never happened in respectable families. In fact they never happened (or hardly ever) in more ordinary families.

Over two generations they had fought fiercely for respectability. They had done everything to earn that respectability. Honest in business, generous to charity, devout to the religious establishment, members of clubs – a good name was their proudest boast. They were not classified yet with the flour milling aristocracy, but they met them socially on a more or less equal basis, provided they were not too pushy.

He went over and tried to cuddle his daughter, as he did when she was small and afraid. She didn't respond; she remained unyielding, her face like granite.

For the first time her mother noticed the old grandfather coming out in her.

'Do we know this man?' her father asked.

'No.' They waited.

'It was Carlo.'

The bitterness like acid seemed to burn through her. The man she loved, who gave her such tender memories, had destroyed her. Never again would she give herself to a man.

Her father asked 'What would you like to do?'

Her mother exploded 'What do you mean, what you would like to do? I'll tell you what you would like to do. You have no choice in the matter. You can go to Dublin to the nuns and they will place the baby. It will get a good home and that will be the end of it.'

She turned to her husband, 'Don't go around asking 'what are you going to do?''

'Take it easy,' he said, 'we want to consider everything.' He held up his hand to fend off another outburst from his wife. 'We have to think of you, Olive.'

Olive's father went back to his office. It was a modest one by most standards. Outside his office was a new Italian cartoning machine, spewing out product. It took the board, laminated it to another board, gummed it, cut it to size, printed it, stacked it on pallets, shrink-wrapped the pallet, counted the contents and dispatched it to an amazed customer.

To some people it was a noisy machine, with a monotonous banging sound, but to him it was a symphony. It produced cartons and profits as never before. It was a poem, it was a thing of beauty.

He sat in his office, but he was not thinking of cartons. His mind was on Olive. There was a problem. He was used to dealing with problems. The correct answer was not always the obvious answer.

In any problem there had to be a minimum of two answers, and if the parameter had to change slightly, there must be three answers. If someone plunged ahead with the wrong answer, it was because of mental laziness or lack of ambition.

Wrong answers were worse than an outbreak of war. They led to wrong decisions or no decision. Olive's father prided himself on his ordered mind. He was logical, organised and to the point. When he had to make a decision he became a great drawer up of lists. The pros and cons were neatly tabulated. He should have been able to come immediately to the one correct and infallible answer. He was a buyer of text books on management skills and read some of them.

In his mind he collated the facts about Olive. Facts were the seedbed of thinking. The right facts led to the right answer. Handled properly the answer led to a decision. It led to profits instead of losses.

Profits were the life blood, the red corpuscles of business. Not to make profits was to deny life and face extinction. He read in the Bible about the man who didn't take his profits but buried them in the ground and for which he was utterly condemned.

Then there was Olive. He pulled himself together; his mind had wandered from Olive.

Consider the facts about Olive.

      A.   She was unmarried.

      B.   She was pregnant.

      C.   She was an acute embarrassment to the family.

These were the parameters. The answers presented themselves.

(A) She was unmarried, but could not get married in the next eight months.

This was the wrong answer. Who said that she could not get married? It was perfectly legal, it was possible. In his mind nay sayers were routed.

(B) She was pregnant.

This was the hardest of hard facts. She could not be depregnated. A visit to Godless England was out of the question.

(C) Family embarrassment.

This would tend to solve itself by the satisfactory conclusion of (A).

The only answer was marriage, carefully stage managed, but where was the potential husband/father?

He stood up and went to look at the cartoning machine. His heart swelled with pride and satisfaction. He placed his hand on it and felt it throbbing with marvellous energy. 'If anything goes wrong with you,' he said out aloud to the machine 'we will look for it, and find it, and fix it. If anything goes wrong with a human being, we hit it over the head, and kick it, and curse it.'

That evening he came in late. Was he hoping the longer he delayed the better chance they had of coming to a decision?

It was quite normal in the house. His wife was writing a letter, Olive was reading. Their small son was doing his homework. Harmony reigned.

His wife signalled to come to the kitchen.

'Well, what is it?' she said.

'It's your way or mine. Send her to the nuns or get her married off.'

171

'And can you do that, get her married off?'

'It's possible,' he said.

'Who is he?'

He answered, 'Respectable, steady job. Not too bad looking. Dull. Reads a lot. Plays golf. Reasonably religious. Moderate drinker. Non-smoker. Five foot eight.'

'Is there any more?'

'Most important of all,' he said, 'not married.'

Despite the drama of the circumstances she could not help smiling.

'And how are you going to get this paragon? Why should this respectable etc. man want to manage a woman carrying an illegitimate baby?'

'I don't know yet, and furthermore don't use the word illegitimate. Somebody could be listening. And try to mend your fences; it's not much fun for her.'

'OK. Another week won't matter. We'll see what happens, but if nothing happens, it's the nuns'.

'Don't forget that she is a grown up woman, and an educated woman, and she might have her own idea about going to the nuns.'

***

Horace Murphy was not well known in Limerick. His only sport was eighteen holes of golf on Mondays. He played with anyone who was free on that day, usually with a cleric or Christian Brother who had the day off. He played for about six months with a retired Presbyterian clergyman over fourteen holes. At the end of the period, neither was sure of the other person's name.

He played on Mondays, because of an obscure civil service rule that certain officials who checked office locks on Saturday morning could have Monday off.

The office locks that required checking on Saturday had long since been superseded by modern safes that required no checking, but the rule remained.

Horace was sure of his Monday morning golf.

He never attended any golf functions or entered competitions. He was not a chatter-up of lady members who came out on Mondays, neither did he frequent the bar after his golf and engage in drollery, or more serious political discussions. The club secretary and steward were unsure of his appearance, but the club professional remembered him as he bought a golf ball every five or six weeks.

Murphy was not married. He was well into his middle age and getting anxious. He wanted a wife, children and some sort of stability in his life. He longed to look at a child's face and see himself looking back. He wanted a family dependant on him, who would look to him for support, guidance, discipline, love and happy times.

He knew what people thought of him. In his office he was called a dry stick, or tight (i.e. mean). Women were suspicious that he never drank or smoked. If he had drank and smoked heavily they would have been more suspicious.

He tried to overcome this weakness by drinking one pint of beer every Friday night. It was no use, he was still looked down upon by women, as a tight (mean), dry stick, who never drank or smoked.

He thought that he might drink two beers on Friday night and it might earn him a reputation as a loveable rogue. It still didn't work.

About this time Charles McGreevy came into his office. It was ten past five and everyone had gone. Horace was entitled to run for the door and slam it after himself, irrespective of any member of the public that might appear.

He doesn't know why he didn't. He knew McGreevy, he had a factory in the industrial estate, and a woman with a refined accent answered the 'phone.

McGreevy arrived in. He had three pages of statistics. The Department wanted statistical analysis, before they would consider a grant for his new machine. Murphy loved figures, statistics, projections, analysis, mathematical modelling. McGreevy had the figures for production, imports and exports, breakdowns for wage both production and marketing, his on cost figures and an estimated figure for overheads.

Murphy licked his lips, he would have loved to spend the weekend digging into the figures.

Quite frankly, he would have enjoyed that more than pretending to chat up some witless blonde, whose boyfriend turned out to be a sixteen stone rugby player.

Murphy said, 'Hello, Mr. McGreevy.'

'I am sorry to come in late, Mr. Murphy.'

Charles McGreevy showed his figures. They were hopelessly out. He was a worried man. Murphy was an official in the Department of Finance (Statistics). They were looked down upon by the regular department who saw them as mere adders and subtractors. They were utterly despised by the department tongs who were ex Blackrock and Clongowes types who talked rugby or even cricket, who feigned ignorance as to a Mayo v. Kerry match and on their annual audit in Limerick, elaborately wiped their desk tops clean with disinfectant.

Horace Murphy and Charles McGreevy sat late that night and talked about business and life. He found that he was unveiling more to the older man.

He was frustrated and even unhappy. His life was mathematics, there was a beauty and order to mathematics and Economic Science. Mathematics was a special sort of language. It fathered Philosophy and Calculus. Before Christ, algebra existed.

He would have loved to have had the opportunity to study higher maths and economics; this would have qualified him to shoot to the top in the department. It could have earned him a doctorate.

174

With that he could have headed the West of Ireland office or even Dublin. In England they knighted their top fliers in the department.

It was not only the issue of promotion in the Civil Service but the opportunity of earning an international reputation as a contributor to learned journals, possibly the authorship of books.

To do all this it meant getting a leave of absence from his work, probably without pay for at least eighteen months. He simply could not afford it. Charles McGreevy listened. That evening he had come in with a problem in figures. Murphy had solved it in minutes.

There was another problem in his mind.

Could Murphy solve it?

***

Mrs. McGreevy was handing around tea and cakes. The china tea set had only been used four times in thirty years.

Mrs. McGreevy was in calm control. Her husband varied from boisterous good humour to an awkward silence. Arthur McGreevy aged twelve, dressed to kill in a flannel trousers and checked shirt, glowered resentfully in the background, missing the Sunday afternoon derby between Arsenal and Spurs. Olive showed a massive indifference to anything that was said or done. Horace Murphy balanced his tea cup and a cake and tried to look pleasant. He discovered when sitting down that he had forgotten to polish his left shoe.

He listened politely to Mrs. McGreevy describing her meeting with the pope in Rome. It wasn't exactly a private meeting, there were two or three thousand there as well as her, but the pope had turned and blessed them. A priest told them afterwards that the Pope had a particular warm regard for the Irish.

Charles McGreevy nodded in agreement. It was a fact well known across the world, he said. Horace Murphy made a comforting sound and looked impressed. Charles made an effort to engage him in polite conversation asked where he came from. Horace mentioned a village near Rathkeale. Mrs. McGreevy said they knew somebody in Rathkeale. 'Who was it Charles?' she asked her husband. He thought deeply for a while. It was a fellow called Mickey. He was a postman. A decent fellow but terribly fond of drink. 'Where was he now?' he asked her.

'I don't know,' she replied sharply.

She had exhausted the charms of Mickey.

Horace had a second up of tea. He said sincerely that it was a lovely cup of tea. Nobody disagreed with him.

They drank their tea, and ate their cakes. The peace of a Sunday afternoon seemed to fill them with a melancholy. It was not cold but not too warm. It didn't rain, but it wasn't sunny.

Horace surreptitiously wiped his forehead. He felt he had to make an effort.

'We had a great sermon from the Canon this morning,' he said. 'It was about the woman who lost the silver coin.'

'Is that so?' said Charles looking interested, 'what did he say?'

'She lost the coin through carelessness. He then went on to say that if we were careless we would go to hell.'

'Proper order!' said Charles.

'That man is too hard,' said Mrs. McGreevy. 'We can all be careless at times.' As she spoke, she bit her lip on seeing Olive. Charles looked at Olive, Horace looked at Olive, Arthur looked away from his TV and looked at Olive.

Horace felt panic rising.

'He went on to say…' mumbled Horace. He couldn't say what the preacher said; he sat in confusion, his mind frozen.

Olive spoke. It was not the voice of a wretched sinner, she spoke forcibly.

'You should ask that Canon to preach next Sunday on the Prodigal Son. It has a happier ending.'

'I remember, I remember,' said Horace, jumping to his feet. 'The Canon said it had a happy ending. They found the silver coin.'

176

'Big deal!' said Mrs. McGreevy.

Horace tried to catch the eye of Olive. She was studiously indifferent. In desperation he turned to Charles McGreevy.

'How do you find business, Mr. McGreevy?'

'Good, good. Very good.'

'That's good,' said Horace.

'Thank God,' said Oliver, 'it's very good.'

Olive spoke for the first time.

'And that's good too,' said Olive. 'It's good that it's good.'

'Watch it, Olive!' said her mother. She wasn't going to take any cheek from a daughter who gave them so much trouble.

Olive stretched her legs and looked as if she would walk out of the room.

'In our business,' said Horace, 'well, it's not actually a business. So in our occupation, well, you would not call it…so in our occupation, but a sort of a service like a…eh…the Army…'

'Are you saying, Mr. Murphy, that the Civil Service is like the Army?' asked Maura McGreevy.

'In a manner of speaking, I suppose yes, but then, of course, no.'

Charles McGreevy nodded his head.

'It's not really like the army,' he said.

'No,' said Horace.

'Ah ha, yes.' The picture was coming clearer. 'More like the Police Force?' asked Maura McGreevy.

'In a sense, yes, like the gardai.'

'The Police,' said Maura McGreevy. Maura's uncles were in the old Royal Irish Constabulary (R.I.C.) and a cousin served as an able seaman in the Navy, so she liked to profess a vaguely unionist outlook which usually took the form of speaking well of the ancient regime (the grandest people) compared to the 'present lot' – horse traders and tinkers.

In McGreevy's house the 'gardai' were the 'Police'.

'Yes, the Police,' said Horace.

177

Anything for a quiet life.

'Do you have a busy time?' asked Charles.

Horace started to think. He wasn't going to be casual with these people. They might seize a word and make something of it like the garda and the Police.

'Busy,' replied Horace. 'Yes, we are busy.'

'But a special busy time when you are extra busy?' asked Oliver.

Horace smelled a rat. If he admitted to them that they had an extra busy time, they might ask him what they did when they weren't extra busy.

This could be dangerous.

Some councillor might ask a question at a meeting. He had a particular dread of 'phone calls from Dublin that usually came in on a Tuesday morning.

He couldn't afford any mistakes.

'A busy time,' said Horace, 'we are actually busy the whole year.' He looked around the room triumphantly. Maura and Olive looked jaded; they did not appear to be gripped by the drama of the public service.

'In business,' said Charles McGreevy, 'it's hard to know which is the worst. Is it being too busy or not busy enough?'

Horace was not sure where this remark might take him. He thought he would play for safety.

He said nothing.

Charles went on, 'The ideal thing of course is when productions equal sales. What do you say Horace, if you were in my shoes, would you strive to increase sales to match the production available, or would you alter production to supply the sales?'

Charles looked at him expectantly. Horace had been holding his breath for almost a minute. He expelled it slowly.

'Yes,' said Horace after a pause. 'That is the problem.'

Horace felt enormously proud. His remark sounded good and it meant nothing.

'What are you two men talking about?' complained Maura McGreevy. 'It's Sunday afternoon and you are going on about production.'

'My dear,' said Charles (he always called her 'my dear' when he wanted to be cutting) 'we are merely considering economics. It's not your cup of tea.'

'Hah,' said Maura, 'so it's not my cup of tea, eh? Well, my cup of tea is a cup of tea.'

Horace thought he would get into her good books. He laughed mechanically, like the clatter of empty milk churns.

'Very clever, Mrs. McGreevy.'

Olive looked at him witheringly. Horace decided he was trying too hard.

'I once got into trouble in school,' said Horace. Everyone stiffened. Mrs. McGreevy gave a sort of squeal like a trapped rabbit. Oliver said nothing, but he abruptly stood up.

Even Arthur stopped lounging in the back and sat up.

Olive did nothing but she looked at him surprised.

'It was primary school,' said Horace, 'there was a girl called Miss Harris. All the boys had to call the girls Miss. She had nice red hair,' said Horace, as if this explained everything.

There was a pause. Oliver waited with his mouth open.

'I called her a name,' said Horace. There was a gasping noise from Mrs. McGreevy.

'Shall Olive and I leave the room?' she asked. Before anyone answered, Horace said, 'I called her Miss Carrot.' There was sound in the room like air escaping from a punctured tyre.

For the first time Olive spoke. 'How perfectly awful!' she exclaimed. 'How unbelievably filthy.' She pointed to the door, 'Leave this house immediately!'

For a second Horace believed her, but with the others laughing he relaxed.

'That was the end of my life of crime.'

Everyone sat easy. The fact that Olive had broken the ice made the difference. Arthur came forward and asked if he could watch television, he wanted to see the last ten minutes of the match. 'OK,' said his father, 'but keep the sound down.'

Horace finished his tea and thanked Mrs. McGreevy. Speaking to Oliver he asked, 'May I have the pleasure of taking your daughter for a walk?'

'I'll have to think about it,' he said, 'but you can go this time.'

Olive looked resigned but she put on her raincoat and they went away.

When they were safely gone Mrs. McGreevy sank into an armchair and lit a cigarette.

'I suppose he is alright.'

'Yes,' said Oliver, 'she could do a lot worse. Of course he has to put the question.'

'And take your money. That lovely money you worked so hard for. A dummy of a man only half as well educated as Olive, and the son of a bus driver.'

'How do you know something like that?'

'Ha!' she snorted. 'How do I know, because I know. I make it my business to know. As far as this family goes, I know everything.'

'Do you know if I was out with a blonde last night?' said Oliver.

She gave a short laugh. 'What blonde would look at you? You were probably going down in the factory singing songs to that new machine and tickling its bottom.'

'What lovely talk on a Sunday afternoon, what refined conversation in the McGreevy household.'

'Shut up.' she said.

'Oh! Will I shut up? I think I will cut some flowers for my mother's grave. My dear mother.'

'I don't want to hear about your mother.'

'Yes,' he continued, 'I'll put some flowers on her grave. She was basically a rather simple person, a good person in a quiet manner. She didn't mind you, even though you spent all day mixing the glue for the laminator. You weren't so particular in those days.'

'I hate you,' said Mrs. McGreevy.

'Don't worry about it. I have to hand it to you, you were a trier. You took two years to get rid of the Limerick accent, though God knows what sort of an accent you have now. But you were determined to get out of that factory and into my bed, and you did it.'

She lit another cigarette and closed her eyes. She didn't mind what he said. When he started ranting, it didn't last long and it didn't matter.

It was Olive that was the problem now. Oliver had made an offer he could hardly refuse.

Horace was to marry Olive in Rome, away from local pip squeaks.

Get a leave of absence for two years. Inevitably he would lose salary for that time.

Oliver could put him on his payroll at £60,000 per annum for the two years.

If he works for a Ph.D. and call himself 'doctor', he would provide a house for him in Limerick.

If he fails, he can buy himself his own house.

It was all he could do for his daughter.

***

Olive and Horace walked down the road. Passing drivers who knew Olive tooted their horns and she raised a hand silently.

'Your people are very fine people,' he said, 'I only know your father, I have great respect for him.'

She didn't answer.

'He would be looked up to in Limerick.'

Silence.

'I would be very glad to be part of the family.'

She seemed to give an assenting grunt, but he wasn't sure.

'Of course I don't know you that well.'

She looked at him angrily. 'And of course, you don't know me,' he said hastily.

They walked farther on through parkland that overlooked the Shannon. They came down to the banks. The place was full of children running and playing. Some families were having picnics. Fishermen fished hopefully. Their boats were tied up, and children were climbing in and out, calling to one another in high pitched voices.

Horace and Olive watched them at their innocent pleasures.

'This could be dangerous,' said Horace.

They walked down to the edge of the river. A fisherman was repairing his boat. Horace spoke to him and repeated, 'This could be dangerous.' He pointed to the children in a boat that was half drawn up on the bank. 'If one of them fell into the lake from that boat, he might drown.'

The boat owner looked angrily at him. 'Why don't you get them out?'

'It's not my boat,' said Horace.

Nevertheless the fisherman ordered the children out of the boat. All came out except one little girl, with golden hair. She was laughing and singing. Eventually she came out too.

'Are you happy now?' asked the fisherman.

'Thank you,' said Horace.

Horace and Olive walked along the path. An evening calm descended on the lake. The birds sang. The setting sun threw long shadows over the peaceful scene.

For the first time Olive showed affection to Horace. She slipped her hand into his and recited:

'Break through the heat of our desire,
Thy coolness and thy balm,
Let sense be dumb, let flesh retire,
Speak through the earthquake, wind and fire,
O still small voice of calm.'

'I was never much for poetry.' He pronounced it 'potre'.

'Poetry,' she corrected him.

'What ever you call it,' he said a bit roughly.

They came to the end of the path, swallows darted and swooped, kingfishers dived for food; the wind made ripples on the water, the still small voice of calm was there.

'Don't say anything,' she said.

She paused, and listened, and felt.

Olive remembered a short story by Maupassant. It seemed better in French rather than the English translation.

A French army officer married a beautiful but shallow woman who lacked any sort of artistic or cultural feelings. One evening he took her for a walk in their garden at sunset, and he was moved as he heard the sounds of the garden, smelt the perfume of flowers and the peace and beauty of the night. His soul was refreshed.

Then she began to chatter in some vain and idiotic manner. He hushed her and asked her to listen to the nightingale. She ignored him and continued to chatter, and in a rage he picked up a lump of wood, beat her and killed her.

He was sentenced to a term in jail. On his release he became a priest.

This story affected Olive. Horace was now chattering. He was talking about whether fish could see or not see in the dark.

This annoyed Olive; the meandering of Horace was altogether useless, it had no merit, culturally or practically. In this quiet and lovely spot, where they might have embraced and stood together as one, all she heard was his blathering.

She pushed him away and ran down the path they had walked up.

She cried bitterly for her fate. She knew what her father had planned for her future. This would be it, to live with a man who loved nothing that she loved, who was deaf and blind to the fine things of her mind, and most importantly who did not understand her and humour her, and could not with a smile or a touch, make her happy.

There was only one man who could do that. It was Carlo. Never again would she know a man like him. She was resentful at the way he left her with child. But she knew that if he walked around the corner, she would forgive him and run to his arms.

The prospect facing her now was that of a respectable and loveless marriage. She thought of her time in Prague, what a difference then and now. She remembered climbing on an empty barrel, waving a flag of some sort (it was her jumper) and crying, "Citoyen á la Bastille"; and now, in the space of a year, she was middle-aged. The Bastille remained.

She sat down on a bench. Horace would come along soon.

He came, as he had to.

He walked over to her. She looked stonily ahead. In no way did she acknowledge his presence. He walked away again and then came back to the bench, cleared his throat once or twice and then returned to the other bench.

He sat down beside an elderly man reading *The Catholic Herald*. Without moving her head she could see him asking some questions. The man looked inside the paper, shook his head and went on with his reading.

Horace returned to Olive. He sat down by her. Neither of them spoke. He reached forward and plucked a daisy and examined it closely. She saw him and thought, *it will take more than a daisy*.

As if talking to himself, he asked 'Have you ever heard about Leonardi Fibonacci?' She was caught by surprise. She didn't know if it was a trick question.

She played for safety. 'I suppose he was the man who invented ice cream.'

Sarcasm sometimes works.

'No,' he replied. 'He believed that mathematics is the soul of art.'

Despite herself she was intrigued.

'What do you mean?' she asked.

'He was as great as the other Leonardo – da Vinci. There are two sets of spirals in this daisy. Twenty one going clockwise and thirty four going anti clockwise. This is known as the Fibonacci Series called after a mathematical sequence discovered by Leonardi Fibonacci.' He stopped, 'I thought you might like to know that.'

She looked at the daisy as if she was mesmerised. 'So what?' she said eventually.

'The mathematics behind this daisy is a thing of beauty.'

She waited. She knew that he would eventually tell everything and make his point.

'The Fibonacci Series,' he said, 'is as follows. You start with the number one and to get it started you add the same number one and one equals two. OK? You then add the last two digits together two and one equals three. Then you add the last two numbers, three and two equals five. Then you...'

'OK, OK, I get it,' she said, 'and what good does all this do to us?'

'Be patient. Remember what I said about this daisy? There are twenty one spirals going clockwise and thirty four going anti clockwise. Now if you counted on the Fibonacci Series and got twenty one what number would come next?'

'I'll make the day for you and say thirty four.'

'You are absolutely right!'

Olive found herself smiling as if she was still a kid in school and had been praised by the teacher.

'Furthermore,' said Horace, 'the same principles works on pine cone scales, the bumps on pineapples, and the leaves of many trees.

185

There is another type of spirals subject to the same Fibonacci Series called Logarithmic spirals, and it can be seen in the curve of elephants' tusks, the horns of wild sheep, and even the claws of canaries.'

'Enough!' said Olive. 'Don't blind me with facts.'

Horace let the daisy fall to the ground. 'My point is that there is beauty in mathematics as much as literature or painting.'

He put his arm around her and she let herself lean into him. They watched some swans fly onto the lake.

'Olive, it's not going to be easy. We are both being humiliated. You have to take me, and I have to take your father's money.'

She looked up to him. 'Horace, we can only do our best.'

They walked sadly home.

Chapter 16

M'Elhinney
Flashback 1970

'The wedding took place in St. Peter's in The Chains Church in Rome, of Horace, son of Patrick and Laura Murphy of Ballylicked, Co. Kerry, and Olive, daughter of Charles and Maura McGreevy of Ard na Greine, The Heights, Limerick. The ceremony was conducted by Fr. Aloysius McGreevy S.J., uncle of the bride, and the honeymoon is being spent in Sorrento.'

The Murphy's were married with circumstance and after a three-day honeymoon returned to London, where Horace commenced studies at the London School of Economics.

Later the big day came. The news was announced and advised by post, although it was first posted up in the college. Horace had achieved his doctorate. He was Dr. Horace Murphy.

Congratulations flowed from his aged parents, the Limerick office, the McGreevy family, the Secretary of the Dept. of Finance, the Minister of Finance, from Lady Mary Henley-Smith (how did she know?) the Institute of Taxation Office and the Paymaster General, Office of the Minister for Trade and Commerce, Secretary of the Central Statistics Office.

In addition H.M. Treasury, Downing Street, invited him to come in any time to discuss career possibilities.

For Horace, it was like being released from jail, it was like a sinner whose sins are forgiven.

Meanwhile, the lease on their flat had four months to go and they might as well keep it.

They explored London and Northern England and parts in between. Three months later they packed up and moved to Limerick. They had an important reason to move. Olive was pregnant again.

***

Maura McGreevy was well satisfied. Although a huge sum of money had disappeared from the family treasure pot, at least it was well spent.

Horace was a doctor, not just a Batchelor as most medical 'doctors' are, but with the much higher status as a 'Learned Father of the Church' and a step considerably above Batchelor of Law, Medicine or Divinity.

Maura McGreevy wasted no time in educating listeners on the lofty qualifications of 'doctors'.

A new baby was born to Horace and Olive. This was a girl. For the first time Olive felt warmth to a baby. All the family rejoiced.

At the initiative of Maura McGreevy a party was given for the new arrival. One Sunday afternoon, the noblest and best of Limerick society assembled at their house.

To Maura's satisfaction, the other 'Fathers of the Church' attended, mainly from academe or Bishops' palaces.

Maura McGreevy dominated the afternoon. She introduced all to all. The only missing guest was their doctor Bill McElhinney.

Horace had a recently made acquaintance with a Dr. Jones and introduced him around and then proudly showed his new daughter. Dr. Jones looked at the baby and then handed her back.

Horace thought, *He is a cool one. He might at least have given her a tickle.*

'Where is McElhinney?' someone asked.

'Don't worry,' said Horace, 'Bill McElhinney has never lost a father yet!'

Jovial laughter all round.

Bill McElhinney sat in his car, slumped behind the steering wheel, and he was not laughing. The noise from Murphy's house caused him to grimace. For Dr. William McElhinney this was no time for rejoicing. As he saw it, it was the curse of curses.

McElhinney was familiar with the jibe that only six people in Limerick could call him by his first name. It was alleged that in his own family his four sons had to call him 'doctor'. He was utterly indifferent to what people said or thought.

The son and grandson of doctors, he drove through the city and walked through the hospitals with a grim determination. He showed the arrogance of one who knows he is always right. His colleagues frequently hated him because they, and the nurses, felt the icy courtesy of his manner; they also felt the sarcastic edge of much of what he had to say.

More wounding still were his silences, an apparent rebuke which was left unsaid. Whatever their efforts, the nurses felt they could never be rewarded with his praise or thanks.

He was said to belong to a secret religious medical society that commanded intense obedience. No one knew, but he had the appearance of a man straining to meet an ideal that might be just beyond him.

He sat in his car watching the guests stream into Murphy's house.

The curse of curses, he said to himself.

A car drew up, disgorging people he didn't know. *The riff-raff comes to town!* muttered McElhinney. *Twenty years ago I wouldn't have looked at them.*

A member of the party attracted his attention, a youngish man. *I seem to know him.* It was Jones, the new doctor. *What's he doing here? Only new to the town, and already sucking up to the Murphys.*

It was beginning to rain and McElhinney felt he should make a move. He knew he was expected before this. Reluctantly he left the car. It was getting dark, he could slip in a back door without being noticed.

He had delivered the baby, as he had delivered scores of babies in Limerick; moreover, many babies had been called after him. *Not that it mattered a damn,* he grumbled. *This is the worst part of a doctor's life. I have been tough on my colleagues; I have been tough on the nurses; I have been tough on my patients, even on my family, but never as tough as on myself. How can I go in and destroy them?*

He listened for a while to someone playing a piano, then a voice singing. There were cheers and claps. Everyone was happy.

Olive was circulating around the room carrying her latest treasure. The oohs and aahs followed her, as did admiring glances from the men. Her London shopping had been successful.

As the second or third round of drinks was consumed the decibel count increased and windows were surreptitiously opened.

The owners/managers of Limerick's top businesses were there, old and new money, both of them glad enough to be seen in the other's company.

Horace was wondering about Dr. Jones. He had met him three weeks ago at the bar of the Golf Club. He found him an amusing fellow, with a fund of stories about hospital matrons and tipsy nuns. A hint or two from Jones had indicated that he was concerned about building a practice, not always easy for a neophyte.

Horace felt important, he was in a position where he could make or break someone's career. A word or two about Jones in the right circle and he could get Jones moving. He felt quite paternal to Jones, which was good. After half-an-hour's chat in the Golf Club he thought he might take Jones under his wing. He felt flattered that the younger man seemed to look up to him.

His own doctor was McElhinney, but it occurred to Horace that he did not give a damn about Bill McElhinney. What had he ever done for him? Jones deserved his chance.

McElhinney knew the house; he walked down to the side where a conservatory was being built; it was half-finished. He pushed open the door and sat down on a workman's bench. In the distance he heard the muted sound of conversation and laughter.

He heard the creek of a door opening and McElhinney looked up. It was Jones.

'Why didn't you tell them?' asked Jones.

'I didn't see you telling them,' replied McElhinney.

'That's stupid! You are their doctor. You know you would have to tell them someday.'

'Is that a fact!' said McElhinney. 'Don't you lecture me. I have delivered three hundred babies in my day. Each one perfect. I don't need advice from an upstart!'

Jones flushed and turned away.

'There is something you can do,' said McElhinney.

'You call me an upstart, and you want me to do something for you!'

'I did, and I'll call you that again,' said McElhinney harshly. 'Go in and tell Murphy I am here, and I have something to tell him.'

'About time,' said Jones.

McElhinney was standing when Horace came in. His figure was half in shadow and his face seemed threatening and mean.

Horace felt he was appearing before the headmaster, and was due a thrashing which he deserved.

McElhinney spoke brutally with an apparent hatred; a nerve on his face throbbed. He looked at Horace as if he was from a lower species.

He spoke of Olive and the baby with all the inhumanity he could muster. It was not his fault. It never was. Horace and Olive must accept Divine judgement.

Horace trembled and nearly fell. Jones appeared from the shadows and caught him and helped him back to the happy sounds of his house.

McElhinney stood still, his knuckles whitened out, his face twisted in agony. *Why is it me? O Lord, my God?*

Horace returned to his guests. His voice was trembling, his face was white.

'I must ask all of you to leave.'

The stunned guests filed slowly out.

Horace picked up the baby and brought her to his room. The remaining guests heard a cry and wild screams like an animal in pain.

They had been advised that their baby daughter was handicapped.

***

Horace was later to say that, given the choice of surrendering his doctorate and having a healthy child, he would sacrifice his doctorate.

In the week that followed, Olive found herself tortured. She felt that fate had conspired against her. She was never to have a marriage/relationship that was normal. Not for her could there be a happy ending.

She had a son who she disliked. Kevin was robust, energetic and at times violent. She tried reading him stories, but half way through he would restlessly seize the cat and throw it through a window.

At play school the teachers complained of his roughness to both smaller and larger children. At a birthday party when he was five Olive left them playing some harmless game, but when she returned Kevin had organised a wrestling competition which he dominated. Some of the smaller children were crying and wanted to go home.

The only consolation was that he was comparatively gentle to his handicapped sister. He tried to teach her to run and jump. A more difficult task was catching a ball. When the ball was thrown, no matter how gently, she tended to open her hands, not close them. She never learnt how to catch a ball.

The utter helplessness of his little sister touched a chord in him. She was not a competitor; her dependence on him was complete. He would never have to fight her and put her in her place. She needed him. He was always willing to lend a hand.

***

That Sunday was like any Sunday. The Riverside Park was crowded as usual. Families were picnicking, children playing, fishermen fishing. Horace and Olive sat on a bench. Kevin and his sister, Maura, were watching some boys playing football. Horace knew it was only a matter of a few minutes before Kevin joined in. Right enough, when it bounced near him he pushed forward and played the ball. Maura toddled off to the boats by the lake, where children were jumping in and out.

A memory stirred in Horace's mind but he stood and watched to see what happened. Maura tried to get in the boat like the others, but she was too small.

Kevin seeing her, left his football and ran to the boats to lift her in. She was delighted to be in the boat, and jumped up and down, as Kevin had taught her.

Kevin stood on the edge of the lake watching his sister. Maura bounced to the rear of the boat, delighted with herself.

She looked into the water, and then fell in.

Kevin was struck dumb. What could he do? He jumped in the boat and ran to the end. He looked in the water. He could see nothing.

Horace and Olive, who had seen everything, ran to the boat. Horace cried, 'Kevin, get in and save Maura!'

Kevin knew he couldn't. He could not swim, the water was very deep, and he did not want to drown.

Horace splashed in and found the floating girl. She was drowned.

Olive was hysterical, she screamed at Kevin. With her umbrella she beat him.

'Why did you lift her in? Why did you lift her in?'

He stood there, and let his mother beat him. He fell on his knees, blood was on his face. And she beat him again, until she was exhausted. And then he ran away.

A nightmare was born.

Chapter 17

Caulfield and Olive

Dear Caulfield,

*I have been following your rugby success in the newspapers
and by word of mouth. It was rotten luck breaking your leg before
the internationals. The sports correspondent of The Times said it
was because you were out of action that we did so badly against
Wales and France.*

*A certain person had bought tickets for Twickenham, and she
was disappointed you were injured.*

*I think you know that she has been seen with a chinless wonder
called Artie Stanley, otherwise the future Earl of Exeter. But don't
give up, he was over here in the summer and was quite useless at
tennis. She has never been quite the same since five years ago, and
is reluctant to come to Ireland. The old wounds etc.*

*You remember that we had a conversation concerning Henley.
My worst fears have come true. He was wretchedly unhappy in the
Navy, and to make it worse he had to serve under the Commodore
who treated him badly.*

He is back here and won't speak to anyone.

*Henley is back here as well and has managed to get into
college. Could you look out for him? Perhaps he could share rooms
with you?*

He always respected and admired you.

Please help us, Caulfield.

Fond regards,

(Lady) Mary Smith.

***

Dear Henley-Smith

I have heard you are taking up academic life and will be joining us next term. Just to tell you, I am rooming with Kevin Murphy (Murph) and our rooms take three. You would be very welcome to join us, and it might save us some drinking money.

Would you be interested in having a go at the rugby team? Murph and I are the only survivors from last year. You used to be big, thick, and fast, so you could be what we want at wing. Let me know.

Give my sincere regards to Lady Mary.
All the best,
Caulfield.

Murphy and Caulfield were unpacking. 'These rooms are getting colder every year,' grumbled Murphy.

'You are not used to hardship, Murph. If you were brought up in North Tipperary you would know what the cold is.'

'To hell with North Tipp.,' grumbled Murphy again.

Caulfield whistled timelessly.

'Any ideas about the team this year?' asked Murphy.

'A couple of fellows from the North. They were schoolboy interpros. last year. They might be handy enough, and there is a fellow from Cork they are all talking about.'

'School boys aren't worth a damn; it will take about two years to get their edges knocked off.'

Murphy was inclined to disparage everything, ex schoolboy stars, coloured players, English players, ex soccer players.

Ex G.A.A. players could be good, as long as they weren't hurlers.

Caulfield hesitated. He knew Murphy had a blind spot going back five years. Murphy had a gift (which was really a handicap) of judging a person in seconds.

A remark from somebody or the way a fellow shook hands determined instantly if he was good, decent, loyal and genuine or else a miserable louse.

'Caulfield, come out with it. You are trying to tell me something.'

'Maybe I am,' said Caulfield.

'I can almost guess what it is,' said Murphy. 'That Brady, of Brady and all the other Bradys, was eating in our house a month ago. He was in Limerick defending some horse thieves or insurance brokers, I am not sure which, when he bumped into my father and he came back for a meal. He told us that our distinguished neighbour was out of the Navy (reasons unknown) and was down for this kip, and was looking for rooms. Come clean, Caulfield. What's going on?'

Caulfield agreed. 'I couldn't help it, the mother asked me, and dammit they are practically neighbours. They only live down the road.'

'*They only live down the road*,' sang Murphy. 'I suppose in the summer evenings you stand chatting over the fence, eh?'

'Henley-Smith is not bad,' said Caulfield. 'In fact none of them are bad, once you get to know them. They can be pretty decent.'

'Pretty decent!' cried Murphy, whistling through his teeth. 'Everyone eh, including that dewy-eyed Miss English Rose Prudence, breaker of Tipperarymen's hearts?'

'Knock it off, Murph.'

'Let's give him a try,' said Caulfield. 'At least we know him somewhat.'

197

'Actually he has played rugby at school. He is big enough to do something,' said Murphy. 'We'll start him in the three As and demote him to the three Bs and leave him there to rot in peace.'

Caulfield was not listening. He was thinking of Prudence.

***

About three weeks later Caulfield was polishing his shoes when a knock came on the door of their rooms. It was Olive, holding a dozen eggs in an egg box.

'Great!' joked Caulfield, 'I'll take them in. Do you mind if I don't tell Kevin?'

Caulfield was struck by her smile, it was warmer than he expected.

He put the eggs away, and when he came back she was gone.

He raced down the stairs and caught up with her at the college gates.

'Let's go to Bewley's for a coffee.'

'Good idea,' said Olive.

Sitting in the café they fell silent, each of them was inadequate. Both knew what they wanted to talk about but they couldn't begin.

Caulfield decided he would be very daring. 'You are an attractive woman, Mrs. Murphy.'

He held his breath. He knew it was bound to come. The frosty look, the narrowing eyes, the stiffening body, the haughtiness.

'Really?' she said.

That was it. One word was enough. Caulfield remembered the old bound volumes of Punch in the rector's study. The Victorian jokes that always ended *'collapse of stout party'*.

He felt collapsed, gauche, a red-faced schoolboy who did not know where to put his hands or feet.

She seemed to smile at him, or was it mockery? No, it was as warm as before. She stretched her arm over the table and touched his hand.

'Thank you,' she said.

He was able to breathe and they started to talk. He told of the love that changed his life six years ago, but he knew now it could not be.

'We sing a hymn, '*O love that wilt not let me go*'. But I had to let Prudence go. The hardest thing was not answering her letter'.

Olive said, 'That was the letter Prudence sent you when she left Ireland. You didn't reply. Why didn't you and what was the letter about?'

Caulfield was relieved to have someone to confide in.

'It's great to have you to talk to, Olive, because you know something of the pain. Even with Kevin it's a waste of time because he will end up making a joke of it. When the letter arrived Aunt Hilda never commented. It was left on the hall stand. It was hours later when I put it in my pocket. I knew Aunt Hilda would love to see it, or even be told. Someday I will tell her.'

'The letter,' continued Caulfield, 'was chaotic. It said one thing, and then denied it. She was going to live in one of Henley-Smith's cottages and grow tomatoes and have a herb garden. We would be together for ever and ever, blah, blah. Then she said she had arranged to go to a finishing school in Switzerland for two years, after which she would come to Dublin and qualify as a doctor and we both could go to Africa, or perhaps Kansas. She was obviously disturbed. Wherever I went, she wanted me to be with her.'

'What else?' asked Olive.

'It was half crazy. She was talking nonsense, but I wanted to believe that nonsense. And above all I wanted to be with her all my life.'

'And is that the reason you didn't reply to her letter?' asked Olive.

Caulfield was breathing in gasps. Olive could see that he was distressed.

'I replied,' he said after a while. 'I wrote exactly nineteen letters.' He paused, and then went on, 'I tore up nineteen letters.'

Olive could hear him sniffling. 'Carry on,' she urged.

'I tried to be logical and sensible whilst loving her with all my heart. It didn't add up, I remembered something Aunt Hilda said. They are miles above us.'

'You have a good prospect of qualifying as a doctor,' said Olive.

'Yes, but even as a doctor could I see her in a suburban surgery, or a small-town practice. Eventually we would destroy ourselves.'

Olive spoke in a low whispering voice. 'You have bared your heart to me, Caulfield. I am going to tell you something that I have never revealed to anyone. I am in love today with a man that I have not seen for twenty-three years. He is the father of Kevin. I will never see my lover again, but I love him for what he was years ago in Prague. You have Prudence. Cherish her memory. Remember the summer of six years ago – the tennis, the laughs, the kisses, how she looked at you – that is the memory you will always love. Reply to the letter and tell her all about that.'

Caulfield was fighting to control himself. He could see Olive weeping.

'People say that I am hard,' said Olive, and she wept more.

Chapter 18

Abigail and Anna

The two men stood outside the hotel. The weather had turned unexpectedly cold with the first easterly winds of the year whipping down the street. They had no overcoats on, as they had left them off thinking the weather was milder. They were shivering.

'Let's get in out of this,' said Murphy.

It was Murphy and Caulfield. They were standing on the North side of St. Stephen's Green, outside the Shelbourne Hotel.

'We are too early,' said Caulfield. 'I don't want to be seen hanging around inside.

We'll go for a walk around the Green.'

'Bloody hell!' groaned Murphy. 'I'll be dead of the cold. Could we not go to the bar and wait?'

'You know we have no money for the bar,' Caulfield reminded him.

'We can order a glass of water each.'

They went across the road and started to walk down the East side. The wind seemed to be in their faces.

To their surprise they met Anna, Caulfield's cousin. They jovially greeted each other. Caulfield congratulated her on her job in public relations.

'I suppose,' said Murphy, 'that it pays very well.'

'Ah ha, ha!' she looked at him, laughing.

Murphy and Anna had met a few times. Caulfield always felt that Murphy fancied her.

'It's not funny,' said Murphy dolefully, 'you are looking at two men, down on their beam ends. We men know what real poverty is. This morning we had to sell our overcoats.'

They shook their heads sadly and shivered.

'Just think we had to sell our overcoats,' said Murphy 'and then we had enough to have a breakfast of dry bread.'

'Oh dear, dear,' said Anna, 'how sad.'

Murphy put his hand in his pocket and took out two coins.

'Do you see those ten cent coins?' Murphy was at his pathetic best. 'If I had more ten cent coins I might buy an apple. Then Caulfield and I would have half an apple and it might get us through until tomorrow.'

Anna opened her purse; she took out four or five twenty euro notes and a ten cent coin.

'I have only one ten cent coin; perhaps you could buy a small apple!'

'She's all heart,' said Caulfield to Murphy. As he spoke, Murphy staggered and Caulfield caught him.

'I hope he is not sick,' cried Anna, her eyes rolling piteously.

'It's not sickness,' said Caulfield in spasmodic jerks. 'But he hasn't eaten for a week. I was lucky, I found three Brussels sprouts in a bin last Saturday, I could have got more, but a dog got in before me.'

Murphy was moaning, 'Tell them I died a Catholic, I am in the tenth day of my fast.'

Anna gripped Caulfield's arm.

'Will we let him go, Caulfield? There are plenty more of those Catholics around, they won't miss one or two.'

'We should fill some food into him. The undertakers don't like skinny corpses.'

Murphy slowly recovered.

Anna said, 'I am stricken to the heart! I tell you what. I'll see you at 1pm. sharp and stand you your lunch.'

'I can smell it already!' cried Murphy.

'That's great,' said Caulfield, pointing back to the corner of the Green. 'You just go down there and across the road to the left, you will see the Shelbourne.'

'Not quite,' said Anna. 'I will go down there and across the road to the right, and I will see Joe's Hamburger Palace.'

There was a groan from the men.

'Tell her,' said Murphy, out of the side of his mouth, 'that it will be full of Catholics.'

'As a doctor – almost – I can tell you that the protein count and the vitamin count is higher in the Shelbourne,' Caulfield spoke portentously.

'Goodbye fellows,' she cried, 'see you in Joe's!'

'At least we can eat,' said Murphy. 'Why can't I have some cousins like her – well fed, well paid?'

As he looked back at Anna walking away he added, 'And good legs, nice bum, good all round distribution. Good teeth, good looks.'

'Did you look into her mouth?' asked Caulfield.

'Good teeth,' repeated Murphy. 'When are you taking orders for that one?'

'Any time, in duplicate,' said Caulfield.

They continued their perambulation around the Green. The wind was still in their faces.

'There must be a reason for this,' griped Murphy. 'Ripley's believe it or not.'

They were avoiding the subject of the day, which was a meeting with Isaac Herzog and his wife Abigail. Isaac Herzog had pressed Caulfield for a decision.

It seemed to any reasonable observer that a decision could be made quickly. A man is a man with instinct. Many could have paid good money for the experience. Some men would have volunteered to do it for nothing.

To be paid generously to conduct the experience with a woman who was almost irresistibly attractive was proof that Santa Claus lived again. Not so if facts were considered.

It might seem that the bonus and advantages were almost universally favourable but no. The essence of the experience was secrecy. If Caulfield was to talk and the media and gossips came to hear then about it his standing would be affected, and his future marriage and family life placed in jeopardy. His children would be the butt of remarks.

Perhaps the most affected would be his medical practice. His reputation as some sort of a stud would follow him everywhere. In the locker rooms where men congregated, he would be the object of never ending hilarity and speculation. Even if he was seen talking to a woman in the most innocent way, in a public street, or even in a place of worship, then the gossip mills would trigger off another round of salacity.

Who guards the guards? (it sounds better in Latin.) Unless she was of a very mature (ahem) age, she might even become the object of the, oh so innocent question and the meaningful look. Of course nature could always take its course, as well and something could naturally develop and who can stand against the power of nature?

'It looks simple.' said Murphy.

They walked slowly around the Green as if unconsciously delaying the meeting.

Caulfield was bothered by something else. He had in a moment revealed all to Murphy. Murphy was a great friend, but old friends get old, they get garrulous and deadliest of all they start talking.

Caulfield could have bitten his tongue off when he told him of Abigail and Herzog. Murphy was generally envious. It was not only money for nothing; it was money for more money. Murphy was reading engineering and he didn't have to worry about female patients.

The knowledge that one other person, even a great friend, knew something so very personal was unsettling for Caulfield.

It was too late now to do anything.

In reply to Murphy's request he was bringing him to the Herzogs. Murphy said something about moral support. He could be something like a second opinion.

Well, maybe he would and maybe he wouldn't. At least he said nothing to Henley-Smith, although he might have been the most discreet of all. They turned the last corner and saw the Shelbourne in the distance. They would be there in five minutes.

Caulfield turned over in his mind the facts, for and against. The fact was that there was more to it than appeared. What was dangerous was what he didn't know.

Herzog's hidden agenda – if there was one – and his own moral attitudes. It was not a mechanical thing like taking a stallion to a mare. He measured himself against Uncle Sam and Aunt Hilda. If they knew, what would they say and think?

He knew exactly how they would feel. It would be a feeling of sadness and disappointment.

He had pleased them all his life in so many ways, they had been more than a father and a mother. Could he at the outset of his career bring that feeling of sorrow to them and to himself?

AT RECEPTION DESK IN SHELBOURNE HOTEL

Mr. Isaac Herzog, please

Yes, we have an appointment

Yes, our names are Mr. Caulfield and Mr. Murphy

Yes, Mr. Herzog is expecting us

   No, we are not booked in for lunch

   No, we are not from the Anglo-Irish Mutual Insurance Company

   No, we would not particularly like to take seats

   No, we would prefer not to excuse you

   No, we did not have a haircut in the Gascon Brothers' establishment downstairs.

No, we did not leave without paying

Yes, we would have paid if we had a haircut, but as we had no haircut, then we did not pay

No, we did not see two Japanese gentlemen in the Gascon Brothers' hairdressing establishment downstairs

Yes, we saw an Australian gentleman leave the hotel.

He was wearing a tartan kilt, brogue shoes, grey stockings with red stripes. He was six foot four inches, he had a scar under his left eye and a tooth missing. His hair was parted in the middle and he was carrying a copy of the 'Roscommon Herald'

No, we did not see the colour of his hair, as we paid him
no attention

Yes, we knew he was an Australian gentleman as he was wearing an anorak with the words on the back, 'I am an Australian gentleman'.

Herzog met them in the lobby. From his suite they could see over St. Stephen's Green and the Dublin Mountains beyond. Herzog went to the window and pointed out the mountains. He mentioned some peaks.

Caulfield was surprised at his knowledge of the Dublin Mountains, and he said so to Herzog.

'Mountains are in our blood,' said Herzog. 'We are men of the mountains, not the sea or the plains, but mountains. 'Unto the hills I lift mine eyes.''

He smiled at Caulfield, 'You know where that came from.'

Said Caulfield, ''My help cometh from the Lord'.'

Herzog moved away from the windows. They all sat down, Herzog looked at Murphy.

'Could you tell me Mr. Murphy, or you Mr. Caulfield, what is Mr. Murphy doing here?'

They looked at each other. Caulfield answered, 'I felt I need some help and advice on the issue. Perhaps I should have consulted a lawyer, but I asked Kevin Murphy. He happens to be my friend.'

Herzog said, 'I see.'

He folded his fingers, and his eyes hooded over, in the way Caulfield remembered in the Italian café.

For some minutes nobody said anything. Herzog appeared to be either sleeping or in deep thought. Eventually he said, 'We saw no good reason to employ a lawyer.'

He looked at Caulfield as if to say, '*the ball is in your court.*' It was the turn of Caulfield to say nothing. He turned it over in his mind. The issue had seemed to him simple. It was yes or no. Payment made, and receipt – so to speak – stamped and completed. Now Herzog was balking at the presence of Murphy

Caulfield thought, *is there an issue there somewhere?* Was Murphy's presence spoiling the deal for Herzog? People like Herzog had a reputation for cunning.

Murphy was thinking, *if this damn thing goes on at this speed, we will be here until tomorrow.* In the meantime, he started thinking of rare medium steak and potatoes with gravy.

'I am disappointed to think that you might want people in to protect your interests. Our agreement was between two people; you and me. It was simple and the terms were generous in your favour.'

'On the face of it,' said Caulfield, 'it was, but the difficulty for me was secrecy. If it escaped my life and medical career could be destroyed. And I had considered that it might be in your interest to let that news escape.'

Herzog looked genuinely shocked.

'Why would I want it to escape? Do you think I want to advertise to the world, that I was unable to satisfy my wife? I would be a laughing stock.'

Murphy decided to speak.

'I think you are right, Mr. Herzog. I would trust you in that regard, but there is always the danger of a breach of secrecy on Caulfield's side.'

'Like from you?' snapped Herzog.

Caulfield looked at his feet. In his heart he agreed with Herzog but he could not say anything. The danger was mainly from his side.

'Or perhaps your rugby friends?' Herzog said, walking over to Murphy and standing over him. 'What about that, Murphy? Some Saturday night in Slats, when you are full of beer, you call out to the lads 'Have you heard the one about Caulfield? He is retired to stud, his sidestep is not what it used to be, nobody buys his dummy, the latest hot shot school boy left him standing'.'

Herzog's words sent Caulfield reeling, it was terribly true. Murphy was a weak point. He should never have confided in him. He could see that crowd in Slats, the baying mob, the shocked silence, and then the hub-bub.

He could see himself staggering through the door, and the road rising up to meet him and the vomit.

But this time there would be nobody to catch him.

Caulfield rose and grabbed Herzog.

'Sit down, please.'

Everybody sat down. In the silence that followed Caulfield could hear the frantic breathing of all. It reminded him of the fight between Murphy and Henley-Smith in Slats, the sweat, the hatred in the air.

There was a knock on the door, and a waiter carried in coffee and biscuits.

'Is there anything else?' asked the waiter. Nobody answered, the waiter left.

Caulfield looked dully at the tray of biscuits and coffee. For some reason, he counted the number of cups.

There were three. Did Herzog order three when he saw Murphy arrive?

A whiff of perfume, and a voice behind him asked, 'Will you have coffee?'

It was Abigail Herzog. She was wearing a black silk ruched jacket over well cut trousers; around her neck a double set of pearls with a gold clasp and plain gold stud earrings.

Caulfield took the coffee and a biscuit.

'Thank you, Mrs. Herzog.'

'Caulfield,' she said, 'call me Abigail.'

Caulfield noticed that Herzog's eyes never seemed to lose her. They followed her around wherever she walked and when she sat down. Caulfield thought she resembled a classic race horse, with long legs, walking delicately, moving her head with aristocratic disdain, the sheen of class enveloping her. The stable hands handled her with awe. It was the first time they had seen perfection.

Murphy introduced himself, 'Kevin Murphy.'

She shook his hand. It was clear that she didn't understand where he fitted in. There was only Caulfield in her immediate plans. Murphy appeared shell shocked, he felt dumb before her. His usual smart alec witticism that he could come up with died on his lips.

She looked at him coolly. She was no pretty shop girl that he might pick up at a perfume counter, painted to the nines with some company's cosmetics, arousing ambition in the mind of the prosperous matrons in town for the day, and causing a sigh with the watching husbands.

'It must be cold outside,' she said.

'Yes, indeed Abigail, we had no coats on and were petrified.'

'I saw you and Mr. Murphy walk away. I was wondering if you were coming.'

'Oh yes, we were coming,' said Caulfield.

'We saw you,' said Herzog, 'along with the mountains. We lifted up our eyes and then the good Lord let us see you with your hands in your pockets.'

'Bully for the good Lord!' said Murphy.

He was getting tired of trying to impress these people. If he could get in a good sarcastic kick in the pants, he could walk out, honour satisfied.

Then he saw Abigail. Herzog saw him watching her and Herzog's lips tightened. He would take care of that Murphy fellow if he got out of line.

Abigail turned to Caulfield. 'Is your mother interested in fashion?'

'I don't think so,' said Caulfield, 'at least not in the fashions we know.'

'And what sort of fashions might she be interested in, yes?'

Caulfield had a premonition that Abigail was not speaking her native language. It tended to be convoluted and stilted. English was not her mother tongue. He wondered again about her background. Possibly it was Russian-Swedish, but it would be foolish to ask.

'My mother's fashions?' pondered Caulfield. 'I never thought of fashions, she never could afford fashionable clothes except...' He stopped.

He thought of a photograph at home in Ballynale. Aunt Hilda had left it in a bedside table in his room. As a small boy he had asked her who they were. She told him briefly, and he never asked again. Only through overheard remarks from visiting relations did he put the facts together.

Herzog and Abigail looked at him with interest.

He was hiding something about himself. Murphy said nothing. He examined his finger nails. Caulfield had told him the bare facts, and it was clear at the time that the matter was closed.

That suited Murphy. He was never too interested. In his own life, there were shadows that he preferred not to think about.

'Except what?' asked Abigail.

Herzog felt sorry for Caulfield. Abigail was dragging out of Caulfield details of a life long buried.

'Except,' Caulfield said, 'in Africa.'

Nobody spoke. Caulfield's answer was so unusual, unexpected that Abigail was silenced. She tried to think what the connection was with Africa.

Caulfield knew he couldn't leave it there. She would want more and more until she had everything.

He could also walk out, but what good would that do? Sometime, somewhere he would have to reveal himself to someone else. It might be better to get it out of the way.

'I think it's only fair, Abigail, if this is a personal matter, we should leave it with Caulfield,' said Herzog.

She looked at her husband with some annoyance. Caulfield had looked as if he was going to talk. Could Herzog not have minded his business?

'Well, I was going to say,' said Caulfield, 'my parents went to Ghana twenty five years ago. I can't remember either of them in Africa, although I call to see my father once a year.'

Abigail and Herzog sat back in their chairs. So did Murphy.

'They lived in a bungalow in a missionary compound. My mother was a nurse, she helped out in the Methodist hospital. He engaged in missionary work amongst the Ashanti tribe. I was born a few years later. I think I was three when we came home. My father was very ill, he was in no condition to look after me so my Uncle Sam and Aunt Hilda took me in. My father was admitted to some sort of a home in Limavady. He has been there ever since.'

Caulfield stopped, but the others knew he hadn't finished. They waited.

'What about your mother?' asked Abigail.

'I have a photograph at home,' went on Caulfield, 'it's the only photograph I have of her. I keep it in my bedside table. My bedside table is... beside my bed... I have an electric light on the table. I used to read a lot in bed at night. In fact I read four volumes of Gibbon's *Decline and Fall of the Roman Empire*. The Rector lent it to me, one volume at a time. I never brought back the volumes, so I have all four of them.'

Silence, nobody spoke.

'I suppose I should bring back the four volumes. Although he never asked me.'

Another silence.

'I should bring them back, the next time I am home. You never know he might want them. Perhaps he had forgotten where they are.'

'What else is in the drawer, Caulfield, what is on the photograph?'

'It's a photograph of me about two years of age. There is also a little black child about a year old. There is my mother all dressed up with coloured cottony clothes. There is a man. And my mother left my father to go with that man. They are now husband and wife. The little black child is my half brother.'

Abigail stood up and walked out of the room. The others kept very quiet. Herzog had hardly moved.

'Does all of this make a difference?' he mused. 'I suppose it doesn't. Yet when I think of it, it does seem to have made a difference.'

Caulfield made no answer.

'Does it, Caulfield? Do you feel it has made a difference?'

'I don't know,' said Caulfield.

Chapter 19

Meet Michal

Caulfield and Murphy stood in the lobby of the hotel. They felt devastated. They hadn't known what to expect, but they didn't think it would turn out as it did.

Herzog had been fair. Abigail was beautiful and gracious until the very end, when she left. Herzog had escorted them to the elevator.

The elevator was out of order. They had to walk down the stairs.

Caulfield and Murphy stood in the lobby of the hotel. What would happen next?

The rain was clearing away, but it still felt wintry outside. As they were leaving the hotel they heard their names being called.

'Murphy, Caulfield,' It was Herzog.

'It didn't go the way I thought it would,' he said.

'It never does,' said Caulfield.

'I have one question. What you told us, is that the full story?' Herzog looked at Caulfield very closely. Caulfield said nothing.

'Well?' asked Herzog.

'I am trying to think. No, there is nothing else. I have told you everything.'

'That's good enough,' said Herzog.

***

They found Joe's Palace, and business was booming. A bouncer at the door with two days' shaves overdue and an unhappy expression, admitted them.

Inside Anna was waiting. 'Hello, 'allo, 'allo!' she cried. She flashed a smile to all.

'Cousin Caulfield has lost his appetite'.

Caulfield glared at Kevin.

Anna knew better than to pry. She chattered on. Someday Caulfield might tell her everything.

'I will order,' said Murphy, reading a menu on the wall, 'a Goliath burger, a cola and chips. All of which is guaranteed to rot my teeth and intestines.'

Caulfield and Anna ordered variations of the above.

The atmosphere was pleasantly warm as the condensation streamed off the windows, and walls and the odour of vinegar and burnt oil created what passed for a Mediterranean ambiance.

'So you are in public relations?' asked Kevin.

'I am three months in my present job,' said Anna, 'I have two responsibilities. One is to keep clients' names in the papers, and two is to keep them out of the papers.'

Kevin banged the table in approval.

'Then we have the politicians who want to look good. Be photographed on their best side, change their shirt if necessary. Try and get them to speak English. It's always an uphill task.'

Caulfield smiled. Kevin roared.

'We are very fond of the politicians; they are always so helpless and pathetic. They need us.'

They mopped their eyes.

'The ones that need us a lot are the bankers,' went on Anna with a merry laugh, 'the poor things are terrified of their AGM. The lights have to be altered ten times before the meeting starts. They want to look stern and capable, but at the same time look like your favourite uncle or Mr. Jones next door.

The Chairman sweats like a horse, but he has a hard sell. He wants to announce good profits, but not so good that people will know they cheated someone. I always like Big Business. They give us a good feed after their AGM, and there is no end to the wine. Sometimes they send us home in taxis after we overindulge. Of course, I am not allowed to drink, but it's amazing what a plate of cocktail sausages can do to you.'

Kevin clapped his hands delightedly

'Then you have the odd bits in between. The Rugby Union gets annoyed because the old chaws can't wear their sheepskins in an over-heated hotel. The fellow with small potatoes in his mouth announces policy. Nobody listens, the bar is closing in ten minutes.

Some soccer clubs are the limit – they ask us to favourably report their big meeting. It takes place in a pub in Merchant Quay. The treasurer can't understand how they lost €2 million. The chairman will explain it all when he comes back from Florida I love it all, never a dull moment! I'm off this afternoon to cover a funeral.'

'How can you cover a funeral?' asked Kevin.

'Simple,' said Anna. 'The undertaker has to pay, but he doesn't. It's the poor stiff in the coffin who pays.'

'We shouldn't be laughing,' said Anna solemnly, but then she laughed. 'The undertaker pays us €800 to get a photo in the paper. If his hearse is included with his name on it, then we get €1,000. And then there is the grieving widow, the relations up from the country, the blonde who appears and nobody knows who she is.'

Caulfield didn't appear to be listening. He was thinking of Prudence.

Anna rose to leave; as she passed by her hand rested for a second on Kevin's shoulder.

***

Anna left. Murphy and Caulfield left and walked back in the direction of the college.

In the distance they saw Henley-Smith. He came back, was delighted to see them.

'We are stony broke,' said Caulfield. 'Buy us a few beers?'

Henley-Smith pulled out a €50 note. 'Will this do?'

'Just about,' said Murphy. 'Where are we going?'

'We'll go to Slats,' said Henley-Smith.

'Slats of happy memories,' remarked Caulfield. He glanced at the other two. Henley-Smith was expressionless and Murphy frowned at him.

'Don't worry, Murphy, we know our manners now,' said Caulfield.

Caulfield's spirits lifted. It was not the end of the world.

'There are times, Caulfield,' said Murphy, 'when a man can go through fire and water and then skate on thin ice, and you can take your life in your hands, and you dice with death, and your number comes up and that's the end of the road, and you know that your chips are down.'

'All at one time?' asked Caulfield.

'Don't sound clever,' said Murphy, 'or I shall respond to your witless remarks in the only way I know.'

'Gee whiz,' said Caulfield 'I'll have to remember all that.'

'Give up that schoolboy gee-whizery,' growled Murphy, 'and use some old fashioned Irish tinkerism.'

They were coming near Slats.

'It's a home from home,' sang Murphy. 'You agree Henley-Smith?'

Henley-Smith didn't reply. He could say 'bye 'bye to his €50 note, and it would be a waste as he didn't particularly want a drink, as a matter of fact he didn't like a drink at all, and it was only when he caught up with a rugby crowd that he had to put his hand in his pocket.

Here it goes, he grumbled, into Slats.

The barman welcomed them. His eyes brightened when he saw Murphy.

'If it isn't Mr. Murphy,' he said genially, 'and how is Mr. Murphy?'

Murphy looked cautions. 'Have we met?'

'Indeed, indeed we have. You see there is the little matter of your account which is gathering dust in my office.'

'Now I know,' said Murphy. 'Now I have you. I understand this thing about Murphy.' He gave a hearty laugh like the man who faced with an intractable problem, suddenly sees the solution. 'I know this man Murphy, not a bad fellow now. My name is... eh... Tomkins.'

'Oh, Tomkins,' said the barman.

'Yes, Tomkins,' said Murphy. 'Tomkins La Touche Tomkins – three names.'

'It's four names,' said the barman.

'Four names?' said Murphy. 'Oh that's right. You are quite right. It's four names.'

'I thought I knew the name,' said the barman sourly.

'Our estate stretches across from Wexford to Kilkenny,' said Murphy. 'I tell you what I'll do with Murphy. I'll give him a bit of a telling off. He's not a bad fellow, and I'll make him come in and settle this account.'

The barman looked resigned.

'Don't forget it, Mr. Tomkins La Touche Tomkins.'

'Leave it with me!' cried Murphy.

It was the afternoon; the bar was beginning to fill up. The unfortunate Henley-Smith paid for his second round. He and Caulfield were having a guarded conversation. It would appear to Caulfield that Henley-Smith did not know of the part that Caulfield had played in getting him into their rooms, and also getting him on the Rugby First's fifteen. He would have to sharpen up to keep his place. Murphy was not the only member to complain. He wanted to do his best for Henley-Smith but since he left the Navy and came to college, the stuffing seemed to have been knocked out of him.

Caulfield met Brady one day in Roscrea. Brady was hinting at something about Henley-Smith, Caulfield didn't get it, and Brady clammed up.

Henley-Smith was telling Caulfield about a society wedding last summer. It was in some big house in Hampshire. The bride was a relation of theirs and Prudence was a bridesmaid. Caulfield was dying to ask a hundred questions about Prudence. How was she? How did she look? Did she ask about him? Had she changed?

Henley-Smith didn't reveal much. He answered she was OK. She looked fine. Can't remember if she asked. Changed? No, not much.

What Caulfield didn't know was that Henley-Smith had been told to shut up about Prudence. Everything was over, the family wanted an end to summer romances. Prudence was being wooed by half of *Burke's Peerage*. She was the deb. of the year.

Despite Caulfield's good looks and charm, she was miles above him, as Aunt Hilda had once said.

Caulfield could feel that Henley-Smith was passing on a message: *to get lost.* Handsome hunks from Tipperary were not in demand this year. He was to concentrate on more local suppliers.

The afternoon was passing pleasantly and the temperature rose to dull the wintry weather outside. There was a babble of female voices outside followed by an invasion of hockey players with faces as red as pippins.

'Where are you going?' said Murphy in mock alarm. 'This is men only unless you start buying beer.' The women shrieked, yelled, cried, laughed, shouted, whispered, talked, moaned, kissed, grabbed.

'You are terrible noisy,' complained Caulfield.

'Throw those women out!' shouted Murphy to the barman.

The barman appeared to be deaf. It was the turn of the women. 'Throw him out!' they shouted. They grabbed Caulfield by the legs, arms, waist. He was immovable. They desisted, except for one who had her arms around his waist. Without looking down at her, he declared, 'Tell me you love me.'

'Later,' she said.

Caulfield looked at her and saw the pretty nurse he knew from the hospital.

'Well, well,' he said, 'it's Nurse – eh Nurse...'

'Nurse McMaster.'

'Of course, you are Nurse McMaster.'

'Michal McMaster.'

'You are the first Michal I ever met, but then I have to start somewhere.'

Michal smiled and he noticed her eyes. They were blue, the same as Prudence's.

Henley-Smith came barging through. He was tired of standing in a corner, buying beer for everyone. He had spent the last ten minutes talking to a girl with a shrill northern accent. He had no idea what she was saying and she kept prodding him with her finger to make a point.

'Who is this gorgeous number?' he demanded of Caulfield, putting his arm around Michal. Caulfield said, 'This is my mother.'

Henley-Smith exclaimed, 'I will take your mother home tonight.'

Henley-Smith hadn't the style or bravura to carry it off. He sank like lead. Michal did not respond and Henley-Smith sounded boorish.

'Michal is my medical colleague. She saves lives every day of the week. Right, Michal?'

'Yes doctor, every day of the week.' She slipped her arm around his waist tighter.

'Come home with me,' said Henley-Smith, roughly, making a grab at her hand. Murphy suddenly appeared.

'Keep your hand to yourself, bud! Can you see you are not wanted?'

Henley-Smith was enraged.

'Who do you think you are? You have been drinking my beer for the last two hours. You have been sponging off me as you always do. So just push off!'

He gave Murphy a push who staggered slightly.

Caulfield could see that bad trouble was brewing. Henley-Smith had a right to feel aggrieved. He and Murphy had three or four pints on Henley-Smith, but given time it would be his turn to get it back. And Henley-Smith had gone over the top by what he said to Murphy.

Murphy was no sponger, neither was Caulfield. Henley-Smith was a child, but Caulfield remembered his last hours with Prudence and what he thought of Henley-Smith that night.

Henley-Smith was one decent guy.

Caulfield came between them. They were two very angry men.

'Please,' said Caulfield. 'Please.'

They looked at Caulfield, and then turned away. He looked around for Michal. She seemed to have gone. As he stood there, the barman tapped him on the shoulder and handed him a piece of paper. He read a message: 'I want to see you alone next Tuesday at 11.00 am. Isaac Herzog.'

The doors of the pub were still swinging. Caulfield went through them and then stopped.

Standing there was Herzog.

He said, 'This is where it all started.' He tipped his hat to Caulfield and went down the street.

Chapter 20

Herzog and Caulfield

Herzog waited for Caulfield. He sat in his favourite chair, situated at his preferred angle to the window. He could see everything that came and went. His coffee was mixed to his favourite blend. His waiter was solicitous. If the manager or any director of the hotel came by, they would not have been treated with as much consideration.

He did not have to click his fingers or tap the table, wave a newspaper or a magazine, raise his eyebrows inquiringly, or delicately cough, to bring attention.

His chair was never occupied when he came to sit down, nor was it ever at the wrong angle.

He did not object to the lull in the conversation when he entered the room. Voices were lowered, whispers were made, heads turned in his direction. Staff did not lounge in his presence; men straightened up, exchanged warning glances with each other, shot their cuffs, and adjusted ties.

He had the supreme advantage, that he knew all staff by their name and by their first name.

Were their children saving up for a bicycle? One was delivered to their house next day. Was a husband going into hospital? A booking was made in the private room of a clinic – fully paid.

At dinner, the Head Chef came out to his table to bid him welcome. He was brought into the kitchen and discussed with him the menu of the day, mixed his own sauces and talked genially with the other chefs. He always left behind an envelope.

He never forgot to inquire about their families, wives and children. He had an uncanny knowledge of their birthdays and names. Was little Marie, the daughter of the pastry chef, fourteen today? A gift was already in the post.

Isaac Herzog sat back in his chair, closed his eyes, and remembered his father who rubbed his hands and spoke tenderly, 'Voszhe iz kleyn yingl?' 'What is it little boy?'

Last night he and Abigail had a fine dinner. They were entertained by a government minister and his wife who were anxious to attract investment.

The food was good, the wine pleasant, the conversation lively and amusing. Abigail with her diamonds silenced the wife, but not for long. Herzog manage to subtly flatter and soon had her smiling. He liked Irish women.

Good as though the meal was, it could never be as good as his mother's which he remembered as a boy. Sometimes he helped her to make the challah bread representing the manna given to the children of Israel in the wilderness.

They dressed in their best clothes and his father and his three sons set off for the synagogue on the Sabbath eve.

On returning his father would kiss his wife, and bless his three sons with outstretched arms. He then praised his wife with almost oriental extravagance.

His wife was deaf.

An atmosphere of peace and holy joy powered the one room dwelling. The toils of the week were forgotten, and the household composed itself to tranquility and gladness.

Herzog thought to himself, *I have gained much, but have lost much.*

His memory shifted away to the coming meeting with Caulfield. *If he doesn't turn up, then it's the end of Caulfield and me.*

But Herzog knew he would come.

He shifted himself more comfortably in the chair. He thought again of Caulfield. It was easy to admire him as it was easy to admire strength and beauty. He admired and liked Caulfield. After all he had picked him.

Apart from his appearance, it was his intellectual gifts. Herzog had studied the examination results. As a former gold medalist, he knew what was what. Caulfield had almost reached the very top, he had never failed an exam. If he wasn't the very best, he was at least very good. More impressively were his social gifts. He scored at debates, used charm, was modest, was not a pusher. He had almost permanent good humour.

If Ireland had been part of Cecil Rhodes' remit, Caulfield would have been a Rhodes Scholar.

At athletics he excelled. A double blue in rugby and cricket. He made records in the high jump and low hurdles.

A white man with a God given right to rule.

One attribute caused Herzog to hesitate.

Caulfield was good looking, he could have been a prototype for the Nordic ideal. Herzog knew how his people suffered from racial madness. The Nordic nightmare in jackboots and whips might return.

Caulfield could not be accused for this, after all he played cricket. And he was not blond. *When all is said and done*, thought Herzog, *all I want is a son for Abigail. A son like Caulfield.*

Herzog checked his watch and compared it to the drawing room clock. He was mildly irritated that his most expensive watch was a minute or two out compared to other timepieces. The other timepieces were always wrong, which exasperated Herzog. It was just as easy to be right as wrong.

Don't get worked up, he said to himself, *an angry man is one down against the opposition.*

Relax, he said again, *you have four minutes left,* and he thought again about Caulfield.

The previous day he had visited his brother Ken. Without giving anything away, he had cautiously raised the issue with him. He had started talking about Jewish tribes in Black Africa and their strange Connubial Customs. Apparently they had developed a rule concerning first cousins and inter marriage. As every Jew knows membership is passed down through the female line only. Where this could not be achieved, marriage of cousins was encouraged so that the bloodline was preserved even at the expense of good genetics.

'So,' said Herzog innocently to Ken, 'in our society if a woman could not marry and fulfil her duty, then surely she would be condoned if she sought satisfaction outside the family? The infant offspring would be Jewish – academically speaking.'

'I presume so,' said Ken.

They talked desultory about a few things, but Ken was preoccupied. He hadn't seen Isaac for months, but then a sudden visit and a somewhat odd subject for discussion made him wonder what was going on.

What is the Old Jew up to? thought Ken. The 'Old Jew' was a nickname the family gave to Isaac. They called him the Old Jew because he was the youngest Jew. Jewish humour is often obscure.

'How is Abigail?' asked Ken.

'Fine,' said Isaac. 'She might be going back to Australia for a visit.'

'She keeps good health, I hope?' Ken's remarks were more than a little casual.

'Australia is a good place for healthy living,' he said.

'Is it?' said Herzog, 'have you been to Australia?' He spoke a little sharply.

'I hear it has a perfect climate,' said Ken calmly.

Herzog stood up. 'Don't worry about her health,' said Isaac curtly, 'but I'll pass on your concern.' He left the house and drove back to town. Now Herzog was waiting for Caulfield, but the sight of Ken's quizzical face remained with him. *It is mad,* he thought to himself, *crazy, dangerous.* They could be made a laughing stock. It would be a gossips' bonfire!

As he sat there, he saw through the window the figure of McNight walking by. McNight was working for the European Union. He liked to stroll up Dawson Street, with a copy of the *Economist* magazine turned outwards.

McNight would go to town on a thing like that. He appeared occasionally on late night T.V. shows, talking of Proust or Joyce. 'Why don't you talk about P.G. Woodhouse?' asked Herzog. McNight strode away.

If McNight got wind of it he could cause endless trouble. Herzog wouldn't put it past him to organize a competition in Latin on the theme of Abraham and Sarah.

Little by little the meaning would be squeezed out, until all fingers pointed to Herzog.

How he hated McNight!

A hand touched his shoulder; and a voice said, 'Enjoying your nap?'

It was Caulfield. They shook hands.

His favourite waiter approached him. 'Coffee please, Patrick.'

'Money still has its uses,' said Caulfield.

'As it always has,' replied Herzog, 'you remember it was only a few months ago, you sat here and listened to my blatherings.'

'Little did I know where I was going that day,' said Caulfield.

'You don't know very much, Caulfield,' Herzog spoke caustically. It didn't take much to rub Herzog up the wrong way. 'Just sit there,' went on Herzog, 'and everything will be made clear. Sit there, fold your hands and remember to say 'yes sir, no sir'.'

'I beg your pardon, Sir. Whatever you say, Sir,' said Caulfield.

Herzog smiled faintly.

Caulfield was preparing to feel outraged. He had come there for a friendly meeting of some sort, and now this man was slapping him down. He felt he was being securely put into his box. He looked at the clock on the mantelpiece. He wasn't late, as he had learned that Herzog was a stickler for punctuality.

'It's a half minute fast,' replied Herzog.

'So it's not that,' replied Caulfield.

'Before you storm out of here in a huff, wait for a cup of coffee. At least you will have something to show for the morning.'

Caulfield found himself chuckling.

'One of us got out of bed on the wrong side this morning.'

Herzog liked this feature of Caulfield. His good humour was never far away. The waiter brought the coffee and biscuits and expertly poured out two cups without spilling.

Caulfield's eyes nearly popped out as he saw Herzog slip a €10 note into the waiter's hand.

He was tempted to say something to Herzog about giving him up medicine for serving coffee, but thought the better of it.

They drank their coffee. Herzog was amused at the way Caulfield seemed to clear the plate of biscuits. Evidentially he had missed his breakfast again.

'I hope you enjoyed your coffee,' said Herzog.

'Very fine coffee,' said Caulfield. Actually it was very strong and bitter. It would never have sold in the Co-Op stores in Ballynale. His Aunt Hilda who knew her coffee would have made short work of such stuff.

The waiter cleared away the coffee.

Both men leaned back in their chairs and waited for something to happen. They eyed each other. It reminded both of them of the Sunday morning in the Italian café. All that was missing was the photo of Toscanini.

Caulfield murmured, 'da, da, de, dum.'

'How is Abigail?' asked Caulfield.

Herzog looked at him questioningly. 'I mean,' said Caulfield, 'she left the room quickly, and I hoped she hadn't taken offence.'

Herzog said nothing.

'Had she taken offence?'

'I will ask her this afternoon, but I am not aware that she took offence.'

'Also, in case you think I have been presumptuous in calling her Abigail, she invited me to call her by her Christian name.' Herzog appeared to be amused.

'Alas and alack, we Hebrews do not have Christian names which we call first names.'

'Oh Oh!' cried Caulfield, 'of course I forgot. Please forgive me.'

Herzog held up his hand graciously

'Forgotten.'

'Actually,' said Caulfield, 'this question of Christian names and first names is a minefield. I was playing tennis a few years ago with a titled woman and I quickly learned that I should address her as Lady Mary and not Mary.'

'If people have a title they are entitled to have it and use it. The head of my London Bank is the son of an Earl, and I have no problem in addressing him as Lord Hendry. Actually I can trace my lineage back to Abraham. I suppose I could call myself Abrahamson, not to mention Isaacson and Jacobson.'

Caulfield asked, 'You have no hang-ups about ancient titles?'

'None,' said Herzog.

People came in and out of the drawing room. Herzog seemed to have nothing to say. Caulfield decided that he could sit it out. It was not the first time that Herzog had strung him along. But this time Herzog was uneasy.

Caulfield decided that it was not deliberate policy on Herzog's part. There was nothing to gain from this sort of shadow boxing. With all his money, was he still a nervous man? The little Jew who got pushed aside by the rugby types. As a student did he feel out of it when the girls brushed him off, when the Caulfields of the day looked through him and around him but never at him?

Now Herzog had a woman who little guys like him didn't deserve to have. He took huge pleasure in dressing and parading her. The beach house and the ski lodge, the cars, and diamonds, the personal maid. He had found her and taken her from nowhere. She was his and only a very stupid man could claim her. Even a flirtatious look could have dire results.

It was not surprising that he looked on her as a glittering investment, emotional as well as financial. Nothing was too much trouble. She was his life.

Herzog suddenly put a question at Caulfield. 'What do you think of my wife?'

Caulfield frowned, and thought deeply.

'She is one of the most beautiful women I've ever met,' said Caulfield.

'One of the most beautiful?' queried Herzog. 'Do you know many beautiful women?' He sounded almost aggressive. Caulfield did not feel like answering. He was not going to exaggerate. He had answered Herzog's opening question. He answered truthfully, he told him his wife was beautiful, one of the most beautiful. He could not bring himself to claim that she, or any other woman, was more beautiful.

Herzog was frowning. This conversation was not going the way he expected.

Caulfield thought to himself. This man window shopped for a woman, he picked up the best looker, dressed her, loaded her in jewels. She had style, class and she was Jewish.

How could Herzog have been so lucky? Her very height was a bonus. Herzog enjoyed being seen with her, enjoyed the way she towered over him. It was the little man's revenge, the rugby hulks gnashed their teeth.

'Out of my way!' he seemed to say to them, and they stood out of his way.

Herzog sat up in his chair.

'Let's get this thing straight, Caulfield,' he said. 'Is Abigail Herzog not the most beautiful woman you have personally met?'

There was a pause.

Herzog spoke again.

'I am not expecting you to speak for all the women in Brazil or Hungary. I am sure they have their beautiful women.' Caulfield nodded, 'Absolutely,' he said.

'Then what is your answer?' asked Herzog.

Caulfield thought the whole thing was absurd. It was like kids arguing who had the biggest lollipop. Here was a grown man acting like a kid. I have the biggest lollipop. Yah yah!

'The answer,' said Caulfield, 'is not simple.'

Herzog seemed to be quite pleased with Caulfield's answer. At least it was an answer, and it was only a matter of simplifying it to a simple answer. At which point grown men can discuss such vital issues as football or the conduct of politicians.

'The thing is,' said Caulfield. He had lately acquired the habit of answering tricky questions with the words 'the thing is'. 'Yes,' said Caulfield, 'the thing is that one's conception of beauty is coloured by one's feelings, one's emotional attachment to the other person. In other words, if one is in love with the other party.'

Herzog seemed to frown. Caulfield went on, 'I put it to you like this. Did Mark Antony love Cleopatra?'

Herzog looked surprised. 'Do you know, I never thought of it. Did he?' he asked Caulfield.

'Actually, I can't be sure,' said Caulfield, 'but the thing is, as human form goes, Abigail is perfection. The woman in my life was Prudence Wolstenholme, whose left ear was slightly out of line with her right ear, or of course, vice versa. However, she wore her hair in such a way that it wasn't noticed. She never knew that I knew. And do you know something?' Caulfield continued, 'I never kissed her on her ears.'

As Caulfield spoke he raised his voice accidentally, and it carried over the room. Many of the morning coffee drinkers looked around, fascinated by a man who was not an ear kisser.

'OK,' hissed Herzog, 'that's enough about ears.'

Ignoring him, Caulfield continued, 'I was tempted once or twice to draw her attention to it, but I feel that, perhaps, it might have been unwise.'

Herzog slapped his knee and roared, 'You were wise beyond your ears!'

Those dozing in their chairs sat up suddenly and Herzog's waiter hurriedly rushed in, but left when everything was in order.

'The thing is,' said Caulfield, 'the most beautiful woman in my life has funny ears.'

'Tell me,' said Herzog, 'have you ever looked at Abigail's ears?'

'I have,' said Caulfield, 'she has perfect ears.'

Herzog let out a sigh of relief. 'We must keep this to ourselves.'

'And now Isaac Herzog, to business. You want to speak to me.'

'Yes, Caulfield, I do. You remember the meeting last week. My wife Abigail left the room. I apologise for her, but what you said was most unexpected.'

'I hadn't planned to say what I did.'

'But it had to be said sometime.'

'Yes Isaac, I know that.'

Herzog twisted in his chair. He looked uneasily around the room. 'I appreciate your openness, and can understand your difficulties... but... however, the fact is... we must consider...all the facts. I am not sure how to say this, but we must have all the facts. If we go through with this and we don't know the facts, then the results could be catastrophic.'

'I am not sure if I am with you,' said Caulfield.

'I think you are with me,' said Herzog. He fell again into one of his silences. He twisted a gold necklace around his fingers. Caulfield didn't know if it was his or Abigail's. Herzog seemed too embarrassed to continue. Eventually he said, 'Well it's like this. Do you know a Professor Wertheim?'

'Yes, I think I do. I have read a book by a Professor Wertheim of Stellenbosch University.'

'In South Africa,' prompted Herzog.

'Yes.'

'Professor Wertheim is the world expert on genetics,' said Herzog.

It was now time for Caulfield to say nothing. A fear which possessed him for years came flooding in. He had tried all his life not to think again and again. He had looked into the mirror, had turned his head one way and the other. He had swept up samples of his hair from the floor of Horan's Barber Shop. He had pressed it between the pages of a book and then months later he had taken it and tried to straighten it. There was no clear answer.

In a hot summer when Uncle Sam and Aunt Hilda went to Kilkee, Caulfield sun bathed on the rocks to see how his skin tanned. To his relief it tanned slowly.

Herzog spoke gently. 'You see what I am getting at? We must have all the facts.'

Caulfield nodded dumbly.

'I am sorry, Caulfield.' said Herzog.

Herzog went on. He was now in full flow. The ice had been broken. He spoke in a low urgent tone.

'You had been honourable to tell us the full story of your Aunt's home, your bedroom, the bedside table, the bedside lamp, the drawer in your bedside table. The photographs in the drawer of your bedside table. The photograph of a white woman, a black man, a little boy who was neither black nor white. The little boy was your half brother.' said Herzog

There was silence.

'Caulfield, that little boy. Was he your full brother?'

Caulfield had difficulty in breathing. For years he had denied it to himself. Now this little Jew had thrown it at him and his world was shattered.

231

He could take no more. He could no longer answer. He could no longer face Herzog. Rising up he ran from the hotel, ran across the road ignoring the busy traffic, through St. Stephen's Green, round and round, in and out, as if pursued by demons, until he collapsed exhausted on a park bench. He groaned as if being tortured.

A little man, in a cashmere coat and a Burberry scarf with sharp intelligent eyes, came up behind him. He put his arms around him, hugged him and said, 'Take it easy, Caulfield. I have more to say to you.'

Chapter 21

The Job

It was the first job that Herzog had gone for since leaving college. He was twenty-four when conferred with his Masters degree. As all beginners do, he felt raw and untried.

When Herzog lived in the tenement after his father's death, he completed his Masters and sought employment. The days of good living were years ahead and on occasion he had to use Passchier's Pawn Shop.

He read with admiration the exploits and feats of one, Jacob Anderson. He used money to control capital and in so doing acquired respect, fear and the trappings of culture. That was where Herzog wanted to be.

As Herzog spoke, Jacob Anderson watched him intently. It was the first time that a Trinity Gold medalist applied for a job. Anderson was intrigued with Herzog; he had never seen such a small man, small bones, large head, delicate hands that fluttered like a butterfly.

When he ceased, and Anderson took up the conversation, Herzog went quiet, he folded his hands limply. His head drooped on his chest; it was as if his entire body was listening.

'All we are,' said Anderson, 'are hucksters exchanging bits of paper. We call it money.'

Isaac Herzog nodded in agreement. He had heard it all before. Anderson liked to play the ordinary bloke; he did everything except crack nuts with his teeth. He was famous for his silences. He left people rambling on, and let them talk themselves into ever decreasing circles until they had talked themselves out of a job, or a deal, or his office.

Herzog had developed the habit of first turning to the financial pages every day. Others had sought out the arts pages, or sport, European news, or the latest from Washington. Herzog had read them last, if at all. Herzog had enough of arts or sports. They were mere fripperies on the borders of life. But the world's exchanges where billions flowed back and forth were the real stuff. Dublin was a backwater, even a minor backwater but Herzog studied the open and closing exchange rates and made his decisions. It was always on paper on what might have been. He sat opposite to Jacob Anderson; he was applying for his first job, and hoped that he might be making his first buy/sell contract in the real world!

The Dublin Stock Exchange was the second oldest after London. It had been a bastion of the Castle Catholics and Anglo-Irish. It was the only commercial institution where a gentleman could buy and sell without the ignominy of being in trade. For years it had been the club of the Protestant cause, but not all Protestants could join. The social division was as strong as the sectarian one.

Jacob Anderson represented the new order. The bulwarks crumbled to his attack.

Anderson was talking. He was definitely the leading force on the exchange. Only on a small exchange could he establish such hegemony. Despite his mantra about bits of paper, he was a deal maker par excellence. He brought people to banks, cut himself in for a share of the deal, much to the irritation of the bank who thought it was all theirs. Financial circles talked for months about a cabal he put together consisting of a prominent politician, new money, old money, new money, himself and a planning officer, to turn scrub land into a shopping centre, which eventually gushed out money.

'Out of the strong came forth sweetness'.

Anderson looked at him, 'What can you do for me?'

'I suppose I can sit at your feet and learn'.

'Not had,' said Anderson. 'I'll take you on for twelve months. Perhaps we will destroy each other in the end.'

They both laughed, but neither of them realised how unfunny that remark was going to be.

'I'll ask Madeleine Herlihy to show you around,' said Anderson.

Madeleine was quite tall, a pale reserved sort of face, dressed fashionably in an old fashioned sort of way, sensible shoes. A diamond brooch worn unobtrusively, just touches of make-up.

She spoke with a Dublin upper class accent; plain and unobtrusive. She conveyed a cool rather remote manner, the men in the firm kept their distance.

Occasionally a rumour might half heartedly go round about Anderson and Madeleine. They were supposed to have been seen at the races. Another time it was the opera. The telephonist thought she saw her getting into Anderson's car and being driven away.

Nobody dared to ask openly. Anderson's attitude was quite different from the way he spoke to her and the rest of the staff.

He liked to play it rough with them. Shouted at them across the office, addressed them by their surnames, spewed out profanity at a dealer when he was on the 'phone to a client. He liked the clients to know who was boss.

Did they complain to each other? Plenty of times. But on one occasion there was a note left on their desks.

'Do you want my money? Do you want my job? If not, leave by the front door'.

His attitude to Madeleine was different. He never mentioned her name, but on addressing her would drop his voice and speak confidentially. He frequently asked her opinion, would then stand still considering it, before passing it onto a lesser minion. She was the only person, apart from Anderson who had a private office. Anderson was not married.

'Please come this way, Mr. Herzog,' Madeleine led the way.

Herzog couldn't but notice that she had almost perfect legs.

'Up these stairs is Mr. Anderson's office, here is mine. This used to be a separate building. There was a separate office before Mr. Anderson took it over. It was called Herlihy-Bennett.'

'And you were one of the Herlihys?'

'Quite so,' she said without any expression.

'There are two old buildings knocked into one. You will find that our present office is a warren of rooms, up and down. There is an old regulation that stock exchange members must have their office within a half mile of the exchange.'

'My family is used to working out of one room.'

Madeleine looked puzzled and then decided it was none of her business.

'Quite so,' she said.

They went through two rooms where about twenty of their staff were checking share certificates against a printed list.

'These are clerks who have to balance the business every day. You will spend some time here first.'

Herzog nodded. The staff was either very young or quite old. Either full of beans and would-be Rothschild's, or old boys washed out after a lifetime of looking at other people's certificates.

'What will I be doing here after forty years?' asked Herzog.

Madeleine froze him with a look.

'You were the first of your people to come in here. Don't make it harder on the others.'

'Thanks for your advice, Miss O'Herlihy.'

'And now,' said Madeleine, 'do you want to see the rest; or would you rather stand there and make wise cracks?'

'By all means,' said Herzog, 'let us see this treasure trove of history, where time stands still, and the peace comes dropping slow.'

Madeleine said, 'Do you know what our agent in New York calls people like you?'

'Tell me,' said Herzog.

'A smart Kike.'

'A Kike!' exclaimed Herzog. 'I have heard of the word. He will have to be careful when he comes here next time. I have my pride.'

'Oh he won't mind,' said Madeleine. 'He is a Kike himself.'

She showed him the rest of the offices, provided a chair and desk for his use the next morning, introduced him all around, and said goodbye.

Herzog left the building and walked around the so called Financial District. The buildings were like Anderson's. Old houses, not quite standing straight, where merchants once sold ship loads of washing soda, tapioca, eider duck feathers, from (as his old school master once told them) every corner of the empire. There was little traffic, a few pedestrians were trying not to fall off the narrow footpaths.

There is a key, said Herzog to himself, *to all this.*

Selling paper certificates is not big money, thought Herzog. *Everyone here knows how to do it, and everyone does it. How does one unlock the door? How does one take the tide at the ebb, which leads onto fortune?*

At the street corner stood a public house so ancient that no name was on the fascia. He went in and ordered a coffee.

An ancient crone behind the counter stood stock still. She didn't move an inch but gazed at an advertisement for Donnelly whiskey. Herzog became mildly interested in the advertisement. *Who were Donnellys?* he thought. *Are they still making whiskey?* Had they all gone into the Priesthood? Was one of them the biggest sheep farmer in the Argentine? Had a pretty daughter of -say- Paddy Donnelly became a nun, or alternatively married the younger son of Lord Roseberry?

There was no end to the possibility of these Donnellys. He wondered if he woke up the old fellow sleeping in the corner, and asked him, could he throw some light on the history of the Donnellys, their life and times.

237

As he was turning over these melancholy thoughts, the ancient drone shuffled away. From the back came the banging and clatter, the groaning of rusty machinery, and a piercing whistling noise.

All this for a cup of coffee, thought Herzog, feeling nervous.

The ancient of days reappeared, this time with a cup containing some coffee. Her hand trembled so much that the alleged coffee was spilling over the cup, into the saucer, so by the time it was left in front of Herzog the cup was sitting in about half an inch of the liquid. Herzog wondered, *Did I really need a cup of coffee?*

The previous day a street collector solicited two euros from him for the under privileged of the Moluccas Islands. 'Can you,' challenged the collector, 'give up your dinner for a slice of bread for the Moluccas?'

It didn't seem at that time to be a fantastic deal, either for him or the Moluccas, but he parted with a two euro piece.

He now wished that the collector was with him, so he could press on him this cup of coffee.

The door opened behind him and he recognized the footsteps.

'Hello, Madeleine.'

'It's Mr. Herzog!' she said. 'Getting ready for the big adventure tomorrow?'

'Sort of,' replied Herzog. 'I have been doing research. Lloyds of London started in a coffee shop, so I have made a start for Andersons. Please accept the first cup of coffee. It will become a sort of a Bloomsday thing.'

'I'll have a gin and tonic,' she said.

'It's not what I expected.'

'Life,' said Madeleine, 'is full of bitter disappointments. Not too much tonic.'

'I don't think I thanked you for showing me around' said Herzog.

'No, you didn't.'

'Well, thank you.'

'Thank you for the drink,' she said.

'Can you tell me something about Herlihy and Bennett?'

'The O'Herlihys once owned a lot of land in Tipperary/Limerick. My father used to go on about them. They were the usual tribal chieftains. There is a big house near Roscrea where they supposedly lived. Actually, I am not too interested.'

'I think you are interested,' said Herzog, 'but you feel it's none of my business or else you are afraid of boring me.'

She looked at him.

'Aren't you the clever little fellow!'

'I don't mind being bored, but don't patronize me.'

'You seem to be forgetting,' she said, 'that from tomorrow you will be jumping through hoops for me. So don't get too uppity.'

'All right,' he said with an air of weariness. 'I suppose this means that I better take you out to dinner tonight and then go back to your place for a nightcap.'

'Ha, ha, ha. You little squirt. I think Jacob Anderson is losing his touch in taking you on.'

'He needed brains,' said Herzog modestly. 'That and good looks,' he added.

'Oh, really?' she said, 'brains and good looks, anything else I missed?'

'The usual things – charm, personality, felicitousness.'

'Felicitousness,' said Madeleine. 'How lovely. We are sort of low on felicitousness in Andersons. I must tell the staff to look out for your felicitousness. Mr. Anderson will be thrilled.'

'And of course,' went on Herzog, 'there is chutzpah.'

'Please tell me about chutzpah.'

'I can't,' said Herzog. 'It's a Jewish thing. If you are not Jewish, you haven't got it.'

'How awful, how terribly disappointing. I so wanted to be Jewish. Get me another drink.'

'What about a cup of coffee?' said Herzog.

The bar served up a gin and tonic.

'Do the staff come in this place after work?' asked Herzog.

239

'This is our watering hole.'

'Does Jacob Anderson join you here?'

'Perhaps on Friday night, but not often, he is not a drinker, but that would suit you, would it not? You have your chutzpah on Friday night as well.'

Herzog looked disgusted.

'There is no such thing as a chutzpah on a Friday night, or any night. Chutzpah is personality.'

'It sounds infectious,' said Madeleine. Herzog ignored the remark.

'Chutzpah is the exercise of bravura, the ability to sail close to the wind. It's the ability to beat four kings with a pair of sevens.'

'I wish you the best of luck,' said Madeleine. 'If you had worked for Herlihy and Bennett in the old days, we might still be here.'

'Leave yourself in my hands and all will be well.'

She looked at him scornfully.

'Don't think you can take on Jacob Anderson. He will have you for breakfast.'

'Cheers!' said Herzog, raising his glass.

***

Anderson sat in his office listening to Madeleine and Herzog, as they moved around through the various offices.

Although he was looked on as a modern man's man of today, he liked the Dickensian nature of the place. He half expected Mr. Pecksniff or Micawber to come through the door. Very few people knew that he was well read. He was going through Dickens for the second time. He had read all of Jane Austen when he was sixteen. But Anderson found it profitable to cultivate the air of a Philistine; his language was uncouth, sometimes barbaric, that grated on the more urbane members of the exchange.

This had the effect of making him more feared than he deserved.

He now watched Madeleine and Herzog. He was not sure about Herzog. Something there did not add up. He was a funny little fellow, but could be dangerous. He was one of these who listened casually but intently. One could see his mind at work. He seemed to sum up one's remarks and put it aside for further use, and dismiss the next one as rubbish.

The tones of Madeleine came through intermittently. He strained to hear its timbre and inflection. He knew he could never have it, not in a thousand years, but then he didn't want it.

He couldn't use it for himself. His own accent was pure Dalymount Park but, like most Irish people, he didn't know he had an accent.

Madeleine was explaining something to Herzog and he was replying volubly. This annoyed Anderson. They were far too chatty for his liking.

When Madeleine showed new comers around, they were usually intimidated and replied with more than a murmur. This one was questioning, joking, putting Madeleine on the defensive.

Anderson had given this little Kike a job, and he didn't seem grateful. That was more than some of the snotty Protestants would do. When Anderson first came for a job, even the Catholic firms preferred a Protestant (provided he was a good rugby player). He vowed he would change all that. He did. He was thinking it would be handy enough to have a scratch golfer on the pay roll. Most of the clients were golfers, and liked a round with – say – a South of Ireland winner, who had to be good enough to nurse the client around before winning on the eighteenth.

'God Almighty,' groaned Anderson, 'why does life have to be so complicated?'

Madeleine's voice came through. She was in an office next door, she was explaining something to Herzog about Reuters and Bloomberg's ex dividend prices and spreads and hedges.

Anderson hardly heard what she was saying. All he heard was her voice. That beautiful, expressionless, monotonous, upper class Dublin voice.

Anderson looked at an auditor's statement. He was the owner of the two biggest office blocks in Dublin. He looked at the net value. He didn't bother to add up the millions.

He was only listening to the voice.

What was he going to do?

There was mother. He visited his mother every day of the week. Five days of the week he had luncheon with her in Irishtown. It was the house he was born in. He remembered the woolly pullovers she knitted for the cold winter days. She was and still is the warm centre of his universe.

He told Madeleine that his mother had begged him for one thing. That he would not marry before she died.

Anderson came to work at eight o'clock every morning. So many times he was in a vile humour. He criticized, shouted, ridiculed and kicked the paper bins. His staff wondered, *why does he have to be so unreasonable?*

Chapter 22

Dr Jellett

Dr. Jellett was a tiny man, almost wizened, but very agile for his age.

'Let us think today of... eh, ethics,' he said, looking up as if counting the beams of the roof.

The class of medical students and nurses yawned and shuffled their feet. The most pleasant summer day induced a feeling of gentle somnolence.

'Let us think today,' said the doctor again, 'of ethics.'

The class straightened up a little.

'Ethics, for the ordinary man,' he went on, 'can only be learned at his mother's knee.'

Caulfield was awake; he opened his notebook and started to scribble but a strange ennui possessed him. Although he made notes he had little interest in them. He felt a tightness squeeze his stomach: this damn thing was killing him. For no reason he felt an overpowering anxiety.

'No profession,' said the doctor, 'is as dependent on ethical behaviour as medicine.'

'No profession,' he intoned, 'is based so much on trust, and because of that no other professional holds in his hand the lives of people, sometimes frightened, frequently in pain.'

Caulfield doodled a perfect rectangle on the heading of his notepaper and then blocked in the word *Ethics*. He had a feeling that Dr. Jellett was watching him. He looked up, but the doctor's attention was elsewhere.

243

Caulfield dropped his pencil, and leaning down to pick it up glanced backwards. The nurse he met in Slats was staring at him. She blushed when Caulfield caught her eye and averted her gaze. *She is Michal,* he thought. *She's pretty.*

'Mr. Caulfield,' said the Doctor, 'do I have your attention?'

A faint titter went around the room.

'We are discussing Ethics.'

'Thank you, sir,' said Caulfield.

He was in little danger of being reprimanded as the Doctor, apart from being Honorary President of the Rugby Club, was a genial host on Sunday afternoons when he invited Caulfield and a few others out for afternoon tea. Caulfield was highly esteemed in his house as he played many games of draughts with Jellett's grandchildren and, to their delight, Caulfield always managed to lose.

Ethics, thought Caulfield. *Is Herzog paying me to be unethical? Is Abigail tempting me away from what I learned at Aunt Hilda's knee?*

Dr. Jellett continued, as if speaking to himself. 'Ethics are a number of rules, easily learned; those things that we sense as being good. We do not learn ethics; they come with the infant in his first bath. What is right and wrong is at the heart of ethics,' said Dr. Jellett to no one in particular.

'Suppose somebody broke into your father's house and rifled the family silver, is that right or wrong?' he posed the question.

Miss Redmond put up her hand.

'Yes, Miss Redmond?'

'It would be wrong.'

'Quite so, Miss Redmond.' She gave a small smile, and tidied the papers on her desk.

'Suppose your father's house was locked and an expected guest broke in and helped himself to a glass of milk. Is that right or wrong?'

There was a silence, they looked at each other.

'Would you like to answer, Miss Redmond?'

She coloured a little, and said, uncertainly, 'Wrong?'

'Quite right, Miss Redmond. And finally – and I won't ask you this time, Miss Redmond – I'll ask one of the Einstein's amongst the men to answer...'

Delighted laughter from the women, the men scowled back.

'Gentlemen, if a policeman with a search warrant was to break into your house, would that be right or wrong?'

He looked around the room; the men didn't want to answer. Dr. Jellett looked down at Caulfield.

'It's your turn, Mr. Caulfield.'

With a world-weary sigh, Caulfield replied, 'I suppose it has to be right.'

'Splendid, splendid, Mr. Caulfield! Although, I must say, last Saturday against UCC you apparently thought that a forward pass was right and not wrong.'

The class erupted in shouts and laughter. Dr. Jellett smirked and Caulfield took it in good humour.

'In ethics,' said Dr. Jellett, 'we know when a thing is wrong; when we are uncomfortable and the referee blows his whistle.'

Caulfield felt like walking out; it was like a blow to his stomach. What Herzog wanted him to do was beginning to feel like a crime.

Dr. Jellett was smiling benevolently at Caulfield, who did his best to grin back. Dr. Jellett could not have known anything, but he seemed to know his ethics and something more.

The doctor hit his stride. 'Let us continue. Whether a thing is right or wrong, good or bad is not absolute but variable. Do you agree?' He looked at the ranks of students; they avoided his glance, and he came back to Caulfield.

'What about it, Mr. Caulfield?'

He felt sick. Was Dr. Jellett trying to get at him? Did Herzog walk him into this? Did Abigail and Herzog mark his card with Jellett, knowing the enormous influence they had in the college?

Perhaps Herzog had got tired of his shilly-shallying and made arrangements elsewhere? They no longer wanted Caulfield – was that it? – and before they got rid of him he had to be crushed.

He felt his face covered in perspiration. Dr. Jellett was perplexed. He had never seen Caulfield under such strain.

'I believe that it is dependant on circumstances or on the social situation,' said Caulfield.

Dr. Jellett sat back in his chair and considered this response.

Finally he replied, 'Good answer, Mr. Caulfield.'

Dr. Jellett gathered his things together and left. The lecture was over.

The students made their way out of the Lecture Hall; Caulfield remained at his desk, his whole body sapped by tiredness, his whole being felt tensed and held in a grip of fear. He was afraid, and he was afraid of being afraid. For four or five weeks he slept badly. He had scrounged a few sleeping pills from the head nurse, but they had only cursed him with weird dreams. He started to over-sleep and woke up tired.

Then he recognized it.

He wept. His whole body shook. Where was his strength and manliness? His body was shaking like a girl's; he was helpless, he had no answer.

For five minutes he sobbed like a baby. To an outsider it looked pathetic and even disgusting.

He was a student doctor, and he knew what it was. It was one thing to read of it in a text book, or hear the droning of a lecturer. He had walked the wards with his lecturer and remembered seeing a giant of a man squeezing his hands helplessly, his huge frame shaking. Now he understood that man.

They had looked at that man dispassionately and with only a mild curiosity. It was one thing to look at someone; it was another thing to go through the valley of the shadow on one's own.

Finally, the tears were over and he felt better and relaxed. His body felt no longer crippled. What was the crying about? It's all over, except it wasn't all over.

As he stood up and turned to leave there was a woman standing in the doorway.

It was Abigail.

How long had she been standing, how much had she seen?

Strangely enough, he didn't mind. He had confessed his frailty, but he had overcome it for the time being. He had disclosed the old men's secret that he was not as tough as a woman.

He threw his books on a chair and went to her. He had still a tremble from his ordeal and as he approached he thought he had never seen such beauty.

From her clothes, to her hair, to her face and hands. Not even Prudence, in all her prettiness, approached her.

He embraced her with passion. She responded and then stood back with a quizzical look.

'Is this what Isaac is paying you for?'

'Don't try and analyse me.'

'I can let you play around and have some fun,' she said, 'but once a child comes, it is over. If it doesn't come, then it's also over. Isaac Herzog has a business and he pays for the best, but don't short change him. And speaking of that,' added Abigail, 'you owe him a lot of change.'

'Give me time, more time. My nerves are attacking me. But it will come.'

'It better,' said Abigail, 'you haven't much time.'

Chapter 23

The Way West

Caulfield was feeling the strain of concentrated study. He walked miles every night after the intense lectures. He wanted to be alone, but he wished he had a dog. There is nothing like a dog for company.

Murphy sensed the stress that he was going through.

'You told my mother you were coming down to Limerick.'

'Yes,' said Caulfield.

'Well, come on,' said Murphy. 'Golf is the game. You have only yourself to play against. Do you want to come down to Limerick for a few rounds?'

'It might lose me a cricketing blue,' said Caulfield.

'You don't have to wear wicket keeper gloves to hold the golf club. Just one little golf glove, and its easier to cheat.'

'It sounds a good idea.'

'I'll give the mother a ring,' said Murphy.

'There is something else,' said Caulfield, 'Henley-Smith.'

Murphy groaned. 'Not him.'

'Could you give him a break? He has gone through some bad trouble. I don't know what happened, but he's out of the Navy.'

'Good for the Navy! But if you insist, then ok, let him come.'

There was a silence between the two men. They were heading into their fourth year. Shadows of the Prison House closed on the growing boys. They still had the special cachet of students, with the aura of Trinity 'men' and a certain amount of tomfoolery was allowed. Nobody could say what paths could lead them where.

The leaves were drifting for the last time, and the new faces of the freshmen were taking over, their voices as raucous as theirs had been.

Murphy spoke. 'Maybe I misjudged Henley-Smith. It's just that he seems to raise my hackles. I suppose he is a decent enough fellow, but he is his own worst enemy. Anything he does, he gets it wrong, and rubs people up the wrong way.'

'Well, thanks anyway,' said Caulfield, 'you ask him – it will be worth more to him.'

'Hurray, hurray, it will make the day for me!' exclaimed Murphy.

Henley-Smith was asked and he came. Enjoying his moment of popularity, he produced three free passes which was a privilege given by the original Railway Company to the Henley-Smiths in 1870, in allowing rights of way over their various lands.

Murphy was thereafter mollified.

As they came within a few miles of Nenagh, Caulfield wandered away and sombrely stood looking through the window. He passed that bridge of a thousand memories, Barneys Bridge.

He remembered every detail, the new hairstyle of Prudence, the bicycles on the road, sitting in the car together, the blissfulness of being so close to her. The contentment that came after Aunt Hilda's tea party.

He asked himself, *what would it be like to see Prudence again?* Sitting on her bicycle waving her arm at the passing train, with that smile that always entranced him.

Well! What would it be like?

He stopped, and then he sadly realised that he didn't know. He would have changed. They would have changed. He would be nervous because she had changed. She would be nervous because he had changed. If she had waited for the train, she would not have waved.

She would have been a stranger sitting on her bicycle.

Caulfield saw a dark shadow behind him.

'I thought you might be here,' said Henley-Smith. He continued, 'I know all about it. You cannot bring her back. Believe me, she did a bit of crying when she returned to England.'

'What happened then?' asked Caulfield.

'It was simple,' said Henley-Smith, 'when she finished crying, she dried her eyes. And that was that.'

'That was all?' said Caulfield.

'Look, Caulfield. I don't want to be brutal. If you don't keep putting something on a fire it will burn itself out.'

Caulfield looked angrily.

'Can you spell the word 'platitude'?' he said to him. Henley-Smith looked pained. He paused for a time to find his words.

'The last time I saw Prudence was last Christmas, when we went over there. She told me something about you and she asked me to pass it on when the time was right.'

Henley-Smith turned as to go away. Caulfield pulled him back. 'What was it?'

The train rattled and swayed nearing Nenagh.

'You are pulling at my belt,' complained Henley-Smith.

'Sorry! What was it she said?'

'When the time is right. It's not right when you are still short with me.'

'I am sorry. I am sorry, now please tell me what she said.'

'OK.' said Henley-Smith, 'now let's take it easy.'

The train gathered speed as it left Nenagh. The carriages swayed from side to side, at the point where they met, and where the WC toilets were placed. Passengers came and went to the toilets, but Caulfield ignored them.

'She told me,' said Henley-Smith, 'that she cried until she could cry no more. She told me that she might never see you again, but she would always have the loveliest memories of you in that summer.'

Caulfield turned to go away. Henley-Smith pulled him back.

'She told me,' said Henley-Smith, 'that when she is an old woman, with a shawl, and sitting by a fire, she would dream and remember that young man, a veritable Galahad, who was the love of her life.'

Caulfield gripped Henley-Smith. He held him tightly and his body was rigid.

'That's it,' said Henley-Smith. 'That is the end. No more tears. Face up to it, Caulfield. You know she has seen you for the last time.'

Henley-Smith spoke harshly. 'What's past is past. You have your memories, and so does she.'

The train slowed down as it came into Limerick.

Olive Murphy was waiting on the platform. Caulfield thought it was nice of her. Kevin kissed her perfunctorily and made an effort to introduce.

'Of course I know you all. Henley-Smith, Caulfield, you are all very welcome. You should have come long before now.' Olive could lay on the charm when she wanted.

There were roars and squeals as the three burly men and two sets of golf clubs plus some cases and a driver sought to squeeze into her two door. The men, except for Caulfield, sounded like kids. It was like the last day of school.

Charles McGreevy had made available the prime site on which the Murphy's had built their house.

Sunday afternoon's invitation to his bowls parties was a highpoint for Limerick society. People who never bowled blossomed out in whites and talked earnestly of bias and so on.

Caulfield was the hit of the party. He ogled the younger women, and was gallantry itself to the older ones.

Yet to the men he was a man's man. In a rugby-mad city like Limerick, the word spread that internationals Murphy and Caulfield were in town. The clubs came around and asked them to come to their pitches and coach the youth.

With the greatest good humour they gave hours on the side step, the pass, some training and tackling without injuring. They posed for numerous photos with the younger fry and signed and signed and signed.

'Enough is enough,' said Kevin. 'We will head for Lahinch in the morning and get some golf.'

Chapter 24

'Phone Call

'Phone call to Mrs. Olive Murphy from Jim Hayes, Manager of Lahinch Golf Club, concerning the behaviour of her son Kevin, and his two friends, Caulfield and Henley- Smith, on the previous evening.

- *Some of the members had spoken to him;*
- *Particularly some of the ladies were offended.*
- *He was asked to call a Council meeting so Mr. Kevin's conduct might be discussed.*
- *Yes, Mrs. Murphy, he would do his best;*
- *Yes, he had a very high regard for the Murphy family;*
- *Yes, he would do his best, but he could not be sure.*
- *Yes, the Council particularly valued the membership of Dr. Horace and Olive;*

But it was very awkward.

- *Some of the ladies were talking of resigning. Mr. Harney said he would consider resigning – those remarks about nuns in Chipping Common were very unpleasant.*
- *In fact, he was never near a place called Chipping Common.*
- *Nobody wanted to suspend members.*

- *Two lady members were suspended five years ago, when it turned out they were maintaining a service of sorts behind the fifth green.*

Of course, that was different.

- *He was only a servant of the Golf Club, he only had one vote.*

- *He personally was hurt by a reference Mr. Kevin made about him and Birkenhead.*

- *Although he was not going to make an issue of it. He was only once in Birkenhead, thirty years ago, when he was helping his father with cattle.*

- *The ladies were very offended by his comments regarding their articles of clothing.*

- *The Bishop complained of being struck by a lighted cigar thrown by Mr Kevin.*

- *Major Rayburn was very upset. He only has one vote, but he is very popular, even if he gets mixed up with his golf scores.*

- *He hoped that the McGreevy's and the Murphy's would understand.*

- *Also, the Honourable Mrs. Tavistock-Ponsonby was deeply wounded by references to her background. To mention things about her father, who was a bookie in Listowel, was hurtful.*

- *She had been advised to consult the solicitor Mr. Brady of Brady & Brady.*

It was not his decision.

- *Yes, he knew that Charles McGreevy sponsored the Open Week;*

- *Not many people would do it; they were a very decent family.*

- *Yes, yes, he didn't mind reminding the members that the McGreevy's felt privileged in sponsoring the Open for many years.*
- *Yes, yes, the Council will know that the McGreevy's are anxious that the Open Week must continue.*
- *The Club manager understood perfectly.*
- *Goodbye and thank you.*

(To Mrs. Murphy, née McGreevy)

The next day the Murphy's house was very quiet. Caulfield and Henley-Smith were down early for breakfast. After the 'good mornings', Olive had toast and glanced through the morning paper.

She wasn't the gracious host of a few days before. The silence was complete. Unanswered questions hung in the air.

After they went to bed the previous night, somebody must have 'phoned, possibly the gardaí. Horace had left earlier that morning. He did not want to pick up the pieces. That was Olive's job.

As for Olive, she was furious. She had the disappointments in her earlier life, now her home had filled a gap. Auctions in Britain and Ireland had been ransacked for good antiques. She knew exactly what she wanted.

She knew the Henley-Smiths through Lady Mary Smith and her set, and more indirectly, Caulfield, who was much talked about. After yesterday there was no chance of him coming to Limerick, which was upsetting.

This left Kevin. It had to be him. It always was him. She was sick of trying to help, sending him out of Limerick to school and college. When the butcher praised him after a good write-up in a big match she vowed never to go near that shop again.

She wouldn't let Kevin bring some of his rugby friends to the house. They were drunken buffoons who could end up dancing on the piano.

Caulfield and Henley-Smith finished their breakfast.

'What are you going to do?' asked Henley-Smith.

Olive was at the far end of the table. She could not have heard them.

'I don't know,' said Caulfield. 'The situation is almost impossible.'

'Maybe so, but we just can't dump him.'

'Well I can,' said Henley-Smith. 'It would give me a great pleasure to dump him.'

Olive folded her paper and came up to the two men.

'You had quite a day yesterday,' she said grimly. 'The little boys had quite a game.'

They hung their heads.

'I was thinking that I might leave today,' said Henley-Smith. 'I don't want to outstay my welcome.'

Olive looked at him with distaste.

'No,' said Caulfield 'we'll stay if it's alright with you, Olive. Let's do something. Could we go for a walk over the mountains or something?'

'You could,' said Olive, 'the Glen of Aherlow is only thirty miles away. It might take you about two days.'

'Oh, good! I hear it's very nice.'

'Or you could always go on to Kerry and try Macgillicuddy's Reeks,' she gave him a grim smile, 'that would take four or five days.'

Caulfield looked thoughtful. 'I don't think we would have the experience.'

'No, I don't suppose so,' she said.

'OK,' said Caulfield. 'We will get this show on the road. I will go upstairs and get this baby out of his cot. Henley-Smith, go into the kitchen and start making sandwiches.'

Henley-Smith was about to protest, but he sighed and headed for the kitchen.

Olive looked at Caulfield admiringly.

'Neat,' she said. 'Very neat.'

Murphy was lying back in bed, his hands over his face. He heard Caulfield's step.

'Get out!' he roared. 'Get out you agricultural lout.'

'Let me know when you are finished.'

'I am finished,' cried Murphy. 'I have given up the best years of my life for you peasants.'

'You need a stout pair of shoes for walking in.' He held up a pair with thick soles. 'These should do for mountain walking.'

Murphy slung himself back on his bed. 'How much do I have to pay to get rid of you?'

'Don't forget your breakfast,' said Caulfield, 'and your old pal Henley-Smith is making sandwiches.'

'It's getting worse,' said Murphy. 'I am expected to go on the mountains with a madman and a nit.'

He went downstairs in his stocking feet carrying the walking shoes. Olive barely looked at him.

'Good morning, everyone.'

Olive, Henley-Smith and a maid were in the kitchen. Nobody answered. He went over to the maid and put his hand on her. 'Hi ya, Bridie, are you happy, Bridie?'

'Kevin!' said Olive sharply.

'Sure we are going to get married, aren't we, Bridie?'

Bridie giggled and looked embarrassed.

***

Kevin, Caulfield and Henley-Smith set off for the Galtee mountains, about an hour's drive from Limerick. Olive saw them off with foreboding. 'What will they be up to now?' she said. 'School

257

boys, cowboys, idiots, probably coming home pushing a crashed car. Half drunk, covered in cow dung.'

'We might be gone for two days,' said Kevin.

'Good,' said Olive.

The atmosphere in the car was one of harmony. Everyone made strenuous efforts to promote universal peace.

'Did you ever see the countryside look better?' chortled Henley-Smith. 'Fresh as a daisy and we still have the autumn colours.' They agreed vociferously. 'Remember the poem?' said Caulfield, 'something about deep autumnal colours.'

They all tried to remember, but were not sure. 'What about mellow fruitfulness?' said Murphy. 'That's it,' said Henley-Smith. 'No,' said Caulfield. 'It was – what do you call it – a host of daffodils.'

They agreed there were daffodils somewhere but it didn't seem to go well with autumn colours.

'I know,' said Murphy. 'It's primroses.'

'No,' said Caulfield, 'primroses are out.'

The atmosphere in the car dropped perceptibly. *It doesn't look good,* thought Caulfield, *if we can't agree on primroses.*

Around a corner they met a farmer's cart half way into a ditch. A police car stood by. All parties looked baffled.

'Tell them to get out of the way,' shouted Murphy. He proceeded to blow the horn and continued to shout. Henley-Smith, like a copy-cat, shouted as well.

Two gardaí appeared and looked threatening. They looked at the gardaí.

'Damned hell,' moaned Murphy.

'I don't believe it!' said Caulfield.

'Get out,' said Murphy to Caulfield, 'and say something, about the weather, about anything.'

The two Gardaí approached with a look of pure pleasure on their face. They were the same garda who were called into Lahinch golf club the previous day. The three men groaned on recognising them.

'Well, well, well,' said the senior garda. As before, he took off his cap, scratched his head and put it on again.

'No doubt we are going to a wedding, are we? Or is it a golf match with the gallant Major? What sort of fun have we planned today?'

The three men looked blankly at the garda.

'We are going for a walk.'

'Oh, I see.'

The garda was enjoying it.

'So you are naturally going for a walk in the car. How else could you go for a walk?'

'You should try going for a run in the car,' said the other garda. 'You can run it downhill and push it up.'

'Great idea, O'Riordain,' remarked the senior garda, 'but I have a better idea. Listen to this.'

He looked at the three in triumph.

'Fill it with water. How about going for a swim in the car?'

The gardaí doubled up at the good of it. The senior garda wiped his eyes. Even the farmer who was in the ditch joined in the fun.

'I have a great idea,' said the senior man. 'Let's play a game.'

'A game?' queried Murphy.

'Yes, any number can play, but three is an ideal number.'

'Look out,' whispered Caulfield to Henley-Smith, 'this is a trick.'

'The game is called cartwheels, and three people who are good and strong have to pull a cart out of the ditch.'

There was a subdued moan.

'And, of course, there is a first prize.'

'Which is?' asked Murphy.

'The first prize is a garda summons, which the garda has discretion to tear up, and it consists of charges of rows and mayhem at a Golf Club and making lewd remarks to lady members.'

'What is the second prize?' asked Murphy.

'The second prize is to spend an indefinite period of time in Limerick garda Station.'

'We will go for the first prize,' said Caulfield.

The three of them reluctantly inspected the cart. The horse had pulled the cart into the ditch, leaving the farmer in an embarrassing situation.

'How did this happen?' asked Henley-Smith.

'Its not part of the game to decide how it happened,' said the senior garda, 'just get it out.'

'Thank you, officer.'

The officer didn't appreciate mild sarcasm. 'Watch it!' he said.

'Do you know what?' said Henley-Smith.

The others looked expectantly at him. Henley-Smith was a landowner, a countryman, an experienced man with horses. They felt that he had an intuitive knowledge of farming life. Pulling horses out of ditches was the thing that they more or less did before breakfast.

Both Caulfield and Murphy felt a keen sense of gratitude to him. He was an OK guy. In minutes he could solve this, and they would be on their way.

'You notice,' continued Henley-Smith, 'that the horse and cart is facing up the road.'

The two gardaí, Caulfield, Murphy, the farmer trapped in the cart, and a number of small boys, looked up the road. They looked up the road as if expecting a premonition. They nodded gravely, wondering why they hadn't seen its significance.

'That means,' said Henley-Smith, 'that the horse and cart was travelling in that direction. So now we know what direction it was travelling in.'

The farmer spoke up. 'I know what direction it was travelling in.'

'Is that all?' asked Caulfield.

Henley-Smith gravely nodded his head.

'Is this an example of rural wit?' said Caulfield.

The garda looked at Henley-Smith up and down.

'So we have solved the question of which way the cart was going. Not that it matters a damn.'

The garda spoke to Caulfield.

'Does this fellow think he is smart?'

'No, he does not.'

'If I thought he did I'd write a docket out now.'

'No need for that, sir,' said Caulfield, 'we are going to get this out now. But first of all, do you know where we could get a tractor?'

Everyone looked around. A small boy was standing in the driveway of a farm.

'Has your daddy got a tractor?' asked Caulfield.

The boy ran crying back to his house.

'Terrific!' said Murphy. 'You seem to have a way with children.'

Caulfield said to Henley-Smith, 'Get in beside that man and lift him out. Don't mind the nettles, they won't sting forever.'

Henley-Smith backed away.

Caulfield whispered urgently in his ear.

'That cop is going to take you into Limerick garda Station. He thinks you got smart with him. This is your only chance.'

Five minutes later the farmer was released, the Gardaí were pleased and Henley-Smith was stung all over.

'This is the second time I have been punished for nothing,' he said.

It was a year before Caulfield would find out what he meant.

Caulfield told Henley-Smith, 'Go up to that farmhouse and ask the man for the loan of a tractor. Tell him you don't know how to drive a tractor, you are not taxed to drive a tractor, you have no driving licence or insurance. He is bound to lend you a tractor.'

Within minutes the farmer drove down his tractor and pulled the cart out of the ditch.

An emotional farewell was said by all.

***

Approaching Tipperary, Murphy pulled up and asked Caulfield to take over.

'You tired?' asked Caulfield.

'Yes.'

'Did yesterday take much out of you?'

'Yes.'

'Do you want to go through with this?' asked Caulfield.

'Yes.'

'Quite a yes man,' said Henley-Smith.

Caulfield turned around and glared. 'Shut up!' he told him.

Caulfield was sorry he had suggested a walking tour. There was bound to be a casualty somewhere, and Murphy was not enjoying himself.

'These are the Galtee Mountains,' announced Henley-Smith. 'Historic O'Herlihy property, from the Galtee up to the Slieve Blooms and down to the Shannon.'

'I've heard this before.' said Caulfield.

'Take off your hats, you stand amongst kings,' said Henley-Smith.

'Tell me,' said Caulfield, 'do you have tuppence worth of Irish blood?'

Caulfield was glad to have an argument. It might liven up Murphy a bit.

'Listen to Caulfield,' cried Henley-Smith, 'descended from Williamite land grabbers, and he asked me if I had Irish blood.'

'Just how much Irish blood, have you?' said Caulfield.

'I am descended from Lady Emily O'Herlihy, as Irish as a greyhound, and my ancestor, James Arthur Henley-Smith, R.N.'

'Where did he come from?'

It was Murphy speaking. Slumped in the front seat, he had listened and didn't want Henley-Smith to get away with too much.

Henley-Smith said nothing. *Let it go*, thought Murphy.

But Henley-Smith came back at Caulfield.

'You asked me, I ask you,' said Henley-Smith. 'How much Irish blood have you got?

'Tuppence worth,' replied Caulfield, 'but what a tuppence worth!'

Murphy clapped his hands.

Henley-Smith was not finished.

'How about you, Murphy, where did the Murphys come from?'

'Will you give it a rest?' moaned Caulfield.

'You started it.'

'The Murphys were Kings of Kerry. When we came to town, the Herlihys were just good enough to hold the bridle of our horses.'

'Like hell!' muttered Henley-Smith.

'OK, Mr. H. Smith. Tell us the story of Captain James Arthur Henley-Smith R.N.'

'He was an officer and a gentleman.'

'Is it true that he got Lady Emily into the family way and then married her?'

'How can anyone sink so low,' said Henley Smith, 'to spread such a vile rumour?'

'For a consideration I shall not mention it to anyone,' said Murphy.

'Thanks for nothing.'

They were coming near Tipperary. A signpost said *'Galtee Mountains. Walkers Only'* The road looked narrow and twisty.

'We will go on,' said Caulfield.

They came to a wider road stating *' Galtee Ladies' View'*.

'We can view the ladies,' said Caulfield, 'it's beginning to sound interesting.'

The road wound upwards, hedges and trees, disappeared. They could see across miles of heather. The view was desolate, only an occasional cottage visible.

They came to the famous *'Ladies' View'*, a small car park, with the same view further on. This is where they come Mr. Hemingway, they come here, they come for the big view.

Caulfield took out a large scale map.

'This is the mountain walk,' he said, 'it comes and goes, and twists and turns. With a bit of luck, they will find our bodies next Christmas.'

They parked the car and locked it.

'O'Herlihy,' shouted Murphy, and raising his hands skyward, 'we have returned, so kill the fatted calves.'

After a hundred yards, they remembered their sandwiches, which they immediately consumed. Off they went again.

They walked in silence for hours. The vastness of the country came to them. Sometimes they walked through mist, and then they broke through to sun and new views.

Henley-Smith went ahead, followed by Murphy and Caulfield.

They had never been in the beautiful Glen of Aherlow before. They met nobody, no 'phones rang.

Three hours later, feet were sore and tired. Henley-Smith pulled up.

'Let's have a pow-wow,' he said.

They took off their shoes. Their feet were tender and blistered. They examined their toes with care.

'Where are we?' asked Murphy.

'About nine miles from anywhere,' said Caulfield. He examined the map. 'If we get to a road,' he said, 'we then have to find our way back to the car.'

'It looks miles away on the map,' Murphy said. 'There is one other thing. That farmhouse.' He pointed down the valley, a tidy looking farmhouse which seemed to nestle in a fold of the hills. 'They might give us a meal and a bed for the night.'

They looked down at the farmhouse. Smoke was coming from the chimney.

They viewed the house without much enthusiasm.

A man came out and walked around to the back of the house.

'Yonder peasant, who is he?' asked Murphy.

'That's strange,' said Caulfield.

'What is strange?'

'That farmhouse,' said Caulfield pointing to it.

'There is nothing strange about a farmhouse.'

'When we stopped here I looked around everywhere and I did not see that farmhouse.' Henley-Smith was about to make a flippant remark but he stopped as he felt a keening wind pick up and mist forming on the mountain side.

Murphy shivered. 'Let's get out of here.'

'I could have sworn there was no farmhouse,' said Caulfield.

As they prepared to move off, a tall woman appeared from the mist, walking silently. The men were about to greet her, but she passed through them and disappeared.

As she did, Kevin cried to himself and Caulfield grabbed him by the arm.

'Let's go,' said Caulfield.

'What's the matter?' asked Henley-Smith.

Kevin and Caulfield didn't reply, but they staggered and slid down the mountainside to the lane near the farmhouse. They groaned, as the stony path seemed to pinch their bruised toes.

The day began to darken, the light in the window of the house flickered and almost disappeared, and a chill possessed their bones.

A stream splashed over the stones as it raced past the house. A stone bridge connected the house to the lane way.

They stood outside the house feeling indecisive.

Before they could do or say anything, the door opened.

'I beg your pardon, ma'am. We were wondering if we could stay for the night? We are willing to pay for bed and breakfast.'

They looked at the woman, her husband appeared, a little girl came and clutched her mother's dress. The little girl had golden hair, and a child's hairclip with pretty stones.

'Of course,' the husband said. The woman led them in. The table was set for five people and a child. They had a meal.

The evening darkened and they sat around the fire talking and gossiping. Murphy was tired and he asked to go to bed.

Upstairs were three beds in a room, neatly made up with fresh linen. They all decided to retire and they said 'goodnight'.

Caulfield lay in his bed, but he was too tired to sleep. He listened to the splashing of the stream outside.

Suddenly Murphy screamed and screamed – 'The child! The child!'

He ran to the window, as did Caulfield and Henley-Smith. They saw in the moonlight the little girl, her hair shining. She was in the stream; she was kicking and beating the water.

They rushed downstairs. The woman was standing at the open door and holding a lamp. Murphy rushed to the stream and gathered up the child. She was breathing and smiling.

The moonlight shone through her hair. He clutched her to himself.

Caulfield and Henley-Smith tried to bring them into the house. Murphy would not let them. She was safe with him.

They gathered together for warmth under a tree.

The sun was well up before the men wakened. Their clothes were wet. The little girl where was she? They looked, they could not find her.

They stood up to go into the house. There was no house; there was only a ruin of a farmhouse with no roof or windows.

They carefully entered the ruin. Nothing in the house looked familiar except what was once a chair and on it was a child's hair clip, with pretty stones.

***

'That was it,' said Caulfield to Olive. 'We didn't know what to do about the child's hair clip. So we left it.'

He continued, 'I never saw Kevin act like it before. He laughed and cried, and threw himself on the ground. We had a job getting him to the car and then home. 'I saved her, I saved her' he kept shouting. Some mighty burden has been lifted from Kevin's shoulders. He is a different man. He even tried to kiss Henley-Smith, poor Smith, he doesn't deserve that.'

'What was the hair clip like?' asked Olive.

'A child's one with pretty stones.'

Olive opened a drawer and took out a child's hair clip with pretty stones.

'That's it!' cried Caulfield, in amazement. 'And there's one other thing that I noticed. The woman who brought us in. All evening she never said a word. She was about fifty, slim build, dark, curling hair, parted in the middle.'

'It sounds like me,' said Olive.

'It was,' said Caulfield.

'And what else was there on the mountain?' Olive asked.

Caulfield moved uncomfortably.

'Nothing.'

'There *was* something,' said Olive.

'No, nothing.'

'You are lying!' said Olive.

Caulfield wrung his hands. He appeared to groan.

'Alright,' said Caulfield. 'There was a woman. Kevin and I recognised her. She was Abigail.'

'No, she wasn't Abigail,' said Olive. 'She was just like Abigail, as she was just like the other women who need punishment. Only she is punished to walk the mountains.'

'What did she do?'

'In her heart she despised the ancient gods and mocked them and so they cursed her to walk the mountains for one hundred years. But when the Christians came the ancient gods were destroyed and there was no one to relieve her of their curse, and so she walks these mountains now for ever – and ever.'

'And what's the story about Abigail?' asked Caulfield.

'Nothing, there is no story about Abigail.'

'It's my turn to call you a liar.'

Olive shrugged her shoulders. 'I have never been on that mountain and I don't believe in fairy stories. Years ago I had a nanny who told us that story. I believed and I disbelieved. There is more in heaven and earth than are dreamed of in our philosophies.

'Ten years ago I got an overwhelming compulsion to go to that mountain and a few yards along the path I found a red coloured anorak printed in the Czech language. It was Carlos. I believe,' she said, 'and I don't believe.'

'That leaves us with Abigail,' said Caulfield. 'What do I believe and not believe about her?'

Olive looked at him steadily for a minute

'There is something that you know about her but I know you won't tell me. She matters and that surprises me because I know that Prudence is very much alive and you will always remember. There is something more in the future between you and Abigail, and that could be dangerous.'

Olive continued, 'Your very niceness is not going to save you from women. What about your mother, do you think of her with a warm heart?'

Caulfield said nothing.

'What about Prudence? All that love and tenderness, but she left you in bits.'

Caulfield stayed quiet.

'And Abigail,' said Olive, 'she wants you the way a tiger wants an antelope.'

'I think it is time for us to go back to Dublin,' said Caulfield, 'these stories are upsetting me.'

Chapter 25

Herzog's Start

Herzog had the run of the place. He said to young Quirke 'Come out for some lunch.' It was 12.50 pm.

When he was questioned for leaving early he would lightly state that he worked Jerusalem time.

He wasn't exactly popular in the office, but nobody seemed to dislike him. He described himself to someone as the best drudge in the practice. Whatever he wanted, he found it easily; clients were impressed at the speed which he could remember facts and figures. Staff were not supposed to tip shares or pay attention to tipsters' sheets, but he had the knack of picking out the salient facts, and let the clients make the decision. The clients were beginning to ask for him. Herzog did not know of it, but he was only two years away from joining the super-rich.

Herzog had taken Quirke under his wing. The staff assumed that Anderson had given Quirke a job as the office junior so he could shout at him.

Ask him a quick question and he tended to stop and stutter. Anderson would stand quietly over him, increasing the pressure. The office staff would squirm in embarrassment.

They went to Mundy's Pub which crowded up quickly. Beef sandwiches, veg. soup, and a biscuit. The working man's lunch.

Anderson usually went to his mother's house in Irishtown where she gave him a bigger lunch than he wanted, but his somewhat baleful influence was at least absent for a while.

'How's it going?' asked Herzog, paying for the lunch.

Quirke had been on the telephone for a week.

'All sorts,' he replied. 'One fellow was looking for money. Two million to buy the Isle of Man.'

'Did we lend it to him? Did you send it up to Anderson?'

'He didn't want to borrow it. Just the full amount in a suitcase. I had a feeling that Anderson wouldn't jump at it. Another fellow wanted to buy a farm. I told him this is not a bank, it is a stockbrokers. He told me his grandfather was a stockbroker, he broke stones on the side of the road. There was nobody else on the 'phone, so I listened. They had Sunday off in those days, and their only recreation was tossing half-pennies at a crossroads. He sounded to me,' said Quirke, 'to be the most decent man I've known.'

'Those were the days.'

'You can keep them,' said Quirke. 'Yesterday, I had this woman on the 'phone, she thought we were a building society. She was going to sell her farm. She wanted to live on the income. She wanted a guarantee income of €300 a week.'

Herzog said nothing.

'She had been in the bank and if she sold the farm for €300,000 and invested in one of their bonds, she would only get €173 per week. She was smart enough; she knew that she could not live on that amount and pay a maid.'

'What's she going to do?' asked Herzog.

'I don't know.'

'Where does she live?'

'Somewhere in Offaly.'

'What's her name?'

'I didn't ask her.'

Herzog gave a deep sigh. 'That's terrific.'

'Why do you want to know all this?' asked Quirke.

'Its beginning to interest me,' said Herzog, 'but what good is it if we don't know her name?'

'I do know her name, it's the same name as mine. She is my aunt.'

Herzog groaned. 'What do you mean by stringing me along like this? You and your idiotic aunt. Come along back to the office.'

They walked back to the office, but Quirke noticed that Herzog was walking slowly and didn't respond much to his remarks. His mind was elsewhere. Even when Anderson appeared he ignored him.

'I want you to know,' said Quirke, 'that what I told you is true.'

'It better be,' said Herzog.

The weather turned baking hot. In his apartment at 85 Dorset Street, Herzog opened all the windows. Mrs. Zeiss had the apartment spotless. He didn't really need her, but as children she used to give them hamantasher (small cakes) on the Festival of Purim. After Mr. Zeiss died, Herzog was sentimental and kept her for nominal duties.

Sunday morning Herzog phoned Quirke. 'It's Sunday morning,' complained Quirke.

'Get moving,' said Herzog.

'They are starting to throw the Christians to the lions. I have a fiver on one of the lions.'

'It's not fair,' moaned Quirke.

They met in St. Stephen's Green, on a bench near the stone bridge. Chubby little girls were carrying small bags of bread for the ducks.

A pretty girl standing on the bridge saw a young man approaching. They ran to each other and kissed.

'Aren't they lucky,' said Quirke sourly.

'It will come,' said Herzog. 'Just for now I want to speak to you. This aunt of yours, is she on the level?

'The Quirkes are famous for being on the level. Honesty is our best policy, except when of course it pays to be dishonest.'

'That's fair enough. OK.' went on Herzog. 'Now the story is; she will sell her farm for €300,000 plus or minus and we have to produce a net income out of that of €400 per week, minimum.'

'Isaac, forgive me for saying this, but won't we be on the level the whole way through?' Herzog looked at him. 'I feel sick at the idea of anything else. It wouldn't be worth tuppence if it meant doing some old woman out of her money.'

Quirke saw his flushed and angry face. 'OK. OK. I only asked.'

'Do you want me to go on?' asked Herzog.

'Of course, Isaac, but I had to ask. Now you have answered.'

Herzog relaxed.

'All right then. Now the question is how do we make €400 per week on a capital of €300,000? If we invested the €300,000 at six percent we could pass on €346.'

The two men looked out across the waters of the lake. The ducks dived for food. It was the ideal Sunday morning and one could hear the bells ringing, as the unco guid headed for church and chapel.

'What is the most we can get?' asked Herzog.

'Four, perhaps four and a half.'

'So three hundred thousand at four and a half is thirteen and a half thousand, or €260 per week.'

'That's the most we can get,' said Herzog. 'It's going to take some trick to turn €260 per week into €400 per week, and get rich for Herzog and Quirke. The more you think of it, the more impossible it seems.'

Quirke looked at Herzog.

'Obviously you know how.'

'How old is your aunt?

'Seventy-one.'

'How old was your father?'

'Seventy-three.'

'How old was your other aunt who lived with her?'

'Sixty-nine.'

'And again your aunt is...?'

'Seventy-one.'

273

'So your aunt is seventy-one, and her relations passed on at the same age.'

'It's our only chance,' said Quirke.

And Herzog said. 'And all we have to do is to go and see your dear aunt and sell her a policy on the idea of the Herzog-Quirke Insurance Company Limited.'

Herzog stood up. 'Go to your church, wherever it is, and say your prayers. We are going to need them all.'

***

Herzog was driving out of Dublin.

'I have never told so many lies,' he said. 'I told Anderson that Lord Iveagh wanted to play golf with him today. I 'phoned Lord Iveagh that Anderson wanted to play golf with *him* today. I told my brother Ken that I needed his car for a Bank of Ireland ad. I told Madeleine that I had a pain in my stomach and wouldn't make it, and you, Quirke, had to go to a funeral in Wexford.'

They made good time through the pastures of Meath and Offaly. Quirke guided them expertly to the Quirke farm, a few miles from the Grand Canal and ten miles out of Tullamore.

'I used to spend my school holidays here every summer. I loved every blade of grass in this country.'

'Do you want a loan of my handkerchief?' asked Herzog, 'or what about a few blades of grass for the office? We will have Madeleine in floods of tears.'

'Not after she learns of your miraculous recovery from stomach pain,' said Quirke.

Herzog said, 'Do they have bog holes around here where I could hide a human body for a few years?'

Despite the raillery, there was an undertone of anxiety. Selling insurance is not a job for the faint hearted. Even when supported by the back up of an eminent Insurance Company and a famous name. Essentially he and Quirke were nobodies. They had the great advantage of Quirke's connection but an inquiry might blow their cover. To all this, was the imponderable fact that success might bring disaster. If Miss Quirke should live to a ripe old age then bankruptcy would inevitably follow and stigma would be with them for a lifetime. It also meant that Miss Quirke would spend her closing years absolutely destitute.

Of all white collar crimes, the one that attracts the most opprobrium is life assurance fraud that affects the old and vulnerable.

Herzog's face became grim as he considered the situation, and drove the last few miles through the midlands countryside.

If he failed his name was mud, despised and hated, seen as a conman, cheating an elderly woman, his name a byword for dishonesty.

If he succeeded, his success would bring rewards for a while, and then disaster.

Worse of all, if his fecklessness led to disaster, who would know the most and be the most wounded? He looked through the windscreen and thought he could see the figure of a little man who never overcharged a penny and sometimes never charged a penny. A man who was proud of his sons, because they represented all that was good and honest. Herzog ground his teeth, and brought the car to a stop.

'What's the matter?' said Quirke.

He looked at the tensed up figure, leaning over the wheel. 'Don't lose your nerve, you can pull it off. We can.'

'OK.' Herzog muttered. He struggled to put the car into neutral.

'Remember this,' said Quirke 'this is our only chance of getting out of middle class poverty. We take our chance with two hands. And also remember if my aunt deals with the bank or anything else, all she will have is €260 per week, deal with us she gets €400 and perhaps more. We have seen the facts; statistically she cannot live beyond another four years.'

Herzog nodded and drove on.

'You mightn't have much brains,' he said, 'but you have plenty of balls.'

'Such vulgarity!' cried Quirke.

The two of them laughed. They arrived at the Quirke's farm. Herzog carefully drove through the stone pillars to the farmhouse.

'I suppose you love every stone in these pillars?' said Herzog.

'Yah, yah.'

It was a plain, handsome house, from cut stone. An overgrown tennis court was on one side. The other side had been a rockery with beehives and an orchard. A Morris Minor car, at least thirty years old and with flat tyres, was parked awkwardly at the corner. A Labrador snoozed on the gravel path and then slowly and arthritically stood up. There appeared to be nobody around.

Quirke approached the door, and paused. It was down on its hinges and he had to lift it to push it open.

'Hello!' he cried.

There was a faint answer. Quirke, familiar with the house, went in to the drawing room on the left. He turned on the switch which lit up the room.

An elderly woman sat there.

'Hello, Aunt Mary,' he said.

'Ah Brendan, it's yourself.'

He shook hands.

'This is Mr. Herzog who works with me.'

He gravely bowed and shook hands.

'Aggie would like to be here, shout for Aggie.'

'Aggie!' shouted Brendan.

She appeared. A shabby looking woman with a hard, suspicious face. Herzog smiled benevolently. He shook her hand. 'You are Aggie, I have heard all about you.'

Herzog thought: *A thieving woman, not to be trusted. Someone has got control here.*

Aunt Mary explained, 'Aggie has been with me for years. I could not do without her.'

Herzog thought: *She couldn't get rid of this Aggie. She interferes in everything.*

Aunt Mary said, 'Please, everyone, sit down.'

Everyone sat down except Aggie and Herzog. Herzog offered his chair to Aggie.

'No,' she said. 'I will stand.'

'Are you sure?' said Herzog. 'Have my chair.'

(She won't sit down, that's a sure sign of aggression. Wants to get away quickly.)

'I was thinking of selling the farm,' said Aunt Mary. 'I would be more comfortable in town.'

Aggie said, 'You could buy a farm nearer the town and it would be comfortable.'

(In other words, buy nothing and I will still run things here.)

Quirke broke in. 'I think buying farms is not going to do any good. What you want is a good income for you to live on.'

(Well done, Quirke.)

Aggie said, 'I am not leaving.'

(She wants to steal the place first.)

Herzog smiled his most winning smile. He spoke *sotto voce.* 'You must have run this house for years. If it was sold we could probably get a good settlement for you, plus your existing job with Miss Quirke.'

(Stop being a nuisance.)

'How much would this settlement be?' she asked.

'Will you leave that with me?' replied Herzog.

(Mind your manners or you won't get anything.)

'I want to ask Mr. Herzog, chairman of the company, to outline the advantages of the Retirement Insurance Policies.

'Thank you,' said Herzog. 'I will take just a few minutes.'

'We specialise in Retirement Insurance Policies so that our members can enjoy an adequate and safe retirement income.'

(Keep on repeating the word 'retirement' and 'income'.)

'There are two main features of this policy. Safety and an adequate pension. There is no point of having a safe return which is also a small return. It's like burying your talents in the ground.'

(Great stuff, Herzog; he noticed the bible on the writing table as well.)

Herzog went on to develop their offer of their superior service compared to bank bonds, etc.

(Don't mention annuities.)

Herzog stopped and asked Aunt Quirke, 'Do you have a gun in the house?'

'We used to.'

He asked Aggie the same question.

'I had a gun in my Da's house.'

'Well, Aggie,' said Herzog, 'would you get your Da's shotgun and shoot every bank manager in the country?'

Herzog, Quirke, and Aggie roared laughing. Quirke shrewdly kept the laughter going until Aggie stopped.

(Herzog winked at Quirke, Aggie was now coming around.)

'These bank managers should be shot. They are selling bonds at 4% that gives you a miserable €230 per week. We guarantee, guarantee,' emphasized Herzog, 'guarantee 350 to 400 per week.'

'Could I get the 400 per week?' asks Miss Quirke.

(This is it, Herzog. Close the deal. You won't get a second chance.)

'Can we guarantee 400 per week?' said Herzog.

He stood ram rod straight, and looked through the window with an air of intense concentration. He turned to Quirke.

'Quirke, can it be done?'

'I don't know,' said Quirke, 'but I know one thing. Aunt Mary is my aunt, and if there is 400 to be had I am going out to fight for it, and to hell with head office!'

(It's home and dry, Herzog. Just wrap it up.)

'That's enough, if Brendan Quirke says 400, we will get you 400 per week.'

Turning to Miss Quirke he said, 'That's it, € 400 per week. Guaranteed.'

'Where do I sign?' asked Miss Quirke.

Quirke drove back through the darkening evening. Herzog nearly laughed the whole way. His nerves almost collapsed from the anti-climax. 'The beauty,' said Quirke, 'is that if she gets more than the 300,000, then it is pure gravy for us.' Herzog told him to pull up.

'Did we do anything dishonourable today?'

'No.'

'Because of us did she get the best price on the market?'

'Yes.'

'Drive on,' said Herzog.

***

On the 1st June, Miss Quirke sold her farm for €330,000. The money was lodged to the Herzog-Quirke Insurance Co. Ltd.

The sum of €400 was paid out promptly every week. By the 5th November they had paid out €10,000.

Miss Quirke died on the 12th November.

The net profit to Herzog-Quirke was €320,000.

At the funeral many people came up to commiserate with Brendan Quirke.

Chapter 26

Epicure Mining

Anderson sat at his desk pretending to read some papers. Madeleine sat at the corner of his desk, her face black with anger. Herzog and Quirke stood with hands behind their backs.

'Sit down,' said Anderson.

'We'll stand,' said Herzog.

They had learnt something from Aggie. Anderson finally looked up.

'Explain yourself.'

'About what?'

'Don't get smart,' said Anderson. You know perfectly well. From the time you told lies to Madeleine and me, to the time that you posed as an insurance agent, to the time you acted without a bond contrary to the Securities Act of 1970, to the time you risked the good standing of this house.'

Herzog replied, 'What about the time this great house risked its name in purchasing a certain property in North Dublin; then when permission was refused sold it and bought it back at half the price, then when a certain planning officer joined the company you bought it and resold it at four times the price, and now units are rented out at twenty five times the price.'

Anderson rose, his voice shook like a corner boy facing an Alsatian.

'Get out!'

'Not just yet. Anything we learnt, Anderson, we learned it in here.'

Anderson sank back. Herzog had the impression that Anderson had run out of steam, was no longer angry. He accepted the situation.

'I may reconsider,' he said, 'but in all fairness there has to be a price.'

He looked at them.

'You used this office and resources to make at least €300,000. I'll take half of it and a promise from you not to try this thing again.'

Quirke and Herzog looked at each other. They smiled broadly, dug each other in the ribs, and went through a pantomime that expressed astonishment.

Quirke said, 'Nice try, Anderson.'

Madeleine looked at Herzog. She seemed to mouth a word.

'Kike.'

Herzog could afford to be generous. He smiled at her.

'We can't share anything,' said Quirke.

'Then what are you waiting for?' snarled Anderson. 'Get out and stay out, and the same for that Jew boy.'

'Hold it now. We have an offer.'

Anderson looked at them sideways. 'Offer!' he said. 'Some offer. You fellows came in here six months ago, with the bottom hanging out of your pants.

'And now you want to come and tell me about a deal.'

Anderson stopped. Perhaps they had some sort of a deal. Quirke and Herzog made tracks for the door.

Anderson spoke up. 'Hold it.' There was silence. The two men came back. 'What's the deal?' Herzog was very smooth. 'Let's forget the shouting and the name calling, and discuss this quietly.'

Anderson looked at his watch.

'I'll give you two minutes, and I don't want any retirement insurance.'

'We can help you to make ten times what we made last April.'

281

Anderson sat very still.

'Ten times, was that what you said?'

'Yes.'

'Go on,' said Anderson.

'Have you ever heard of a place called Australia?' asked Herzog.

Anderson threw away his pen as if he wouldn't need it again.

'Madeleine, have you ever heard of a place called Australia?'

'No,' said Madeleine.

'There you are,' said Anderson, 'there ain't such a place as Australia.'

'Very funny,' said Herzog.

'You have one minute.'

'There is something in Australia that's a gold mine. Except it's not a gold mine, it's worth nothing, but it's fantastically valuable if we sell it, and we can sell it without buying it.'

There was silence.

Anderson took a deep breath. It was the air of a man who has had a difficult day at the office.

'Madeleine, can you translate any of this gibberish?'

'I remember something about Australia. There was a 'phone call in from someone who wanted to buy it,' she said.

'I remember now. How much does this fellow want to pay for it, Herzog?'

Herzog gave a nervous laugh. He seldom got mixed up like this, he better start again. 'I'll start again,' he said.

'Start again?' questioned Anderson, 'I thought you were finished. This fellow wants to buy Australia, let's see what he will give us. You could check with the London market. Maybe Brazil is for sale too?'

Herzog remained calm. Anderson was enjoying himself and so was Madeleine. He waited until he was breathing easily.

'There is a mine quoted on the London Stock Exchange, in the mining section, called Epicure Mining. It has been said that someday it will be the biggest nickel mine in the world.

Herzog looked around. Anderson and Madeleine were listening intently.

'There is but one snag.' They waited.

'There is not a mine called Epicure in Australia. Even the Australians have a name for an Australian nickel mine. They call it 'a hole in the ground owned by a liar'.'

Herzog finished: 'It seems this mine is just a hole in the ground. If any of this is true, it could be the greatest bear market of all times. But we have to move – now.'

Anderson looked impressed and cautious.

'Maybe so, but who has checked all this?

'Who is this guy, Shenk, who runs Epicure, and seems full of himself?'

'A lot of questions, a lot of ifs and buts,' said Anderson.

'Should we leave it?' asked Herzog.

'No,' said Anderson. 'We follow this one. If it's half true, we can sell it short, and share it fifty-fifty.'

'That's big of you,' said Herzog.

We need you out there to check it. We have only a few days.

Anderson's eyes were glinting. He was like a tiger that smells the spoor of its enemy. He was on the prowl. Win or lose, he would be there at the finish.

'Mr. Shenk,' he whispered, 'we shall see Mr. Shenk.'

Chapter 27

Nickel and Gold

He was in the dead centre of Australia, in Alice Springs. He was dried out like a pancake. He had pains in his neck and shoulders. He had dust up his nose and in his ears.

'You seemed concerned,' said a stranger sitting near by.

'That's what you call putting it,' said Herzog, rubbing his eyes after three days of driving into a glaring sun.

'What's the problem?' asked the stranger.

'A man called Anderson, a liar and a thief. He is the problem.'

'There's no shortage of those sort here.'

Herzog thought: *how profound.*

The two of them sat in the colonial comfort of the Commonwealth Hotel in Alice Springs.

'Alright,' said the stranger, 'let's start at the beginning.'

Herzog was thinking: he was facing the biggest opportunity of making real money. It was in his grasp. It was slipping away.

Quirke wanted a nice house with a garden. Herzog wanted more. Should he be satisfied with a bungalow and a white picket fence and rhubarb for the Garden Show? There was nothing wrong in that, in fact nations were built on it.

Herzog tried to count the odds. *It is no time to play cute. I should be careful with a total stranger talking double-talk, but I won't get anywhere talking to no one. I might as well bet the bottom dollar. I'll get nothing by doing nothing. I have to chance it.*

He started to talk to the stranger and he kept talking.

'It was my deal from the beginning to the end,' he told the stranger. 'I spent a weekend analysing the returns on the London Stock Exchange. I wanted to see if there were any discrepancies in the current share values compared to the previous twelve month opening values. I hit pay dirt with Epicure Mining. Twelve months ago it opened at twelve cents. The current value is $91.36 Australian. The stock was watered, and in the background was a shady character called Shenk.

Obviously they were going to sell it short if we didn't get in before him. They quietly bided it up over twelve months while the Stock Exchange went to sleep. It should be ready to sell short any day, even tomorrow. There's a fortune crying to be made,' said Herzog. He shifted in his chair and continued, 'I told Anderson what I had found. He jumped at it and sent me out to Australia to report back. But he put a lock on my money so I couldn't trade. It was a perfect double-cross.'

'I think we can do business,' said the man, 'Will you wait? I will be back in an hour.'

'What is your name?' asked Herzog.

'My name is Drofinan or Mister 5%.'

So that's Drofinan, thought Herzog. *He is no friend of Anderson.*

The stranger – Drofinan – returned. He sat down facing Herzog. He said nothing, but looked at him.

Herzog knew it was favourable.

'It's OK,' said Drofinan. 'You assign me your €300,000. I'll sell two million in Sydney and London. The market will probably not be able to sell that quantity, unless Anderson is putting buy orders at the same time. Thanks to your e-mails, they should. By close of business here and London, these gentlemen should be screaming. We will have about twenty three million to share. I'll be reasonable, fifteen for you and eight for me.'

'You are all heart,' said Herzog. 'The whole thing could have been made and lost in minutes. For a while I trusted Anderson, but he outsmarted himself. He bought my story of the nickel mine that was no mine. Then he sent me out here. He wanted me to get an up-to-date story on Epicure and also to get me out of the way so he could block my money and prevent me from trading. In selling short, only one man makes real money – the first man to sell.'

'There's one other thing,' said Drofinan, 'you were very trusting in this deal.'

'I had no choice.'

'Good going,' said Drofinan. 'Would you like to buy a bank?'

At the moment, I could hardly buy an ice cream.

This is a bank you could do things with, and it's a small Manchester bank. The name is Grim Brothers. You can have it for three of your millions.

"I'll take it" said Herzog. 'It will be Grim Brothers and Herzog. Can I ask you something, Drofinan? How did you so conveniently make an appearance here?'

'I got a 'phone call from an old friend asking me to help you.'

'Abigail?'

'Yes, my former wife, and your future one.'

***

She smiled, Yes, I am Abigail.'

'Abigail, will you marry me?'

She looked at a funny little man who came no higher than her shoulder.

'Of course,' she said, 'I will.'

It was the first time that Herzog had taken an interest in women. He was in a matter of seconds bowled off his feet. Abigail Liebnecht was amazingly blessed in looks, style, and personality. She had an indefinite glow that captured him. The wonder for Herzog was that she responded to a little man with apparently little to offer. He was small and frail, she was tall and willowy. She responded to his rash question with a rash answer: 'Yes I will.'

That evening they dined.

He told her his history; the horrors of Kiev; his father's tenement; his academic success; his reason for Australia. The letter from his cousin, Eli, in Melbourne.

She told him how her mother and sisters hid in the Polish marshes, living off nuts, frogs, birds' eggs, and dandelions.

They fled from the Nazis, and then the Russians. On the whole the Russians were better. He Nazis wanted them dead, the Russians only wanted their bodies.

Her mother told her they fled westwards with the hoards of refugees, and they linked up with the Americans and British. They were the best of all. They wanted their bodies too, but were willing to pay. Some years later, Abigail was born in Paris.

'And now you are here,' said Herzog. 'The survivor of survivors, in sunny Australia.'

Abigail raised her glass. 'next year in Jerusalem.'

Ten days later, Isaac Herzog and Abigail Leibnecht were married in the Tel Isaac synagogue. Isaac's brothers from Ireland were present, together with his cousin, Eli. His brother, Ken, proposed, "May the children of a strong man be like arrows in his quiver".

Mrs Abigail Herzog (née Leibnecht) became ill after the ceremony and was admitted to the Royal Infirmary, Melbourne, for a few days.

Regret was felt at the death of Mr. Shenk, Chairman of Epicure Mining Company, one of the most important nickel mining companies in Australia.

Drofinan

He was a man whose face held a thousand secrets. He moved with a grace as if boneless. His hooded eyes took in a whole room; they tended to frost over if asked too many questions.

He was Armenian.

As an infant his father was hidden in a kitchen oven, temporarily safe from the marauding Turks. His father's first memory on being taken from the oven was the swamp of his mother's blood on the kitchen floor.

His father's voice would drop to a whisper as he described the Turks.

Who was his companion, Hildegard? For a man like Drofinan getting a woman like her was easy as hailing a taxi. But she was no floozy.

Sometimes Drofinan made it easy for someone to cheat, then he had the excuse to destroy. He traded in armaments, enriched uranium, information and oil.

Drofinan travelled in the Middle East, was guide and advisor to sheikhs. He was a westerner who was trusted by the Arabs. Drofinan protected them from the grey numbers men of London and New York. Five per cent of an oil company was little enough reward for him.

He walked without leaving a shadow. He left no footprints.

Chapter 28

M'Night

Anderson waited for Herzog. He had the air of a man who was controlling himself with difficulty. His reputation was now in question.

The gossips in the Exchange were trying to fill in the pieces. There was something about a scoop in insurance, which Herzog snapped up from under his nose, and then somebody sold Anderson short in mining, and he had to take a bath running into millions.

Mr. Anderson, it was rumoured, was extremely irate.

Madeleine was reading Rothe's column in the *Financial Times*. The columnist was being lyrical about the demise of Epicure Mining. It opened on Monday at $91.36 Australian and closed on Friday at seven cents. For dealers who were lucky not to be affected, the rise and fall of Epicure had a certain charm.

On the London market, the fall of Epicure was a signal to the colonials that they had no right to be messing in things beyond their means. The suits of Threadneedle Street smugly advised New South Wales diggers to stick to digging.

However this disappeared rapidly, when it was seen that the diggers had a healthy disrespect for mines containing the word 'Nickel' and it was the investors of the mother-country who lost most.

'Talk about 'Black Monday',' said Madeleine, 'this is it! We are in the eye of the storm.'

Madeleine read the paper, and her mind was confused. She had admired Anderson, and overlooked how he could cut corners. After all, everyone seemed to make something out of his deals. To her he was like an Elizabethan Free Booter. What he did wasn't quite right, but it brought home the gold plate.

But the Epicure business was different. It was outrageously crooked. Stopping a client's account was tantamount to stealing it, under the rules they must release the funds when requested.

Anderson lied when he did not release the funds. His excuse – that he thought they belonged to someone else – was feeble. Madeleine did not overlook the fact that Anderson paid her well (she deserved it), appeared to fancy her (but wasn't sure), would probably marry her (nothing certain), she liked him, (not always). She was admired when on the floor of the exchange (so what).

She left ostensibly to go to another office, but actually to go for a walk and get some fresh air.

***

She went down College Green and then into Trinity. *I wonder if they're playing cricket?* she thought. She remembered nostalgically of watching her father and brother in the old days, playing on opposing teams.

They made such a big thing about being gentlemen. Her father's club was indisputably all gentlemen. Her brother's club – alas – was sons of trades people.

She liked the company of gentlemen. She was not, she insisted, a snob. But she liked the language, the understatement – the body manners.

Heaven was a place where men stood in the presence of women. Hats were worn to be taken off. Men and boys' trouser pockets were not for keeping their hands in. Right handed gloves were speedily removed on shaking hands.

There was nothing better, she thought, than to be a woman in the company of a gentleman.

***

Back in the office, Anderson was in a state of fury. The President of the Dublin Stock Exchange had sent for him. He was looking for an inquiry into the events of the past week. So many people had got stung and they all bayed for blood.

What enraged Anderson was that he suffered more than anyone. Why did they not investigate Herzog? Of course he was not a member of the D.S.E., but Andersons were. So Andersons were investigated for being skinned alive, while Herzog laughed all the way to the bank.

His language bounced around the offices.

Thinking of the bank made him pause. He had heard a rumour that Herzog had bought a bank from Drofinan.

If it was Grim Brothers of Manchester he could have kicked himself. Grim Brothers was small going nowhere, but it was solvent. It was owned by the old Cotton millionaires of Lancashire. Anderson had often eyed it, but he had missed out on hearing it was for sale.

Curse Drofinan, Curse Herzog.

Drofinan! His lips curled. That wop had crawled out of a cesspool in the Middle East. He met him once and he hated him. Drofinan had a knack of making him feel small. Once when Anderson had tried to buy the Advocato Biscuit Factory, he found that Drofinan had gone in before him and owned a third.

In the end, his syndicate had to pay twice the price of the entire building for just Drofinan's third.

The syndicate was very critical of Anderson, and many of them never dealt with him afterwards. Curse Drofinan, curse Herzog, curse that little pup, Quirke!

***

Madeleine stood under the trees in College Park, mesmerized by the click of bat against ball.

As a child she liked to watch her father who, with a touch, could send the ball anywhere. In the evening when the shadows lengthened the applause tinkled around the ground, the essence of polite approval. Some of the players – future District Commissioners and tea planters – leisurely strolled around, holding their girls' hands, their long dresses billowing gently in the evening air. That seemed so long ago. When her father was bowled (he played first man in) she walked to the pavilion and sat on the steps waiting for him. She listened carefully to the voices and tried to match them up to the players who came to bat.

Now, the only sound was that of voices and the distant murmur of Dublin traffic. She could never figure it out in detail, but within the grassy rectangle of the cricket pitch was a world of ordered privilege.

No one ever saw barefoot children there, or tired old women with plastic bags of groceries or alcoholics sleeping under a tree.

They belonged to another city with different voices and the language of the stranger.

She liked the older world, but she was now living in the world of Anderson.

Madeleine went to the pavilion. In her father's time nobody stopped her as they always knew who she was. *I wonder if anyone will stop me now?*

Nobody did.

Someone called Caulfield was batting. There was a round of applause as he reached his fifty. 'Jolly Good!' exclaimed a player, waiting to bat. 'Jolly Good' he kept calling, even for a feeble effort.

Everything was 'Jolly Good'.

Caulfield was caught in the slips for fifty-five. 'Is that 'Jolly Good'?' said Madeleine to this fellow. He was beginning to retort when he took a closer look at her.

'Everything is 'Jolly Good', Miss Smart Pants.'

'Oh,' cried Madeleine, 'if my poor mother could hear that.'

Ten minutes later they exchanged names and Madeleine knew she was talking to Henley-Smith, he of the O'Herlihy Clan, which she, Madeleine O'Herlihy, found to be a very pleasant coincidence.

Caulfield wasted no time in meeting the new girl.

When Henley-Smith went in to bat, he scored exactly two runs.

'You see,' said Caulfield to Madeleine, 'he wasted no time in getting back to you.'

'Jolly Good!' she said.

***

The match was drawn. Caulfield loitered in South Anne Street, surveying a display in men's outfitters and beginning sentences to himself that started with the word 'if.'

'If I only had them,' he muttered. 'Them' were white cricket flannels. His own were held together with white shoelaces.

As he stood, the window reflected a man. The man didn't move. He remained standing, the man still didn't move.

Caulfield moved to another window. The man followed. Caulfield turned to him

'Hi there!' said the man.

'Hello,' said Caulfield shortly.

'I know who you are,' said the man.

'Who am I?' asked Caulfield.

'You are a friend of Herzog; I used to see you in the Shelbourne.'

'That explains everything.'

'I don't like Herzog.'

'I am sorry,' said Caulfield, 'I can't do a thing about that.'

'You are getting fresh, mister.'

'Now that's a thing *you* can't do anything about!'

'OK. We seem to be getting nowhere.'

Caulfield didn't reply.

The man took out his cigarettes. He opened the pack, but the pack was empty. He crushed the pack in his hand, and let it fall on the ground. Caulfield looked at the pack on the ground and then he looked at the man.

'I think it's your pack,' said Caulfield

'I don't want it. It's your pack. You pick it up.'

Caulfield put his hand on the window for support.

'You must be a pretty tough guy.'

'I don't want any trouble from you,' said the man, 'but pick up that cigarette pack.' Caulfield looked at him for some time. He walked away slowly.

When Caulfield got to Grafton Street he looked back. The man was still standing rigidly staring after Caulfield. Caulfield thought, *what could he do?*

In College Green he stopped to talk with a woman who was in his year. The shadow of a man came behind him. It was the same man. He was holding a full packet of cigarettes.

'I want to warn you about Herzog. He will make use of you.'

'Oh?'

'The wife is no good.'

'Why not?'

'That's my business, and don't ask questions. He wants you to do a job on his wife, and don't ask questions.'

'What's your name?'

'McNight,' said the man, 'and don't ask questions.'

Caulfield looked at the man. He seemed to be perspiring, a slight tremble was in his hand. Caulfield recognised the symptoms.

'Would you like a coffee?' he asked him.

'I wouldn't mind.'

Caulfield looked at the girl.

'What about you, Julie?'

'Sure' she said.

They walked a few steps up Dame Street and came to a small coffee shop. Inside a waitress came to their table.

'Three coffees, please,' said Caulfield.

'I don't want coffee,' said McNight.

'Would you like tea?' asked the waitress.

'No.'

'Cocoa, a soft drink, club orange?'

'No,' he said.

Caulfield asked him.

'What would you like?'

McNight dropped his cigarettes on the floor.

'Pick up my cigarettes,' said McNight.

Julie and the waitress looked at Caulfield. He bent down and picked up the cigarettes. He showed the greatest good humour.

'There are your cigarettes,' he said.

The waitress brought two coffees.

'Where's my coffee?' asked McNight.

The waitress went away and brought another coffee. As she did, McNight stood up to leave.

'Be very careful,' he said, 'you may be walking into something.' And he left.

A tall, well-dressed woman came into the coffee shop and recognizing Caulfield she approached the table. Caulfield stood up and pulled out a chair.

Julie looked at her, and decided it was time for her to go.

The woman sat down.

'Would you like coffee?' asked Caulfield.

Abigail smiled. 'You students must be loaded if you can stand four cups of coffee.'

Caulfield spread his hands out. 'The fact is, Abigail, I am fantastically wealthy!'

She looked at the white shoe laces holding up his trousers. 'So I can see! You buy only the best quality shoe laces.'

They both laughed.

Abigail became serious.

'Time is running out – when is what taking place, and when is where?'

Caulfield was silent for a moment.

'I could say now, but there is something stopping me.'

'So it's off?'

'No,' said Caulfield, 'but now I got a shock. The guy – he says his name is McNight seems to know something.'

'We know all about McNight. He tipped a waiter in the hotel for his information. McNight is finished!'

'Finished', thought Caulfield, *who is finished?*

'For twenty years that man has been spreading malicious rumours about Isaac. He put up with it; Isaac could only hate him. I followed McNight from Grafton Street, and then you came on the scene. Did you see the tremble in his hands?'

Caulfield nodded.

'Poor McNight,' said Abigail indifferently, 'he is one of life's losers. Some people don't deserve it, others deserve it in spades.'

Abigail stood up. 'Make up your mind, Caulfield, because I can turn against a person very quickly!'

'Even Adonis?'

She smiled mirthlessly and left the shop.

The following day the newspapers reported that Alistair McNight, Director of the European Union office in Dublin, had accidentally fallen into the river and drowned.

Chapter 29

Death of McNight

The next day Caulfield cancelled his lectures. He was devastated by the news of McNight. What did it mean?

He decided to telephone Abigail. The call was answered by an expressionless male voice that said Mrs. Herzog was out of town.

'Mrs. Herzog was in town last night,' said Caulfield sharply. The male voice hung up.

Caulfield walked over to the small coffee shop where he had last seen McNight and Abigail. He sat down, as if he could seek enlightenment. A voice spoke.

'Do you want tea or coffee?'

There were two men, five foot eleven inch in height, with bony faces, hard eyes, calculating looks.

'Who are you?' asked Caulfield.

'Never mind, Caulfield. Where were you last night?'

'I was here.'

'We know that,' said one of the men, 'just tell us where you were.'

'For the second time, I was here; and then I walked across to my rooms in the college and I read for a few hours before bed.'

'We'll ask you for the last time, where were you last night?'

'Look fellows, take it easy! I walked down to O'Connell Street bridge, walked along the river to the Ha'penny Bridge, crossed the bridge and came back to college, where I read and went to bed.'

'It's beginning to sound better, Mister,' said the man who hadn't yet spoken.

A waitress brought two cups of tea to the men. 'Tea or coffee?' asked one of the men.

'Coffee,' said Caulfield.

One of the men spoke to the waitress. 'Who was on duty last night?'

'Betty,' said the waitress.

'Where's Betty now?' asked the man.

'She quit,' said the waitress, 'this morning.'

The two men looked thoughtfully at each other.

'Was Betty not happy here?' asked one of the men. The waitress shrugged her shoulders, put empty cups on her tray and walked away without speaking.

'Can you fill us in on Betty?' asked one of the men.

'Not much,' said Caulfield. 'We had been married two years, had seven children; went mountain climbing last Christmas, lost three of the children and never found them since. Betty was saving up to take opera lessons.'

One of the men looked pained, the other whistled soundlessly.

'Caulfield – or Mr. Caulfield, I don't think it matters too much – you can help us, or we can go to another place that's not so comfortable. You can guide us and help us make that decision.'

Caulfield sat silently, nodding his head as if he was agreeing with himself. 'OK, this has something to do with Alistair McNight. In case you are wondering, I read about it in the paper this morning. I met him in South Anne Street looking at a shop window, and then later outside here. I invited him for coffee, and Betty – you remember Betty, don't you? – well, Betty brought us cups of coffee. Mr. McNight decided that he didn't want his cup of coffee and he walked away, much to the disappointment of Betty – you remember Betty.'

'Carry on, Caulfield.'

'Oh yes, I nearly forgot this one; McNight was perspiring and his hand was trembling and I recognized it – as a medical student – that it was stress related. I only speak as a student.'

Caulfield fell silent, as if there was nothing more to say. The men sat still, waiting, as if there *was* more to say.

'And so...?' said one of the men.

'That is so,' said Caulfield.

The other man gave a weary sigh. 'Why does it have to be like this? Mr. Caulfield, would five minutes be enough to put your affairs in order and then you can come with us. No need to bring anything, we can give you a complete change of clothes.'

'When do I get dinner?' asked Caulfield. The two men shook and laughed at the good of it.

'Did you say *dinner*?' asked one of them.

This triggered the other man to shake helplessly. '*Dinner*!' he said, 'after three days you will be entitled to the four o'clock sandwich; you will find it extraordinarily nourishing.'

Caulfield rested his head in his hands.

'I'll try and remember. I met McNight in South Anne Street and then I met Julie in College Green, and then McNight came along and we all came in here. And when we were in here we met Betty – you remember Betty – and then McNight went away.'

Caulfield could hear the ticking of a clock in the coffee shop.

'Oh, I remember,' he added, 'Julie went away.'

'You're nearly there, Caulfield,' said one of the men.

'Oh, there was another – a woman. She was a Mrs. Herzog, the wife of a banker. We talked for a minute about this and that, and then she went away; and that was that.'

'What was this and that about?'

'Her husband is giving a big party for the Rugby Union, nothing important.'

'Not quite good enough, Mr. Caulfield.'

'If it is not enough you should ask for Betty, she was here – you remember Betty, don't you?'

Caulfield stood up and walked back to the college. The two men sat on and drank their tea.

Caulfield went to his room and lay down on the bed. He was feeling disturbed by the conversation the previous night. McNight was no fool, even accounting for his hatred of Herzog; McNight was strong academically, a man of his calibre did not live by delusions.

He thought of what McNight had said: *I want to warn you...The wife is no good... He wants you to do a job... He will make use of you... Be very careful.* Did all this mean anything? McNight was issuing a stark warning, was there any substance behind it?

If there was no trouble with hidden warnings, then McNight was fooling himself. On the other hand, if McNight was on to something it could mean real trouble for Caulfield.

What Abigail had said sent a shiver through Caulfield. *McNight is finished,* she had said. *Finished?* thought Caulfield at the time, *who is finished?* It was all too much.

He tried telephoning Abigail again. The same male voice answered and Caulfield left a message, 'Tell Mr. Herzog I am going to Ballynale in Tipperary. It seems a long time since I visited my family. I should be back in a day or two.'

Caulfield packed his suitcase and some soiled linen that Aunt Hilda would wash. He wanted to get away, and there was only one place to where he could flee and that was Ballynale.

He would be safe in Ballynale, amongst his own people he. In his old bed he could sleep soundly and forget the fears that screwed his body and reduced him to a sobbing child. He had felt the fears returning, but Aunt Hilda would hug him and bring him peace.

He ran down the steps carrying his own suitcase and at the bottom he saw his nemesis. He was waiting with arms folded.

'Not so quick!' said Herzog. 'I got your message. You look like a bank robber leaving town.'

'I have had my fill of this Al Capone stuff. I want to get back to the green grass of home.'

'OK,' said Herzog, 'I'll have you driven down in the Bentley, but on the way I want a heart-to-heart conversation, so we both know what's happening.'

'That sounds reasonable, as long as there are no tricks.'

'When you are ready to come back, let me know.'

Herzog took Caulfield's suitcase and they waited in College Green. His Bentley came smoothly by and they got in.

Herzog pulled the connecting window closed.

'Now, start at the beginning,' he said.

'First, you tell me what is the truth about McNight,' replied Caulfield.

'He is dead, and that is the only truth that matters, and the rest of the truth is that he drowned himself, and a bit more of the truth is that he was a sick man, and the last bit of the truth is he was suffering from manic depression, stress … you should know what it is.'

'We have been studying it, I know a bit.'

'More than a bit, my friend. Your surrogate wife told me of your weakness in the lecture room, when you were her little baby.'

'Damn!'

'Don't mind,' said Herzog. 'She has to tell me everything – that's what makes her so adorable. That's what makes McNight and people in your condition so dangerous.'

Caulfield sank back in the leather upholstery. He almost forgot what Herzog had been saying. A gentle heat played around his ankles; music came from somewhere.

'Before we get to Ballynale, we have to understand each other.'

'I want to know the full background to McNight,' said Caulfield.

There was no answer from Herzog. He lit a cigarette and opened a window.

'You have to realize that I was the last person to speak to McNight,' went on Caulfield, 'and you and Abigail were the last people he talked about. One way or another, we are up to our necks.'

'Right,' said Herzog, 'one thing at a time. The first is what you know and which you haven't told me yet, and the next is what I know.'

Caulfield told him, what McNight had said and did and then what Abigail said. 'It's your turn, Herzog.'

'I have known McNight since we were freshmen,' said Herzog. 'He represented everything that I despise in a man. He hated me and because of that I hated him; there wasn't a lie that he didn't make up.'

'Abigail told me that,' said Caulfield.

'When I married Abigail he went bananas; he couldn't accept that I got a woman like her. He was so full of hate that he attacked her with anonymous letters. He said she worked as a prostitute and worse. He sent letters to my best customers saying I was sending copies of all their correspondence to the Revenue Commissioners. There was no end to it. He hated me so much that I hated him back; I felt that I was losing my reason.'

Caulfield said, 'Two cops questioned me this morning. If they could hear what you are saying now they would put you under arrest.'

'Is that because I have the biggest motive?' asked Herzog.

'That's right,' said Caulfield.

The car journeyed through the Irish Midlands. The engine was barely audible. Herzog seemed to have gone to sleep.

Caulfield thought, *could Herzog have done this?* The answer was 'no'. He could not imagine him doing it. What about Drofinan? He could have arranged it with his hired killers. Speaking of which, those two policemen in the coffee shop were rather peculiar; they knew all his movements from the night before. How did they know to wait for him in the coffee shop this morning? He could see the faces of the two tough men, one man and the other man.

It was about half-an-hour later that Caulfield broke the silence. 'Do you think someone pushed him into the river?'

Herzog moved his legs and then lit another cigarette. 'Perhaps it could be you.'

'Thanks for nothing!' said Caulfield.

Herzog pushed open the sliding glass panel and tapped the driver on the shoulder.

'Stop here, please, and get cigarettes.'

The driver pulled up at a shop and bought a packet. Caulfield remembered. The driver handed the packet back to Herzog who dropped it on the floor.

'Pick up my cigarettes,' said Herzog.

'Who told you?' asked Caulfield.

'First Abigail, and then Betty. You could have drowned him,' said Herzog. 'Because he humiliated you with the cigarettes.'

'I wouldn't know how to kill anyone,' replied Caulfield. 'I am essentially a peace-loving person, except once when a Welsh forward tried to kick me in the face, and furthermore *I* never admitted to hating McNight.'

'I wanted to be sure,' said Herzog. 'Your behaviour was odd, skitting down to your bolt hole in Tipperary – that won't do you any good. I called for you to-day because I wanted you to face the music and get over with it. It should be over by to-morrow.'

'Then who did the job?'

'One person,' said Herzog, 'himself. He hated himself, as well as hating me. When you talked to him in the coffee shop he was having an attack of the jitters; he felt he had no future – his hand was trembling, remember? He verbally attacked me in that coffee shop last night; he made sure he had two witnesses – Julie and Betty, the waitress. They couldn't forget him after all that stuff of ordering coffee and not drinking it. Then the exhibition of making you pick up his cigarettes.

'In his mind he had publicly insulted you, why would you not want to kill him? And if the gardai could not have made a case of murder he would have scored anyway; the fingers pointing at the famous rugby player and the wealthy banker. We would not have been charged – only ruined.'

'What was your alibi last night?'

'McNight 'phoned me about ten o'clock to give me his plans. He sounded regretful, even sorry, that it was ending this way. I begged him not to do it, offered him help, but he hung up. I telephoned the police, but it was too late – they had just got the news.'

Caulfield felt that Herzog was weaving a web. From the beginning, Caulfield could see that there were unanswered questions concerning the whole business of Herzog and Abigail.

He thought of the first time he met Herzog in Henley Hall at the tennis-cum-birthday party and how Herzog had buttered him up. Herzog referred to his wife who was in Australia – OK, there was no reason why she shouldn't be there.

A bell rang in Caulfield's mind. What was going on?

Caulfield had been working in Emergency Admissions and a small boy with his father, had come in with a broken arm.

It turned out that the father was a brother of Isaac Herzog, who let it drop that Abigail was sick in a Melbourne Hospital.

Caulfield had never forgotten that dinner party and the radiance of Prudence; but his most vivid memory was of Herzog and his blazing eyes as Caulfield told a not very funny joke of a Jewish jeweller. *I'd hate to be,* as he thought then, *lost in the jungle with that man!*

He liked Herzog, who was basically straight, but he could be too smooth and there were times when half the truth was worse than a lie.

As they drove into Ballynale, Caulfield said, 'It was a bit of a coincidence, was it not, that the police got the message about McNight just seconds after you had been speaking to him.'

'Get into this hick town of yours,' replied Herzog, 'and tell them all what a smart fellow you are!'

'Don't be rude,' said Caulfield, getting out of the car with his case, 'I told them that years ago!'

CHAPTER 30

Home

It was fair day in Ballynale. Although livestock marts had put many fairs out of business, the Ballynale Fair fought a rear guard action against the curse of progress.

Caulfield felt safe in the quiet village, and even safer in the company of Aunt Hilda and Uncle Sam.

They were delighted to see him and ravenous for news. He supplied the latest intelligence on her nephew (his cousin) who was the minister in the family, also his two cousins (her daughters) Anna and Sarah. Then Hilda's sister, Mary, who taught Irish for thirty years, and who boasted for having slapped three bishops for inattention. Then their former neighbours: the two misses O'Dohertys, who, after they closed their shop in Ballynale, went to live in Clontarf. 'How are they?' asked Hilda. 'Very odd,' said Caulfield. 'I used to meet them when I went jogging in Clontarf. If I stopped to say hello, they would reply that they had no money for me, and what did I do with their dog, and complained that the gardai followed them everywhere.'

'Oh dear!' said Hilda.

'Do you know who I share room with?' asked Caulfield. 'Henley-Smith from Henley Hall.'

'A mighty lump of a lad,' said Uncle Sam.

'I heard some story about him,' said Hilda.

'I don't know the full story,' said Caulfield, 'but he had to leave the Navy.'

'Was there a scandal?' asked Hilda.

'No.'

'Really?' said Hilda, quite disappointed.

The fact that she was a regular church goer didn't mean that she didn't enjoy a scandal.

'Do you ever see the Commodore?' asked Caulfield.

'Now and then,' said Sam, 'a lot of the starch seems to have been knocked out of him. At one time he would sit up ram-rod straight, barking out his orders. Now he lounges back in his seat looking miserable.'

'He has a problem,' said Caulfield, 'and so does his son Henley-Smith. Sooner or later it shall be told,' he added, in sepulchral tones.

'I have been trying to get Henley-Smith into hard training. Murphy and I are the only two internationals from college. In fact, we are the only two internationals from Leinster. The two existing wingers, Elliot and Fitzpatrick are crocked. There is an outside chance Henley-Smith could make it.'

'Does he want it?' asked Uncle Sam.

'He does and he doesn't. If he did want it enough and got it, it would be the making of him.'

'The other fellow in our room, Kevin Murphy...' said Caulfield. He was about to continue when he noticed a dead silence, and then he knew, and he knew that they knew. Uncle Sam looked grim, Aunt Hilda looked sad.

'We believe he is a nice fellow,' said Uncle Sam.

'He is,' said Caulfield knowing that his answer was irrelevant. Niceness didn't come into it.

'And he is a rugby international with you?'

'Yes, and he is a feared man in four countries.'

Did it make a difference? thought Caulfield. *No, it didn't make tuppence worth of a difference.*

'How long have you known?' asked Hilda.

'For some time. Kevin didn't say anything except in a jokey sort of way, and Anna always seemed to be coming and going.'

'After a while it became obvious that when I saw one, the other seemed to be around.'

'Did you say anything to them?'

'I said to Anna, 'one day you will be walking a stony path'. I think she cried a bit.

Later I thought I should say something to Kevin. I did, and after three seconds he told me to shut up. 'We are grown up', he said, 'and we don't need lectures'.'

'You were only trying to help,' said Uncle Sam.

'Perhaps, but I wonder if anyone can help.'

'In my day,' said Aunt Hilda, 'mixed marriage was a greater sin than adultery – on both sides. I remember my father telling us girls that he would rather see us bringing home an illegitimate baby than a Catholic husband.'

Caulfield felt profoundly depressed. Kevin was his best friend, Anna was a beloved cousin. How could he come between them, and yet he felt keenly for Aunt Hilda and Uncle Sam. He shared in their grief and worry because it was inarticulate. They were simple and good people.

They just felt and wept.

Kevin was a fine man and would make a good husband, a good provider, the maker of a happy home.

It didn't matter.

Anna was a homemaker; her laughter would fill the house, a provider and moulder of her children.

It didn't matter.

The obscure tribalism which curses the Irish in different ways, which being invisible is strong, and even fanatical, will someday dissolve.

But not yet.

Uncle Sam gave Caulfield a push. 'Stop daydreaming.'

Caulfield pulled himself together. 'Sorry, I was thinking of them.'

Aunt Hilda came over to Caulfield and kneeled down at his chair.

'Dear Caulfield, thank you so much for all that you have meant to us, and for the way you kept an eye on Anna and Sarah in Dublin.'

Caulfield started to protest but Hilda put a finger on his lips.

'Yes, you did. And thank you for the way you can help Anna.' She smiled. 'Do you remember the way you used to say your prayers? You always mentioned Anna and Sarah. Amen and Amen. You used to say two Amens, one for Anna and one for Sarah.'

Caulfield tried to smile.

'In time,' he said, 'this problem will disappear.'

He went upstairs to his old room. It was all there. The bed, the bedside table with a bible on top, the lamp, the drawer in the table. Inside a photograph, slightly faded and creased.

For twenty-five years it had laid there, in the darkness of the drawer, like a ticking bomb, like a sore that would not heal, like a nagging tooth, like a worrying conscience.

For the umpteenth time, he looked at the photo. At the woman, she was his mother; at the man, was he his father? At the little boy - was he his brother? Was he to carry this burden forever?

Aunt Hilda called him for tea. It was just like the old days except Anna and Sarah were absent. Caulfield could tell, as he came down the stairs that they would have bacon and egg, griddle bread and cherry buns. After the statutory bread and jam, it finished off with chocolate cake.

The conversation followed a lazy path of chat about the new minister, the death of ninety-four year old Mr. Rafferty, the rector's wife who gave birth to twins, the sergeant's wife who scandalized the town about her carrying on with school boys, and the threat that the bank might close down its branch.

For Caulfield's part, he gossiped about the rugby and cricket team. How he played against Sir Ralph Webster-Brabazon's (the British Ambassador) Select XI. And the terrible trouble they had in not bowling out Sir Ralph Webster-Brabazon before he had scored at least thirty. The morning of the match (a great social occasion) officials of the Department of Foreign Affairs came over and warned the College Captain that a major diplomatic incident might be created if the Ambassador was bowled out at an early stage.

Caulfield told Aunt Hilda and Uncle Sam about his best athletic achievement, the low hurdles. The low hurdles, he explained, was not necessarily inferior to the high hurdles. Sheer speed was an advantage in low hurdles; in high the gifts were different. Aunt Hilda only understood about half of what he said, but she admired the modesty and hope of youth.

Caulfield spend the next two days revisiting his old haunts, and then duty called him back to college.

Caulfield decided to take Herzog at his word. He phoned and left a message with the expressionless male voice to organize a lift to Dublin.

'If you come early, Isaac, you can have some of my aunt's rack of lamb – genuine kosher'.

Herzog replied, 'Delighted to accept, but I absolutely refuse to pay.'

Uncle Sam and Aunt Hilda were astounded at the little man. Caulfield saw how he could turn on the charm, especially for Aunt Hilda. He compared her rack of lamb with that of his mother's, and compared his mother to Hilda.

'There is not a day,' he said, 'when I do not think of my mother. I lived for her, she lived for us. We men are weak; it is only women who can give us strength.

As he talked he wolfed down his rack of lamb and asked for a second helping. Uncle Sam was dazed at his excitable performance. Herzog turned to him as he might have been overlooked.

'Men like you are the backbone of the country, Mr. Sam; strong wives, strong religion, respect and faithfulness and a good neighbour to all.

Uncle Sam gulped.

'There is nothing greater, Mr. Sam, than two people who create a happy home.'

He turned to Aunt Hilda.

'I could sense it the moment I came in, Aunt Hilda – you have what money cannot buy, a good and a happy home.'

Hilda was nearly in tears. 'Thank you, Mr. Herzog!'

'Please call me Isaac.'

Over coffee, he glanced around the room and noticed the photograph of Anna and Sarah holding a large silver Hockey Cup.

'Your cousins?' he asked Caulfield.

'Yes, indeed. They are Sarah and Anna; the crowning moment of their school life.'

'The taller of the girls is Anna?' asked Herzog.

'Yes! How did you know?'

'Because I saw you one day in Nassau Street, lecturing her with some vigour. Really, Caulfield, you are too young to be pompous!' (*Laughter*) Herzog smiled. He had these people in the palm of his hand.

'Talking of Anna,' said Herzog, 'did I hear you say something about her working in public relations?'

'Yes,' said Caulfield, 'she works for Whipple, Ogster Heffernan.'

'I don't believe for one minute that anyone is called Ogster or Whipple, but give her this.' He handed over a business card. 'Tell her to come and see me. We might do some business.'

'Oh, thank you, Isaac!' said Aunt Hilda.

Herzog bid them well with an old world courtesy; he bowed to Hilda, 'The meal you get from a woman in her own home can never be equalled in a restaurant.'

As he left the room his hand rested on a large Bible. 'Ah, yes,' said Herzog, 'the Book of Books; we Jews and Christians live by this Book.'

'It was my grandfather's Bible,' said Hilda.

She almost wept.

Caulfield, overcome, forgot to say goodbye.

The Bentley purred silently away.

'How do you do it?' asked Caulfield.

'It's the oriental coming out of me; but I believe your Uncle Sam and Aunt Hilda are about the finest people I have met.'

'What about your own parents?'

'Change the subject,' said Caulfield.

The day was still bright although the chauffeur had put on his side lights; the big car ate up the miles.

'Regarding McNight,' began Herzog, 'the case is more or less closed. A witness saw him head for the water and was within a few feet of him as he went in. The witness telephoned the police and then disappeared.'

'And that witness was you.'

'The witness did his best to save him. End of story.'

'OK,' said Caulfield. 'I'll buy that story.'

'And now,' said Herzog, 'I want to know what McNight said to you outside that coffee shop on the night he died. The *whole* truth this time.'

Caulfield said, 'I will always remember his words: *the wife is no good, Herzog will make use of you, I don't like Herzog, be very careful.* I don't know what they all mean but I want an explanation before we complete our deal.'

Herzog seemed to collapse into the corner of the car; he breathed heavily and gave a little groan. The car stopped outside the college.

'Get out!' he said. 'I'll send for you when I need you.'

'I am not ready to get out,' said Caulfield. 'I have been thinking about McNight. What he said was not the raving of a mad man, he had something on you.'

'Get moving,' said Herzog to the chauffeur, 'drive anywhere.'

Caulfield continued, 'I can ignore what McNight said about you making use of me, and that he didn't like you. But he warned

312

me to be careful, and I didn't like what he said about Abigail. I didn't like it, and I can't ignore it.'

'That she was no good?'

Caulfield turned away from Herzog. 'I didn't say it.'

'Are you saying,' said Herzog, speaking very deliberately, 'that you agree with what he said when he called Abigail a prostitute?'

Caulfield violently shook his head. 'No, no, no! Please Isaac, don't even think that! You know she isn't and so do I. When McNight said she was no good it could mean anything. It could mean that she was – a – bad cook, for example.'

Herzog started to laugh. 'That proves it! Your Aunt Hilda is the best person in Ireland!'

Caulfield smiled weakly. 'Isaac, I have got to know the answer to this: why did Abigail keep going back to Australia?'

'It could be anything; she could have been going back to see her dentist.'

'You know it wasn't that.'

'Someday I will tell you all, but now I am tired. I will leave you back to college.'

Caulfield saw a great sadness in Herzog's face. He was worth millions; he had a car that Caulfield would never have; he had won all the prizes of life; he had everything and nothing.

Herzog longed for his father to come and rub his hands and say tenderly, *'Bentshn da zun'*

The car stopped in College Green and Caulfield opened the door. On an impulse, he grabbed Herzog and hugged him. 'We will meet again, Isaac,' and he left him.

Chapter 31

Microbes

Dun Laoghaire pier was the best walk in city or country. The surface of the pier was easy and pleasant to walk on. Dog droppings were relatively rare. There was little danger of putting one's foot through the twisted roots of a sapling, and the overrated pleasure of kicking piles of leaves was never indulged.

The air was clean and – well – airy. For city dwellers, the salty tang combined with the harsh crying of sea gulls, gave all a feeling of brisk good health.

It was impossible to be bored. The panorama of boats, yachts and dinghies provided an ever-changing pattern for the viewing public, and behind the harbour, were further delights of mountains and hills.

Nothing is ever perfect for long. Those of our benighted species might feel acutely uncomfortable if they met others that they knew while walking on the pier. Does the mature gentleman, soberly dressed, conservatively shod, his thinning hair cunningly and precisely laid across his cranium, show symptoms of anxiety? Do his eyes dart here and there, viewing the oncoming citizens, who apparently do not carry the burden of responsibility that he has. Who are these oncoming citizens, in the distance, now only as big as a hand?

Are they Uncle Tom and his wife Mary, or the bank manager and his daughter, perhaps the chap with a locker beside you in the golf club? The fellow down the road whose dog barks. Your barber, the milk man, the wife's maid.

It could be the over diplomatic rotter who sees and cheerily calls your name whilst completely overlooking Sandra, or is it the sanctimonious hypocrite who at the point of making eye contact, turns and points out the fascination of a train entering a station forty degrees to the right not noticing your presence or Sandra's.

The philosopher might consider why such an admirable citizen, whose affairs have never been brought to the attention of the Revenue Commissioners, who shows a sound set of opinions relating to politics and the social order, should show erratic behaviour while indulging in the simple matter of walking. The philosopher, being a man of ordinary talents and modest ambitions, has arrived at a conclusion that shook the scientific world, that two plus two equals four.

Now the sight of two together makes more than the sum of its parts.

Our citizen views all comings and goings. Is there anything unusual in the way he tends to walk three feet ahead of his walking partner, or on some occasions three feet behind?

The borough of Dun Laoghaire whose concern for the local citizens is a matter of public congratulation, has observed two unusual facts: that many walkers suddenly run to the side of the pier, turn their backs on the oncoming traffic, take off a shoe, and seek by banging same to dislodge a stone. This exercise can take up to five minutes.

Our town engineer is studying the phenomenon that there are no stones on the pier in the morning, and no stones at night. How then does a stone get into somebody's shoe during the day? The philosopher, who was called in for a second opinion, also commented on the number of nieces who walked on the pier with their uncles and who were later seen holding their hands in licensed premises.

***

315

Kevin Murphy brought Anna to Dun Laoghaire and, like a million couples before them, walked hand in hand down the pier. It was an almost perfect day.

They felt like an adulterous couple. They were not married, or even engaged. If they met friends there was a slight raising of the eyebrows. Nobody said or implied anything untoward. A civilized chat took place but, seconds after leaving, a grunted commentary would start and stop, and someone might indulge in a whistle.

They walked to the end of the pier and gazed out to sea. Kevin put his arm around Anna and pressed her into him. She did not resist. 'Kevin' was the only word she could say. They looked out at the sun setting on the horizon. Their faces were sombre.

They loved each other, but they also loved other people, they knew the pain they could cause other people. They sought desperately for a solution.

The weather was turning nippy and they walked back on the lower ramp of the pier. A man and his son were tying down their yacht.

Man: Will you tie down the canvas, Andy?
Boy: OK, Dad.
Man: Will we sail tomorrow?
Boy: Oh sure, Dad.
Man: Will we sail to America?
Boy: (laughing) Not yet, Dad.
Man: Some day, eh?
Boy: You bet, Dad!

They listened to the father and son talking, laughing and joking.

'That's the way it will be with us.'

This time she cried. Kevin had a phone call from Limerick. His father sounded matter of fact. Someone had seen Kevin with his girl, a pretty girl. Of course nobody has ever seen a fellow with an

316

unpretty girl. Father and mother were pleased, (so they said). You should bring her down to Limerick. (Oh sure.)

Question and question, except the one question.

Wait for the big question and give the big answer, or give no answer, which is the big answer.

Then the silence.

They met friends on the street, in the café, the shop, the bus. Marvellous! Terrific! they cry. So happy for you, the big date? Nothing as vulgar as asking about religion.

Just a simple, where did he/she go to school? *Oh – silence – ah.*

Anna and Kevin were enraged by well meaning platitudes. *There's no problem. We are all Christians, what's the problem? Let the children decide, there's no difference, we all have the same God, there's no problem.*

In their hearts they thought; we have at home a father, and a mother, uncles and aunts, priest and minister, church and chapel, harvest services and holy days, Sunday school and Corpus Christi, Epiphany and Little Christmas.

There's no difference, except the difference.

***

Anna and Kevin walked up Haten Road; they remembered that a girl from the office, Nan Pride, lived here and they called.

'We were inspecting the pier,' said Kevin genially. 'I am sure it will last another year.' There were smiles and a welcome all around.

It was an old fashioned household, Mrs. Pride brought in an old fashioned supper. Small scones with dabs of raspberry jam, swiss roll cake and plain biscuits. Mr. Pride wore his slippers, smoked comfortingly on his pipe, and nodded and puffed in time with Kevin's pontifications. Beside him lay the *Radio Times*, a rock of safety in a darkling world.

Their son, at homework, frowned into his algebra book Kevin was tempted to offer help with his equations, but he let it go.

The Prides felt comfortable and safe. Their world was solid. Abroad the dictators were ranting, unions in the country were always looking for more, but the government was steady, they knew what they were doing.

Kevin and Anna were asked where they came from. Limerick and Tipperary were inevitably given. Mr. Pride was well satisfied. He knew the counties. Two good counties, sound people, both counties, the finest people, decent people. Very decent.

They went home.

***

Dr Jellett chaired the meeting and introduced the distinguished visitor, Dr Hector Fassenberger.

The occasion was the Annual Harold Ferguson Memorial Lecture, in memory of a long-forgotten alumnus, one Harold Ferguson, MD... The learned doctor had pioneered the study of yellow fever and earned his doctorate on the thesis, "Yellow Fever: Prevention and Cure".

Dr Jellett surveyed the assembled audience and within a few seconds could estimate who was absent. Those misguided enough to enjoy alternative entertainment could expect a certain rigour in the marking of their next examination paper.

The late Ferguson's family had made money out of nickel mining in Canada and left a fortune to the college on condition that a memorial lecture was held annually, with the complete medical school in attendance.

Dr Jellett cleared his throat and stood up. The murmurs of conversation died away.

The show was on the road.

'Ladies and Gentlemen, I have pleasure in introducing Dr Hector Fassenberger, Head of Clinical Pathology in Melbourne University.'

Caulfield didn't move. The bell that rang before was to ring again. What was it that made him involuntarily hold his breath and sit in absolute stillness? Caulfield pondered on the sinister roll call: Melbourne, Abigail, Australia, Herzog, microbes, McNight, Dr Jellett.

Fassenberger was pale in appearance and slightly built, and coughed delicately from time to time.

'Ladies and Gentlemen,' he cried, 'Fellow doctors, Members of the Senate of Dublin University – greetings.'

He put his hands into his pockets and then took them out. He looked around the hall and coughed once or twice, as if he had forgotten what to say.

'I am going to...' he hesitated. 'I am going...' he stopped and looked up at the ceiling. His lips moved but no sound came forth.

Dr Jellett frowned. Had he lost his notes or his speech? What was the matter with him?

Caulfield was also puzzled. Was this part of his act, or was he simply unwell? Did he forget where he was, or had he over-imbibed at lunch? He felt vaguely sorry for the man and wished he could bring it to an end.

Then Fassenberger started to speak; his voice was low and virtually inaudible beyond the front row. It gathered some strength as he talked and Caulfield could hear some words and then some sentences. With growing confidence the speaker took a step forward and then another one back; he even held up his hand to make a point.

Dr Jellett relaxed; they would get through this lecture somehow.

'The esteemed Harold Ferguson,' said Fassenberger, 'who died almost a century ago eliminated Yellow Fever in the tropics. It was never a problem in this country.' He waited for the expected laugh;

319

for some reason it raised the roof when he lectured in Melbourne, but here in Dublin it was met with an indifferent silence.

He ploughed on.

'My speciality is venereal disease, known as syphilis. I suppose it is not a problem in this country?' He waited for the laugh.

The laugh never came, Fassenberger began to panic. Again, he put his hands in his pockets and took them out. Everyone waited; eventually he continued.

'Do you know that venereal disease destroyed the Roman Empire?' He looked at the audience – apparently they didn't know.

'The Legions collapsed,' he went on, 'because an invisible microbe did what the Persians, Turks and Germanic tribes could not do.'

In the audience a faint sigh was heard; a man whispered to a woman, who giggled. Dr Jellett glared down the hall and wrote a name into a notebook.

'The women who followed the legions were known as camp followers; they were a bigger threat to the Empire than spies or the chariots of the Arabs. Their weapon, deadly on themselves and on their clients, was a microbe.'

Dr Jellett looked astonished as Fassenberger suddenly walked over to him.

'I can't continue,' he whispered.

'My dear Fassenberger, would you like to sit down? Perhaps a glass of water…?'

'Thank you so much,' said Fassenberger. He drank some water.

The audience moved uneasily on their seats; they had no idea of his indisposition.

Caulfield was not feeling well either. Although the doors and windows were open the air was stuffy, and many of the audience were tempted to slip out. Some had heard the lecture before.

Dammit! thought Caulfield, *why can't he get on with it?* His clothes were feeling sticky and his feet sweated. *Thanks for nothing to the distinguished visitor.*

'I remember when I was in the Panama Canal the natives were dropping like flies. That's what I said, the Panama Canal... Oh, I am sorry, it wasn't the Panama Canal, it was...' he struggled to find the word, 'the Corinthian Canal, was it? Perhaps it was the Manchester Ship Canal?'

The audience horse-laughed, but their hearts were not in it. Dr Jellett looked dismayed.

Caulfield felt a headache coming on. He hadn't a meal for two days, and he began to shiver. His head buzzed and he felt dizzy.

He saw Herzog going up to the dais; M‘Night crept up, hiding behind a grand piano. What could he do? He shouted Abigail. Everyone was calling; they were on their feet and pointing their fingers at Caulfield.

Jellett and Fassenberger ignored the taunts and they kept on talking. Herzog wept. Fassenberger changed the subject. He was talking about gonorrhoea. Caulfield could not believe it. The man took off his trousers and exposed himself to the nurses who shrieked and fainted. Caulfield drew the attention of Jellett to this – he did nothing except cadge Herzog for cigarettes.

Then Caulfield saw a figure. It was Abigail. What a wonderful woman; how he loved her passionately. She was running across the Melbourne Cricket pitch in a storm of green and purple microbes. Jellett was shouting now (at least he would do something) but he was being attacked by enormous wasps; he wrote down all their names in a notebook.

It was quiet at last. The students lay down on the ground in a deadly silence. Caulfield rose to speak and held up his hands. 'My little children, these things I write onto you that you sin not.' Immediately the students erupted as one and headed for the door. They roared hideously and screamed to get out of the building.

Women and children were trampled underfoot. Caulfield was threatened and pelted with prunes.

'Ah ha, Caulfield!' said McNight. He took off his cravat and waved and waved and the bees came in greater numbers. Kevin was on the ground covered in black babies.

'Caulfield,' he cried, 'help me!' but they came in greater numbers. The black babies were six feet deep, covering an area of two tennis courts.

The noise fell away. He was sitting peacefully in his seat in the lecture Hall. A few students stood round him, looking concerned. He had almost fallen on top of a woman – it was Michal. She smiled at him and surprisingly she kissed him. 'Thank you,' said Caulfield, 'what a lovely thing to do.'

Assisted by Michal and some of the students he pushed himself out of the hall. The fresh air revived him but then the front square began to spin around; his legs felt weak and …it was night.

***

Voices from a distance. An authoritative female voice giving orders. A voice like Henley-Smith's was querulously asking questions. Kevin's voice was close and then faded away and disappeared. Caulfield faintly saw different coloured balloons that melted into nothingness and then returned in obscene shapes like grinning microbes. His bare arm was pricked and he grimaced as a hot needle plunged into the muscle of his arm. He sank back into the darkness.

He came to, and found himself in his own bed. His eyes focused and he tried to make out the time. Four o'clock – it was either morning or afternoon. He staggered out of bed and went to the window, looking down on the front square. His legs felt watery; what was the matter with him?

The square was deserted and asleep; so it was morning. Caulfield felt angry with himself. He had always been proud of his athleticism and fitness; he seldom had a day's sickness, At the peak of his manliness, he was now trembling before the onslaught to his mental and moral being. *If only I stayed in Ballynale I could have lived a cleaner life.* Look at Aunt Hilda and Uncle Sam, how much he admired them, how much he loved them. He remembered the stories Uncle Sam used to tell him when he was tucked up in bed. And how much Herzog had admired them. He thought of that girl, Michal – could she help him? *Whatever I want, I can't do it on my own.* He went back to bed.

***

The room was shaded by Venetian blinds; one window was clear and open and Caulfield could see through to the roofs of adjoining buildings. *Are the roofs of Dublin similar to the roofs of Paris,* thought Caulfield, *the Parisian roofs about which the poets sing, the artists starve and the sophomores from Duluth or New Jersey clasp their hands in ecstasy?*

'Mr Caulfield!'

He sat up. 'Sorry I was day-dreaming.'

The doctor smiled indulgently. 'We can all daydream.'

'I was dreaming about the roofs of Paris.'

The doctor was unimpressed. He scribbled a note into his file.

'You were about to tell me about your mother. Many problems derive from mothers.'

'I haven't seen my mother for twenty years. She handed me over to my father's care when I was three, and then got rid of both of us. He came back from Africa in a state of collapse and was sent into a home. I got to see him every Christmas but he doesn't know me.'

The doctor spoke softly. 'Can you remember, was this a great shock to you?'

'I don't think I felt it. My uncle and aunt took me in. They were, and still are, wonderful. My old life in Africa seemed to fade away.'

'I find it strange that you remember nothing. Even at the age of three something should remain. The fact that you felt no shock might mean that you succeeded in burying it.'

Caulfield said nothing. The doctor waited. Why should he say anything about his father? He was six years old before the truth started filtering through. Unconsciously, he clenched his fist and tapped the side of his chair. The doctor watched.

'There was a thing about my father, but it has nothing to do with my problem.'

Caulfield stopped; he knew he had given it away, now he had to finish it. 'The thing is, I'm not too sure who my father is. I know who my mother is, she is the one who went native in Ghana; she left my father for an African. But who is my father? Is he an African, or is he a man in a mental institution? He could also be a miner in the Ashanti gold mines.'

'Surely not?' asked the doctor.

'Sometimes I think I am too tall to be an Irishman, and those mines are run by white South Africans.'

Caulfield gritted his teeth; he grasped the arm-rests of his chair and the doctor noted the intensity of his speech.

'It's no fun not to know who one's father is. Even the worst is better than nothing.'

'Not so,' said the doctor. He looked through his notes and made alterations. 'From what you have told me, you are under pressure from many sources. Your final examination is coming up; you are feeling the pinch as you are effectively an orphan; you are coming to the end of your career in athletics, which was your life for so many years – it's a lot to worry about. You haven't said anything about your relationship with women, which potentially can be a major source of angst.' The doctor paused. 'Do you wish to consider this factor?'

Caulfield shook his head.

'Are there any financial problems?' asked the doctor.

'I am as rich as any medical student.' They both smiled.

'As one doctor to another potential doctor, you know that I am bound to absolute discretion so you should free to tell me about the women in your life.'

For the first time, Caulfield brightened up. 'I was madly in love when I was seventeen. I was an ordinary country fellow who was good at tennis. She was straight out of Debrett. There will never be another one like her; although I have a new girl who is very nice and I will probably see her again. There will never be one like Prudence. I will always carry that space in my heart for her. She said to a friend that when she was old she would remember me as the Galahad she loved. As for me, when I am a cantankerous old man I will remember the princess who was radiant at sixteen.'

As Caulfield spoke the tears welled up in his eyes and then fell, almost silently. For five minutes he wept for the days that could never be recalled.

The doctor sat in silence. He knew the tears would have a healing effect and would temporarily relieve Caulfield from the tensions that bound him.

When Caulfield finally dried his eyes he asked the doctor, 'Can I ever be released from this curse?'

'Absolutely, yes! You may carry this around with you for a lifetime. It's there; it will be part of you as the colour of your eyes. But it will be controlled and your life will be perfectly normal.' The doctor wrote out a prescription. 'This will get you out of jail! However, I think there is more to say – especially about your relationship with women…' the doctor smiled at Caulfield, '…but I won't press you on that now.'

Caulfield felt grateful to the doctor who had given him hope and had shown sympathy at a dark time. As he walked back to college he remembered the doctor's advice: 'Get fit' he was told, 'do a two-mile jog in Clontarf; take your medication and come and see me again.'

I think I will call and take this Michal for a walk, thought Caulfield, *the sun is coming out. It will be a lovely evening.*

Chapter 32

O'Mahoney

The sensation of McNight passed away, and Caulfield returned to his studies. He continued to place himself under the care of his Doctor and his panic attacks subsided.

Caulfield and Murphy were invited to lunch by the celebrated O'Mahoney.

O'Mahoney said, 'Perhaps you could shave a week before the dinner and, if it wasn't pushing it too much, how about an inch or two off your nails?'

They considered the matter gravely, made inquiries regarding O'Mahoney's ancestry, and accepted.

O'Mahoney played an influential if obscure part in the Irish Rugby Union. He was not an executive, or a blazer, but he had perfected the art of getting in the way of important decisions, and was considered invaluable when it came to resisting anything that looked like progress.

Despite this he was an amiable fellow and, because of his shareholding in the distillery that bore his name, the reputation of Irish hospitality was held in high esteem in rugby playing countries.

One of his phobias was that the selection of members for international duty should be selected from twelve clubs (no more).

This was agreed enthusiastically by the twelve clubs, but treated with considerable reserve by the remaining forty or so.

O'Mahoney was never elected to any office in the union; in fact he never stood for any, and contented himself with being generally indispensable.

They met O'Mahoney in Jurys. Although not the same as the Shelbourne, it had the unmistakable rugby ambience, being at the other end of Lansdowne Road.

'What are we here for?' said Murphy,

'It's money, whiskey or women,' remarked Caulfield.

'It's not women, I have the only one I want. As for money, if offered I will take it reluctantly.'

'The instincts of a gentleman!' murmured Caulfield.

O'Mahoney appeared. He waved and ushered them toward the bar.

'Murphy, Caulfield! You are welcome.'

He was mine host writ large.

'We can never refuse free food,' said Murphy.

'You are welcome to the free food,' he cried, and waving a glass of O'Mahoney twelve year old, 'all you have to cover is the drink.'

Murphy and Caulfield laughed a little apprehensively.

'Very kind of you to ask us out,' said Caulfield.

However O'Mahoney was a man of generous impulses, he was that sort of man beloved by the Irish, always the first to stand a round.

'We are going to have some lunch,' said he, 'and then we will talk some serious stuff.' The meal as usual was uninteresting but substantial.

O'Mahoney being a man of means was given to standing dinners. He developed to a fine art how to use hospitality to cultivate friends and influence.

His few critics were forced to admit that the guiding force in his life was rugby football, and the rugby of some years ago.

'You two fellows represent the very best in the game,' he said to them.

'Do you remember,' he said to Murphy 'the match against the Welsh, we defended for five minutes, maybe six? How many tackles did you stop them with?'

'Eleven or twelve.'

'Eleven or twelve,' repeated O'Mahoney. 'Horatio on the bridge had nothing like it.'

Murphy shook his head. 'Could I do it this year, I doubt it.'

O'Mahoney punched his arm.

'You have two good years left.'

He looked at Caulfield.

'How many years have you left in the game?'

'One year,' said Caulfield.

O'Mahoney looked thoughtful.

'You may be right. This Nolan chap in Lansdowne is hard to keep down.'

'He is a very fine player,' said Caulfield.

'Remember,' went on O'Mahoney, 'you have one thing he hasn't yet.'

Caulfield looked at him.

'Memory; a lot of people I talk to will not forget that try against France two years ago. You collected the ball under your own goal post, you ran virtually two lengths of the field and touched down under the French goal post.'

'There are tries,' said Caulfield dreamily, 'and THE TRY.'

Caulfield pressed his fork into the table cloth. It made nice parallel lines.

The questions buzzing in his head were, *what are we doing here? What does this man want? Next thing we will be on about is the playing fields of Eton.*

'When I was a kid,' said O'Mahoney, I remember reading in a school book, the very English words that ended:

'Play up, play up
And play the game.'

'Do you look back to your school days as happy days?'

'Very,' said Caulfield. 'To coin a new phrase, they were the happiest days of my life.'

Murphy looked at Caulfield. Fortunately he did not know the Eton Boating Song.

'Some years ago,' said O'Mahoney, 'I proposed at the AGM that the international team should be selected from the top twelve clubs, or twelve oldest clubs. I was in earnest.'

'I read about it,' said Caulfield. 'It was never a starter. Even fifty years ago it would have been so-so.'

'Right,' said Murphy.

'Those clubs,' continued O'Mahoney 'would have had the muscle and prestige to push it through. All that was lacking was a driving force.'

He waited for a response, but none came. Murphy and Caulfield looked blank.

'It would have brought Irish rugby back to the great old days. Particularly to the time when thirteen Irishmen beat fifteen.

O'Mahoney's eyes glistened.

'There were giants in the land in those days. We walked off that field and Twickenham rose to us. That was sportsmanship. I would love to replay that match, but times have changed.'

Caulfield was reluctant.

'We can't go back.'

'That's the oldest cliché in the business,' said O'Mahoney, 'but people do go back, and times need not change.'

He glared at them. But seeing their dejected mien, relented.

'OK fellows, we will leave it. Tell us instead how by much we are going to beat the old enemy.'

They had second helpings, and it seemed clear that O'Mahoney had another dog's bone to chew.

'In the past, not so far away,' said O'Mahoney, 'it's not generally known that a certain influence was brought to bear on who was selected for international honours.'

'Now I knew how I was selected,' said Murphy.

'Why did you have to tell us?' moaned Caulfield.

O'Mahoney laughed on cue.

'We had a system,' he went on, 'for the so-called big five selectors, two from Leinster and Ulster and one from Munster. They were susceptible to being advised.'

'You were not slow to advise.'

'Exactly,' said O'Mahoney. 'These selectors were ex internationals and consequently not over-endowed with grey matter.'

Caulfield said to Murphy, 'Murphy we better quit when we are still ahead.'

Everyone laughed.

'We always feel sorry for these selectors. Most of them had played one match too many.'

'Ha, ha, ha.'

'It was the golden era of string-pulling and they were pathetically grateful for any advice you could give.'

'Being the Christian you are, you were not slow to pick the team for them.'

'Are we not here on Earth to help our fellow man?'

O'Mahoney looked beatifically to the ceiling. Murphy and Caulfield bowed their heads. O'Mahoney continued.

'We had a sort of rule of thumb. We picked three from the universities, five each from Ulster, Leinster and two from Munster. If Munster started moaning, we might give them one of the university places. There was a sort of a dispensation for Ulster.

'Four out of five had to be Prods. We made an exception once or twice, particularly if an RC had a father in the British Army. Then we had two RCs, and we could have a problem in keeping them apart in the scrum.

331

'Another time, a promising scrum half out of Ulster threatened to push the proportion out of control, but we got a tip off that he was non-practising. So he got in, but only just.

'It was tricky enough as well in Munster, where not having a Limerick player could cause a civil disturbance.

'The attitude of the crowd had changed. Remember the silence when the place kickers lined up to take a kick? Now they roar like banshees trying to upset the kicker.'

Murphy said, 'That's not a big thing. The kickers always say that a dead silence is worse than a roaring noise.'

Caulfield agreed.

'I don't care,' said O'Mahoney, 'it's the motive that matters!' His voice was getting angry. Caulfield and Murphy were making no effort to be agreeable.

'We and Scotland were always proud of the number of professional men on the team.' He pointed his finger at Murphy.

'Ours came from the twelve schools/twelve clubs. Get it?'

Murphy got it. He nodded dully.

When would this crank give up? He looked at Caulfield. He was examining intently the pattern on his coffee cup.

'We were playing Scotland at Murrayfield. McAfee of Scotland – a great friend of mine delightedly told me, that they had five lawyers on their team. 'Is that so?' I said, 'we have six doctors.''

He punched Caulfield playfully. 'McAfee turned pale. He didn't speak to me for hours.'

'Now,' continued O'Mahoney, 'let's go back to the twelve top schools. It was simple in the old days.'

Murphy was ready to take him on.

'Why was it simple?' he asked.

'Simple. The twelve schools you know who they are, you went to one of them. They made you what you are.'

'Across the world those twelve schools are better known than the counties of Ireland. Do you know what those twelve schools have been called?'

Caulfield and Murphy shook their heads. Both men in open debate would have dismissed O'Mahoney out of hand. But they were fascinated to hear more.

'They have been called the 'Jewels in the Crown' of Irish rugby.'

O'Mahoney sat back. He had those men tied up. They had gone to these traditional schools which were traditional boarding and rugby schools, then on to a most traditional college, which along with the schools were out-and-out rugby dominated. They could not deny what they felt in their bones.

'Those were the days!' said O'Mahoney wiping his eyes.

'Unfortunately, we can't go back.' said Caulfield again.

'Fortunately, we can.' said O'Mahoney.

They looked at him.

'And that is why I am having you to lunch.'

Murphy and Caulfield looked at each other with surprise.

'Are you softening us up to tell that we are being dropped?'

'It happens to all of us sooner or later,' said O'Mahoney portentously. Then seeing their crest fallen faces, he smiled and punched them on their shoulders.

'Don't worry,' he cried, 'it's not you fellows. Maybe in five years time.'

They relaxed.

'That is the unfunniest joke of the year,' growled Murphy.

'Now listen to me, there is another problem. We have a problem in the back line, Fitzpatrick and Elliot, are out injured. Admittedly Fitzpatrick can be as thick as a ditch, but he will be hard to replace. The other wings in Ulster and Munster are clodhoppers, no damn good to anyone. There is one player and it's worth looking at him.'

He looked at Caulfield and then at Murphy. Caulfield furrowed his brow as he went down a list of possibles. It was Murphy who spoke.

'You must be mistaken.'

'Name a better one,' said O'Mahoney.

Caulfield finally got it. 'Henley-Smith!' he gasped.

Murphy looked away in disgust.

'You have it all wrong. Anyone would be better.'

O'Mahoney shook his head.

'Have another look.'

Caulfield spoke thoughtfully.

'He had a useful game last Saturday.'

'Do you think he could mark Bleddyn Davies?'

'Nobody could.'

The luncheon party sank into reflective silence.

'We have little choice.'

O'Mahoney continued. 'Could you fellows not put some fire in his belly? He has the speed and the strength, all he wants...'

'All he wants is to stop being yellow,' burst out Murphy.

'You have said it!' said O'Mahoney. 'Can you fellows do it? Can you scare him into it?'

Caulfield spoke quietly. 'I would like to try.'

O'Mahoney droned on.

'You have to give him credit for one thing. He learned his game in a school that was not for pot hunters.'

Murphy laughed and grabbed O'Mahoney's arm.

'You are hurting my arm.'

'So you went to Stonyhurst?' asked Murphy.

'Yes, and I am proud of it.'

'And that's the place,' said Murphy, 'that takes decent, thick Paddies, and turns them into little Englanders.'

'That could be a great improvement,' said O'Mahoney.

'And,' said Murphy, 'we can walk off the pitch on Saturday week, beaten hollow, but all singing:

> 'Play up, play up
> And play the game.''

Chapter 33

Michal

Caulfield and his fellow students followed the learned and respected Dr. Jellet down the antiseptic corridors of the hospital.

The hospital was a triumph of Victorianism and Caulfield loved every piece of it.

He had grown up as a student doctor within its walls. It was his home from home.

He had the feeling that as he listened to the learned doctor, that somebody was watching.

Somebody was. It was Michal McMaster.

'Well hello,' he said. It was the most original thing he could think of.

'How are you?' he asked as they later walked through St. Stephen's Green.

She smiled and held his hand.

'Such a lovely day,' he enthused.

She linked his arm.

'Are you safe?' he asked one day as he rowed a boat out of Greystones Harbour.

Her eyes said it all.

'You have lovely toes,' he said later, as he dribbled a handful of sand over her bare feet.

'One flower for another,' He whispered as he pinned a rose to her coat.

'What do you say?' he asked.

'I will,' she said.

'Thank you, darling,' he said.

Michal was his and he loved her. The struggle of the years was over. A contentment possessed him. A new period in his life took hold. A happiness that was real and living.

Aunt Hilda was ecstatic; Uncle Sam gruffly approved. The engagement was in the paper, and strangers rushed to shake hands as they walked through Ballynale.

After morning service the congregation ignored the minister, and queued up to wish the couple good luck.

Henley-Smith phoned. He wanted them over for Sunday lunch. 'I am not cycling,' joked Caulfield, 'I'm too old.'

'Bring Uncle and Aunt, and they will have to give you a lift.'

On the journey over Caulfield fell silent as they passed over Barney's bridge.

There were some things that he was not ready to speak about.

In Henley Hall the reception was warm. Caulfield fell silent again, memories crashed in, but yesterday memories. Today was today.

There was a surprise. Henley introduced his girl, not yet fiancée, one Madeleine O'Herlihy. She was tall, reserved but cordial, spoke in the Dublin upper class way. 'A distant cousin', she said about Henley-Smith.

'From about three hundred years ago,' she added, smiling.

'Of course! We've met,' said Caulfield. 'At cricket in College Park. How much did you score that day, Henley-Smith?'

'Let's go into lunch,' he said.

***

They were in their rooms. Murphy was desultorily cramming for his final. Caulfield was getting his things together. He would soon get rooms in a hospital. Henley-Smith looked down at the goings on of the quad with a total lack of interest.

Murphy and Caulfield exchanged looks. Caulfield pointed to Henley-Smith's back, but Murphy shook his head. It wasn't his day for playing the Good Samaritan. Caulfield took a deep breath.

'By the way, Henley-Smith, that was a good game on Saturday.'

Henley-Smith didn't reply.

'You left O'Neill standing.'

Henley-Smith made a grunting sound. It could have meant anything.

'Are you training for the cup matches?'

Another grunt.

Murphy smiled broadly, and silently clapped his hands.

Curse him, thought Caulfield. *If he won't talk, what can I do?* As if responding, Henley-Smith left the window and went outside to the landing. They heard his steps as he went downstairs.

'That's that,' said Murphy with some glee. 'We gave him a pressing invitation to play for his country and he left with his nose in the air.'

'It's your turn next time.'

Caulfield ran down the steps after Henley-Smith. He thought he saw him with Madeleine, as they left the college grounds.

To his surprise he walked into Herzog.

'Hello stranger!' said Herzog. 'Congratulations and all that. When is the execution?'

He meant his wit for the best, but he succeeded only in irritating Caulfield.

'Soon, soon,' he grumbled, 'but at the moment I am looking for Henley-Smith.'

'You missed him; he walked by with a cool figure in grey tweed. I was furious, he had absolutely no time for me. Who does he think he is anyway?'

'It's a disgrace,' agreed Caulfield, 'but the figure in tweed is a person of some importance. She possibly will become Mrs. Madeleine Henley-Smith and she is not to be trifled with.'

'I thought I knew her,' said Herzog. 'She used to be the Girl Friday of a Mr. Anderson, the stock broker. She caused me some grief in my day.'

They stood on the busy footpath of College Green, occasionally having to hold on to the railings to prevent being knocked over.

'We must sit down and finish our talk,' went on Herzog. 'Your big football match will be next week, and it might be your last game.'

'How did you know?'

'People talk,' said Herzog.

'I have the price of two pints in my pocket,' said Caulfield. 'If you are nice to me I will let you purchase the next two pints. Provided you buy the first two pints and I will therefore have the option on the next two at a time and place of my choosing.'

'Splendid. Let's go!'

Herzog stopped. 'Could you say that again?'

'Keep moving,' urged Caulfield. 'This place is full of pickpockets.'

They ended, as many people do, in Byrnes. Caulfield looked gloomily at the top of his glass. 'I won't be coming in here much more. College days will be over; rugby days are coming to a close. I have signed up the prettiest girl in the hospital, and I have to keep her happy.'

He pondered for a while. 'I think she will keep me happy.'

'We all have that job, Caulfield, and you have a better chance than most,' said Herzog. Then after a pause, 'I have to ask you Caulfield, what has happened with you know what?'

'You mean my step-brother in Ghana?'

'Yes.'

'You tell me how I stand with the beautiful Abigail.'

'The offer is still open,' said Herzog. 'We both have thought deeply.'

'*The offer is open!*' said Caulfield. 'You make it sound like a container-load of grapefruit.'

Caulfield stretched out his hand onto Herzog's arm.

'Sorry,' he said. 'I didn't mean it like that.'

Herzog's face was angry.

'Don't ever speak like that again!'

'I won't,' said Caulfield. 'Let's say one thing at a time. She knows everything. I told my girl everything. And then I asked her, 'Will you?' She said, 'I will.' I asked if she still loved me. She said, 'I do.'

'I asked her what she would do if she had a brown baby. She said if it was our baby she would love it. She said if it was a black baby, she would love it. She said if it was any sort of a baby, she would love it and love me. I told her I would always love her.

'We prayed that day, that we would be blessed with a healthy baby. We didn't specify colour.'

Herzog listened. All the anger had left him.

'Did you tell her about Abigail?'

'No,' said Caulfield. 'How could I? That's something I could not tell her. No woman could accept that. It goes against everything they believe in a man.'

'What you say is true,' said Herzog, 'but sometimes a thing is so true that it fails to make sense.'

'You have left me behind,' said Caulfield.

'In Africa people own and share everything in their village. We would say you can't take my spade or cooking pot, but to the natives it's theirs. They just take it.'

'And wives are like cooking pots?' asked Caulfield

'More or less,' said Herzog. 'There is a sort of exception, wives and cows are owned by the chief.'

The two men sat at the bar cogitating on the oddities of human nature.

Caulfield finally spoke. 'I think this would be a hard sell to put over our women. I think we should stick to our present system.'

Herzog agreed. 'I never cared much for cattle anyway, not to mention cooking pots.'

'Does Abigail fully know what the odds are?'

'No, but neither do you. It's impossible to guess what the result will be. It might not be the next generation. It could be the fifth or tenth or never. One thing is certain... it will never go away. It will lie waiting to strike, or *not* to strike!'

'Where did you learn all this?' asked Caulfield.

'Your Professor Wertheim spent a weekend with us. Sorry, we did not ask you, but there was no point.'

'Did Abigail talk to him?'

'All the time.'

'There's always a danger that Abigail and I become involved.'

'No danger,' said Herzog.

'You are pretty sure of yourself.'

'Absolutely.'

Caulfield gave a little laugh.

'You have a good brain, but let's face it you are not Casanova.'

'I am not thinking of that,' said Herzog, 'but I have a friend called Drofinan. He is not subject to the laws of this country so we do favours for each other. Two of his staff were over here after McNight died.'

'And they spoke to me in the coffee shop,' said Caulfield. 'Now I get it!'

'You get it,' said Herzog. 'Now listen to me, you promised me an answer immediately.'

'There *will* be an answer,' Caulfield assured him.

'You have seven days,' said Herzog. 'We have waited long enough. We are not waiting any longer.'

They ordered another two beers.

Herzog heard footsteps behind him that sounded familiar.

It was Madeleine, and she was with Henley-Smith.

Herzog affected a pained reception. 'Why do you have to follow me into pubs all the time?'

'Actually I have come to fancy your gin and tonics. I'll have another one, thanks very much.'

'Listen to her,' he said to the two men 'what nerve, considering that she sacked me out of Anderson Stock Brokers.'

The barman put up a gin and tonic.

'Who ordered that?' said Herzog.

'You did,' answered Madeleine. 'Thanks.'

Caulfield grinned. 'She is well able for you, Herzog! We will come back later to pick up the bits of you that are left over.'

He spoke to Henley-Smith.

'What do you mean by running away? Murphy and I wanted to talk to you an hour ago. Come on back to our rooms.'

Henley-Smith looked uncertain.

'Come on this way.' Caulfield pushed him out.

***

Herzog looked quizzically at Madeleine.

'He went quietly, didn't he? Like a lamb to the slaughter.'

She raised her eyebrows.

'And he is the man you are going to marry?'

'Very likely, most likely. Almost certainly. Any day now.'

'Just say 'maybe''.

She didn't reply, but fiddled with the ice cubes in her glass.

'Why will you marry him?'

'What cheek, how dare you! Actually I will marry him, because he asked me.'

'He has two thousand five hundred acres of the best land, a fine mansion, socially prominent, right?'

'I suppose so.'

'In other words, he wants to marry his mother.'

She did not reply

'And that's the reason against. And if he wants to marry his mother it doesn't leave space for a wife.'

'You are great,' said Madeleine, 'at selling people short.'

'Think about it,' said Herzog. 'I am no psychologist, but you want a man who is a winner; you don't want a man who is a coward and gets fired from the Navy for being one.'

Madeleine sat up straight on her bar stool.

'What do you mean, what do you know?'

'Nothing,' said Herzog. 'I know the right man for you.'

'Hurry up and tell me!' gasped Madeleine.

'He is absolutely perfect for you,' went on Herzog. 'He is a liar, a cheat and a thief.'

'No good,' said Madeleine with a sweet smile, 'you are married already.'

'Not funny. This man is Jacob, the son of Isaac and he is his mother's favourite son.

It's fantastic, is it not?'

'What are you talking about?' she asked.

'Genesis,' said Herzog. 'It's a truly wonderful coincidence. You worked for Jacob

Anderson, he was the son of Isaac and his mother's name was… what?'

Madeleine bit her lip. 'It was Rebecca.'

'Jacob was no saint; he was a liar, a cheat and a thief. And yet he was a giant in history. Jacob Anderson is a giant. Marry a giant and not a milk pudding.'

'It's unbelievable,' said Madeleine, 'after all you two have done. You have fought like cats, and you want to send me back to him. He would kill you if he could.'

'I don't think so. Jacob Anderson is a bigger man than you think.

Anderson will never forgive you. He is a great hater.'

'Madeleine, tell me. Has he asked you to marry him?'

Madeleine didn't reply. Then she said, 'Yes.'

'And Henley-Smith wants to marry you, or thinks he wants to.'

'Yes. I've heard what you said. Henley-Smith is not a genius, he is not what you call a giant, but he has decency and kindness.'

'Madeleine, do something with me. Next Saturday Henley-Smith will be playing rugby for Ireland. Come with me, and after the match make your decision.'

Madeleine shook her head. 'I'll be going, but not with you. I'll have another gin and tonic.'

***

Henley-Smith looked resentful as Caulfield pushed him into their rooms.

'What the hell is all this about?' Murphy was apologetic.

'Caulfield went over the top. Sorry about it.'

'You are sorry. He is sorry. I don't know which of you is the greater hypocrite.'

'Look, I said we were sorry. But there is a very good reason. We have to have an answer first thing in the morning.'

'Like hell!' said Henley-Smith.

'Just listen,' said Caulfield. A silence fell over the room. Henley-Smith yawned and appeared to go to sleep.

'It's like this,' said Murphy, 'we have been asked by a man called O'Mahoney. Do you know him?'

Henley-Smith shook his head.

'It appears he went to Stonyhurst.'

'I have it!' said Henley-Smith. 'Somebody is in jail. He wants money, food and a bed for the night. He is welcome to your bed, Caulfield. Good night, everyone.'

'Shut up!' said Murphy.

'Perhaps it is the saintly Father Paulus. He was forever running short of whiskey.'

Murphy ignored him.

'O'Mahoney is a selector of sorts for the match on Saturday. He is interested in asking you to play on the wing.'

Murphy and Caulfield waited for a reaction. Henley-Smith snored. He was fast asleep. Caulfield looked at the supine figure. 'I think we should break one of his legs and let O'Mahoney get someone else.'

They viewed with considerable distaste the snoring figure.

They went to their beds and after undressing soon drifted off to sleep.

***

Caulfield was wakened in about twenty minutes although it seemed like four hours.

Henley-Smith, still in his street clothes, was shaking Murphy and shouting in an effort to waken him. This alarmed Caulfield, for Murphy still had a reduced tendency to suddenly flail about if abruptly wakened. Caulfield ran to Murphy's bed and attempted to pull Henley-Smith off.

There was general consternation, and loud banging from downstairs, indicating the wrath of the tenants from below.

Murphy was understandably enraged. Nobody likes to be wakened up suddenly. The sight of a fully dressed Henley-Smith standing on his bed and shouting gibberish touched an emotion similar to terror in Murphy's heart, and he assumed that (1) the place was on fire or (2) some sort of police raid was taking place.

Caulfield managed to get Henley-Smith off Murphy and spread-eagled him on the floor. It turned out that Henley-Smith was inquiring about a Father Paulus and was attempting to get more information regarding the same cleric from Murphy. Henley-Smith mumbled an apology, but Murphy was not in a mood to accept apologies, especially as he was fully awake and found it difficult to get back to sleep.

The brouhaha subsided, and it looked as if a relative calm was restored. The cries and knockings from below fell silent. But to coin a new phrase, they were still in the eye of the storm.

Henley-Smith was found asleep in Murphy's bed. He slept with a gentle snore. When an inspection of Henley-Smith's bed showed a standard of hygiene inferior to the average Bengali Prison cell, Murphy became possessed with a fierce and righteous anger. He took off a leather belt and proceeded to lash the recumbent posterior of Henley-Smith. First with his right arm (fifteen lashes) and then with his left arm (twelve lashes).

He stopped his punishment and to general amazement he and Caulfield observed that the lashings had practically no effect. Henley-Smith had hardly moved.

They examined the belt. It was of genuine leather. Henley-Smith's trousers had been pulled off. He had taken the full force of the lashes. A feeling of helplessness possessed them.

They got into bed. Caulfield noted with gratitude that Murphy had accidentally got into Henley-Smith's bed. Caulfield had the comfort of his own.

***

It was early. The sun streamed through the window. Henley-Smith was wont to shrewdly observe that this was the sign of morning and a new day.

He poked at Murphy.

'Breakfast,' he said. 'Do you want a rasher and sausage or two of my eggs?'

Murphy looked at him blearily.

'Are you Henley-Smith?'

'Of course.'

'Then get out,' muttered Murphy.

'I'd like you to know,' said Henley-Smith, 'that I own a rasher and three of the eggs.'

A voice came from inside Caulfield's bed. 'Will you two shut up, I'm trying to sleep.'

They looked over at Caulfield's bed; a huddled figure under the blankets stirred restlessly.

'That's where he is!' said Henley-Smith. 'I was wondering what happened to him.'

'Who's sleeping in my bed?' asked Murphy, getting out.

'And who's sleeping in my bed?' said the mother bear and Henley-Smith.

Murphy stood up carefully, put on slippers and a dressing gown. Washed his hands and face and came back to the table.

'Someday, Henley-Smith, you will tell a joke that makes people laugh. The moon will be blue and dragons will stalk the earth.'

'I have asked you already, Murphy. Do you want a rasher and sausage or two of my eggs?'

'I will have two eggs.'

'Then have some manners and restrain your biting wit.'

Caulfield surfaced and followed Murphy to the table.

'Good morning, everyone.'

The other two looked at him.

'I suppose it is good morning.'

'Just about.'

They finished breakfast in silence. The bread had no butter, the tea had no sugar. Caulfield finished his rasher, bacon rind and all.

'Now gentlemen, kindly explain.'

Henley-Smith looked at them. He was unamused.

'There must be an explanation of how you behaved like hooligans last night.'

'Listen to him!' said Murphy. 'You went bananas.'

The two of them sat silently, with heads in their hands, devoured by gloomy thoughts.

Murphy pulled himself up. 'I beg your pardon,' glaring at Henley-Smith. 'Your behaviour last night was execrable.'

'That's a great word to use!' said Caulfield. 'I'll save it up for future use.'

'You aroused the crowd below; you attacked me when I was sleeping. I had to sleep in your bug-infected bed.'

'I am getting to the stage,' went on Henley-Smith., 'when I don't find it hilarious to see snow balls thrown at elderly gentlemen or buckets of water pitched out of windows.'

They kept their silence. It was difficult for grown men to defend rural flights of humour. As they sat, the telephone rang on the ground floor, and then a voice called for Caulfield. He went downstairs and came back three minutes later. He sat down, and immediately began to speak.

'OK, Henley-Smith, let's get one thing established. We were no angels last night, but neither were you.'

Henley-Smith looked blank, but said nothing.

Caulfield went on.

'That caller on the phone wants to speak to you at 10am this morning in the Shelbourne. We will go around with you and stay with you until he says what he has to say.'

'This is going to be another big gag,' said Henley-Smith. 'What is it going to be this time? The donkey in the bath, eh? Maybe a consignment of glass hammers.'

Murphy shook his head.

'Grow up, man!'

Henley-Smith calmed down.

'OK, I'll go with you. I think we have all passed the age of practical jokes.'

Murphy stood up. 'We all leave here at the time of 9.45 am and head for the Shelbourne.'

As they walked, Caulfield counted.

'Today is Tuesday, tomorrow is Wednesday and then it's Thursday, and after that it's Friday, and on Friday, we get our caps, pay for the jerseys and the socks, and provide our own boots, and on

348

Saturday, after a fine lunch, at 2.45 pm we run out for the twelfth time on the grass of Lansdowne in front of forty four thousand people. After the match, if you are not crippled, or in hospital, you will be stood a first class dinner. PS. Black tie, and you pay for the black tie.'

Chapter 34

Court Martial

Henley-Smith was walking on air after leaving O'Mahoney.

'I dreamed of it but never thought it would come.'

He skipped and jumped so that pedestrians looked askance, 'I've got to celebrate, let's go to Slats and celebrate.'

'No,' said Caulfield, 'we won't celebrate before the match.'

'We won't celebrate after the match either,' said Murphy sourly.

'Fellows,' intoned Henley-Smith, 'this is a big, big day. It's a new beginning for Henley-Smith, for Dublin University, for the four corners of this great little country.

I want to thank you for what you have done. You preened me up, you gave me a chance, you must have twisted that O'Mahoney's arm. You gave me a break.'

Whilst Murphy had walked on to just within earshot, Caulfield had stopped and listened to the big man. Henley-Smith spoke from his heart. Caulfield had made a chance for him. It was once in a lifetime. With Fitzpatrick, Ireland's best winger injured, he would never have an opportunity like this again.

Caulfield grabbed his arm. 'Give it all you have on Saturday.'

'I will, I will.'

The two men hugged each other, and went on to join Murphy.

He was not a cynic, or a bucket of cold water. Murphy had no objection to Henley-Smith as a man, but he wanted to win.

The match against England was one they usually expected to lose. Once every five years they won against the odds. This year it was a toss up; they had a home game, but would miss their injured winger, Fitzpatrick.

Murphy felt he was carrying the hopes of fifty thousand. The young school boys and the old chaws. They were depending on him, he was their hero; they travelled from Limerick, Cork, Belfast, chanting his name, waving flags. He felt utterly crushed when he let them down. He felt a cold anger against the 'Play the game' brigade. He only had room in himself for victory.

'We'll go back to college,' said Caulfield, 'and walk around the place, and see where it all started.'

Reluctantly they passed by Slats, and headed for college. The news of Henley-Smith's selection must have made the radio news. Many of the pedestrians smiled and clapped. Henley-Smith graciously acknowledged their salutes, but Murphy grumbled. 'In my time I could hear people asking 'who's Murphy?' When I was selected even my mother 'phoned up and asked if it was me.'

Caulfield was beginning to sober up and think of the consequence of Henley-Smith's selection. His weakness was defence. Putting it bluntly, he shirked his tackles. He was as Murphy said – yellow.

If Henley-Smith flagrantly missed a tackle, a mighty groan would echo around the stadium. This would have a disastrous effect on the team's morale. He hoped it wouldn't.

For other reasons Caulfield hoped that Henley-Smith would shine. He remembered the celebrated tennis match against him in Roscrea. They were only school boys, but triumph eluded Henley-Smith. He experienced defeat and disgrace for much of his life. There was his dinner party, which was held against him. The birthday party where he first met Prudence and the sympathy that Henley-Smith showed him at that time. He had also first met Kevin Murphy and the three of them formed a loose, if chaotic, relationship.

They walked through the college to the playing fields. The second fifteen were playing a scratch match against Lansdowne.

The Lansdowne winger, cut inside, jinxed his way out and easily outpaced the opposition for a try.

'Who is that fellow?' Caulfield asked a spectator.

'His name is Nolan,' he said.

Caulfield saw the pride in his eyes.

'Are you his father?'

'Yes, Mr. Caulfield.'

'Next year he will be playing in Lansdowne Road and I will be watching.'

The spectator nearly wept.

'It is very good of you to say that. Thank you, Mr. Caulfield.'

The three men walked on and sat down. A groundsman was trimming the cricket square although the cricket season was three months away.

'It was an October evening, a Saturday. The days were shortening. A typical October Saturday afternoon rugby day. Does anyone remember the score?'

'Yes, it was 12-3,' said Murphy. 'We won despite a forward pass from Caulfield.'

'Certainly not! It was getting dark and the referee was bursting to get to the jacks.'

'Like a sporting gentleman you should have handed the ball to the referee, and asked him to call a scrum.'

'The referee didn't give a damn about a forward pass,' said Caulfield. 'All he wanted was the match to end and get to the jacks.'

'Mighty acts come from small details.'

'Profundis,' said Murphy.

'If that is supposed to be Latin, then it isn't. You forget that the Jesuits taught me Latin in a real school.'

'I suppose Fr. Paulus taught you when he was sober.'

'Could we change the subject?' said Caulfield.

'I am thinking of that match, it was dusk, and we first made contact with Herzog. I saw him standing in the shadows but thought nothing of it at the time.'

'That reminds me,' said Murphy, 'when I was leaving this morning I met Heizog. He has invitations in the post to us for a reception on Friday before the match, in his suite at the Shelbourne.'

'I heard something about this,' said Caulfield. 'He is putting the team up in the hotel overnight. It's great. It's years since I had breakfast in bed.'

'Eight pm.' said Murphy. 'By 11 pm we must all be tucked up, in good time for the joust next day.'

Murphy looked at Caulfield

'I asked if I could bring three guests for the evening.'

Caulfield yawned. 'Anybody we know?'

'I think so.'

Nothing was said. Caulfield seemed to lose interest. He looked intently at the greens man cutting the grass and wondered how he got the edges so exact. Then it was as if he remembered something.

'Who are they?'

'Your cousin Anna and her mother Hilda, and my dear mum, Madam Olive.'

'No! I warned them to stay away from a loose character like you. Are congratulations in order?'

'Maybe they are, and maybe they are not.'

Henley-Smith spoke up.

'That sounds a bit like the forecast of Saturday's match.'

'I hope the answer is 'yes',' said Caulfield, 'and I will have the honour of being the first to shake your hand.'

'Thank you, my good man.'

'Have you met Aunt Hilda, as I call her?'

'Not yet. The ice will be formally broken tomorrow. If you hear screams coming you will know that Auntie Hilda has heard the news. It might be a good idea to go to the pictures.'

'You fellows are lucky enough,' said Henley-Smith. 'You seem to have your romantic life cut and dried. I seem to be sinking into something up to my neck.'

He sat on the bench between the other two. He looked miserable, the euphoria of earlier in the day had dissipated. He was beginning to go through a familiar mood of failure and disappointments. He had let down himself at sport, at school, in his career. At college he was the butt of corner boys who allegedly were students. The institution which he respected as a producer of gentlemen, was now distrusted by the police because of their inability to behave in public.

Everything was black, common and second rate.

Caulfield put his arm around him.

'It's not so bad. You have gone through a hellish two years, but you have come back. Things will pick up. You will play a great game on Saturday.'

Henley-Smith shook his head in disbelief.

'I don't know. The match will be on T.V. and I know my old man will be watching. I have never played well when he watches.'

'I think you will,' said Murphy.

It was the first time that Murphy had praised or encouraged him. It gave Henley-Smith a lift, and he felt better. Murphy realised he needed encouragement and some praise.

'We'll support you,' said Caulfield. 'It will be like any other match, you'll forget the crowd.'

Henley-Smith smiled wanly, but his spirits started to fall again.

'It's alright for you fellows. Your girls will be whooping and shouting for you. They will give you a lift, even though you can't hear them.'

'So what?' asked Murphy.

'I can just see myself. Trying to field a high ball, the English pack thundering down, and I will be thinking of my girl, maybe she will, maybe she won't. That will do wonders for me.'

Despite the pathos the men could not help laughing.

'It's too, too sad!' exclaimed Caulfield.

'The only thing we can do,' said Murphy solemnly, 'is for us to get this lady, give her a bit of a talking to, perhaps break her arm, and ask her to be reasonable.'

'That's the answer!' said Caulfield.

They were laughing again, but Henley-Smith remained glum.

Caulfield came back to him.

'This girl of yours, is she the one I met here in the cricket pavilion last summer, and later in your house?'

'The very one! An ice cool brunette, perhaps too cool, but I am mad about her.'

'There is no problem,' said Caulfield comfortingly. 'Just snap your finger and she'll fall into your arms. Have you told her how much you love her?'

'Not exactly, but I strongly hinted at it.'

'You hinted?' asked Caulfield. Murphy's mouth fell open and he turned away. Caulfield showed consternation. There did not seem more to say.

'I know what you are thinking,' said Henley-Smith. 'You think I should rush her and sweep her off her feet – huh, maybe send her some poems, and a bunch of eleven roses – huh.'

Murphy broke in, 'I would take it easy on the poems, the roses sound like a good idea.'

'You can't go wrong with roses,' advised Caulfield.

'The thing is,' went on Henley-Smith, 'that a rotter called Jacob Anderson is keen on her. He is filthy rich, although Herzog took him to the cleaners, so it's between the two of us. She said something about making a decision over the weekend. She asked me for a ticket for the match and I had to spend an hour explaining why a scrum scrums. She surprised me by asking 'what is the difference between a ruck and a maul?' Actually, I am not too sure.'

Henley-Smith seemed to sink into depression again.

'It's too bloody awful,' he moaned. 'Everything is in a mess. I hardly get a civil word from my father; he takes his meals in the kitchen after the servants are finished. My mother thinks she is

355

dying from something, stays in bed all day reading the Bible. Aunt Miriam is dead. Elizabeth just moons around doing nothing. I was delighted when I was chosen for Ireland. Now it doesn't seem to be a big deal.'

He stopped. 'What I want is a good wife to cheer me up, someone…' he stopped, 'someone who could cheer me up and make me feel good. Yes that's it, someone to make me feel good.'

His voice trailed away. The two men looked at each other, they were horrified. This man was unfit to play a club game let alone an international.

'That's why I would love to have Madeleine. She is so calm, so strong, when I am with her I feel calm and strong. I begin to feel good, yes I feel good. She cheers me up. It's a great feeling when she cheers me up. I want to marry Madeleine.'

'What happened about your father?' asked Murphy.

'Who says anything happened to him?'

'No one! I am only asking.'

'You need not ask,' snapped Henley-Smith.

'Take it easy,' said Caulfield. 'It was you who said that you couldn't get a word from him, and he had to eat in the kitchen etc. and so on. There seems to be something wrong when you mention his name. Every time you mention it you seem to get screwed up. You grit your teeth and your voice changes. What is it about your father? It would be better if you told someone.'

'Get if off your chest,' said Murphy.

He looked out at the cricket square. It was quite perfect. How did the groundsman get it so perfect? How did his father have to destroy his family?

'I was court martialled,' said Henley-Smith, 'for cowardice. They court martialled me because I didn't kill myself, because I didn't pick up a live unexploded bomb, which exploded seconds later. There wasn't one officer present at that court martial who had done such a thing, but they were not on trial. I was and my family was disgraced.'

'How old were you?' asked Murphy.

'Twenty.'

'Twenty!' said Murphy, 'and they expected that of a twenty year old?'

Caulfield said, 'I don't understand something. If you were court martialled for what you deserve why did your father have to go into seclusion? Surely he could have given you a thousand euro and a remittance and shipped you off to East Africa.'

'Good question!' said Murphy.

'That is the question,' said Caulfield.

'Did your mother not help out?'

'She said that every time she saw me she felt sick.'

'You have had a funny family.'

'It all started on the destroyer HMS Essex; we were cruising off the coast of North Korea, and came under fire from their shore batteries. I told you about the unexploded shell that landed on the bow of a ship. I was supposed to have risked my life in picking it up and throwing it over.'

'And you didn't.'

'No. But Seaman McNeill did, and was decorated.'

'I am sorry to keep bringing in your father's role in all this. Was he on the ship? Was he a Commander and Captain of the ship?'

'Yes. He was standing by the shell as it landed. He retreated back and went below. I was on the bridge and saw it all. I reckon that McNeill saw it and reported the incident. He must have paid McNeill to say that it was me. Basically I took the rap.'

Murphy tried to console him.

'You were brave enough to take the rap. You sacrificed yourself for your father's reputation. That took courage.'

Henley-Smith clenched his fists and stood up and looked to heaven.

'If it was only that easy,' he moaned. 'Do you think it was courageous to take the blame for the old man? For me to accept a reputation as a coward and live with it? The court martial said I

357

lacked bravery, but it would have taken more bravery to indict my father and let the world see him as he was.

'I took the easy way; I let the world see me as a coward and left the Navy. The old man has not got off lightly. Every night as the wind blows, he hears the sound of the typhoon, he feels the fear of the ship under fire, he hates himself as he remembers bribing McNeill.

It's no wonder he wants to eat with the servants.'

Henley-Smith drooped his head. Murphy suddenly stood up. To the amazement of the other two, he placed his arm around Henley-Smith and hugged him.

'I have realized, Henley-Smith, that you may be a braver man than any of us. You are going out onto the pitch of Lansdowne Road on Saturday afternoon, and on that pitch Henley-Smith the winger is going to bury Henley-Smith the coward.'

Chapter 35

Denouement

Caulfield was sitting on the window ledge of their room, which overlooked the front square. He saw people come and go; junior dean, lecturers, visitors with cameras, the provost's wife, a man with a dog, three women in white with tennis racquets, an elderly clergyman in danger of tripping up – anybody and everyone.

Caulfield was feeling pleasantly relaxed after a strenuous workout. Life was good again.

A man, tall and burly, entered the square; he stopped and looked around uncertainly, as if he was a stranger. Taking a piece of paper from his pocket he turned it one way and another, and then looked up at the apartment rooms.

Caulfield sensed immediately that the man was looking for him. The man walked slowly over to his apartment and again checked the drawing on the paper. He entered the building and his steps could be heard as he climbed the stairs.

Caulfield was alone in the apartment, but he was unafraid for now he knew the man. It was Herzog's chauffeur who had driven him down to Ballynale. He felt a twinge of regret as it occurred to him that he never thanked the man, though it was Herzog's car and petrol. Come to think of it, he had never thanked Herzog either.

Caulfield's door was open and the man walked in without knocking.

'I am to drive you; they are waiting for you in Sandycove.'

'They are waiting in Sandycove?' asked Caulfield. 'Why Sandycove? Is it James Joyce the fearful Jesuit who wants me?'

The man seemed impervious to Caulfield's wit.

'No, it's Mr and Mrs Herzog.'

Caulfield could have haughtily told him that Mr and Mrs Herzog were at liberty to come in to see him, but he was not one to stand on his dignity. He followed the man outside and they drove away, Caulfield enjoying again the luxury of the Bentley.

At a distance Caulfield could see Herzog curled up in a deckchair, protected by a stone wall. Abigail was not in evidence but he knew she was there, possibly sheltered by the rocks; hidden but ready to come out, prepared to present the final demand, to play the final card, to judge the gambler's throw. *She will be here, armed by her beauty and style,* he said to himself, *I haven't a chance.*

Herzog opened the door for him and Caulfield stepped out. 'Thanks for the lift Isaac.'

They walked down the road, away from the rocks. Caulfield asked, 'Where are we going?' 'Nowhere,' Herzog said.

They walked on.

'You can say *"No"* and walk back to the college,' said Herzog. 'You can say *"No"* and forget about twenty-five thousand deposited in your bank account. You can say *"No"* and forget about a fellowship in college.'

'It's not like you, Herzog; you never used a sledgehammer before.'

'I can't help it. We have waited and waited. We overlook your African brother and half-brother. I treated you like a son.'

He stopped and grabbed Caulfield's arm. 'I came to look upon you as a son; you were everything to me. Abigail looked on you in a different way, not quite like a son. I took that chance with you and Abigail; both of you behaved and respected me and earned my respect.'

'I have nothing but the greatest respect for you,' said Caulfield, 'and it wasn't just your Bentley and the millions in your bank, not even the gold medal; but you can't expect me to go blindfolded into this. I have to say *No* when I don't know the full story.'

'Why can't you accept what I say? You are not in danger.'

'You are asking too much,' said Caulfield.

They stood on the promenade and let the on-shore wind whip in and chill their bones.

'Alright,' said Herzog, 'let's go back.'

This time they walked slowly. A woman stepped out from behind the Bentley. She was a tall woman dressed with casual elegance in a Russian mink coat and hat.

'Its been over a year since I saw that,' said Caulfield. 'It was the night you rescued me in Slats.'

Herzog grunted; he wasn't listening and he wasn't taken in. Abigail looked at Herzog but he didn't respond and she knew that nothing had happened.

'Caulfield, come this way,' Herzog went to the end of the wall and started to climb the rocks. It was getting dark and Caulfield was sliding from one rock to another; it would be very easy to slip and break an ankle.

'What the hell are you trying to do?' grumbled Caulfield.

'Take it easy and I'll tell you something.'

'Big deal!' said Caulfield. 'Tell me that the rocks are hard and the sea is wet.'

'I came out to this place on the day my mother died. I didn't know where I was going but I climbed the rocks and gazed out to sea. I wanted to forget everything. I wanted to be part of this ocean and lose myself in its immensity. Since then, when I am disturbed or helpless I have come here to seek direction. That's why I am here. What do you know about Abigail?'

'Nothing.'

'When I married Abigail she had just divorced Drofinan. There was a reason. Drofinan had played around and paid the price.'

'I know,' said Caulfield, 'he could have destroyed the Roman Empire.'

'Eh?'

361

'Carry on – I don't like the sound of it, but we'd better get it over.'

'Don't be smart,' said Herzog.

'Sorry, sorry; but what is next?'

'Abigail became infected with syphilis.'

Caulfield gave a cry like a wounded deer; his feet slipped and he tripped over sharp-edged rocks. He was about to fall but gave a despairing jump and landed on the wet sand. The incoming tide washed over his feet.

The chauffeur, who had been watching them carefully, ran over and picked up Caulfield and together they helped Herzog down off the rocks. They hobbled back to the Bentley.

Abigail said, 'What is going on?'

'You know what is going on,' said Herzog, 'I told him everything.'

'Yes, he told me everything,' said Caulfield.

'And what is *everything*?' asked Abigail.

Caulfield was tired of diplomacy. 'He told me that you were infected with syphilis.'

There was a silence. They could hear the crashing waves on the beach. The chauffeur behind them jumped from one foot to the other in agony, having overheard the exchange.

Herzog turned to Caulfield, grabbed him and tried to shake him.

'I tell you the truth! Abigail does not have it anymore.'

Everything happened so quickly; Abigail cried and Herzog bundled her into the car and shouted to the chauffeur, 'Drive back to Dublin!'

Caulfield was left standing by the beach, feeling hard done by. It was going to be a long walk to College Green.

He was seething. *How could they have led me up the garden path? Abigail was infected, or was she?* Even if she was, he knew she could be cured with antibiotics – it was as simple as fixing a broken collar bone.

The same could be said of Herzog; a dose of antibiotics should have left him a new man. It could have cleared up in no time – but there had to be more.

Herzog had not walked around Dublin on that Saturday night for nothing. He propositioned Caulfield, had driven him to Ballynale in an expensive car, chatted him up in Henley Hall, and got himself into a twist over McNight. Abigail was never far away, she even turned up at the college races in a green chiffon dress that had everyone gasping; a peck on the cheek was his reward for coming second in the high-jump.

His mind went round and round. *Dammit,* thought Caulfield, *I will be back with that doctor sooner than I thought.* He trudged back to college and tried to fit the pieces together in his shattered mind. *Take Herzog,* he thought, *his conduct would be understandable if he contracted syphilis in the years after he married Abigail. And then there was Abigail: had she contracted v.d. before marriage and unwittingly infected Herzog? No? Yes? Don't know?*

Perhaps Abigail had looked at her five-foot-one-inch husband and was unhappy at the thought of producing five-foot-three-inch children? It would take three generations to get some height into the Herzog's. These Jews like to strike a hard bargain; Herzog might not pay for a family of midgets. Caulfield's head was bursting; it would soon be as bad as that nightmare of the microbes.

To his surprise he was nearly home. As he came into College Green he stopped. The Bentley was parked outside with sidelights on and somebody sitting in the back.

'Well, hello, hello,' he said to Herzog.

'Sorry; but come back to the hotel and have some dinner.'

'No, but you can come into my pad and have some tea.'

Not for the first time Herzog was taken by Caulfield's good humour; he should have been in a spitting rage, but here he was – all smiles.

They went into the rooms. Herzog turned up his nose. 'Do people live in this place?'

Caulfield grinned and said, 'it has everything except a sewing machine!'

Henley-Smith was absent and Murphy was snoring with his mouth open. Caulfield made tea.

'I have a very confused idea in my head as to explain the events of tonight. It's you or it's Abigail.'

Herzog didn't reply, but finished his drink. 'That's very good tea,' he said.

Caulfield nodded his head. 'It is excellent tea.'

'Nothing like a good cup of tea,' said Herzog.

Caulfield sighed. 'That's what we came up here for – a nice cup of tea.'

'It's quite simple,' said Herzog. 'As a young man I played the fool. I contracted the disease. I thought I was cured. I was, but then I wasn't.' Herzog settled back in a chair and spoke in a low, tired voice.

'I met Abigail. She had been married to Drofinan, so she was no shrinking violet. She also discovered that Drofinan was no Lion of the Bedchamber and she dumped him and took a chance on me. The rest is history.'

'Tell me the history.'

'It's coming. I am tired of living a double life. I am tired of lies. At first everything was hunky-dory and then it happened. She was infected with syphilis. I suspected the worst from her but then the doctors found that it was from Drofinan. He was being treated at the same time. I didn't have it. I had something else – something called Chlamydia.'

'Which causes sterility,' said Caulfield.

'Trust a medical student to know that! I might have been better off with syphilis. I rushed to get treatment for Chlamydia, but it was too late.' Herzog gave a bitter smile. 'I suppose I sold myself short.'

'Is that the lot?' asked Caulfield.

'Abigail started to go back to Melbourne for a check-up every five or six months until she was completely in the clear. She had got such a fright that she continued to have tests for a few years. She preferred to go to Melbourne than have the tests in Dublin – it was more confidential there.'

Caulfield moved uneasily.

Herzog continued. 'One day I was leaving the Melbourne Royal Infirmary with her and who did I see standing on the steps but…?'

Caulfield said, 'A guess – was it McNight?'

'It *was* McNight, with the dirtiest smile I ever saw on any man's face.'

'And so you pushed him into the River Liffey!'

'I never pushed him. I never laid a finger on him. I just brought him to the edge and as he went down the steps I told him that he was the most miserable creep I had ever known. And so I have to be celibate for the rest of my life. I don't mind too much; I am married to Abigail and that's everything. I have to live the life of a saint, but so does the pope and he seems to manage!'

Herzog stood up and went over to Caulfield's chair. 'I beg of you, Caulfield, on my knees I beg of you! I want you, and so does Abigail. She wants a son called Herzog and so do I. Is it so terrible what we want?'

'I don't know what is moral any more. I have a girl called Michal McMaster. I think I love her; I think I will marry her. Can I betray the one I love?'

Herzog looked at him with something akin to scorn. 'Wise up, pretty boy, and don't be so holier than thou, and don't be so high and mighty, and don't give me that line that you *think* you will ask Michal to marry you, and you *think* she will say *"yes"* and you *think* you will live happily ever after.' Herzog's voice rose to a shout. 'Let me tell you something; you can't betray her because you are not married to her. You are not one flesh and perhaps never will be.'

Caulfield could not think of a reply.

Herzog sensed that Caulfield was weakening.

Caulfield was tired of the moral struggle; he was sick of wrestling with ifs and buts.

'Go back, Caulfield, to that Family Bible of yours and see how the prophets of old slept all over the place. Even David had ten concubines and half a dozen wives, and Abraham slept with his wife's maid and then turned the maid and her son out of the house – lovely people they were!'

Caulfield's hands trembled. The brutal words of Herzog lashed him, leaving him at the point of no return. In a tense and hoarse voice he said, 'I suspected for some time what you have just told me, but there is something else that you don't know. It's another thing that is hidden from you and Abigail.'

Herzog uncertainly walked a few steps.

'My girl, Michal, is friendly with a nurse in the Misercordia – they play hockey and tennis together, and so on. This girl let it slip that Abigail was in for tests in the Misercordia. None of this was known to you, and they know nothing of our arrangements.'

Herzog grabbed Caulfield by the arm. For a small man, he had a powerful grip.

'Easy on, Isaac, let me tell you. I phoned Seamus Brennan who I knew in medical school. He is interning now in Misercordia. I asked him if I could get a look at Abigail's file, and reluctantly he showed it to me. The file seemed OK – just about.'

Herzog relaxed his grip.

'The trouble with me,' went on Caulfield, 'goes back to when I was sixteen and I went into hospital with a torn cartilage. It came from a bad tackle in school rugby.'

'So what?' Herzog asked.

'They discovered then I was resistant to a certain virus. Relax, Isaac, it need not be that bad. But you can see if Abigail did pass on a virus to me I would have no protection, no resistance. I would be crucified for life. I could never marry Michal. I could never marry anyone. Surely you can understand now why I have been dragging my feet?'

Herzog took Caulfield's hand in his own

'It's been a long struggle, Isaac, but now I can do as you ask.'

'When?'

'By the end of next week.'

'Where?'

'I won't tell you, but you will know.'

Herzog stepped back and held out his hand; Caulfield moved forward and took his hand and shook it.

CHAPTER 36

At last, Abigail

After a cold shower, Herzog put on a silk shirt. It slipped smoothly down and around him.

Abigail had bought a dozen of them from Charvet & Pavs, with ties to match. He didn't want to tell her that his tastes were essentially plebeian. He was delighted to see her clad in designer clothes, but he had a longing for the ordinary in his own wardrobe. He remembered his shoes as a boy, which let in water and left his socks soggy, sticking to the shoe sole.

When he came in for a bicycle he had to tuck his long trousers into his socks. In that way he got them wet at both ends. He handled the Charvet shirt with disinterest. As a twelve year old he had two shirts. The one he wore and the one his mother washed for the Sabbath. He loved the new shirt after his mother's washing. He could not describe it, but he knew it was special.

Charvet shirts were alright, but they had no soul.

'Who is this woman Madeline?' Abigail asked.

'If she came in sackcloth she would have style.'

'Is that so? Maybe you could get me some sackcloth.'

Herzog pretended to be amused. 'Your ancestor, David, was no stranger to sackcloth.'

'Zip up my dress,' she commanded.

Herzog went to the door and called, 'Patrice.'

A Filipino maid came in.

'Madam would like her dress zipped up.'

There were times when Herzog hated himself. Who was he that he couldn't zip the back of his wife's dress? He tried to console his conscience that he had driven himself to the top, and had to work all the time to stay there.

Some idiot had pompously told him that the top of the mountain was dangerous; the winds were strong and bitter, and if you fell it was difficult to stand up.

Abigail was silent after the incident, and when the maid left the room she said, 'Are you not overdoing it?'

'I suppose ... I don't know why I did it.'

'I have noticed that lately you are trying to prove yourself as an important man.'

Herzog didn't reply.

'This party to-night,' said Abigail, 'is a bit over the top.'

Herzog didn't reply.

'It's a long way from Dorset Street,' said Abigail.

'The best parties I was ever at were in Dorset Street – every week,' said Herzog.

She turned around to him. 'Alright, darling, I won't spoil this party, but from now on could you, and you only, zip up my dress?'

'I will.' He kissed the back of his wife's neck.

'Thank you,' she said, 'and remember, it's only a short distance back to Dorset Street.'

***

It was the biggest splash of the year. The great and the good drove up in their Mercedes, BMW, Lexus and lesser breeds. Herzog had begun to make his name. His bank on St. Stephen's Green featured more and more in the financial pages. It had the glamour of a private bank and the distinction of being able to take on the household established ones, which until recently had sniffed at the upstart.

New premises on St. Stephen's Green excited wonder and respect. People asked how was it done? The small investors who bought its capital were bemused at its growth and thrilled at its profits which were very real. The small investors who became capitalists spoke with a swagger, rejoiced in their shrewdness at having outsmarted some of the suits on the stock exchange.

They were important and significant players (a new word) in having provided capital to the house of Grim Brothers and Herzog, and when they met annually to wolf down plates of smoked salmon and bottles of red wine, they expanded their waistlines as well as their self esteem.

The red wine might not (definitely not) be Burgundy A.C. and the salmon – alas - never experienced the rigour of the North Atlantic but the heavy hitters (another new word) appreciated a growing dividend as good compensation.

There was a certain beauty in a stock where the price and the dividend increased exponentially. Despite nay sayers in the press, the strength of the bank was annually confirmed by results.

Not every captain of finance/industry was able to boast of Herzog's academic standing. Not that Herzog would boast, but somehow his gold medal distinction emerged.

It was Herzog's party and it seemed every one was coming. There was no doubt that the great attraction was Abigail. Although she was not a recluse, she was not well known and tended to cultivate her interest in history and art in private.

No one ever saw her leading a horse into the winner's enclosure or exposing her breasts in the seedier clubs. If she declined interviews, it was mainly because of Herzog's instinctive antipathy against publicity; the echoes of Kiev and Lithuania still resonated.

Herzog, like all Jews, enjoyed a good party. He enjoyed showing off Abigail. He took a personal interest in her clothes, jewellery and style. He insisted that Abigail remained close to him when he moved around. On meeting and talking to his guests he went to some care to involve her in the conversation, and was delighted if she tended to dominate some guest who might have a special interest in history, art, languages.

Some people might comment to Herzog that after talking to him for a while they tended to forget his small stature and insignificant appearance. The well meant compliment failed to please him, at no time was he insignificant.

Herzog and Abigail's experience of the haut monde had been limited. They rose through classes which defied definition. The world had changed, certainties had dissolved. Herzog's ambition was that Abigail would be a *Grand Dame* in the Viennese tradition.

In the melting pot of change it was virtually impossible to separate classes and talents.

How do you classify a pop musician, a supermarket magnate, a titled farmer, a briefless barrister, a professional golfer (top and listed internationally), a prostitute, a prison governor, a bank director, a computer geek, an unfrocked priest, a cook's son, Duke's son, son of a belted Earl?

Herzog and Abigail stood at the door of their apartment. The butler called out the names of the guests, an army of servants took away coats, etc. to a separate room. Abigail was more than brilliant. She was stunning. Her diamonds, once the property of a Maharani of India, were supplemented by emeralds and pearls.

The mixture of her own beauty, her jewels, and the exotic splendour of the designer dress flown in from Paris created an overwhelming sense of occasion. She did not patronise or condescend but showed a natural friendliness that disarmed everyone.

Caulfield met her alone for the first time that evening. He whispered, 'I see the rose of Sharon and the lily of the valleys.'

Abigail smiled knowingly. 'I know where that comes from, and there is more to come.'

Herzog and Abigail were at the door when Mr. Kevin Murphy, Mrs. Olive Murphy, Miss Anna de Paul and Mrs. Sam de Paul were announced.

Kevin made an effort to be at his charming best.

371

He introduced his mother to Anna.

Anna introduced her mother to Kevin.

Caulfield introduced Aunt Hilda to Olive.

Kevin introduced Olive to Anna.

Abigail and Herzog were all smiles and graciousness.

Anna was goggle eyed at Abigail's diamonds.

Abigail was breathless at Anna's outfit.

'I wish,' she said, 'I could wear lavender like that.'

Kevin took Anna's hand and said to Hilda, 'Mrs. de Paul, I would like to ask you for Anna's hand in marriage. We want you to know that we wish to get married in Anna's church in Ballynale and perhaps your cousin in Dublin might marry us, assisted by my cousin Jack who is a curate in Kilkee.'

The tears and the kissing lasted five minutes.

'What we do after that,' said Kevin, 'is for us to decide.'

Caulfield heard the news. He was first to congratulate Kevin. The rest of the team rushed forward to congratulate the pair with all the finesse that rugby forwards reserve for these occasions.

'Now you know,' said a voice, 'the difference between a ruck and a maul!' It was Henley-Smith and he spoke to Madeleine by his side.

Behind him was Anderson.

There was a sudden silence. Herzog and Anderson faced each other. Most people in the room knew something of the tension between them. Herzog moved forward and held out his hand.

Anderson took his hand.

'This is an opportunity for me to say something I have always wanted to say,' said Herzog. 'You are Anderson and I am the Brother Grim.'

Famous divines, eminent sceptics, teachers of French, Jews, epileptics, consultants and brokers, farmers and lover, models whose legs end up at their shoulders.

They all came to Herzogs party.

***

Caulfield felt tired and got to his room at 11.30pm. The music from the suite below played louder and he could hear the laughter of people and the sound of breaking glass. The team manager had ushered them all to their rooms at 11.00. He didn't want the blame if they produced a sub par performance in Lansdowne Road.

Caulfield felt he would like a bath. There was one with golden taps, and he ran the water until steam half filled the room. He soaked in the hot water and started to think of his life, his childhood in Africa. Would he ever go back and see his mother, who had disposed of him and destroyed his father?

He thought of his life at school, his boyhood and boarding school. He realised he had been extraordinarily lucky. His gifts in athletics and sports, which opened doors everywhere. The new love in his life, Michal.

The bitter sweet memories of Prudence which never died, and sometimes wakened old wishes.

Great friends like Murphy and Henley-Smith. How much he owed to Aunt Hilda and Uncle Sam.

The countryside of Tipperary, the friendly people.

And Michal, who was on night duty. He had 'phoned her to tell her that he loved her, and she kissed him goodnight over the 'phone.

He thought of the match tomorrow. It could be his last hurray, tomorrow he was being marked by the new English hit-man, at the best it could be a draw. The loss of Fitzpatrick on the wing was crucial. He was glad Henley-Smith was getting his chance, but he was playing a league above himself. If he shirked a tackle, he was gone for good.

Caulfield luxuriated in the bath and he silently thanked the little man who made it possible. He had come out of nowhere into his life. Born into a cold water tenement, their lives had become intertwined, as had the lives of Henley-Smith and Prudence and

373

Kevin and Olive and the McGreevys, and Anna and Michal and Hilda and Sam.

They had shaped his life, he had shaped theirs. They would not have been the same without him, or he without them.

His chapter was closing. The new chapter opened on Monday.

Caulfield got out of his bath. The team manager had ensured that there was nothing in the rooms to read, so he turned off the lights and lay in the darkness.

Time passed, and he was asleep. People left and cars pulled away. Silence was complete.

Then he heard her voice, humming gently in the adjoining bathroom. For a moment Caulfield felt uncomfortable. Any moment now she'd walk out from there, ready for him.

Then she will come to me.

What will she say?

What will I say?

The poetry of the Torah, thought Caulfield.

The Holy Scriptures that says it is good.

The act of creation that the Lord blesses.

I must speak to her in the beauty of language, thought Caulfield. *It is no time for harshness or force.*

He picked a lily from the vase and placed it on the turned down satin sheets. The sweet smell that filled the air was the fragrance from the flowers. His senses were intoxicated by them. His heart was pounding, waiting.

He heard the doorknob turn.

'Caulfield,' she whispered.

His strong arms circled her waist. Her womanly scent filled his nostrils.

There came to him the words of the Prophet.

"How easily you were led – it is the Lord Yahweh who speaks – you behave no better than a bold faced whore. An adulteress welcomes the strangers instead of her husband".

374

"Yes," said Ezekiel, "whoring with your lovers and your filthy idols, and giving them your children's blood."

"No," said Solomon. "No. They are good and decent people. She is the lily of the valleys; the rose of Sharon. He is like a gazelle or a young stag leaping across the mountains. I speak for them, and I know them."

She had washed her hair and it hung damp around her shoulders.

He pulled aside the bedclothes and she slid in. Her body was cool and perfumed. He leaned over her.

"She walks in beauty like the night of cloudless climes and starry skies."

She raised her arms and pulled him down.

'Don't be restless or afraid, my darling. We will give ourselves to each other. You will give me a child and it will be beautiful.'

'How would Solomon describe it?' asked Caulfield.

Abigail closed her eyes and smiled.

Its eyes will be like the pool of Hershon.

Its nose like the tower of Lebanon

Looking towards Damascus.

How lovely its little arms.

How blue its eyes.

'Just like you,' said Caulfield.

'Blue eyes like yours,' said Abigail.

Abigail gave a happy little laugh.

'It will be a gorgeous baby. I can hear it laugh and gurgle. I can feel its little fingers. I can hear it cry for me, and I will come,'

She hung on to him tightly and then gradually relaxed. There were tears in her eyes.

'Don't leave me, Caulfield.'

'Of course not.'

"Who is this that appears

Like the dawn

Fair as the moon

Majestic as the stars in procession"
'How lovely,' said Abigail.
My lover spoke and said to me,
Arise my darling,
My beautiful one, and come to me,
See the winter is past
The rains are over and gone
Flowers appear on the earth
The sound of singing has come
The voice of the turtle is heard in our land.
They both smiled in the darkness.
The following morning she was still there.
She whispered sleepily.
You are beautiful my love,
Comely as Jerusalem,
Terrible as an army with banners.
She kissed him and left.

Chapter 37

The day of the Match

From early morning the traffic was noticeably higher. As the morning progressed, so did the traffic. Foreign and domestic accents were heard. Handcarts and trailers made an appearance. The police came and looked benevolently at the passing scene. Important looking men, wearing earphones, talked vigorously to invisible gremlins: Lansdowne Road on the day of the match.

It was a Saturday, the day before Sunday. Some people called it atmosphere, others said you could eat and smell it. From central Dublin to the southern suburbs, gnarled red faced men left their houses uncustomary early. It took them four hours to travel five miles. Like medieval pilgrims they paid obeisance at sundry watering holes. Piously they remembered the fallen and spoke of the giants of old who entered Valhalla.

It was not only an old man's day out. Cheery faced schoolboys, with the scarves of a dozen famous schools, jumped on moving busses, clattered up and down the steps, and chattered in high treble voices. The passengers sat resigned, they knew the reason. It was the day of the match.

Closer to Dublin centre the dulcet tones of the Home Counties, would be heard or the borders of Scotland, or the Welsh valleys, would be more prominent depending on the opposition. The hotels that lived for this annual infusion were allowed to break the tiresome rules of licensing and late hours. With extra consumption the visitors came to love the Irish, and were entertained by maudlin songs and verse about *Kathleen Macushla* and *Galway Bay*. Many a tear rolled down a furrowed cheek, on the day of the match.

Before the Match

It was a common delusion suffered by young men that women attending a rugby international were exotic and beautiful creatures, creating a veritable Ascot of style. In fact married women who no longer had the need for pretence, flatly refused to go and were satisfied by hearing the final score on radio.

The unmarried women who were still in the marriage market, had the difficult task of wearing anoraks, woolly caps and fur lined boots, and still looking glamorous.

The challenge was cheerily met by converting themselves to blondes, clothed in mink, prettily painted, long legged, and content to supply the goods on offer.

As the average male clothing consisted of anoraks, the blonde in the fur coat stood out, and it was assumed that either her name was Cynthia, or she was on a retainer from a gossip columnist.

Escorts of such women took a certain pleasure in retailing the gaffes of their companions.

During the following Monday coffee breaks, the gloom of a February day was lifted by recalling their queries.

'Why is the ball not round?' said one.

'What goes on in the scrum?' said another.

'Why do they wear those funny caps?' said a third.

Three minutes to the Match

Overhead the crowd was banging with their feet. It might have been an excess of enthusiasm or a calculated effort to disturb the opposition.

For a first time player, it was intimidating. The television in the corner helped no one, sundry pundits weighed up the pros and cons. Their substantial girth which had developed since their days of glory, wiggled and spilled over their chairs. They spoke as prophets and seers, and their forecasts expanded on the television were met with profanity from the players.

Caulfield, one of the senior men, went around the room, consoled the beginners like Henley-Smith and the new fellow from Cork. 'Relax,' he said, 'let the Brits sweat. The Welsh beat them by twelve points; they panicked and put on seven new fellows for this match, all of them raw.'

'Sure, sure,' they agreed desperately.

'We will take it easy,' said Caulfield, 'and then we will hit them.'

'Good idea,' said the fellow from Cork. Murphy, lacing up his boots, shook his head sadly.

The team manager came in, to utter a few last words of wisdom.

None of the players heard him or paid him any attention. Their main concern was to play as well as they could and avoid letting the crowd laugh and jeer.

As the stands filled up, the roar of the crowds increased. Everyone looked at the clock, they had three minutes.

'We are coming back as winners,' shouted Caulfield, raising his fist.

The team roared their agreement. It was uncanny how the spirits of the team suddenly lifted. Call it leadership, call it nothing, but Caulfield sent a surge through the fifteen men. He had inspired them to go out and play above themselves to play and to win.

379

Henley-Smith edged over to Caulfield. He had something on his mind.

'I've got to tell you something. She is here in the stands. They flew in this morning.'

'What do you mean?'

'Prudence, and Madeleine and Anderson.'

Caulfield swore. 'What's going on?'

'Herzog told me at breakfast. Anderson fixed it. He arranged this a week ago. If I have a good game Madeleine will leave her seat before the end. She will wait for me. Anderson thinks I will be a flop.'

'And what about Prudence?'

'The three of them will sit together in the Presidential box. You can't miss them.'

Caulfield looked incredulous. 'The Presidential box?'

'Don't ask me how he fixed it. Anderson can fix anything.'

The bell rang. The match was on.

'What about Prudence?' asked Caulfield.

It was too late.

The Match

Caulfield was no stranger to Lansdowne Road, but as he ran out for the eighteenth occasion his mind was in a state of turmoil. He had led the team on seven occasions, but this time he nearly forgot the protocol of introducing the President to the team.

What was Prudence doing here? He had never seen her since she waved goodbye on the Barney's Bridge. She might have gone secretly to Twickers to catch a glimpse, but that hardly counted. How did she get involved with Anderson? Neither he nor Prudence had ever known or met him. There was something sinister and mean about the man. Why could Anderson not mind his own business?

Caulfield was a firm favourite with the home crowd, and with most of the visitors. His natural skill and personal geniality made him an ideal captain and for the ceremonies involved.

As the President returned to the box, and before the kick off, Caulfield took a quick look. He recognised Madeleine immediately but was not too sure about the others, a man and some woman, she must be Prudence. As he looked, the woman waved a white handkerchief. The wind blew it away.

Caulfield cursed to himself. This was going to be a lousy game.

If he could get Anderson he would kill him.

England kicked off and almost immediately swept forward to the Irish goal line. The Irish forwards were inept, they seemed sluggish, without ambition; Kevin was leading the pack but appeared helpless to rouse them. The two new forwards who had been stars of last year's team at eighteen stone each, looked pathetic, lying up against the scrum and letting themselves be pushed everywhere by the rampant Saxons.

Caulfield was almost hoarse in trying to lift them. He urged his half backs to kick and get their kicks in. Until they left their own twenty-five it was useless to try and run the ball.

The inevitable happened. A loose maul, five opposition forwards pushed the two big Irish off the ball and scored. The remaining Irish appeared to walk leisurely over to the scene to survey the wreckage.

Caulfield was livid. It was the worst performance of an Irish fifteen under his captaincy. It was no consolation that Henley-Smith could stand at the wing with nothing to do. The battle was fought amongst the forwards and the Brits had correctly decided that they had the upper hand there. They threw everything into the war and got a soft try.

Their policy would seem to be: keep it tight, get another try and a few penalties and on the turn, walk off with eighteen or so points to spare. In the second half they could throw the ball around and enjoy themselves. The Irish team looked like a beaten side. At half time they trudged into their locker room with drooping shoulders. Eighteen points down and were hardly ever out of their half.

The silence of their fans outside was deafening. The Saxons were singing *Swing Low, Sweet Chariot*. As Caulfield went down the tunnel he looked up to the Presidential box.

It was Prudence alright. She was talking animatedly to Anderson. Madeleine caught his eye. She appeared to mock him.

'Look at the superheroes! The big boys have given them a spanking.'

Caulfield waited for Henley-Smith.

'Tell me quickly the whole story,' said Caulfield grabbing his arm.

'Anderson is going to double cross Herzog. He hasn't given up. He is in with an Italian bank and they are going to sell Herzog short. The market will be outraged. No bank ever sells another bank shares short. But Anderson doesn't mind, and the Italians hope to pick up what's left for nothing.'

'But Herzog is a wealthy man. The bank is very strong.'

'Herzog says that the strongest bank can be destroyed by a rumour,' said Henley-Smith.

'That's terrible, but what has it to do with us? What is Prudence doing here?'

'Anderson is a madman. He wants to destroy everything to do with Herzog; not only his business, but you and I, and our girls Madeleine and Michal, Quirke and his girlfriend, and even my father, the poor devil.

'He brought Prudence here so that you could go for her again and destroy Michal; he is grabbing Madeleine, who he played around with for years, telling Madeleine that he could not marry until his mother died. Herzog checked it out. There wasn't a word of truth in it. What's happening today is that the women have decided that they will leave, say ten minutes before the final whistle.

'If Madeleine leaves it means she is leaving Anderson and I am to have her for ever and ever amen.

'If Prudence leaves the stand, its goodbye to you and thanks for the memory. You go back to Michal.'

'I was never away from Michal.'

'That's the stuff! Just remember if she wants to talk to you, she will stay in the stand and you should come to her.'

'Madeleine will come to you if you score two tries.'

'Any chance of you passing the ball out to me?'

The team coach came charging down the passage. He was furious.

'What do you think you are doing?' he roared and gave them a dirty look. 'I am trying to get you fellows to waken up and not chit chatting out here.'

The bell rang. The rest of the team came out with hangdog expressions.

'Just look at them,' moaned the coach. 'It's like Napoleon's retreat from Moscow.'

None of them laughed.

'We can win this match and we will win it,' said Caulfield.

There was a perceptible squaring of shoulders. They had heard this gung-ho before. On one occasion it had worked. Caulfield led out the team to tepid applause. It was Ireland's kick off. The fellow from Cork was given the kick. He made a terrible mess. It sliced away to the left into an almost empty section. Two Brits were there and the unknown Henley-Smith. The Brits erupted. They had two to one advantage. Their winger and a centre against a lumbering giant which a commentator had unkindly described Henley-Smith.

It would be the softest of soft tries.

It was, but not in the way expected.

The English winger decided to pass inside but missed his man, and Henley-Smith running up, intercepted and ran over unopposed.

The Irish stand almost forgot to cheer, but when the truth sank in, Henley-Smith was greeted like Caesar returning from the Gallic wars.

The effect on the Irish was electric. They had been lucky, they would be lucky again. The Brits looked as if they had a body blow. The play moved into their half, Caulfield came into his own.

Ragged English forward play let the Irish get the ball cleanly to Caulfield who made the opening for Henley-Smith. It was not a difficult try but still a try. Henley-Smith didn't fumble, or drop the ball, he wasn't caught by the full back. Henley-Smith deserved the try. Two trys on his opening game. He walked on water. Two penalties from the fellow from Cork and the score was 18-18.

Caulfield looked at the clock. Five minutes to go. At the same time he saw the President's box, Anderson was on his own, the women had left.

Caulfield pointed to the box and grinned at Henley-Smith. It was going to be their day.

Two minutes to go came the moment of truth. England pulled themselves together with some superb passing from the English pack saw their prop, seventeen stone and seven pounds, bearing down on full speed on Henley-Smith. Caulfield stood almost stationary. There was nothing that he or anyone else could do. Henley-Smith was on his own. He met him almost full on. He turned the Brit over out of touch and out of the game. Henley-Smith lay stationary, a trickle of blood coming out of his nose.

Henley-Smith the winger had buried Henley-Smith the coward.

The referee blew his whistle. He had a minute left and two minutes of injury time. Henley-Smith was bleeding and semi-conscious, according to rules he had to be carried off.

The referee ordered an Irish scrum. He decided to hold up play to see if Henley-Smith could resume. He couldn't, he was out cold and still bleeding.

Murphy

Murphy stood almost in the centre of the pitch. His chest was heaving from the strain of the combat. Both sides had found extra resources to make that final effort for victory.

For Murphy a draw was a defeat. To give so much for nil-nil was mockery to the brave men who had given all.

He had to admit that Henley-Smith had proved himself. He was lying unconscious, with blood on his face. How could he tell him when he recovered that a draw was enough?

Murphy loved the physical contact of rugby.

When going down for the first scrum, he would catch his opponent's eye and whisper, 'OK fella, any nonsense and you have a broken neck.'

Murphy played the game to its limit. In the boiler room of the scrum, he felt high and lifted up amidst the brutal power of men clashing in battle.

The backs were no strangers to physical contact, but they were blessed with speed and guile. It was a man to man contact where one ran against another, mocked him, deceived him, left him on the wrong foot, passed the ball, or didn't pass the ball. Caulfield would then bring in the strike force of the other centre and a winger. They assaulted the bailiwicks of the enemy, which for a second they hated. They struck with overwhelming force. The opposition desperately regrouped. They had four against three, but the fellow from Cork came from nowhere and glided through outstretched hands to carry the ball over the line and fall upon it.

There was heard the cry of the Mongols on the walls of Peking.

'That,' said Murphy, 'is rugby!'

Final Whistle

The referee blew for the finish. Murphy who had stood in a daze, realized that the game was over.

A great win chortled the newscasters, small boys ran on to the pitch to slap the players' backs. But as the Captain of Ireland trudged off he knew it could be his last season, if not his last match. It had come home to him during the game that he had lost a yard of pace. His famous side step had resulted in an ignominious tackle, his dummy a little too obvious.

From the age of twelve, rugby had been his life. Some other game would take its place, but he had no regrets.

Uncle Sam used to say, that as a door closes, another will open.

He was on the crest of a new world, new people, new faces and a new life.

Amen

It was a typical February Saturday rugby afternoon. Dusk crept across the rugby pitch and pockets of mist gathered in places. The spectators drifted away.

Henley-Smith found his feet again and struggled to walk back to the dressing rooms supported by Murphy.

He was offered the assistance of a stretcher but on Murphy's urging refused it. He must walk back in triumph and not be carried.

The three stood in the middle of the historic ground. A small man in a cashmere coat with quick intelligent eyes watched them from the touch line, a tall woman dressed with casual elegance in a Russian mink coat and hat, linked his arm.

In years to come, the old chaws would reminisce of heroics in the past and battles long ago.

***